USA TODAY bestselling author **Debbie Herbert** writes paranormal romance novels reflecting her belief that love, like magic, casts its own spell of enchantment. She's always been fascinated by magic, romance and gothic stories. Married and living in Alabama, she roots for the Crimson Tide football team. Her eldest son, like many of her characters, has autism. Her youngest son is in the US Army. A past Maggie Award finalist in both young adult and paranormal romance, she's a member of the Georgia Romance Writers of America.

Addison Fox is a lifelong romance reader, addicted to happy-ever-afters. After discovering she found as much joy writing about romance as she did reading it, she's never looked back. Addison lives in New York with an apartment full of books, a laptop that's rarely out of sight and a wily beagle who keeps her running. You can find her at her home on the web at www.addisonfox.com or on Facebook (www.Facebook.com/addisonfoxauthor) and Twitter (@addisonfox).

or (
e. ers:

rdshire

Also by Debbie Herbert

Appalachian Prey
Appalachian Abduction
Unmasking the Shadow Man
Bayou Shadow Hunter
Bayou Shadow Protector
Bayou Wolf
Siren's Secret
Siren's Treasure
Siren's Call

Also by Addison Fox

The Colton Sheriff
The Cowboy's Deadly Mission
Special Ops Cowboy
Colton's Deadly Engagement
Cold Case Colton
Colton's Surprise Heir
Silken Threats
Tempting Target
The Professional
The Royal Spy's Redemption

Discover more at millsandboon.co.uk

MURDER IN THE SHALLOWS

DEBBIE HERBERT

DEADLY COLTON SEARCH

ADDISON FOX

MILLS & BOON

First Published in Great Britain 2020
by Mills & Boon, an imprint of HarperCollins*Publishers*
1 London Bridge Street, London, SE1 9GF

Murder in the Shallows © 2020 Debbie Herbert
Deadly Colton Search © 2020 Harlequin Books S.A.

Special thanks and acknowledgement are given to Addison Fox for her contribution to *The Coltons of Mustang Valley* series.

ISBN: 978-0-263-28032-6

0520

MIX
Paper from
responsible sources
FSC™ C007454

This book is produced from independently certified FSC™ paper to ensure responsible forest management.

For more information visit: www.harpercollins.co.uk/green

Printed and bound in Spain
by CPI, Barcelona

MURDER IN THE SHALLOWS

DEBBIE HERBERT

Many thanks to all of you who have purchased this book! I hope you enjoy reading this as much as I enjoyed writing it. It was such a privilege to visit the Okefenokee Swamp while researching this book and experiencing all of its wild beauty firsthand. I'd also like to dedicate this book to my wonderful agent, Ann Leslie Tuttle of Dystel, Goderich & Bourret LLC, for all of her encouragement on this and every project we've worked on together over the years.

Chapter One

Wild. Mysterious. Primordial.

Bailey throttled the ATV's accelerator, describing to herself the view she saw along Trail Ridge. She smiled in satisfaction as the wind whipped away the sweat clinging to her face and bare arms. Even though she hadn't discovered the Okefenokee Swamp until her teen years, she considered herself a true "swamper" in spirit, if not by birth. The primitive wildlife refuge had been a personal haven during her troubled adolescence, a place to soothe her battered mind and body. It still brought her peace.

An eagle soared above, its huge wings spread as it swooped down to the top of a nearby pond cypress. Quickly she gathered her binoculars for a closer look. An unfortunate squirrel dangled from the bird's marigold beak. But, hey, we all had to eat—including baby eaglets. As a park ranger, she'd often witnessed the relentless need to hunt or be hunted, to kill or be killed in the eternal quest for survival.

She brought the ATV to a stop and hastily noted the location and time in her log. Tracking eagles and gopher tortoises was a part of her duties in monitoring protected species. That done, she lifted her binoculars again in time to spot the adult eagle bringing the food to the giant nest that housed his mate and two eaglets.

Heat scorched her arms, and the humidity blanketed her skin. She swiped perspiration from her forehead and clutched the ATV keys, ready to move on.

Loud staccato warbling pierced the air, and several sandhill cranes soared upward, crashing through a clump of saw palmettos. Appropriately known as the "watchmen of the swamp," these birds let out a distress cry that alerted other creatures. More birds took flight, and even a couple of deer grazing along the blackwater shore went running for cover. Curious, she raised her binoculars and scanned the area from which they'd come but saw nothing unusual. Perhaps an alligator had lumbered near their nest. But normally, in that case, the cranes would hover above, squawking at and even swooping down on the gator to drive it away from their eggs or hatched babies.

Bailey hopped off the ATV and made her way down the embankment toward the wide, swampy patch of water that, several miles ahead, formed into a canal that led to the Suwannee River.

The sound of something dragging across the sand was followed by a loud swish of water. Perhaps she'd been right. It was a sunbathing gator returning to the water trail. Near the white sand shore, Bailey caught sight of the disturbance.

Not an alligator. It was a man. Dressed in camo, he navigated a long, slender johnboat, sluicing a paddle through the waters.

"Hey, there," she called out in a friendly greeting.

He didn't turn around, and she frowned. Why hadn't he answered? Was he illegally hunting gators or turtles?

"Hey," she called out again, determined to check his fishing license. "Hold up. Park management here."

His head turned slightly, allowing her to glimpse only a distant profile, but his olive-colored brimmed hat shaded the upper part of his face. Instead of turning around and obeying her command, he pulled the engine throttle and sped off.

Anger flushed her face. The man was definitely up to no good, but he had her at a disadvantage and knew it. She'd never catch up to him in the twisting, winding waters. Bailey pursed her lips, frustrated as he slipped out of reach. By the time she fetched a boat, he'd have disappeared like a snake in high cotton. Her gaze swept the area, looking for a trotline or other signs of illegal activity, but there was only the drag mark of his boat in the sand and muddy footprints by the water's edge.

Her gaze traveled further, and she squinted at the railroad bridge, nearly overgrown by reeds and marsh grass. Had he gone for a hike on the Thirteen Bridges Trail? Usually, that place attracted a younger crowd drawn by the old ghost story—and a place to party. But she might as well take a look anyway and see if the mystery man had left any clues as to his identity.

It'd been months since she'd last walked the trail. She trod heavily on the near-rotten bridges—merely old crossties over wetland—and recalled the legend about a wailing woman searching for her lost baby. Supposedly she and her infant had been murdered out here not long after the Civil War.

Personally, Bailey thought it a bunch of nonsense, brought on by inebriated, highly suggestible kids—although she considered herself fairly open-minded about the supernatural. How could she not be? Her best friend, Lulu Atwell, was an older Seminole woman who told her tales of Native American lore that often defied rational explanation.

At the end of the trail, the tiny abandoned church still stood. She pushed open the door, surprised at its resistance. Given its age and condition, it should have been falling off its rusty hinges.

She squinted at the sudden darkness. Only two small grimy windows admitted filtered sunlight. Stale, moldy air twitched her nose. Her eyes adjusted, and she focused on two metal cots in the twenty-foot by thirty-foot room.

What the heck? This old place had always been empty, except for the occasional beer and liquor bottles strewn over the rough pine floor, relics from parties. But this?

Prickles washed down her spine as her mind immediately jumped to a story that had dominated the news for a couple of weeks. Two young women, sisters, had been reported missing. They were last seen kayaking away from the outfitter store in Folkston, Georgia—her town—located only seven miles southeast of an Okefenokee Park entrance.

This couldn't be related to those women—could it? No way.

Still, she couldn't shake off the weight of dread that crushed her lungs. Bailey squared her shoulders and marched to the beds. Thin, urine-stained mattresses lay atop the rusting cot frames, and she pulled up one of them.

A bundled strip of gray cotton was stuffed along one of the railings, looking like a mummified mouse.

Oh, no. As she looked at what appeared to be a gag cloth, bile rose in her throat, and her hand beelined for the leather sheath of her knife at her waist. But she wasn't thinking of the missing women. Instead, her mind leapfrogged to the past. As much as she'd suppressed those memories, they now flooded in.

And she was *there*. Sixteen years old and lying on the damp concrete basement floor, her face and body grinding into the cold concrete with its faint scent of mold.

Above, the whistling snap of a belt before it descended. And as much as she tried to brace for it, she could never prepare for the burning sting. Or the screams muffled behind the dirty piece of cloth gagging her mouth.

No, no, no. That was long ago. I'm all grown up and safe. Even as she repeated the mantra to her trembling inner child, her body refused the comfort. Bailey ran out the door, leaned against the side of the church and vomited. That done, she breathed deeply—long, slow breaths—as she took in her surroundings. The eerie beauty and isolated environment of the swamp assuaged her anxiety as nothing else could. It was her sanctuary. Always had been, even during those dark days.

Resolutely she pushed away from the rotting boards and squared her shoulders. Nothing could erase her past misery, but if someone had been hurt in this abandoned ruin, she'd do everything in her power to bring the abuser to justice.

Bailey pivoted, reentered the building, and went to work. A damn shame there was no cell service in this remote area, but her cell phone wasn't entirely useless. She dug it from her pocket and videoed the entire room from top to bottom. She noticed not another clue of foul play, but if this place was a crime scene, no doubt forensic experts would find microscopic details that she could not. And she was positive something bad had happened here. A heavy energy pervaded the church, seeping into her bones with the chill of certainty.

Briefly she debated collecting the gag cloth for safekeeping but decided against it. Best to let law enforcement gather it and keep it uncontaminated in their chain of evidence. It should be safe enough where it was. Unless… She recalled the man speeding away in the boat.

Innocent outdoor enthusiast or illegal fisherman—or something worse? It was possible the man could return.

She shook her head and left the evidence as it was. Instead she walked around the building to check for anything else unusual. At the back of the church was a graveyard of over a dozen crumbling headstones with mostly unreadable etchings. A rusted metal fence sectioned off a patch of long-forgotten graves. Purple pickerelweed and yellow-eyed grass choked the monuments to the dead.

Next to the cemetery was a maze of waist-high boxwoods that formed a labyrinth. Many believed that walking labyrinths was a gate to one's inner self, that its circular structure, combined with its spiral, meandering paths, led to a meditative peace and awareness. Had the mystery man traversed through here for his own nefarious purposes? Could there be another surprise in store?

In the interest of thoroughness, she'd take a look. Besides, she'd always been curious about the maze. She'd heard that no teenager, no matter how drunk, had ever dared to enter, as it was also—no surprise—believed to be haunted. General legend had it that to enter meant you'd be forever lost. No one returned alive.

Bailey entered the maze, boots scrunching against river pebbles that made up the path. Only a handful of weeds managed to push through the stones. The old English boxwoods that lined the maze were slightly overgrown but must have been a miniature variety not to have totally grown together over the years. Dutifully she walked the curves, searching left and right for foreign objects or anything out of place—a wrapper, a tissue, a sock. Soon, she'd reached the end of the labyrinth, where a large tea rose shrub bloomed at its center.

She inhaled the unexpected floral bouquet before her—but spiritual enlightenment? Nope. She felt none of that. Then again, searching for crime evidence probably emitted too many negative vibes, especially after the horrible memories that'd resurfaced only minutes ago. Turning to exit, she caught sight of silver glimmering from a nearby tupelo tree. What could this be?

Bailey pushed through one of the boxwoods and strode to the tree for a better look. The bit of silver flashed in the sun from high above, tantalizingly out of sight. Again, armed with the cell phone, she turned on the camera and zoomed in.

The lens of a small security camera blinked back at her.

Bailey gasped and took a step backward. "What the heck?" she muttered.

Nothing about this old chapel and graveyard was valuable. Besides, this was a wildlife refuge, not private property. No one had a right to set up surveillance equipment. Maybe it had been left to catch teenage trespassers? No, that didn't make sense. If park management had bothered to initiate security measures, she'd have been the one to install the camera and monitor its feed.

Which meant…she wasn't sure exactly what, but it couldn't be good. On its own, the discovery would have been perplexing, but when combined with the discovery of the cots, and the gag, it could only mean trouble.

And that man in the boat—was he connected to all this? Again, Bailey silently cursed that she hadn't had immediate access to her own boat.

What if you had? an inner voice taunted. *What might he have done to you?* She swallowed hard. Her mind leapfrogged to yet another dreadful realization. The man hadn't just seen her in person. She was now recorded on his camera. *Not like I'm defenseless*, she reminded herself, patting the knife at her waist. She was no longer a scared, trapped teenager at the mercy of her foster father.

The roar of a motor pierced the relentless cacophony of insects. She whipped around, trying to pinpoint the direction. The rumble came again, closer. Another ATV, she decided. Nobody was allowed to ride through here without specific authorization. So either this was another park employee or someone more ominous. Had the man in the boat circled around and landed? Was he now driving toward her?

One thing she knew for certain: she wasn't going to wait to find out. Bailey scrambled to the front of the church and sprinted toward her ATV parked near Trail Ridge, only twenty yards away. The other vehicle was almost upon her as she cranked the engine and hit the accelerator. If it turned out to be another employee, she'd look foolish, but for now, safety trumped pride.

Risking a quick glance in the mirror, she saw a man in dark sunglasses. The determined set of his jaw, along with the increased speed and direct aim of his ATV, told her that he meant to overtake her. The question was… why?

Unfortunately, the winner in this chase would come down to who drove the faster vehicle. Sadly, her decade-old, bottom-of-the-line ATV would be no match in this contest. The park had a limited budget, and speed was never a consideration in purchasing a serviceable ATV to roam the swamp.

He passed on the left and frowned, signaling her to stop.

Bailey tamped down her uneasiness as she regarded the interloper. He was dressed all in brown, some kind of uniform evidently, but not the park's. For the second time that day, she caught a glint of silver in the scorching afternoon sun. Only this time, she didn't need to zoom in with her cell phone to see it.

Pinned to the shirt on his right upper chest was a six-pointed star badge—the Charlton County Sheriff's Office. *Whew.* Bailey hit the brakes and jerked to a stop. How could they have known she was on her way to call them once she reached her cabin? Unless this area was already under suspicion and they were watching it. Which could explain the security camera. They might have placed it there in the hopes of nabbing a person of interest. Perhaps this officer observed the man exiting the chapel and then slinking off in his boat. Naturally he'd come to investigate.

The moment he turned off his ATV and faced her, Bailey quipped, "You're a day late and a dollar short."

His forehead creased, and he removed the dark sunglasses. Olive green eyes, the color of faded camo, regarded her in consternation. "Excuse me?"

"I said you're a little late. Your man's already slipped away by boat."

His frown only grew deeper. "Man? What man? I haven't a clue what you're talking about."

This time it was her turn to frown and regard him in confusion. Bailey cocked her head to the side. "Haven't you been watching the old church?"

He gazed over his shoulder at the abandoned structure and then faced her again. "Nooo," he said with a slow, deep drawl. "What makes you think that?"

"But…" She bit her lip, puzzled. In her seven years as a ranger, she'd encountered law enforcement officers only three times. Once, when a local child with autism had gone missing—thankfully, he'd been discovered hours later, unharmed and swimming in the alligator- and snake-infested Suwannee River. The second time had been when a camper had suffered a heart attack, and his family had sent out an SOS flare in the dark of night. The third, of course, had been the recent massive descent of cops, firefighters and volunteers who had combed as much of the 438,000 acres as was humanly possible to search for the missing women.

"Why are you here then, Officer..." Her glance fell to the stitched letters under his badge, searching for a name. Horror closed her throat as she read it. *Dylan Armstrong.*

For the second time that day, the worst memories of her life resurfaced in an unexpected floodgate that, once opened, refused to recede. She hardly ever thought about that troubled time in her life, yet now, in the space of less than an hour, fate had punched her in the gut twice.

Coincidence?

Bailey believed in many things—that places like that old church contained a certain energy left from its history, that the Okefenokee held mysteries deep within its primitive fortress, that certain plants and animals often appeared at critical moments as messages from the universe. But most of all she believed in signs—not coincidence. And the fact that her past had twice been thrust in her face in rapid succession was a bad sign indeed.

"Ma'am, are you okay?" he asked, exiting his ATV and standing directly in front of her. He wasn't frowning now. Instead, his forehead was creased with concern. Those unusual olive-colored eyes—so like the elder Dylan Armstrong's she remembered—appeared kind and trustworthy, inviting her to accept his help.

But she wasn't going to be fooled. Not again. Not ever again.

He opened a bag tied to the back of his ATV and pulled out a water bottle, then thrust it into her hand. "Perhaps you're overheated? Dehydrated?" he suggested. "Happens all the time out here. Drink this, you'll feel better."

Anger replaced surprised horror and she shook her head. Did he take her for an incompetent idiot? For God's sake, she was an experienced ranger and knew to stay hydrated in the smothering heat. And even if she was thirsty, she'd never accept anything an Armstrong had to offer.

"I'm perfectly fine," she answered icily, effectively cutting off his overture. "What are you doing riding the land? Did you obtain a special permit?"

"Of course I did."

She'd just see about that. Bailey turned the ATV key and the motor roared to life. "Good day, Officer."

"Hey, wait a minute. What did you mean about the man speeding—"

His words were drowned out as she throttled the accelerator and the ATV wheels spun in the dirt, spraying clumps of soil onto his uniform pants. She watched him through the rearview mirror as he scowled at her, hands on his hips. But he made no move to follow, and the tightness in her chest eased as she drove around a bend and his tall form disappeared altogether.

She'd head straight to headquarters and report everything she'd seen at the church to her supervisors, as was her duty. In turn, it would be their responsibility to contact the sheriff with those findings. If Armstrong complained about her odd behavior today, she'd insist that she'd bypassed him in order to report everything directly to her own supervisors. The sheriff's office had their chain of command, and she had hers.

With any luck, she'd never have to set eyes on Officer Armstrong ever again.

Chapter Two

What the heck was that woman's problem?

Dylan brushed the dirt from his pants and climbed back on his ATV. He briefly considered overtaking her again—no doubt he easily could—but then what? Listen to more of her crazy talk? An encounter with a man had spooked her. His gaze drifted to the church. It stood abandoned as always. Another few years and the perpetual damp of the swamp, combined with the aggressive kudzu, would reduce the place to rubble.

His fingers twitched on the throttle. Annoyed as he was, he'd seen a moment of pure fear in her wide eyes. Come to think of it, he'd seen the woman around town a few times. Cool as ice, that one. He'd run into her at the grocery store once and had idly taken in her long, toned legs as she bagged apples in the produce aisle. Some sixth sense of being watched must have alerted her to his attention, and she raised her eyes, catching him gawking. Unfazed, he'd offered his customary breezy smile and waved. Instead of responding to his innocent flirtation with a smile—a reaction that, frankly, he was used to from women—she'd pulled her full lips into a tight line, abruptly turned her back on him and jerked her shopping cart in the opposite direction.

Jeff Aiken, his best friend since preschool, had hooted

with laughter and nudged him with an elbow. "Don't think she was impressed with you, dude. You're losing your touch."

"Who is she?" he'd asked, checking out her shapely ass.

"Bailey something-or-other. Heard she works at the park and lives near it like a hermit. Not exactly friendly."

"That's a shame." He'd shaken his head, eyes still on the woman, lips curled in a rueful grin.

Jeff had grabbed a six-pack of beer and tossed it in his cart. "Stop acting like you're still in junior high, and let's get a move on."

The memory jogged him to action. Abruptly Dylan changed his mind and gave chase, the wind whipping his face as he accelerated. Bailey what's-her-name wasn't getting away so easily this time. If the ice queen was rattled, he wanted to know the reason.

In less than five minutes, he spotted her, riding as fast as that run-down ATV could manage. He gunned the motor, and her head swung around for an instant before she faced forward again, never slowing. Dylan drew alongside her and motioned her to stop. Surprisingly, she obeyed. He exited his ATV and approached where she sat, her arms crossed and her lips pursed just as they were at the grocery store long ago.

"Appears we got off on the wrong foot, Bailey."

Surprise melted the stone-wall face, and she narrowed her eyes. "How do you know my name?"

He lifted his palms and shrugged. "Folkston's a small town. We bumped into each other once before."

"If you say so."

At her quirked brow, he realized she had no memory of the grocery store incident, which sent his ego into a nosedive. Still, he gave a determined smile, pushed the sunglasses to the top of his head, and held out a hand. "Dylan Armstrong, Charlton County Sheriff's Office."

She hesitated a moment, then reluctantly took his extended hand. He tried not to notice the effect of her smooth, warm palm in his grasp or imagine her sleek, tanned body hidden under the khaki uniform—it was hard enough not to stare at her exposed long legs in those shorts as she straddled her ATV.

"Bailey Covington," she said in exchange, withdrawing contact a beat too soon for politeness. At least she hadn't wiped her hand afterward.

"You didn't give me a chance to explain why I'm here," he said in his most professional voice, determined to keep his gaze from sweeping down to her legs. "I'm sure you're aware of the two women who've gone missing in the area. We're still searching as much ground as we can with limited manpower."

A shame that the chopper and boats they'd initially used had proved fruitless in the search. Too many places to hide in this wilderness.

"Of course I'm aware of the missing women."

"So, this mystery man of yours, do you think it's related?"

"Possibly. I'm on my way to make a report of what I found today, just in case."

He strove for patience. "Mind sharing?"

"I'm sure my supervisors will be more than happy to allow yours full access to the report. See you around, Officer Armstrong."

With that, she again started the ATV and took off in a cloud of dirt, leaving him staring after her.

Rude, yes. But instead of being irritated, he inexplicably grinned. Never one to back away from a challenge,

Dylan flicked his sunglasses back down and returned to his ATV. "Go on and run. You haven't seen the last of me, Ranger."

WHEN DYLAN ARRIVED at the station, Jeff, his old friend and now a sheriff's deputy, glanced up from the paperwork on his desk and nodded at the sheriff's door. "Boss wants to see you ASAP."

Bailey's report must have already been filed and read. That was quick. Dylan knocked briefly on the closed door before striding inside.

Sheriff Franklin Chesser was frowning at his computer screen. "Weren't you patrolling today on Trail Ridge?" he asked with no preamble. "You didn't see any unusual activity?"

"Only an encounter with a closemouthed, annoying park ranger. I assume you're reading the report that she told me she would file with her boss?"

Chesser turned the monitor so that it faced him. "Take a look at this video she filmed."

Two bare metal cots were haphazardly strewed in the otherwise stark interior of the church. The lens zoomed in on a dirty strip of cloth lying on a rusted metal frame. The footage shook as Bailey Covington exited the church and scanned the area outside. The final shot was of a security camera perched in a nearby treetop. Then the monitor faded to black.

He and Chesser eyed one another uneasily.

"Think it has anything to do with the missing women?" he asked his boss.

"Can't help but make that leap." Chesser replayed the video, and they watched again in silence.

Chesser closed the video. "I have to be realistic,

though. Could be squatters using the cots, and that camera might turn out to be a poacher's."

"Maybe," Dylan agreed.

A dubious silence hung in the room.

"Going to call in the state police again?" Dylan finally asked.

Chesser sighed and drummed his fingers along the scarred pine desk. Dylan understood his dilemma. When Mary Thornton and Amy Holley first went missing, it was determined they were last seen renting kayaks at an outfitting store at the Suwannee Canal entrance. State police had responded en masse. Dozens of them, along with local volunteers, had combed the river where the women had set off. Several boats and even a chopper had searched for six days.

All fruitless. They hadn't unearthed a single clue.

"Let's do some preliminary work first. I've already spoken with the park manager, Evan Johnson. You and the ranger who filmed this can work together collecting evidence and canvassing the area for more. Bring back that camera, and let's see what we've got."

"I don't need the ranger for any of that."

"It's called interagency cooperation, Dylan. Politics. Forging partnerships. Besides, she could prove helpful. Johnson claims she knows the swamp like the back of her hand."

"Not like I'd get lost out there," he muttered. "I've lived here all my life." It wasn't that he didn't want to see Bailey again—he did. But Dylan resented the implication that he *needed* her assistance.

"Johnson's the territorial type and wants his ranger to be involved in the investigation. Not a bad idea, either. If those women, or their bodies, are out there in the wilds, she'll know better than anybody how to track them. Take one of our dogs, too. See if you can pick up a scent."

"I could collect evidence a whole lot quicker without her," Dylan muttered again in protest.

"Go," Chesser said, using a voice that brooked no more argument. "Everyone else is busy catching up with other cases after spending so much time on the search. Bring back the evidence, and we'll take it from there."

"I'm on it." Dylan shoved to his feet.

"Thanks, kid," Chesser said gruffly. "You know I think of you as my right-hand man. Job will be yours one day soon. Your dad was one of the finest cops in the whole state of Georgia."

"No hurry." Dylan meant it, too. He was more than content to work as a deputy and learn all aspects of the job before running for sheriff. He'd already spent over three years on beat patrol and then five more years as captain of the K-9 unit before landing his current position. He wanted to win an election on his own merits, not on his late father's name and connections.

Dylan quickly collected a beagle, Ace, from the K-9 unit along with a plastic evidence bag filled with two swatches of the missing women's clothes. Ace settled into the cruiser with him, brown eyes dancing with excitement, muscles taut and quivering in anticipation.

"Going to earn your keep today, boy," he said, smiling at the beagle's happiness. Ace had always been his favorite dog to work with.

At the park entrance, he obtained special permission to borrow one of their jeeps and, beagle in tow, returned to the abandoned church. At least Ace was enjoying the outing. His black nose was lifted high in the air, taking in the scents, tail thumping loudly on the seat. Compared to being cooped up in a kennel, this was doggy nirvana.

The late-afternoon sun scorched Dylan's skin, and his dark brown uniform felt suffocating as he gathered the collection kit. Lucky for Bailey, her uniform was lighter colored, and she had the option of wearing shorts instead of pants. Speaking of the she-devil, Dylan spotted her slowly roaming the churchyard, mucking up footprints or whatever evidence might actually be at the scene. He suppressed a sigh and approached on foot, the beagle trotting at his side, eager to get to work.

Bailey watched them, no welcoming smile on her face for him or his dog. Evidently she wasn't thrilled to be working with them, either.

"We meet again," he said pleasantly.

"Might want to keep an eye on your dog," she replied in a flat greeting. "Hungry gators and venomous snakes, you know."

He kept his polite smile in place. "Nice to see you again, too."

"I'll show you where the camera's located."

Ace offered a friendly yip, but Bailey ignored him and abruptly turned, leading the way to the back of the church.

He trudged through the brackish plants, Ace close at his heel, sniffing away. Bailey came to a sudden standstill and pointed up at a tree. "There's the camera."

"Hold this for me a sec." He thrust the clothing sample bag and evidence kit in her hands.

"Why? What are you—"

"Going to take that thing in," he answered, snapping on a pair of plastic gloves and grabbing an empty baggie.

"You think that's wise?" she asked, frowning deeper and casting a wary eye on Ace.

"Did you think we'd just leave it here?" he asked, eyeing the tree for a moment before he found a toehold and pushed up onto the first low limb.

"But if you take the camera, won't it spook the owner from returning?"

"Can't leave it and do nothing." Dylan climbed higher until he came eye level with the camera, which was fastened onto the end of a branch with zip ties. He dug a utility knife from his pocket and inched forward on the limb.

Ace barked and scratched at the tree, not happy at being left behind.

"You could do surveillance instead of removing the camera. See if he shows up again," Bailey suggested, shouting to make herself heard from several feet below.

"Kill me now," he muttered. She might not mind living and working outside in the boondocks, but as for himself, he couldn't imagine anything more miserable than camping in this snake-infested land, slapping at bloodsucking skeeters and biting flies all night in the suffocating humidity.

He popped open his knife blade and slashed through the tie, then carefully bagged the equipment before scrambling back down the tree. Bailey's hands were on her hips, her look reproachful.

"Hey, if you want to hang around here day and night to see if someone shows up, then more power to you," he said.

"Maybe I will."

She lifted the chin of her heart-shaped face, a stubborn gesture he secretly found more amusing than annoying.

"Don't get any wild ideas," he warned. "It's not safe for you to attempt something dangerous out here all by yourself."

"And to think I've managed this job on my own just fine for the past seven years."

"Have you ever been out in the wilds with a possible kidnapper before?"

"Well…no. Not that I'm aware of, anyway. But who knows what lurks out there?"

Apparently the woman hated to admit a possible vulnerability, but Dylan had to allow that he was the same. "I'm not questioning your courage," he said gently. "Not many people—man or woman—are cut out to work in a swamp full of reptiles."

Something fierce flashed in her eyes before she shuttered an emotion brewing below the surface. "My guess is that the reptiles are far safer than some humans." With that cryptic remark, she nodded at Ace. "Want to check out the church before your dog roams further out?"

"Sounds like a plan."

He followed her to the front of the building, doing his best to keep his eyes from drifting down and staring at her butt, and keep his brain focused on the job at hand. As Jeff had once said, he wasn't in junior high anymore. Not like he hadn't seen plenty of action over the years, either. Maybe it was Bailey's total lack of interest in him that roused a primitive need to make her respond to him.

Inside the church, he breathed a sigh of relief at the slight drop in temperature. Ace trotted past them both to get to the cots. Bailey hastily swept to the side to avoid the brush of fur against her legs.

Sudden understanding flashed. "Are you afraid of dogs?" he asked.

Her reply was much too swift and charged with vehemence. "'Course not."

She was lying.

"Ace, come," he demanded, snapping his fingers and pointing to the door.

The little beagle swiftly complied, even if his chocolate eyes protested the order. Ace planted himself in the doorway, his body taut, eagerly awaiting the signal to search. Dylan faced Bailey in time to catch the slight whoosh of breath escaping her throat, signaling relief.

Keep Ace from drawing too near Bailey again, he mentally noted. Ace would never harm her, but even if he told her so, it wouldn't take away her fear. Whatever encounter she'd had with a dog in the past, it must have been bad to be leery of a beagle—they were like the teddy bears of dog breeds.

Bailey cocked her head at the cots. "What do you think? Suspicious or not?"

"The sheriff suggested it might be squatters or hunters using this place. Catch many trespassers out here?"

"It happens. But it's not hunting season, and I've never come across something as permanent as cots. It's always blankets or sleeping bags."

She stepped to one of the cots and leaned over, pointing at the strip of cloth on the metal frame. "And then there's this."

Dylan gathered the cloth, placed it in a separate baggie and took close-up photos of everything.

"My fingerprints are on the mattresses," Bailey admitted. "I flipped them over looking for clues."

"I'll make a note of it and get your fingerprints, so we can rule you out in a search." He dusted black powder along the metal frames and mattresses, then stood and scanned the room. There were traces of dusty footprints inside, but they were blurred and of all sizes. Nothing distinctive. This place must still be a hangout for bored teenagers.

"Maybe the cots are for—" he hesitated a beat and plunged on "—you know, overly hormonal teens using this place to party."

Skepticism etched Bailey's face. "Kids today don't use it near as much as they did back in my day. But I understand that particular motive can't be ruled out."

Had she ever used this location for such a purpose? he wondered. But he tamped down his curiosity with determination.

"Now what do we do?" she asked.

"Time to let Ace do his thing."

Dylan swore the beagle grinned in happy anticipation. He withdrew the bag containing the cloth swatches. Bending on one knee, he held the swatches out, and Ace's black nose twitched as he sniffed experimentally.

"Seek," he commanded.

Ace made a beeline to the cots and whimpered as he placed his paws on the mattresses and barked.

"Bingo," Dylan whispered. This was the first big break in the case—and an ominous one at that. But after two weeks, no one expected the women to show up unscathed.

"Those women were here, then," Bailey softly stated, eyes focused on Ace.

"Appears so. I'll load the mattresses onto the jeep, and at the station, we'll cut them open to see if there's anything inside. We'll also check for blood and other DNA markers."

"I want to be there when you do."

He shrugged. "Suppose that's fine. Your boss made it clear he wants you involved in the investigation. But lab samples will be sent to Atlanta, and our forensics sample work is usually undramatic."

"I didn't know that. Just inform me if there's any major finding, then."

"Of course. I'm going to have Ace sniff around outside and see what we can find."

This time, Dylan led the way. The beagle ran past

him and, nose to the ground, drew them to the side of the building and then behind. Ace methodically made his way to the labyrinth.

"I did a quick walk-through earlier," Bailey offered. "Nothing jumped out at me, but there could be something small I missed."

Bees happily hummed around the gallberry plants and swamp gum trees, oblivious to the violence that had potentially been perpetrated in the maze. But he was getting ahead of himself. Perhaps the women had merely made a pit stop along the riverbank when they spotted the church and then had simply explored the area.

At the dead end, Ace hurried to the blooming tea rose bush and frantically began digging. White sand sprayed into the air.

A buried body or two, perhaps?

Unguarded, Bailey glanced at him, her brows raised and her blue eyes filled with dread.

"Why don't you wait for me in the church?" he suggested.

Wordlessly, she shook her head and switched her gaze back to Ace's frantic pawing. Slivers of gold glinted in the waning sun. Dylan knelt and picked up a thin chain with his gloved hands, recollecting a detail from the case. Both of the missing kayakers had been wearing gold necklaces. One had a cross on it, and the other woman's had a claddagh. He'd bet anything there was a murderer on the loose and in possession of both those charms.

"A trophy," he breathed.

Bailey was beside him, her shoulders brushing against his. The contact warmed the cold chill that had prickled down his spine.

"I thought killers kept trophies to relive their crimes," she said.

"They do. Not sure why a chain was left behind and buried. If this is a trophy, and we don't know that it is, the suspect will have some warped reason in his sick head. Maybe to mark the spot where he killed one or both of them."

"As good a reason as any, I suppose." He felt her tremble beside him. "Though I'm still going to hold out hope both women are alive."

He held no such optimism. Not that he needed it to sustain him in a serious crime investigation. Instead, it was the need for justice that drove him.

Work completed, Ace lay down and awaited the praise due him.

"Good boy." Dylan patted him and then rolled the necklace in the palm of his gloved hand before sealing it in an evidence bag. The sun beat down on his back, and the honeybees droned as they collected nectar. The scent of roses perfumed this unholy spot where two women might have met their death. He and Bailey grew quiet, a shared moment of respectful silence.

Violent death had possibly marked this spot. Now to test that theory and stop a killer before he struck again.

Chapter Three

"Sounds like a tough day. A creepy day."

As usual, Miss Lulu succinctly summed up everything in her tidy, no-nonsense way. Bailey rocked on the older woman's front porch glider, bare feet dangling, and sipped from a mason jar of sweet tea. In the deepening twilight, fireflies danced and glowed like drunken pixies. For the first time in hours, she felt relaxed.

"It wasn't the most fun I've ever had at work," she allowed.

"Could be dangerous," Lulu warned. "You living alone in the middle of nowhere."

Bailey snorted. "You've been doing the same most of your life. Besides, we have each other for neighbors."

Their cabins were nearly a quarter mile apart, and Bailey was glad to have her as a neighbor. They were kindred spirits, even if over three decades apart in age.

Lulu nodded, smoothing back her black hair shot through with silver. "And we have our shotguns. In case of trouble."

Bailey dearly hoped she'd never have need to use the weapon. Until a couple of weeks ago, she'd only imagined raising it in case of an encounter with an aggressive black bear.

Much as she'd enjoyed the evening and the supper of

duck fried rice and collards, it was time to shove off. Lulu always retired early and rose with the sun.

"I'll get the dishes," Bailey offered. As Lulu started to stand from the rocker, Bailey gestured for her to stay. "I've got it. Least I can do after all your cooking."

Ignoring Lulu's grumbling, Bailey reentered the cabin. She filled the chipped enamel sink with hot water and a squirt of dishwashing liquid. Truth be told, she enjoyed washing dishes. As her hands soaked in the warm water and fragrant pink dishwashing liquid, she gazed out the window. It was like a prayer, a meditation, as she cleaned and rinsed each plate before placing it, glistening, in the drying rack. But the piercing headlight beams of an approaching truck dispelled her peace. This wasn't exactly a hospitable stretch of road she shared with Lulu. Unpaved and wracked with deep mudholes, it led nowhere.

Faint consternation gave way to deep misgiving when the truck stopped abruptly halfway between her and Lulu's cabins.

"Expectin' company?" Lulu asked, entering the kitchen to stand by her side.

"Not hardly. You?"

They both watched and waited, but no one emerged from the vehicle.

"Nope. I don't like this," Lulu muttered. "Not after what you found in the church today."

"Where are your binoculars? I can't make out who it is."

"Binoculars, heck. I'm gettin' my shotgun."

"No need for all that," she chided, though she'd be lying if the thought of a loaded weapon didn't offer some comfort. "Let's see what we're dealing with."

Lulu reluctantly thrust the binoculars into her hands.

Bailey raised them. At the familiar shock of sandy hair, she groaned.

"Who is it?"

"One of Charlton County's finest. Name's Dylan Armstrong."

"What's he doing parked here?"

"That's what I aim to find out."

Lulu's dark eyes narrowed. "You sure it's safe?"

Another reason she felt close to this woman. Their mutual mistrust of lawmen. Lulu had never enlightened Bailey as to the exact reason for her mistrust, but she'd assumed Lulu had suffered from the same callous treatment she'd once received while seeking help from the law. Treatment she'd experienced thanks to Deputy Sheriff Dylan Armstrong *Senior*.

There it was. A third time in one day that she'd been forced to recall a past she'd rather forget.

"Everything's fine," Bailey assured her. "I'll send him on home."

"Take this with you." Lulu nodded at a covered plastic bowl filled with leftovers.

"You don't have to—"

"Take it."

"Still got enough for Holt if he drops by later?"

"Maybe. He was due to finish his latest tour yesterday. Haven't seen hide nor hair of him today though."

Holt Rucker, Lulu's special friend, worked as an expedition guide through the swamp and other wilderness areas. His schedule was erratic, but it seemed to suit his needs and unencumbered lifestyle. "Surprised he isn't already over," she said.

Lulu raised a brow but didn't comment. Bailey couldn't figure out the exact nature of their relationship. Holt often slept over, but Lulu refused to categorize him as a boyfriend and never complained about their casual arrangement. Evidently, the older generation had their own version of "friends with benefits."

"I made plenty of food."

Bailey knew when she was beaten. "Yes, ma'am. Guess I'll head on back and tell my stalker to hit the road."

Outside, the scent of gardenias and honeysuckle wafted through the air, soothing her jitters at the coming confrontation. She'd barely made it to the dirt road when his engine turned over and the headlights cut through the darkening sky. What was he doing out here? She hadn't asked for protection. Unless there was some break in the case already?

The truck skidded to a stop by her side, and the passenger door flung open.

"Hop in, Bailey. I'll give you a lift."

"Why are you here?" she asked bluntly. "Any news on the missing women?"

"I wish."

She stood unmoving. "Then why?"

He ran a hand through his hair. "Just keeping an eye out for you. Saw you head over here so I parked halfway, trying to keep an eye on both cabins. Don't get all huffy."

"There's no need." She didn't want to be beholden to any man, especially this one.

"Come on, Bailey. You know better. You were seen today."

"From afar. My hair was pulled back in a ponytail, and my hat kept my face shaded."

"Still, there can't be that many female forest rangers in the park. Correct?"

"Just me," she begrudgingly admitted.

"Shouldn't be too hard to get your name from the park

website, and then…" He let his voice trail, allowing her to follow the silence to its logical conclusion.

She had to admit that Dylan was right. With the internet, nothing seemed safe or private these days.

"I have a shotgun. I'm good."

"Okay. Just humor me, then. Get in the truck, and I'll save you a few steps."

Sighing, Bailey climbed in. If she didn't, she'd be arguing with him all night. At least that yipping dog wasn't on board. True, the beagle had sported a friendly, eager face, nothing like her foster father's trained attack Dobermans, but she respected that the animal still had a mouth full of sharp teeth. Once bitten, forever shy.

Dylan whipped the truck around, and she balanced the plastic dish in her lap as they rumbled toward her cabin, which was almost as rustic as Lulu's—with the exception that Bailey's had an air-conditioning unit. After a long day of patrolling the wildlife refuge, the last thing she wanted was to return to a hot, stuffy cabin in the evening.

He parked in front of her house and stared into the gathering darkness.

"Now what?" she asked.

"You invite me in?"

She let out a laugh. "Are you seriously inviting yourself to spend the night?"

"Not the way it sounds." Even in the dark, she detected a flush on his neck and face.

"Go home, Dylan. We might be working together, but I don't know you well enough for sleepovers, and your truck's going to get mighty uncomfortable."

"Wouldn't be my first stakeout. I'll survive."

Stubborn, stubborn man. She opened the door and slid out. Guilt pricked her for an instant, but she hardened her heart. If he wanted to act like a fool, that was on him. "Have you even eaten supper?"

Immediately she wanted to kick herself for asking. This wasn't her problem.

He picked up a bag of trail mix from the dashboard and rattled its contents. "A complete meal of protein, carbs and fats."

Impulsively, she thrust the plastic container at him. "Here's real food. If you don't have any plastic utensils in your truck, I can bring you out some."

"I'm all set." Dylan flipped open the glove box, revealing a stash of napkins, salt and pepper packets, a bottle of hot sauce and plastic forks. "Never know when these might come in handy."

Her conscience clear, Bailey shut the door. "Still say you should head on home."

She felt his eyes on her as she walked across the yard and opened the cabin door.

"Might want to start locking up your place," Dylan called out.

Bailey didn't bother responding. He was right, but she'd managed to figure that out on her own without his advice.

Was she really at risk? The unknown man had viewed her from a distance, after all. He'd seen her general body shape and long hair pulled into a ponytail. In the bedroom, Bailey let down her hair in front of the dresser, letting the brown locks flutter a good six inches past her shoulders. She was past due for a haircut, anyway. Bailey retrieved a pair of scissors and commenced cutting.

Five minutes later, she critically surveyed her handiwork. It would do. The bobbed length lay halfway between her chin and ears. A practical summer cut that would be cooler and also fit her wash-and-let-it-be style.

Like most evenings, Bailey plopped into bed and read, although tonight getting into the book proved difficult. Every so often, she swept aside the curtain and spotted Dylan still parked outside in the truck. At last, she turned out the light, determined to fall asleep. The morning work would start at dawn.

Familiar night noises of cicadas, frogs and owls lulled her unease. She touched the leather cord around her neck and ran her fingers over the charms Lulu had strung on it for blessing and protection—a crow feather for strength, power and wisdom, two turquoise beads representing friendship and an obsidian arrowhead for a hunter's alertness. Four items total, four being a powerful number symbolizing the four moon phases. As she sank into the gray oblivion of sleep, she hoped they'd keep her safe.

Excited barking.

The pungent scent of wet fur, an ominous growl and then nearby panting. Hot kibble-breath.

The dogs were almost upon her.

Bailey sprang to wakefulness, cotton bedsheets clutched in her hands. Blood pulsed in her ears as she searched the darkness for her location. She was home. Safe in her own room. Quickly she rose and went to the kitchen for a glass of water. As the tap filled her cup, she stared out the window over the sink. Moonglow tinged the trees and grass with a silver hue. With a start, she remembered Dylan and padded over to the den to look out the front window.

His truck was in the same spot, but she couldn't see him. Perhaps he'd lain down in the seat to sleep? Some protector. Come morning, she'd be sure to give him a hard time. Her hand found the smooth barrel of the shotgun she kept lodged near the front door. Its hard, cool surface reassured her that she could take care of herself if need be.

Instead of returning to bed, Bailey threw on a T-shirt and shorts and headed to Dylan's truck, determined to send him home. If he drove off now, he could still catch a few hours' sleep in a comfortable bed before they began another search. She rapped sharply on the driver's side window. "Dylan?" she called, not wanting to scare him— not too bad, anyway.

No answer. Man slept like the dead. What kind of cop did that on a protection detail? She peered into the back seat.

Empty.

Chills skittered down the back of her neck and spine. She slowly turned to face the cabin. A man was crouched near the swamp hibiscus by the east wall. Dylan? Impossible to make out from the inky shadows. An urge to angrily confront him warred with the fear that this might be someone else entirely. Although, did it matter who lurked there? What did she really know about this Dylan Armstrong? Precious little. Except for the fact that his father had been a no-good, heartless liar who'd turned his back on a terrified teenager who'd sought his help.

She cursed herself for not taking her shotgun. A weapon was no good if she forgot to carry it in the middle of night. Especially after she'd been warned she might be in danger.

The figure straightened and approached. He stepped away from the shrubs and into the wide expanse of the lawn, and the moonlight glinted on his sandy hair.

"What are you doing outside, Bailey?"

As if he had the right to question her movements. Resentment coupled with a healthy dose of cynicism kept her on guard. "What are *you* doing creeping around my cabin?" she countered.

He was close enough now that she saw the flicker of annoyance in his eyes. Well, he was no more irritated than she. Dylan had no business—

"Someone was out here," he said, cutting into her indignant thoughts. "I saw movement and heard noise in the shrubs. Which, by the way, are way too tall and need trimming. A giant could hide in that jungle."

She ignored his bossy commentary and cut to the chase. "What noise?"

"A rustling not caused by the wind. I climbed out of my truck, and whoever it was took off for the woods out back. You didn't hear me yell for him to halt?"

No, there'd only been the nightmare.

"So, he got away," she breathed, uselessly fixing her gaze on the dark tree line.

"At least I noticed him before he torched your cabin."

Her heart skipped and squeezed at that bit of news. "How do you know his intention?"

Instead of answering, Dylan motioned for her and walked back toward the cabin. Through the damp grass, she followed, arms hugged about her waist. Within ten yards of the shrubs, she halted abruptly. A gasoline odor permeated the night air, overpowering the sweet smell of honeysuckle and gardenia. Under one of the shrubs was a discarded gas container.

She rubbed her arms against the wave of cold that swept her from head to toe. If Dylan hadn't been here...

Unless *he'd* been the one who doused her cabin with gasoline.

She tried to think rationally, warring between what was either paranoia or a healthy suspicion. But why would Dylan have done such a thing? Yeah, she had no use for his father, but it didn't mean that the son was a killer trying to deflect suspicion from his murderous secrets by playing a hero.

"I guess thanks are in order," she said reluctantly.

A rueful smile played on his lips. "Must have killed you to say that."

Chapter Four

Bailey sipped coffee as she and Dylan peered down at the huge map spread out on the conference table at park headquarters. The park land was vast. Over seventy islands dotted the map, along with two major rivers and a stream of waterways twisting throughout the Okefenokee.

"What, exactly, are you looking for?" Dylan asked. His tone was less than pleasant. He slouched in a chair, legs sprawled before him. A sexy stubble—Bailey couldn't help the errant thought—graced his jaw, which he wearily rubbed.

She probably looked every bit as discombobulated as Dylan, but she'd never admit to anyone just how shaken last night's events had left her. Either she was a random victim or a possible killer knew her identity. Regardless, after the cabin was nearly torched, they'd left immediately and had come to the park headquarters.

"Not a morning person?" she asked Dylan with fake cheer.

"It's not morning yet." He yawned, glancing out the bank of dark windows on the east wall.

"Sure it is. I see a few sun rays on the horizon." Bailey took a perverse pleasure in antagonizing him. "Why don't you go home, shower and change clothes?"

"I've got clean clothes in my truck. Is there a place to shower in this building?"

"Yep. I'll show you where it is."

"It can wait until a few employees show up."

Did he plan to stick to her like glue until the suspected kidnapper was found? Heaven help her. "Suit yourself," she said with a shrug, turning her attention back to the map. "To answer your earlier question, I'm looking for a hiding place."

Were the missing women still alive—or at least one of them? After all, there was a gold chain unaccounted for, which bugged Bailey. Why did the kidnapper only bury one of the necklaces in the labyrinth?

Where else could he have taken a victim? She stared at the map and shook her head in despair. So many places to hide. The swamp offered a wealth of opportunity for someone knowledgeable of its twisting secrets.

Not to mention the twelve thousand alligators that called this area home, any one of which could easily drag a human body to the bottom of the swamp and feast, leaving only the bones scattered beneath the blackwater's calm surface.

She couldn't dwell on that depressing reality.

"What's the sheriff's office's game plan for today?" she asked.

"They'll send out more officers and a few cadaver dogs to better comb the Thirteen Bridges area. They've already sent your findings to the forensics lab in Atlanta. Boss put in a request that they expedite the tests. We'll see."

"Think there's anything stuffed in those mattresses?"

"No. They already checked." He held up a hand, warding her off. "I know you said you wanted to be there, but we'd had a long day and—"

"It's fine."

Dylan tapped his knuckles against the map. "Got any ideas on where to go from here?"

She slowly sat down across from him, clutching the warm coffee mug between her palms. "Depends. Anything you can share about the investigation that hasn't been reported to the media?"

"Unfortunately, no. As reported, when the women went missing, we didn't rule out foul play. Their overturned kayaks were found almost nine miles from the outfitter store, in a side waterway off the Suwannee River." Dylan squinted at the map and then pointed a finger. "Right there."

Bailey dutifully marked the spot with a black Sharpie.

"The women were experienced kayakers," Dylan continued. "Friends and family swore they always carried compasses and used them for navigation."

"And now we're close to proving there was foul play."

"That being the case, we always suspected the kidnapper was someone local and familiar with the area."

"Of course. So, this man possibly likes to keep women hostage in sheltered, remote areas. Apparently gagged and maybe bound in some way." She didn't even want to think what he did with them as they lay helpless.

"That appears to be what we're now dealing with." Dylan poured more coffee. "But why now? There've been no other violent crimes connected to the park."

"Could be this guy's first offense," she suggested.

"Maybe," he said, though his doubtful scowl indicated that he didn't agree with this theory.

"If so, then it sounds like we're describing a younger man. Someone who's never before acted on his violent urges." She paused. "Or someone who's cleverly covered up his past crimes until now. Have you had reports of other missing persons in this area?"

Dylan hesitated. "People disappear from time to time. Runaway teenagers, spouses who up and leave their significant other with no trace. Most of these cases are quickly resolved. But the wildlife refuge cuts through miles of the Georgia-Florida border, which encompasses a large number of people. It's entirely possible there are open missing person cases. What are you suggesting?"

"That Mary Thornton and Amy Holley might not be the first victims."

The theory lay bare before them—tantalizing and horrific.

"Can't help wondering if more trophies lie buried, scattered about like his personal treasures." Her own words made her shiver.

From the front door came the harsh sound of metal scraping metal—a key turning in the lock.

Dylan leaped to his feet, all semblance of exhaustion erased. His hand went to his sidearm as he rushed to the door.

"If they're using a key, they must work here," she said, tamping down a burst of adrenaline, even as her hand reached for the knife at her belt.

"Or it's somebody picking a lock."

Dylan flattened himself against the wall by the door and motioned for her to do the same. The gun's safety lock clicked off, and he held it in his right hand, finger on the trigger.

Another jiggle of the key, and the door squeaked open. A tall, rangy man dressed in khaki stepped inside. Her boss. Bailey let out a heavy breath and strode to the door. "Evan! You're here early."

Thick brows rose on his rugged, tanned face. His skin

showed the signs of a lifetime spent outdoors, but even so, it didn't detract from his appeal. Close-cropped white-silver hair emphasized cornflower blue eyes. He flashed a grin, perfect white teeth gleaming against olive skin.

The grin died the moment he spotted Dylan holstering his weapon. "You must be the deputy that Chesser assigned to work with Bailey."

"Correct." Dylan's face was guarded, his eyes suspicious. "You always arrive so early to work?"

If Evan noticed the lack of warmth from the cop, he showed no signs of offense. "Not every day we're called in on a criminal case. How's the investigation going?"

Bailey quickly filled him in.

"Where do we go from here?" Evan asked. "Wait for forensic confirmation that the necklace belonged to one of the women?"

"We've put in a rush request to have the prints and DNA tested, but it could take days. Weeks, even. The office is chronically short staffed."

"Sounds like there's nothing more to be done." Evan nodded at Bailey. "Ready to report back to your regular duties?"

"No." It wasn't like she wanted to spend more time with Dylan and his yippy beagle, but if there was the slightest possibility that one of the women was alive, she had to continue to search.

Both men regarded her with raised brows.

"I'd like a few more days to search."

"Search for what?" Evan asked.

Dylan's eyes flashed with understanding, and he gave a slight nod. "There was only one necklace found. So where's the other?"

"Exactly," said Bailey. "Couldn't hurt to check out a few more places. The kidnapper's shown he takes advantage of old structures to hide his victims." *Until he kills them*. She pushed the disquieting thought away. "He's obviously familiar with the area, so he'd know where there are plenty of old cabins and sheds." She paused a moment when the thought hit her. "Like on Billy's Island."

"Wouldn't that be too obvious? Too risky?" Evan asked, frowning. "The place is popular with tourists."

"Only the western end of the island," she objected. "On the opposite side are several rusted metal sheds and a couple pine buildings left abandoned from the old timber company."

Evan's lips pressed tightly together. "Needle in a haystack."

Her spirits sank. He wasn't going to let her continue assisting the law enforcement officers. How could she return to the same old duties when her talents and knowledge of the area could help solve this case?

"The sheriff's office is game," Dylan said. "If your agency is no longer interested in participating in a joint search-and-rescue venture, I'm sure Sheriff Chesser will understand. Although, it'd be a shame not to have Bailey's assistance. I wasn't even aware of those abandoned structures on Billy's Island."

Very slick. Dylan had appealed to her boss's pride. Grateful as she was for his tactic, it served as another reminder to be wary of the guy. His open, boyish face and manner didn't mean there weren't a few tricks up his sleeve.

Evan held up a hand. "Never let it be said we didn't provide y'all our full cooperation in this matter. Bailey, you're free to work with them over the next week. After that, check in with me, and we'll decide where to go from there."

"No time like now." She cocked her head at Dylan,

eager to be on their way before Evan changed his mind. "There're sandwiches in the break room fridge. Let's pack a lunch."

BY THE TIME they picked up Ace and settled into the small motorboat, sunrise was in full bloom, its coral rays brightening a path down the winding water trails. The coffee-colored water, infused with tannin, was dark but clear. The stream was only three feet deep, yet the current was strong and pulsing beneath the boat's floorboard.

Bailey sat at the helm, navigating the narrow lane bordered by lily pads—all while keeping a wary eye on Ace. Every minute, the stubborn dog edged a tad closer, creeping forward on his belly, brown eyes earnest with longing.

"He's very well behaved," Dylan offered.

"So you say," she grumbled, angling her legs away from the pup. "Keep him by your side."

Dylan patted his leg, and Ace scooted back by his feet. "I'm curious. Are there many places in the swamp that have old abandoned buildings?"

"Several. There's the old Chesser homestead and Floyd's Island. A few other locations off the beaten path as well. We used to have more but the forest fire in 2011 wiped them out."

"Everything in the swamp is off the beaten path. Any special reason we're going to Billy's Island first?"

She glanced at him from the corner of her eye, debating whether to reveal her other reason. He'd no doubt find her amateur theory amusing. After all, she was a forest ranger, not a detective.

"Go on," he urged. "I'm listening."

Bailey touched the obsidian arrowhead that lay against her breastbone, then skimmed the crow feather and turquoise beads. So what if he laughed at her idea? Her self-worth wasn't based on anyone else's opinion—especially not one named Armstrong.

"Maybe one of the reasons he used the church is because there's such a strong legend around it. Lots of folks are afraid of the place."

"Not the teenagers who use it to party," he pointed out.

"They don't use it much anymore. Not like when I was growing up around here. The place is mostly avoided. And then there's the labyrinth, where he buried at least one token." She hesitated.

"Go on," he prodded.

"Maybe he has a bizarre sense of the holy, or a need to defile sacred places."

Dylan rubbed his chin and then gave a quick nod. "Are you thinking of the Native American mound at Billy's Island?"

Just then, the oak platform dock emerged from around the bend, and she steered toward it. "Yes. Plus, the island also has its share of supernatural tales and resident ghosts."

"Chief Billy from the Seminole tribe. I know that one." Dylan chuckled. "Supposedly he was murdered here and comes back to haunt unsuspecting campers."

Their boat bumped against the dock, and she expertly tied a rope around a metal cleat to secure it. "Don't forget about Bigfoot, the Skunk Ape and the South Georgia Pig Man," she added.

"Not to mention UFO sightings and alien abductions. Got it."

A reluctant grin tugged her lips. He was surprisingly easy to get along with, so she'd have to keep her guard up.

She climbed out of the boat with the metal detector and trowel, while Dylan exited carrying Ace and an evidence kit in his arms. He had the dog once again sniff a bag containing clothing samples from the missing women, and her passing amusement vanished.

They stepped onto land, and her boots sank an inch in the damp, unstable peat deposits. Native Americans called the swamp "land of the trembling earth" for just this reason. It made for inconvenient footing, but still, she loved the smell of the wet bog, and this brief stretch of morning before the smothering heat and humidity descended like heavy blankets.

"Should we go to the Native American mound first?" Dylan suggested.

"That works. We can check that and the cabins before hiking over to the old industrial area."

Ace darted ahead of them, eager for the day's hunt. And it would be grueling work. The island was four miles long and one and a half miles wide.

"I can't help thinking about that lost man," she blurted.

Dylan faced her, grimacing. He apparently knew exactly what she was talking about. "Strange things happen out here, no denying that."

Swampers still remembered the lost man. In 1996, he was lost for forty-one days in the swamp, despite a massive search that included helicopters equipped to detect infrared body heat. Finally, he emerged on Billy's Island, dehydrated, confused and exhausted. Theories ran rampant. A few of the crazier ones suggested an alien abduction that resulted in a memory wipe.

Ace quickened his pace as they approached the deserted village. Nearly five hundred people once lived and worked there in a doomed timber operation at the turn of the last century. The swamp eventually defeated all efforts at industrialization, and Bailey couldn't be sad about that. Too many magnificent cypress trees had been hauled away.

Although most of the old homes had gone up in flames, rusty bathtubs remained as well as other relics—a silent testament to the hardy folks who'd tried to tame the wild land. Ace eagerly sniffed each of the tubs, his twitching nose low to the ground. Occasionally his head rose, and he lifted his nose high, discerning some new bewitching scent to be investigated.

Bailey turned on the metal detector and absently arced it over the ground as she and Dylan followed Ace.

"He's not finding anything," Dylan observed as Ace scurried from one leftover relic to another.

Beep beep beep. The detector emitted a solid stop-and-go sound that she recognized.

"It appears that I have, though." She bent her knees and pocketed a handful of pennies and dimes.

He shook his head and chuckled. "Is that penny-ante change even worth picking up?"

"It's the thrill of the treasure hunt. I've found plenty of cool stuff over the years—thimbles, eyeglasses, Confederate coins—but don't worry," she assured him. "I'm fully aware that we're searching for more grisly mementos today."

His eyes widened. "Actually, that's pretty cool. Any of it valuable?"

"Probably not. Whatever I've found in the wildlife refuge, I've turned in. They're on exhibit in the park's visitor center."

They continued roaming, watching as Ace explored the oxidized steel frame, axles and fenders of an old car. The metal detector's continual hum was occasionally broken by choppy beeps as it scanned junk targets.

"How do you know it's not signaling something that might be useful?" Dylan asked.

"Years of experience. Asymmetrical objects like pull tabs from cans or iron objects make that noise. We're searching for jewelry. Specifically, a missing necklace and cross and a claddagh charm." She regarded him uneasily. "Do you think I'm wasting everyone's time, like Evan implied?"

"You have to admit it's a long shot. But a waste of time? No. If there's any possibility of finding one of the women or any clues about their fate, it's worth exploring."

Bailey let out a sigh, not even realizing until that moment that she'd been feeling so tense. If Evan had refused her request, she'd have searched alone during her off days. But searching now, with a cop, was way quicker and more efficient. Even if he wasn't the cop she'd have chosen to work with.

"Thank you," she murmured, oddly transfixed by his warm, understanding gaze. Her breath caught in her throat and her stomach gave an unfamiliar lurch as they stared at one another for several heartbeats.

Dylan abruptly whistled for Ace, and they set off down the dirt path that led to the Native American mound and, further down, to the forsaken site where the timber company had left its old equipment and the railroad tracks laid down to ship out the cypress. Lucky for her, Ace pretty much ignored them as he trotted several feet ahead, sniffing as he went.

The sun began to pummel them, and Bailey patted her face with a handkerchief.

"The heat's brutal," Dylan complained. "How do you stand it every day?"

"You get used to it."

He stopped and chugged half a bottle of water before

calling Ace over. A small plastic cup in the evidence kit served as a makeshift bowl for the dog, who eagerly lapped up the water. Bailey watched, taking a judicious swig from the canteen she kept strapped on her shoulder. Dehydration was always a concern during the swamp summers.

"How much farther?" Dylan asked, putting the cup and empty bottle in a plastic bag.

"We're almost to the mound. Just around the next bend."

They resumed walking the road, which was nearly grown over with trees and brush. She found her eyes drawn to Dylan several times, studying his features. In addition to the unusual eye color he shared with his father, there was something about his strong jaw and broad shoulders that resembled Armstrong Senior's. As far as temperament, Dylan had the same easy smile and sincere expression on his face. One that promised *you can talk to me* and *you're safe with me*.

All lies.

A sudden spurt of anger quickened her steps. Dylan upped his pace and shot her a quizzical glance.

"Something wrong?" he asked.

Bailey drew several deep breaths. Logically, she knew it was unfair to visit the sins of the father on the son, but the knot of resentment remained tight.

"Just eager to search the mound," she lied. Ignoring his skeptical frown, Bailey kept her eyes forward. "And here we are," she said, pointing at the hip-high mound.

"Easy to miss. It's even more overgrown than the time I came here on a field trip in junior high."

It was true. Marsh grass and saw palmetto covered the small mound. Dylan again had Ace sniff the cloth samples. As the dog began his search, Bailey turned on the metal detector and combed the area, small sections at a time.

"My office is going to furnish me with a detector tomorrow, so I can help you at the next location," he volunteered, walking around the perimeter of the mound.

"That'll save time."

Dylan pointed at a pair of dilapidated sheds nearby. "I'm going to take a quick look inside those."

She watched as he walked over, Ace following at his heels. He gestured for the dog to sit, then cautiously peered in the entrance of each shed.

Moments later he returned, shaking his head "no" at her questioning look.

She'd expected as much but was still disappointed. Bailey continued sweeping the mound until the machine's hum shifted to a beep. Her heart rate increased as she bent low to the ground, and then slowed as she eyed a half-dozen bobby pins, so rusted she almost feared she'd get tetanus by merely touching them.

"What do you have there?" Dylan crouched beside her.

"Probably nothing to get excited about. They most likely fell out of the hair of some long-ago tourist."

"I'll bag them up, just in case."

His bare forearm brushed hers, and she became hyperaware of his nearness, of his masculine scent of leather and sandalwood. Ace's body pushed between them, and she jumped to her feet with a startled gasp. Immediately, she cleared her throat in a belated attempt to cover the sound. Ace sniffed experimentally at the bobby pins, then meandered off.

"Since your dog had no reaction, those definitely didn't belong to the missing women, right?" asked Bailey.

"Seems unlikely," he agreed.

"I'll start checking the opposite end." Had she led them on a wild-goose chase after all?

Half an hour later, as she was almost ready to admit defeat, the metal detector emitted a strong beep. Bailey arced the tool, pinpointing the location, and sat on her haunches, trowel and probe in hand.

Dylan stepped in front of her, his tall figure providing a modicum of shade. Even Ace ran over, eager to be in on the action. "Let's see what you got there."

Bailey stopped and eyed the dog warily. Dylan snapped his fingers and pointed behind him. Ace obeyed the silent command, head down and issuing only a slight whimper of protest. The probe beeped again, revealing the hidden object's shallow depth.

Dylan handed her a pair of plastic gloves—"Just in case," he murmured—and she donned them before carefully lifting a scoop of dirt and sifting through the clumps. Her fingers pressed against a hardened circular object. Possibly a pebble... No, its center was hollow. She finished brushing away the dirt and held it to the light.

A white-gold ring, its solitary diamond gleaming impossibly clear as she held it victoriously between them.

"Engagement ring?" Dylan suggested. "Heck of a place to lose it."

She opened her canteen and trickled water over the ring, then wiped it on her shirt until it shone. The ring was etched inside. "'Forever,'" she read. "'L.S. & R.K.'"

"Initials don't match our women," Dylan noted.

"True." Yet her skin felt tight all over. "How do you lose an engagement ring out here? It's not a campsite, no reason to ever take it off. This feels—" she mentally grasped for the right word "—deliberate."

Dylan shrugged as he dug out his cell phone. "Maybe someone recently divorced threw it away in a fit of disgust?"

The camera flash exploded, and she placed the ring in the evidence bag he held out. "You'll check it out, though, right?"

"That's why we're here," he said. "Are we finished with this mound?"

"As good as any one person can be with one metal detector. It's not much farther to the sheds."

"Good. Let's get a move on. We'll wrap it up here, then boat back to headquarters and grab a bite to eat. I want something more substantial than a sandwich. I'll email the photo to Jeff, a friend of mine in the office, and have him do a quick search on the ring. See if it has any significance in an ongoing investigation."

She couldn't ask for more than that. But the whole time they trekked to their next location, Bailey couldn't help feeling like everyone was merely humoring her wild whim.

Pride be damned. If nothing turned up, she'd at least tested her instincts. So what if Evan and a couple of people in the sheriff's office were secretly annoyed? She could live with that.

Ugly rusted machines sprung into their line of vision, jarring in the otherwise pristine wilderness. Railroad tracks lay twisted on the ground like iron snakes, weeds and marsh grass growing between the slats. All were relics from an ill-conceived attempt in the 1920s to conquer the swamp by draining it, selling its timber and shipping it out by rail.

The formidable Okefenokee Swamp had won that

battle, and the company had cut its losses and admitted defeat.

Ace ran to one of the two sheds at the edge of the site, both in serious disrepair, each precariously tilted to one side. They hurried to catch up with the beagle and entered the first shed. Stale, humid air hit Bailey, and she breathed deeper, trying to suck the oxygen out of the heaviness. Ace looked back from his sniffing, but Dylan stayed silent, and the dog returned to work, weaving a path to the right corner of the shed. It didn't take long till Ace pawed at the ground and barked—once, twice, three times. He'd found something.

Chapter Five

Dylan's throat went dry at the dog's signal.

He tried to quash the adrenaline of excitement spiking his blood. It could be a false alarm.

"Ace only has rudimentary training as a cadaver dog," he cautioned Bailey when she questioned him. He took out his cell phone and hurried to the corner. "Certified cadaver dogs go through eighteen months to two years of specialized training."

The dirt floor was packed solid except for Ace's recent pawing. No evidence of recent digging here. Yet Ace sat immobile, muscles tensed. Dylan snapped two quick photos and stuffed the cell phone back in his pocket.

"What do you believe your dog's found?" Bailey asked, rubbing her arms nervously. "Do you think…" Her voice trailed off as though too horrified to verbalize what they both wondered.

"Do I think someone's buried here? There's no evidence the earth's been recently disturbed, so it can't be the women we're searching for. It might not even be a body. But yeah, Ace has definitely found something."

Bailey licked her lips. "What's the next step?"

"We bring in a cadaver dog. If it finds human remains, then this place will be crawling with a team of forensic experts."

"I don't know whether I want them to find bodies or not," she admitted softly, her breath ghosting the side of his neck.

"Always better to know. For the sake of the victims' families and to catch the killer. We may have a serial killer on our hands. If we do, we've got to find him ASAP and prevent other deaths."

"Yes, of course."

"Let's not get ahead of ourselves," he cautioned. "We'll go back to town as planned and report our discoveries."

But Bailey stayed rooted, eyes focused on the hard patch of ground. "You don't think the two missing women are alive, do you?"

"No."

She finally faced him. "But you hear stories on the news about different guys kidnapping women and keeping them locked in a basement for years. Maybe our guy has them hidden away."

"Those are huge news stories because they're rare," he argued. "This situation is different. The wildlife refuge has no permanent residential housing. Even if he found a place to hide victims, he wouldn't have easy, constant access to them."

Her chin lifted. "He might still not want to kill them both straightaway. The guy might keep one or both around temporarily. It's only been two weeks."

He gazed into her hopeful, optimistic eyes, which weren't jaded from years of investigating brutal crimes. She wanted so badly to believe that those women were out there, alive and waiting for rescue. Much as he didn't want to destroy her hope, it would be cruel to encourage false optimism.

"We don't have concrete evidence yet that there's been foul play," he said. "Those women could have fallen out of their kayaks. We both know that can be deadly in these waters."

Alligator food. Bailey would get the point without him spelling it out so crudely.

Dylan whistled for Ace to follow him. The dog obeyed and slowly walked forward, occasionally craning his head backward, a barely audible mewl escaping his throat. Bailey gave Ace a wide berth and strode ahead of them. Outside, he drew a deep breath of fresh though sticky-hot air, glad to leave the sweltering shed behind.

The ride to headquarters was quiet, the boat puttering through the narrow water trails. The bit of breeze it created provided a welcome relief from the late-afternoon sun. Ace curled in his lap and fell asleep. Dylan rubbed him behind the ears, and Ace issued a contented moan without opening his eyes. "Good job today, boy," he murmured.

Bailey appeared absorbed in her thoughts, which was fine with him, as his own mind kept looping through the day's discoveries and what their implications might be.

Once in town, they agreed to eat at Fat Man's BBQ. On the shaded restaurant patio, they had the place practically to themselves. Dylan emailed the engagement ring photo to Sheriff Chesser, along with an account of the dog's possible find at the shed. Ace settled at his feet with a biscuit and bowl of water as they dug into their platters of pulled pork, beans and coleslaw.

"Anything for dessert?" the waitress asked as they finished their meal. "Got some homemade pecan pie this afternoon."

"I'm in. You?" he asked Bailey.

She nodded, and he almost wanted to applaud her for not remarking on the pie's gazillion calories. Not that she had anything to worry about. Her figure was lean and toned, no doubt aided by her vigorous outdoor job.

"What made you go into forestry?" he asked curiously. "Seems to be a field dominated by men."

She shrugged. "Can't imagine working in an office. Being outside, mostly working alone, that's more my style."

"Those the only reasons?"

"It's peaceful."

He waited, but she didn't volunteer more information, so he prodded further. "Thought you'd mention saving the environment. I pictured you being into the whole conservation thing."

"'Course I am."

Again, she didn't elaborate, apparently content to dine in silence. "Are you always this quiet, or does something about me rub you the wrong way?"

"Yes."

Genuine confusion gusted through him. Bailey obviously wanted to avoid clarification. "Yes to what—both?"

The waitress returned to their table and set down two pie slices. Dylan pushed his aside as Bailey dug into hers.

"I'm solitary by nature," she said around a mouthful of food.

"I'm not talking about that part. I sense I'm not exactly your favorite person." Confusion gave way to irritation. "Why the attitude with me? I took your side this morning when your boss wavered on whether you should be included in a search."

"Let it go, okay? It'll make the rest of our work week go by more smoothly."

Sighing, he dug into his own pie. Did it really matter if she had some unknown grudge against him? Or maybe it wasn't him per se. Maybe…

"Did you or your family ever have some run-in with my dad?" he asked her.

That had happened to him a few times before. Once from Tommy Vaughn, a guy in high school whose father had been arrested for theft. Another time, nearly three years ago, from Vern Ashcroft, whom his dad had arrested for assault. In both cases, Tommy and Vern always treated him with a mixture of resentment and embarrassment.

"A run-in," she repeated slowly. "Yeah, you could say that."

He let the matter drop. First opportunity, he'd check the police computer database for an answer. Dylan slapped a credit card on the table when the waitress brought the bill. "My treat."

"I'll pay for my own." Bailey dug out her credit card and placed it next to his. He opened his mouth to remind her of their truce, but she spoke first. "It's getting too late for another excursion. We'll have to regroup in the morning."

"You got another place in mind?"

"Floyd's Island," she said immediately. "There's an old hunting cabin that could be used as a temporary shelter, and there's a huge Native American mound nearby as well."

"Even I've heard of that mound. The old timber company cut through a large portion of it to build a railroad." He rolled his eyes. "They claimed to have found giant-sized skeletons, which, conveniently, disintegrated almost immediately upon excavation."

"Such a skeptic," she said, her mouth twitching up at the corners—evidently unable to suppress her amusement. "Georgia's ancient race of giants. The tourists love that story. Too bad we don't have any giant bones in our little museum. Just the usual pottery and bead mound relics."

The waitress gathered their cards. "Be right back, sugar."

"Exactly how many isolated cabins and old mounds are there in this swamp?" he asked.

"Last count, there're seventy-four mounds in all."

He almost choked on his soda. "Surely you don't want to explore every last one of them?"

"Only those near old buildings." Bailey smirked and then added, "Lucky for us there aren't that many shelters left. Besides Floyd's, we could also explore Chesser Island. That should cover our bases."

"Okay, then. We can call it quits for now. I'll procure a metal detector, and early morning, we can meet at—" His cell phone rang, and he answered it with a grimace of apology to Bailey. "Armstrong here."

"Come down to the office. Right away." Sheriff Chesser's voice was tight with urgency.

"Sure. What's up? Did you get a hit on the ring?"

Bailey's eyes snapped to his, pie forgotten. She motioned to the waitress and quickly signed her bill.

"Yeah. It belonged to a Lisa Shaw, who disappeared just over four years ago. I'll give you more details once you get here."

"We're on our way."

Bailey shoved to her feet as he signed his own receipt. Ace sensed the excitement in the air and perked up from his nap, refreshed and curious.

She waited until they were in his car before asking, "Who did the ring belong to?"

"A woman who disappeared three years ago. Lisa Shaw. Does the name ring a bell with you?"

"No. You?"

"It's teasing the back of my brain, but I can't recollect why."

"Maybe Evan remembers her." She got out her cell phone to call, but he shook his head.

"Better wait and let the sheriff keep Evan informed."

She sighed and dropped the phone in her lap. "I hate all this chain-of-command bull."

Dylan didn't reply, yet he couldn't agree with her more. However, if they both wanted to remain on the case, then they had to follow protocol.

With light traffic, they were soon inside the busy sheriff's office, where noise from the jail, located at the back of the building, provided a constant background hum. They slipped inside Chesser's office, and he motioned for them to have a seat at his conference table, where he already had a laptop set up, its screen illuminated with an enlarged photo of the ring they'd found.

Chesser opened a file. "Lisa Shaw disappeared on April 16, 2016. She and her sister left Birmingham on a Thursday morning and traveled to Amelia Island for a weekend getaway. On Saturday morning, at approximately seven a.m., she told her sister she wanted to go on a boat tour of the Okefenokee. Her sister preferred to stay on the beach, so Lisa left on her own. She was never seen again."

Chesser took a photo from the file and slid it across the table to them. The woman looked to be in her midtwenties, blonde and smiling like the world was her oyster. Nothing like the two sisters who'd disappeared two weeks ago. Lisa was short and plump with carefully applied makeup, a lacy top and curled hair, while Mary Thornton and Amy Holley were both brunettes with the long, lean build of experienced kayakers. In the photos of the recent missing women, neither had worn makeup, and their hair had been pulled back into casual ponytails.

Was he wrong trying to draw comparisons among the women? Had they all met a similar fate from the same abductor?

"We've got a cadaver dog and his handler arriving in the morning from Atlanta," Chesser informed them. "If there's a body in that shed, it'll be a circus around here. Just like it was in the initial search for the missing women."

"Do you want us—" Dylan pointed between himself and Bailey "—to continue searching more locations or join in with other state and federal police when they arrive?"

"Maybe." Chesser cast a curious look at Bailey. "What made you want to search this particular locale?"

"I thought Evan had already explained my reasoning." Her arms were crossed in a defensive stance. So he wasn't the only one who drew Bailey's ire. Could it be all cops she disliked? Or maybe she had issues with men or even people in general.

"I'd like to hear it from you." Chesser paused. "If you don't mind."

The *don't mind* part was a polite euphemism for *that's an order*. He meant for her to explain her logic. Apparently Bailey came to the same conclusion.

"After finding the necklace at the labyrinth and the cots in the old church, it seemed possible to me that the women had been held there and that an abductor buried one of their necklaces in a spot that must hold a sort of ritualistic attraction. Based on that, I wondered if the women might still be alive and if he might be taking them from place to place in the swamp. Places that contain abandoned structures. Bonus points if there were an archaeological or mystical area nearby."

Dylan eyed her with renewed respect. Her theory was as good as anything else law enforcement had come up with. "Modern death artifacts mixed with ancient bones," he remarked.

Chesser and Bailey regarded him with reproach.

"Too early to say if anyone's been murdered," Chesser said. "We'll take matters day by day. Do you have other sites to visit?"

"Floyd's Island and then Chesser Island," Bailey informed him. "Chesser isn't as remote, so it's less likely to have been used." She regarded him curiously. "I take it you're descended from the original settlers?"

"There are dozens of us Chessers around the area," he confirmed. "Hearty progenitors, my folks. Had to be to arrive at a massive swamp and believe you can settle and conquer it."

Dylan had never heard him speak of his connections before, and the pride in his voice was evident. His boss turned to him. "Contact me as soon as you finish tomorrow. Anything special you require?"

"It would help to have a metal detector. Might make scanning an area easier and quicker."

"What about dogs? I can have Captain Woodard join you with more of them."

Bailey's back stiffened a degree.

"That's not necessary," Dylan said easily. "Ace is doing a great job all by himself. What we do need, though, is a cop to watch Ranger Covington's cabin this evening." Dylan quickly filled him in on the previous night's would-be arsonist.

Chesser's face darkened with concern, and he nodded. "Of course. Can't help but wonder if everything's connected. Hopefully we'll have answers soon. And if you change your mind about the dogs, just say the word."

"Thank you," Bailey said. "How much longer before forensics runs the test on the necklace we found yesterday?"

"They're short staffed and running behind but if a body is found, this matter will take precedence. There will be lots of public pressure to solve the case quickly."

"We could be dealing with a serial killer," Dylan said, verbalizing the elephant in the room.

The office went unnaturally quiet.

"One day at a time," Chesser reemphasized. He rose, signaling the meeting was over. "I'll give your boss a call and fill him in," he said to Bailey.

They exited his office and reentered the hum of the main room, where officers sat in cubicles. Jeff waved them over. "Where you been, man? Your sister's called three times already."

"Janie?"

"It's your niece's third birthday. Big party—" Jeff glanced at the clock hanging on the door across from them "—starting in about fifteen minutes."

Heck, it had completely slipped his mind.

"You go on," Bailey said. "I can catch a ride home with my neighbor."

"Why don't you come to the party with me? Plenty of cake and ice cream."

"No, thanks." With a small wave at Jeff, Bailey spun on her heels and started off.

"See you in the morning," Dylan called after her. He fought the urge to blow off the party and follow Bailey home. But Chesser had assigned an officer to watch her cabin that night. Surely she'd be okay between then and nightfall.

Jeff winked at him and lowered his voice. "Those legs. I remember her from the store years ago. She's still not impressed with you, dude."

"Give her time."

Despite the outward show of confidence, Dylan wasn't so sure.

"Better get a move on it. Janie's waiting," Jeff reminded him.

"Do me a favor. Run Bailey Covington's name in our system and see what shows up."

Jeff raised a brow. "That's highly irregular. Why?"

"Someone tried to hurt her last night. I want to know if there's anything in her background that would provide a clue as to who might have a motive. She did hint about a prior run-in with the law."

"Still waters run deep, huh?" Jeff rubbed his chin thoughtfully. "I'll call you later and fill you in."

Chapter Six

The scent of smoke and bacon wafted through the stagnant air as Bailey tied up their boat at Floyd's Island. Bright-colored kayaks in lime, red and yellow banked the shoreline.

"Still some campers around. Cooking breakfast before they shove off," she noted.

Her right shoulder ached as she lifted the metal detector onto the dock. Lugging around the machine for hours yesterday had taken a toll.

Dylan placed Ace on the dock and then gathered up his own supplies. Ace's toenails scrabbled across the old oak boards, and Bailey held her detector in front of her like a shield to prevent him from rubbing against her legs. On the boat ride, Dylan had kept him by his side, but the clever bugger was taking advantage of Dylan's momentary distraction to try to win her affection.

Bailey was having none of it.

"That bacon smells amazing," Dylan said as they walked onto land.

"Sure beats the trail mix we had for breakfast."

"Don't forget the cake."

They'd gotten up early enough without having to worry with cooking a meal. Instead, Dylan had arrived at her cabin with two huge slices of leftover birthday cake from his niece's party. She'd eagerly gobbled up the sweet treat. The handful of trail mix had been a guilty nod to ingest a bit of nutrition.

During the dawn boat ride, he'd regaled her with stories of his family—the cute niece, Laurie, who'd jumped up and down with joy at every present, his sister, Janie, who'd scolded him for arriving late, and his brother-in-law, Shawn, who was also one of his closest friends. Bailey suspected that his casual chatter was an attempt to lighten the mood of their potentially morbid search, but all the talk of family merely brought up buried resentments. She'd never had siblings or a father in her life. But that was bearable. Plenty of people grew up entirely well-adjusted without them. She and Mom had done fine until her mother was diagnosed with lung cancer and died less than six months later when Bailey was sixteen years old. With no living relative willing to take her in, Bailey had ended up in foster care. It had been a sad, scary time but what she couldn't bear was living with her foster father, Edgar Slacomb. The only blessing of that miserable period of her life was that it had lasted less than three years. But back then, each day had felt like a month. Every night, she'd mark off the completed day on her calendar with a thick black marker, gouging the innocent white square in much the way that she imagined inmates would cross off the days until reaching the end of their sentence.

Bailey strode quickly to the fire ring, inhaling the misty morning air, reminding herself that she was a free woman who refused to let the past define her present.

Two couples sat near the fire, sitting atop their neatly rolled sleeping bags, munching on bacon and toast. They hadn't booked the cabin so they must have slept on the ground. Their eyes rounded as they noted her ranger outfit and Dylan's cop uniform.

"Morning, Officers. Is there a problem?" asked one of the men, who shoved to his feet, brushing crumbs off his shorts.

One of the women grinned. "Y'all look like you're set for a treasure hunt."

Bailey acknowledged them with a quick nod, her stride to the cabin never slowing, as Dylan exchanged pleasantries with them and asked questions about how long they'd been in the area and if they'd witnessed anything unusual. Digging the key from her khaki shorts, she unlocked the cabin door and entered.

The spacious, four-room interior smelled faintly of lemon and cypress. It'd been cleaned only yesterday for visitors arriving later that afternoon. Built in 1925 as a hunting cabin, it was listed on the National Register of Historic Places and was a popular rental, even though hunting had been outlawed since the late 1930s. The gigantic stone fireplace gave it a cozy lodge feel, and she bet plenty of tall fish tales and hunting stories had been woven in that den.

Methodically she walked through every room, checking underneath cots and opening closets. Unless Ace was able to sniff out a trail, this could prove a wasted trip.

The front door squeaked open and then clattered shut. "Find anything out of place in here?" Dylan called.

"Nothing." She walked back to the den. "I checked the log earlier. It's been cleaned three times in the past two weeks for different renters."

"Ace still might be able to find a trace if the women were ever here. Isn't that right, boy?" Dylan patted the beagle before opening the bag holding the cloth samples from the missing women. Ace sniffed experimentally. "Go find," Dylan ordered.

The dog lowered his head and began his job. Dylan, too, began a search, looking over what she'd already covered, opening cabinet drawers and lifting sofa cushions.

Bailey strode to the back window, staring at the woods, which formed a solid line only a few feet from the back wall of the house. It felt as though the woods were encroaching upon her, a smothering heaviness asserting its wild dominion over humans and the shelters they erected. Just as the ocean reclaimed inches of shoreline every year, the swamp also seemed to slowly swallow up islands of dry ground until one day, the land would completely disappear into the morass. She pictured the bodies of the missing women slowly sinking into quicksand, gobbled up inch by inch until only a few air bubbles marked their spot—and then that, too, vanished.

She shook off the depressing notion and returned to the task at hand. Until, or if, the bodies were found, there was always hope.

Had the abductor been bold enough to break and enter a cabin popular with renters? If so, he'd taken a substantial risk. Maybe that was part of the thrill for him, though. Pushing the limits in his own arrogance, always believing he could stay a step ahead of the law. Good. The more the man imagined his crime trail invincible, the sooner he'd slip and leave behind a vital clue.

"We've got nothing," Dylan announced at last.

"Is it even worth checking out the mound, then?"

He shrugged. "Might as well while we're here. Floyd's the largest island in the Okefenokee. Maybe ruling it out is at least a step in the right direction. Narrows the search a bit."

With lower spirits than when they'd arrived, they

hiked to the mound just as the kayakers shoved off into the water trail.

The half-moon-shaped mound was several feet higher than the one at Billy's and desecrated by a swath cut from the old lumber company. Evidently in that era, people had no respect for preserving the sacred heritage and artifacts left behind by past civilizations.

Bailey retreated to one end of the mound, Dylan the other, slowly canvassing the area until they met in the middle. Ace did his usual thing, and Bailey was relieved by his total focus on the search. He wouldn't try to make friends with her while so absorbed.

Two hours later, the search ended. Dylan held up the evidence bag to the light—a broken necklace chain, three mismatched earrings and a rusted brooch. Ace gave the items a dismissive sniff.

"Doesn't look too promising," Dylan said.

She rubbed the back of her clammy neck and sighed. "Wild-goose chase."

"We haven't searched the cabin grounds yet."

Bailey took a swig from her canteen before nodding briskly. "Guess we should get to it."

"I have a better idea. We need a break. Let's motor over to Billy's Island and see what they've uncovered before heading to town. We'll turn in this bag at the office—" he held up their meager findings "—and then we can have a long lunch and return to Floyd's late afternoon when it's not so hot."

Even though she was acclimated to the heat, the idea of resting sounded too good to pass up. And she was more than a little curious if anything had been discovered at yesterday's site. "I've been thinking about their dig all morning," she admitted.

"Me, too."

Bailey pointed to the two-way radio hitched at his belt. "They haven't told you anything?"

"We're out of radio range. Lost it about a mile and a half before landing at the dock."

They made their way back to the boat, and she imagined the scene they'd find at Billy's, men with shovels, chipping away at the ground in search of grisly human remains. Not the kind of job she'd ever relish, but she had tremendous respect for the trainers and dogs who performed the task.

The boat motor whirred to life, and she navigated onto the waterway, glad for the wind against her face. Even Ace appeared tuckered out. After lapping up a bowl of water, he snuggled against Dylan's feet and immediately lapsed into a deep sleep, complete with loud snores and grunts.

If only she could fall into sleep so effortlessly. The past night, she'd tossed and turned more than she'd slept, remembering that an unknown person had tried to douse her cabin with gasoline. Could the abductor have figured out her identity so easily? Or was it someone else entirely? A chill ran up her spine as her mind focused on a potential suspect.

"What are you thinking about?" Dylan asked.

She gave a start, flushing as she met his curious gaze. No sense in withholding the truth. "Wondering who poured gasoline around my cabin. I'll sleep better once they've been arrested."

"Still no idea who it could have been?"

She hesitated a heartbeat. "Not really."

Dylan's eyes tightened. "But you have a suspicion."

The man was far too observant. "It's far-fetched. Crazy, really."

"Lay it on me."

"I'd rather not. I can't go around accusing someone with no evidence to back it up."

"Come on, tell me."

She could see he wasn't going to let it go. Bailey navigated the boat around a fallen tree, not wanting to face him as she explained. "It's just… I'm not on good terms with the foster family I lived with in high school. Especially the man."

She couldn't—wouldn't—call him *father*.

"I see."

She darted him a quick glance, relieved to see on his face calm acceptance and not the pitying look she so despised when she'd discussed her background with others. Not that she ever much did. Even Lulu only knew a few bits and pieces from that miserable period of her life.

"It's stupid to point a finger. It was a long time ago. No reason for him to suddenly stalk me or try to hurt me—" *again*, she added mentally "—after all these years."

"He still live near here?"

"Not far. In Waycross." The larger town, with a separate park entrance, was about thirty miles west of Folkston.

"What's his name?"

"Doesn't matter."

"Come on. I'll check him out. I can at least eliminate him as a suspect if he has a solid alibi for the last few days."

Right. Like she'd ever trust an Armstrong again.

"The time for police help with that creep has long gone by. Besides, if he still means me harm, he's had plenty of opportunity to hunt me down over the years." The words soured her throat. Even she could hear the scalding bitterness in her voice.

"I see," he said again.

"You see nothing."

"What's that supposed to mean?"

"Not a thing. Forget it."

"Heck, no, I'm not forgetting it."

Silence stretched between them, broken only by the boat motor and the chatter of birds and insects.

"Bailey," he said softly. "Look at me."

She did. And the compassion in his olive eyes made her breath catch.

"Sounds like your foster father was a real piece of work. I wish someone had intervened on your behalf. A cop, a teacher, a friend. Anybody."

"Hard to make friends when you aren't allowed to socialize with anyone your own age. And confiding to a teacher was out. They homeschooled me."

Dylan winced. "I'm sorry. So they kept you isolated, which is typical with abusers. Wasn't there someone you could have reached out to? A social worker? The police?"

"Oh, I reached out, all right." Dylan opened his mouth to ask the obvious question, but she rushed to distract him. "Why are you so curious? Do you think he might be the arsonist?"

"We should take a hard look at anyone with a violent history. Thought we had already done that, actually. And if he's capable of setting your cabin on fire while you were asleep inside, maybe he's capable of these other crimes as well. I wouldn't rule him out."

Edgar, a killer? Bailey mulled over the possibility. Had he graduated from abusing foster kids to the crime of kidnapping, and perhaps even murder? Somehow, she couldn't picture him doing it. The man was too stupid and too lazy to stalk women in the wilderness and then manage to elude police. But setting fire to her cabin? She could believe that.

"I don't believe he's our guy. He's more of an opportunist," she said slowly. "Younger victims and easy access to them is more his style."

Dylan frowned. "He's not still fostering children, is he?"

"No. I turned him in as soon as I moved away. My report, along with social worker suspicions on a girl who lived there after me, got him and his wife removed from the foster care system."

"Glad for that, at least. Hope you pressed charges."

"I didn't. But he can't ever foster more children, and I'm good with that."

"So he doesn't have a record, then."

"Never got caught committing a crime that I'm aware of."

At the sharp bend in the water, their boat suddenly sidled alongside an alligator basking in the sun. It hissed at them and slunk away into the marsh grass.

"Sorry, Gimpy," she called out. "Wasn't paying attention there."

"Gimpy?"

"He only has three legs. We suspect a turtle feasted on the missing one."

His brows rose, and his lips twitched in amusement. "You actually name these gators?"

"Yep," she said, relieved to note that Dylan was distracted from their earlier conversation. "There's Big Momma, Burt, Bessie, and the one that hangs out by the mouth of this trail is called Gatekeeper. He keeps a close guard on his territory."

"So, we humans are merely visitors here?"

"Absolutely. Bears and gators rule this swamp."

Dylan rubbed his chin, gazing out at the water prairie of lily pads and cypress. "I know they're shy of humans, and there's never been a case of a gator attack out here, but if they came across a dead body dumped overboard by a killer…"

"Not their preference, but food is food."

Only the sound of the boat motor broke the hum of swarming insects and chirping birds as they both chewed over the reminder that one or both of the missing women might be cached below the tannin-stained water, reduced to a mere alligator feast.

At last, they banked on Billy's Island, where several boats had docked. Uniforms were everywhere, swarming around the dilapidated shed, shovels in hand. Ace barked, his dark brown eyes alight with excitement. He started to trot ahead, but Dylan called him back to his side.

"Does this mean…" Her voice trailed off, unable to say the words.

"Probably." His face was grim as they strode over to the group of cops.

Bailey hardly knew what to hope for. She desperately didn't want to think of anyone buried in the wilderness, but if they were dead, then finding the bodies was the best thing for their grieving families.

The stench hit her before she was even close enough for an update, a thick wall of putrefaction stronger than anything she'd ever experienced, powerful enough to make her eyes water and her lungs choke. She'd never been exposed to a rotting corpse before, but no one had to tell her what had been dug up in that old shed.

She knew.

Chapter Seven

Dylan cast a worried look at Bailey. Even for seasoned law enforcement officers this was a grisly, disturbing scene. He tried to shield her view when several men lifted a plastic body bag to carry to an awaiting boat. But Bailey stoically stood her ground and took in everything, even if her face had paled and there was a slight tremble in her hands.

Dylan spoke to one of the officers and learned that the body was female and had been buried for several years.

"We should return to work," Bailey said, heading back to their boat.

"I think we've done enough for the day," he said, but she ignored him.

Resignedly, Dylan sprayed his arms and neck with insecticide. It felt like saturating his body with poison, but if he didn't want to get chewed up by swarming yellow flies, he had no option.

The sun set low, and he'd tried to dissuade Bailey from returning to Floyd's Island, but she'd insisted they complete their search of the cabin grounds before calling today's effort a total loss. Tomorrow, they'd regroup and decide where to go next.

"Waiting one more day to search isn't critical. After finding that body, we'll probably be flooded with more cops and volunteers, starting tomorrow morning," he said. "It's not all on us."

"Good. We could use their help."

He tried to adopt her pragmatic attitude. Privately, he found all the extra help annoying, as state and federal cops homed in on his territory and acted as though they possessed superior intelligence and skill. He might be employed in a rural county sheriff's office, but he and his coworkers knew this land and the local swampers better than any outsider.

They left the metal detectors on the boat and headed toward the cabin. The machines wouldn't be needed unless they discovered something of a suspicious nature that warranted a closer look.

At the cabin's rear, Ace perked up, yipping in high-pitched squeals. Dylan exchanged a quick, surprised glance with Bailey, and then they hurried to catch up to the dog. On the back porch, Ace paced the old wooden boards, a whimper warbling through his chest before he stopped in front of a weathered kindling box and gave three deep barks.

Quickly, they both donned plastic gloves and carefully climbed the rotting porch steps. After a snapshot on his cell phone, Dylan moved the box aside.

Nothing. His shoulders rounded in disappointment.

No, wait—did that pattern of chicken scratching in the wood mean anything? He bent closer, using the cell phone as a flashlight.

The letters *A M* were gouged in the rotten wood.

Short for Amy? The missing Amy Holley? More scratchings were below the letters, and he squinted, trying to decipher their meaning. Bailey took his arm, directing the light beam further up and to the left at another etched marking.

HELP

He sucked in his breath.

"She's alive!" Bailey swiveled her head toward the forest as though expecting Amy Holley to materialize from its dark depths.

"At some point she was, yes," he cautioned. "Doesn't mean she still is."

"What else did she write?"

He studied the floorboard, unsure how to decipher the crude, irregular markings. "Looks like she tried to make a circle with some kind of drawing inside of it."

"A tree?" Bailey suggested, cocking her head to one side as she gazed intently down.

"Maybe?" But it was a guess. "What did she use to write with?" he muttered, then glanced around, spotting a sharp rock nearby. "Aha," he breathed, gathering it into a baggie.

"Great. Her prints should be all over that," Bailey said.

She had been right after all. Until a dead body was found, there was hope. Whoever held Amy against her will hadn't killed her immediately.

Ace growled, and Bailey suddenly jumped to her feet. "Did you hear something?"

He scrambled to his feet as well, hand automatically traveling to his sidearm. Dylan shielded her with his body, scanning the woods in all directions for signs of movement. Ace continued growling, baring his fangs at an unknown menace. "What did you hear?"

"A rustling behind us. Could have been a deer," she offered skeptically.

This was supposed to be only a search for clues, not a cat-and-mouse game with a killer. He needed backup, and there was no way to radio for help. They were sitting ducks, an open target, for whoever was out there, watching, maybe even taking aim at them.

A whistling buzzed near his ear, and Dylan threw his body over Bailey, knocking them both to the ground. An explosion sounded above them, and wood shards rained down. Ace charged off the porch.

"Crawl to the side of the cabin and make a run for the boat," he breathed into Bailey's ear.

"But what about—"

"Just do it. I've got your back. Get in the boat, head back and radio for help."

Bailey crawled away, and he followed, gun raised. She dropped to her feet at the edge of the porch. "What about you?"

"I'll hold him off. Go on."

She glanced at him doubtfully as another shot rang out.

"You're my best hope," he told her, knowing it was the only thing he could say to get her to leave him.

With a reluctant nod, she took off running.

Dylan crouched by the side of the porch steps and discharged his weapon in the direction from which the shots had been fired. Little chance his bullet would hit the attacker, but he wanted to demonstrate he had his own firepower. He'd put up a fight.

"Get back," Dylan ordered Ace.

But the beagle was having none of it. He stopped running, though, and began barking furiously, eyes and ears focused on the woods.

Another shot rang out, and Ace fell to the ground with a sharp yelp of pain. The sound filled Dylan with fury.

"This is the police! Give yourself up!" he shouted.

In response, yet another round exploded, hitting the porch railing only inches from where he crouched.

His ears strained in the ensuing silence. Why hadn't he heard the boat motor?

The ominous quiet settled, thick and cloying, grating on his nerves. At least with gunshots firing, he had an idea where the shooter was. But now? He could be anywhere, sneaking up on him from any direction. Ace whimpered and limped to him. Blood trickled down his right haunch.

Dylan scooped Ace into his arms, rose up a couple of feet and made a run for the front of the cabin. A shot exploded in the gathering twilight, and he braced, expecting to feel searing pain. Grateful he didn't, he reached the front of the cabin, where Bailey ran toward him.

"Fuel line's cut," she called out breathlessly. "We're stuck."

They were so screwed.

"Get in the cabin!" he ordered.

Bailey held up the keys, already one step ahead of him. He covered her back, gun at the ready, as she undid the lock.

"Backup's on the way!" he yelled into the darkness. "Don't be stupid. Drop your gun and step forward with your hands in the air."

The door creaked open, and they quickly stumbled inside.

"Run to the hallway," he told Bailey. There were no windows there, and she'd be safe for the time being. Dylan locked the door and assessed the layout. The two largest windows faced the front and back of the cabin, but there were also two small side windows.

"I'll keep watch at the back while you watch the front," Bailey volunteered.

"You're not armed. Just get in the hallway."

She didn't bother answering, and she didn't move from her position flattened on the wall next to the back window.

He quickly turned his gaze to the front and watched the lengthening shadows darken in the swampy gloam. Four shots had been fired. Which meant their attacker had at least two left. Just enough to kill them both.

An eerie cacophony of pig frogs, cicadas and God-knew-what-else began their night songs. His eyes and ears strained, trying to pick out the tiniest rustle or shifting of moonlight in the darkness. He heard a roaring sound and started, until he realized it was only the pounding of his blood in his ears.

Ace gave a low moan, laying his head on Dylan's right shoe. Poor guy. The dog needed a medal if they came out of this alive.

Time slowed, the night growing impossibly darker by the second. How long had they been standing there, poised for disaster? Could be sixty seconds, could be an hour.

"I think he's gone," Bailey said softly. He could barely discern her silhouette in the short distance between them.

Why hadn't their attacker taken another shot? Maybe the guy was used to controlling vulnerable civilians and not exchanging potshots with an officer of the law. Or maybe he'd believed the lie about backup arriving at any moment.

"Gone where?" he asked. "He's out there somewhere under cover of darkness. Watching and waiting."

"It's past time for me to check in for the end of my shift. Evan knows we're here at Floyd's. He'll come."

"Ditto. Chesser will raise an alarm as well."

"Evan warned me I was cutting it close time-wise, coming out so late in the day." Her voice was flat and heavy.

"I take responsibility for that. It was my idea to check at Billy's and then break for lunch."

"No, I'm the one who insisted we return."

Not that it mattered. They were a team. "Guess neither of our bosses is going to be too happy about a night rescue operation."

"What if—" She hesitated. "What if our rescuers walk into a trap? There's no way to warn them about the shooter."

"Don't worry. They'll be prepared for the worst."

Ace gave a louder whimper.

"How badly is your dog hurt?" Bailey asked.

"Appears to be a flesh wound, though it's bound to hurt like heck."

The whir of a motor broke into the background drone of the swamp's night creatures.

"Have they come for us already?" Bailey asked doubtfully. "Or is that our attacker escaping?"

"Either way, it's good news for us."

He waited, eyes focused forward, straining to see if anyone approached. There were no lights, no shouts, no one calling their names.

"Pretty sure it's our guy slipping away," Dylan said at last. "Too soon for the others to have raised the alarm and made their way over. We might as well have a seat and wait for them. Let's go over here," he directed, walking to one corner of the den. "We'll sit together facing outward, and if anyone comes in unannounced, I'll have us covered."

Awkwardly they settled on the floorboards. Ace scrabbled to join them, then plopped down between them with a whine. Dylan felt Bailey stiffen beside him, and he reached to move Ace to his other side, but she crisply said, "Leave him be."

His hand paused. "You sure?"

"He's injured. Shifting him will cause more pain."

As though sensing Bailey had made a concession on his behalf, Ace plopped his head on her knee and licked her skin.

Bailey flinched, then let out a rush of breath. "Yeah, yeah. Don't get used to it, buddy," she said gruffly.

He licked again, and that time, she accepted the overture, if not warmly, at least stoically.

Ace was definitely making headway in his campaign to win Bailey over. Day two, round two went to the dog. His money was on Ace for the eventual win.

"How soon will the body at Billy's be identified?" she asked.

"Should be an easy match, what with the teeth and skeleton all in one place."

"I'm afraid it's going to be Lisa Shaw."

"Me, too. It's the first record they'll check." He turned to her in the thick darkness. "Thanks to you. Your idea to search for trophies in a specific location might be the break we need to find our guy. He's certainly getting nervous. Tonight's attack proves it."

"I'm going to ask Evan if we can ban camping and outdoor activities in the swamp for all civilians until we catch the killer."

"He won't like that. Neither will local businesses that profit from the tourism."

"Evan can at least ban overnight excursions and issue a public warning to day visitors."

"Don't worry. Once news gets out that a body was found, which has probably already happened, it'll deter outdoor enthusiasts."

"Good."

They lapsed into silence, and he was intensely aware

of her warm breath and the brush of her forearms against his, hot and sweet and intimate. She stretched out her legs—those long, lean legs that he never tired of seeing. Heck, he hadn't even known he was a leg man until he met Bailey. Absently he brushed his fingers over Ace's head. The dog was napping, a good sign that the pain had eased. A sudden thought had him frowning.

"You really plan on returning to your cabin this evening? Not sure that's wise."

"I'll be fine. Don't sleep outside my place in your truck again. We'll need a good night's rest to maintain our energy and focus tomorrow."

"Will you at least consent to an officer providing drive-by patrol again?"

"That works."

So, she just didn't want *him*. "Hey, while we're stuck here, mind filling me in on whatever grudge you have against me?"

His words weighted the air, and he watched her fingers tap against her thighs in a dance of suppressed agitation. Just when he gave up hope of her responding, Bailey let out a long sigh.

"It's nothing you've done. I shouldn't hold it against you."

"Hold what against me?"

"I did reach out a long time ago about my foster father. To a cop."

Outrage washed over Dylan. "And he didn't intervene?"

"Nope."

No wonder she had no love for law enforcement. "He should have. We're here to protect the vulnerable. There's no excuse for his behavior. Who was it?"

She shook her head. "He's no longer on the force."

"That's good, at least." Probably some temporary officer who wasn't fit for the job and either quit or got fired. He wondered if it was anyone he might have known. Off the force or not, he'd love to rip into the jerk. "I'd still like to know his name, though."

"Let it go. I have, or I'm trying to, anyway."

Dylan swallowed hard. "How bad was the abuse, Bailey?"

Again, she paused so long he didn't believe she'd answer.

"Never mind, it's—"

"A few beatings," she said, interrupting him. "It was a long time ago. I'm over it." Her shoulders rose in a dismissive shrug, but her effort to minimize the horror didn't fool him.

He inched a hand over and laid it on top of her fidgeting fingers. "I'm sorry for what you went through," he said simply.

Her body became as hard and unyielding as a statue. Had he made a mistake touching her? Moments passed, but instead of withdrawing, she turned her hand over and squeezed his fingers. The silent acknowledgment eased the underlying tension that had bubbled between them from the start. Here, under the cover of ink-black darkness, she'd bared a little of her soul, and it humbled him.

Ace's muscles violently twitched in the throes of some dream, and he jerked to a sudden awakening. His warm tongue lapped at their linked hands, and Bailey withdrew from his grasp, easing away to put a few inches between their bodies.

While she was in such a mellow mood, Dylan decided to push his luck with one more question. "Why are you so afraid of dogs?"

Her mouth snapped open, so quick he knew it was a knee-jerk defensive response.

"It's okay. Nothing to be embarrassed about. You're certainly not the only person who fears them."

Bailey stood and strode to the front window, flattening her body against the wall before venturing a peek outside. "Let's just say I have a healthy respect for their bite."

"Because you were bitten?"

"Hmm. Still no sign of rescue," she commented.

He let it drop. Enough true confessions for one evening.

"Shouldn't be too much longer. It'll take about an hour for them to get here once they realize we never returned."

"Less than that. Evan will use the airboat. That should cut at least twenty minutes from the trip."

"Airboat?" He perked up. "You have an airboat? Why haven't we been using it? Geez, it could have saved us a ton of time."

"It's only for emergencies."

"Why?"

"It's bad for the environment and the wildlife."

"Yeah, well, isn't our search an emergency?" he grumbled.

"In the beginning, but not after the initial search was called off. Everyone gave up hope."

"And now we have leads. I'll have my boss speak to yours about getting us that airboat." A steady rumbling sounded from afar, and Dylan scrambled to his feet as Ace growled. "Don't step outside until we know for sure who's out there."

But Bailey was already halfway to the door. "I can tell from the sound that it's the airboat. Which means Evan's driving, and we're safe."

"We're not safe." Dylan hurried to the door and

blocked her exit. "It's a long shot, but our attacker might still be in hiding. Ready to pick us off one by one."

"Then I have to warn them of the danger."

"Chesser's with Evan and I'd bet at least a couple more officers. He'll caution everyone to be on their guard."

They faced off in the stale opaqueness of the cabin, their breath mingling. A flush of heat scoured him as he absorbed the tingling nearness of her body so close to his own. She was affected, too. He could feel it in her sudden stillness and quickened breath.

Light flashed through the grimy windowpane, breaking the spell. Now that their rescuers were closer, he could make out the distinct sound of at least three different boat motors.

Help had arrived en masse.

Footsteps pounded on the boat dock, and floodlights lit the cabin. Chesser's voice abruptly boomed over a megaphone: "This is the police! Come out with your hands up."

Bailey raised a brow. "*Now* can we go?" Without waiting for an answer, she pointed at Ace. "Might have to carry him out."

He whistled, and Ace slowly limped to his side. Dylan scooped him into his arms, careful not to touch his wound. "Me first in case anyone is excessively trigger-happy," he said. "And be sure to keep your hands raised when you exit."

He ignored her exaggerated sigh and cautiously opened the front door, one hand behind his head, the other holding Ace. "Officer Armstrong," he called, stepping out. "Ranger Covington is right behind me."

The beam of a floodlight pierced his eyes, and he squinted at the dark, murky shadows of the officers. Someone barked out an order to cover all sides, and feet shuffled as officers formed a U-shape to defend themselves from every angle. Evidently, they were taking no chances that he and Bailey weren't in extreme danger. Dylan imagined this was what it felt like being rescued in a jungle during a covert military operation gone wrong.

"Are you two alone?" Chesser's voice still boomed over a megaphone, but he was much closer.

"Far as we know," Dylan called out. "We were attacked but believe he's left the area."

"Bailey, are you okay?"

He recognized Evan's voice.

"I'm fine," she called.

A dark figure emerged from the cluster of rescue workers, and Evan swiftly stepped forward and draped an arm over Bailey's shoulder. "You sure you're okay?" he asked gruffly.

A swift bolt of irritation crackled down Dylan's spine. Was Bailey's boss a little too touchy-feely with his employee, or was he imagining it? He'd taken an instant, irrational dislike of the man from the start, so perhaps he was reading too much into what was, after all, merely a side-armed hug.

He quickly filled the sheriff in on what had transpired as the officers made their way to the boat dock.

"We're closing in on him," Chesser noted with grim satisfaction. "First thing in the morning, I'll send Jeff and another officer to gather the spent shells and run ballistics tests. By then I hope we'll also know the identity of the body we dug up."

From the corner of his eyes, Dylan watched Evan, still with an arm over Bailey's shoulder, guide her to the airboat. His proprietary manner annoyed the heck out of Dylan, but for now, he'd let it go. He got in Chesser's boat.

The trek back to the park entrance was noisy as everyone chatted all at once about the day's discoveries and offered theories about the possible killer.

Alligator eyes glowed red whenever boat lights hit them on the water. Startling how prevalent they were as they slithered through the murk at night, hunting their prey. Was their killer also out there, eyeing them from a safe perch?

When Dylan's boat arrived at the park marina, Bailey and Evan were already there, waiting. "When and where are we meeting in the morning?" she asked him as he stepped onto the dock.

"Let's meet at the sheriff's office. Come as soon as you can. I'll be there."

"Shouldn't we take Ace to a vet first?"

"I'll have one of the K-9 officers take him immediately," Chesser volunteered. "If the vet doesn't keep him overnight, he'll be fine in our kennel."

"Kennel?" she asked, rounding on Dylan. "I thought he lived with you."

"No. Never has."

"You mean you work with this dog and then let him be shut in a kennel all night?"

"He's always lived like that. He's used to it."

Her lips pursed in an angry line. "Ace can stay with me if he doesn't need to stay with the vet. He can alert me in case of an intruder."

"That isn't necessary since you're—" He bit his tongue before saying the words *afraid of dogs*. "Like we discussed, you'll have a drive-by patrol this evening keeping watch on your cabin. You don't need Ace."

"He doesn't deserve to be alone all evening."

Her insistence surprised Dylan. Clearly, compassion won out over her fear.

"I want to do this," she said quietly. "He and I will get along just fine by ourselves."

Brave words. But Dylan suspected that what he had in mind for their work the next day would require every bit of her fortitude, and then some. Truth be told, she'd probably rather face their mysterious killer than what he had planned.

Chapter Eight

Despite the early hour, the sheriff's office was abuzz when Bailey entered the crowded room. From the litter of coffee cups and empty fast-food wrappers, she suspected that many of the officers had pulled an all-nighter. They were huddled around a massive whiteboard with black chunks of text and photos, like honeybees swarming a gallberry bush. Her eyes immediately caught Dylan's, and he rose from the massive conference table.

She walked closer to the board, curious about the suspects and theories. Bubbly smiles radiated from a photo of Mary Thornton and Amy Holley as they stood by their kayaks, ready to embark on a new adventure. Underneath were the names of their husbands with question marks—she supposed the closest of kin were always suspects—and then a list of all the employees of the adventure outfitter company. She scanned the names, then stopped at a familiar one: *Clay Slacomb*. Blood pounded in her ears, and she bit the inside of her lip to ground herself.

There was only one name worse than Armstrong, and that was Slacomb.

"Everything okay?" Dylan murmured beside her.

Without replying, she abruptly exited, and he followed her into the hallway. Out of the group's earshot, Bailey rounded on him. "Tell me about Clay Slacomb. Has he been questioned?"

"Slacomb." Dylan rubbed his chin. "The outfitter employee? Yeah, they all were questioned, but nothing stood out with any of them. Why?"

"Interrogate him again."

His eyes sharpened. "What makes you suspicious of this guy?"

She disliked discussing her past, but she couldn't keep silent. "That abusive foster father I mentioned yesterday? Clay is his brother."

Dylan's face set in hard, determined lines. "Has Clay ever laid a hand on you?" he asked. His eyes had turned hard and cold, and his voice was the aural equivalent of sharp, pointy icicles.

She drew a shaky breath and fought back the ridiculous twinge of shame. "No, but he witnessed the abuse firsthand and he…laughed. Someone like that, well, I wouldn't put anything past him."

He reached a hand out as if to touch her, then dropped it back by his side. "I want the name of Clay's brother, too."

"Edgar. Surely you don't think they acted together?"

"We can't rule anything out. Given their history, though, I'd put either one of them at the top of the suspect list. Listen, Bailey, I'd wanted us to question your foster father today, but if you'd rather not be present, I'll certainly understand."

See Edgar again? Her throat tightened as she pictured his angry, pinched face. The man had always acted ticked off at the world, ready for the tiniest provocation—one wrong word, one microexpression of disrespect on anyone's face—to detonate his temper. His brother was cut from the same cloth. The pair of them acted as though everyone had cheated them out of what they were entitled to—and they were determined to make everyone pay for that transgression.

"I'll go with you," she said flatly.

"You don't have to. Take the morning off, and I'll come pick you up when I'm done."

"No, I'm going, and that's that."

Dylan slowly nodded. "If you're sure."

"I am. And you'd better have another officer question Clay while we're speaking with Edgar. If not, he'll warn his brother of our suspicions. We don't want to give Clay time to prepare. Or possibly flee."

"Gotcha. Be right back."

Alone in the empty hallway, she shivered and rubbed her arms. How would Edgar react when he saw her after all those years? Was he still furious at her for filing a report against him? Stupid question. Of course he was. Nobody could hold a grudge like a Slacomb. For over a year after she'd left his house and spoken against him to a social worker, she'd received late-night phone calls. He'd called her a worthless fool, promising that she'd pay for her lies. When she'd threatened to file a restraining order against him, he'd finally stopped. Since then, she'd had no contact. Occasionally, in town, she'd see him or his wife, but she'd turn her back on them and avoid eye contact.

"Ready?" Dylan returned to her side, and they marched to his patrol car. "Where does he work?" he asked. "Think he'll be there or at home?"

She gave a derisive laugh. "He's too antisocial to actually hold a job. That would entail working alongside other people and reporting to a boss. No, he supposedly works from home. Runs an auto repair business out of his garage, but his place is so remote he doesn't get much business."

"And where's home?"

She gave him the address, and they slipped into silence as they left downtown Folkston and headed toward Waycross. Near the town limits, they turned off onto a dirt road, and then soon spotted the sprawling ranch home and the property that she'd vowed never to set foot on again.

So much for famous last words.

A pack of Dobermans stormed toward their car, barking furiously.

Her throat went dry, and her fingers dug into the door handle. "Watch out for the dogs. They're vicious. He lets them roam unless someone's booked an appointment at his shop."

Dylan popped open the glove compartment. "Grab a can of mace. If he doesn't control his dogs, I'll shoot them if they move to attack."

"Oh, they'll attack all right. That's what he's trained them to do." Wherever the pack roamed, Edgar was sure to be nearby. Her eyes scanned the property.

A figure stood in front of an open shed, clad in a white sleeveless T-shirt and baggy jeans streaked with grease. A cigarette—unfiltered and hand rolled—dangled from his thin lips. He squinted at them as he ran a hand through his thinning brown hair, which had more silver in it now than when she'd seen him last.

A cop car pulling up at his house was probably the most unwelcome sight Edgar could imagine—until he spotted her stepping out of the vehicle. Bailey surmised that he didn't want to see the likes of the woman who'd put a stop to his gravy-train foster care money. Not that the system provided much in the way of compensation, but he'd pocketed it all and in return provided only a closet-sized room and meals of peanut butter sandwiches.

He and his wife, Millie, needed the money since his mechanic business was slow. Edgar was great at fixing vehicles, but he lacked customer relation skills. Which was to say, he ripped them off as much as he thought he could get away with, all the time sporting a smirk that did nothing to endear him for future business.

"Last chance to change your mind," Dylan said.

"No way." To her surprise, she found herself actually looking forward to this confrontation. Edgar wasn't so scary when he was outnumbered and in the presence of an armed officer. Her hand instinctively strayed to her necklace, and she stroked the soft crow feather. *Courage.* The cool, hard obsidian arrowhead lay heavy on her breastbone. *Power.*

The Dobermans surrounded the car, jumping up on the passenger doors, their nails scraping metal. Their pointy faces snarled by the windows. Her fingers curled into her palms. She'd rather face ten Edgars than one of those beasts.

"What the heck," Dylan muttered.

"He always keeps a pack. Trains them to attack at his command. And trespassers are always fair game."

"That him standing over there?"

She nodded, and Dylan lifted a megaphone to his mouth. "Call off your dogs, or I'll shoot them."

Edgar scowled and barked an order for them to "git." They retreated a few feet, bodies taut and mouths snapping as she and Dylan stepped out of the car. Bailey gripped the mace can tightly. Too bad she hadn't had it years ago when Edgar had sicced the pack on her. Good thing Ace was still at the vet that morning. These Dobermans would have chewed him up as an appetizer.

"Cage your animals," Dylan ordered. "Immediately."

Edgar scowled but ordered the dogs to the house. Mil-

lie magically appeared at the door and ushered them in.
She was still a mousy brown ghost existing in the shadows, obeying Edgar's every command. Bailey almost felt
sorry for her. *Almost.* But the woman had certainly never
spared her any mercy during her time in that house. A
bit of the tension in her belly unfurled as the last of the
dogs entered the house and the door closed behind them.

"Whatcha want with me?" Edgar asked in gravelly,
abrupt tones. Even his voice was mean, hard and dam-
aged by a two-pack-a-day habit. He cocked his head at
Bailey but addressed Dylan. "What'd you bring her for?
We ain't on the best of terms."

"We're here to question you about the two women who
recently went missing."

Edgar's face mottled, and his scowl deepened. "That
ain't got nothin' to do with me. What kinda stories that
bitch been telling you, eh? The truth ain't in that one."

"Let's keep this civil, Mr. Slacomb. I won't tolerate
that kind of language about my partner."

"She a cop now?" Edgar spit on the ground before
sparing her a malevolent glance. "Don't see no badge."

"Ranger Covington is assisting me in this matter, and
you'll accord her the same respect as you do me."

Which meant nothing to Edgar, because the man had
no respect for anybody. He folded his arms and regarded
them sullenly.

"I understand you know the area well," Dylan continued. "Have a johnboat you use for fishing the swamp?"

"Yeah. So? I got a license. No crime there."

"Heard you like to fish along the orange water trail
by Billy's Island," Dylan noted. "We found a body there
yesterday."

"What? You tryin' to pin somethin' on me? Can't a
man fish in peace no more?" Edgar rounded on Bailey.

"What kind of nonsense you been tellin' the law 'bout me? Why, you little—"

"That's enough," Dylan cut in.

Anger overcame her initial timidity, and Bailey stepped in front of her former tormentor. "Shut. Up," she said slowly, her words measured and clipped. "For once in your miserable life, try listening and using your brain instead of antagonizing others."

Edgar flung the cigarette from his mouth and ground it into the dirt with the toe of his black boot, no doubt wishing she were beneath it instead of the cigarette stub.

"Where were you three evenings ago?" Dylan asked.

Honest surprise flickered in the man's tight face. "Where I always am. Here. Go ask Millie if ya don't believe me."

Bailey stepped away from him, clicking her tongue. As if his wife would do anything but parrot Edgar's every assertion as truth. That milksop of a woman had given up on life years ago. Maybe a better woman than Bailey could forgive and forget Millie's silent acceptance when Edgar chastised her and the other foster children…but no. In Bailey's eyes, Millie's unprotested witnessing of the acts condemned her alongside the husband she chose to stay with.

"Any other witness to that?"

"No, just me and Millie watching the TV." Curiosity won out over belligerence. "Why? What happened three nights ago? Another woman gone missing 'round here?"

"Someone tried to burn down my cabin," said Bailey.

He blinked, and then snorted. "Well, it weren't me."

"Would you mind taking a polygraph test on your whereabouts that night?" Dylan asked.

"Heck, yeah, I'd mind."

He nodded and switched tactics. "Did you ever come across Amy Holley and Mary Thornton while out fishing?"

"The missing women? Seriously, you tryin' to pin murder on me?" Edgar swallowed hard. "I may a been a bit harsh with some foster kids in the past, but that don't make me a murderer."

A bit harsh? Bailey bit her tongue to keep from interrupting Dylan's questioning.

"What makes you believe they were murdered?" he continued.

"You said you found a body. I assumed…" Edgar's voice drifted off, and for the first time, a certain vulnerability crept in.

Dylan didn't reply, just stared him down.

"C'mon, man, I ain't done nothin'." Edgar's voice switched to pathetic cajoling.

"What about Clay?" asked Bailey. "You think he's capable of committing a violent crime?"

Edgar shot her a look of pure hatred before turning to Dylan. "No. No way. Do we need to get us a lawyer or somethin'?"

"Not if you haven't done anything wrong." Dylan's hands went to his hips, drawing attention to his sidearm. "But if you were the one outside Ranger Covington's cabin two nights ago, you best not ever go near there again. Anything happens to her or her property, you're our number one suspect."

"So that's what this is about. It ain't got nothin' to do with them missing women."

"In my experience, a man with a history of violence against women who lives in proximity to where two went missing at least warrants an interview."

"Are you done now? I told you everythin'."

Dylan nodded. "We're watching you. Have a nice day."

He turned as though to leave, then swung back around. "Better start keeping your dogs under control, too."

"I ain't broke no law. There's no leash law out here in the county."

"Doesn't matter. If I believe they pose a clear threat to the community, I can send the humane officer here to round them up."

"The dog catcher?" Horror sagged Edgar's face.

Bailey knew he cared about those dogs more than any person, even his wife and brother. He'd trained them from pups to be aggressive and to "protect" him and his property.

"I'll keep 'em in the house or in the fenced backyard," Edgar grudgingly conceded. "But they wouldn't hurt a fly."

The bite marks scarring her right thigh were a testimony to that lie.

As Dylan headed to the cruiser, Bailey stood her ground until Edgar made eye contact with her.

"Liar," she said simply. "And we both know the kind of man you really are. What you're capable of doing."

She let the dead weight of her words fully settle between them, daring Edgar to deny the truth. He gaped at her, apparently at a loss as to how to respond to an adult Bailey, one who was no longer powerless and silent.

Bailey returned to the car and slammed the door shut, allowing herself one last glance at Edgar leaning against the garage, shoulders slumped, and then at the old ranch house, where Millie's pale face peeked out from behind a dingy lace curtain. Several huge dogs surrounded her, teeth bared and barking furiously. Bailey turned away and breathed more freely as the car rumbled down the dirt road and again entered the county highway.

"You okay?" Dylan asked her at last.

"I'm fine, actually." It'd been unexpectedly satisfying to confront Edgar, to show him that she was no longer a defenseless child he could bully. She even suspected that Dylan planned the whole thing to give her an opportunity to face her demons from a position of strength. But she was nothing if not truthful. "To be honest, though, I don't think Edgar's our guy. Now, Clay, that's another story."

"Let's see what's happening on that end." Dylan punched out a number on his cell phone. "Jeff? Y'all talked to Clay yet?" Pause. "What time is he due back? Ten minutes, okay. Hold on."

Dylan lowered the phone and shot her a quizzical look. "Clay's out giving a private boat tour, but he's due back in ten minutes or so. The outfitter shop is on our way back to town. You want to talk to him, or should we let someone else?"

"I vote we interview him, too."

Might as well cut down another Goliath from her past. Seemed she was on a roll today.

Chapter Nine

He was late.

Dylan paced the loading dock, impatient to question Clay.

"He'll be here soon, don't worry," Greg Ridley, the owner of the outfitting company, assured him.

"Tour guides don't follow exact schedules," Bailey explained to Dylan. "Sometimes we'd take a little longer exploring with the guests, depending on what they were interested in seeing. I used to work here," she explained at his raised brow. "Afternoons and summers in high school, then summers in college. I loved every moment."

He imagined she'd love any job that got her away from the Slacomb residence. No wonder she loved the swamp.

"One of the best guides I ever had," Greg said, beaming at her as though she were his own daughter. "She started off working the concession stand, graduated to running the store merchandise register and then transitioned to tour guide. Kind of hate she got her forestry degree and left us, but Bailey deserved more than I could give her at this outfit."

They all stopped talking and gazed at the water trail's mouth. The sound of the approaching flat-bottomed boat could be heard before it was seen.

"Is there a problem with Clay Slacomb I should be

aware of?" Greg asked. "He's well qualified and polite enough with the tourists, but I have to admit he's a loner. A bit of an odd duck. Has no interest in getting to know his coworkers. He shows up five minutes before a scheduled tour and immediately leaves once it's over. No hobnobbing with anyone."

"We're just questioning people familiar with the area," he answered evasively.

"Notice you're not questioning me or anyone else on staff this time," Greg said, tugging at his long gray beard. "If the man has anything to do with those missing women, or has some knowledge he hasn't shared, he's a real liability for my business."

Greg was an aging hippie who passionately loved nature and wildlife. He and his wife, Alma, had settled into the perfect business, an ecoadventure outfitting company, which allowed him to spend most of his time outdoors and earn a comfortable living.

The boat chugged into the shallow waters and headed for the dock. A middle-aged couple clad in T-shirts, shorts and baseball hats sipped cans of soda. A lean, scruffy man with rusty hair and a beard sat at the helm, dressed in long sleeves and long pants. Swampers knew to cover their limbs before venturing deep into the marsh. Clay had the same build as his brother—wiry and small of stature. Although one was a redhead and the other had brown hair, they both had a wary look on their faces and dark eyes that shone with suspicion and constant shifting, as though they were trapped animals pursuing an exit strategy.

He'd seen Clay from a distance over the years. The man had been brought in from time to time for public drunkenness, bar fights, disturbing the peace and, last year, a few domestic disputes. He'd never crossed the line resulting in a physical assault charge, but his girlfriend at the time had felt justifiably threatened and called for help after each incident. Thankfully, she'd decided enough was enough and split.

Had Clay sought new women to bully? And had that escalated to abduction and murder? So far, he was their best suspect.

The boat bumped against the platform and Greg started over to the dock.

"Don't mention we're here," Dylan said. "We'll wait for him near your store."

Greg nodded appreciatively. "Might not look good for business to have cops around waiting to question my employee. Thanks."

Dylan hadn't done it for Greg's benefit, but if it helped out a guy who'd befriended Bailey when she'd most needed a friend, then he was glad. As Greg hurried to the dock to lend a hand tying up the boat, Dylan motioned to Bailey, and they retreated into the shadows of the outfitter building.

The older couple exited the boat first, surprisingly spry for their age. The woman made a beeline to the restroom on the far side of the building while the man went inside the store. At the dock, Clay unloaded a cooler and then hopped aboard the platform. He scooped the heavy cooler up in one hand, and it tilted his body to the right as he made his way up the dock.

Once Clay was within six feet of them, Dylan stepped out of the shadows.

"May I have a word with you, Mr. Slacomb?"

Clay stopped dead in his tracks and regarded them warily. "Eh? What's this about? I ain't done nothin' wrong."

"We're not accusing you of a crime. We merely want to ask you a few questions—"

"Did that bitch call and file a complaint? I knew it! Flaky as heck that one."

Dylan removed a notebook from his front uniform pocket. "May I have the name of this woman?"

"You don't know?" He shook his head. "'Course you already know it. You're just messin' with me."

Paranoid little dude, Dylan decided. He'd play that card to his advantage. "Name, please. Cooperate with us and we'll get to the bottom of this."

"Nancy Mims," Clay admitted grudgingly. "We been out a few times. I swear I thought she was at least nineteen. How was I supposed to know she weren't seventeen yet? Anyways, we got in a fight and I might have pushed her away when she came at me, all jealous about another woman I was talking to. I left Nancy there at the bar. Spiteful little witch. What kind of lie she done told you?"

Shoving an underage girl? It was all the excuse he needed. Dylan shut the notepad and stuffed it back in his shirt. "Let's discuss this at the station."

His only warning was the microsecond that Clay's eyes shifted to the left. The cooler dropped out of his hand followed by an explosion of ice and soda cans rolling along the sidewalk. Clay ran, fast as a twitchy rabbit exiting a fox's lair.

Damn it. Dylan took off after him, determined to overtake Clay before he reached the tree line only twenty yards away. Bailey sped along beside him and he shook his head. No way he'd compromise her safety with a desperate man.

"Stay back and call for backup," he ordered, never breaking his stride.

"Gotcha," she called out.

The sun flashed on Clay's coppery hair, urging Dylan forward like a beacon. He had to get the guy before he disappeared into the woods. Clay reached the first copse of trees and never looked back, darting into the wilderness like a hunted animal.

Dylan plunged into the dense underbrush, felt palmetto needles slashing through his pants and flaying his legs. Not far ahead, he heard Clay's heavy footfalls as he ran. Twigs snapped, and branches whipped as he ran deeper.

"Stop," Dylan called out. His shoes sank an inch into the wet peat. Water seeped through the leather and sucked the bottom of his shoes more with each step, slowing his progress. Clay, he remembered, had been wearing knee-high wading boots. A tactical advantage—along with his intimate knowledge of this area.

Another flash of red broke through the thick shadows. Clay was at least fifty yards ahead of him now.

"Stop," he called again. "I just want to talk to you."

More frantic rustling as the suspect leaped and skipped further into the Okefenokee. And then silence.

Blood rushed through his ears, a whir louder than the swamp's constant buzzing of insects. His chest was on fire, burning with each deep breath. He strained his ears to pick up any noise, but all he heard was his own labored breathing sawing in and out of his chest.

Stupid, stupid move on Clay's part. Did he really think he could escape a manhunt? But then, nobody had probably ever accused him of being too bright. The man was only making it harder on himself when he eventually was caught. Mentally, Dylan added fleeing a cop to the bevy of charges Clay was about to be slapped with.

He pushed forward. If the suspect was within hearing distance, perhaps he still had a chance to persuade him to give up his flight.

"Come on, Clay. Let's go to the station and talk this

through man to man. What do you say? Running from me doesn't look good for you. If you're innocent like you claim, all of this can blow over. By tonight, you'll be back home."

An even more profound silence greeted his words. "Damn it, Slacomb. Quit this foolishness."

Twigs snapped somewhere close to his right and he spun around, drawing his gun. "That you, Slacomb? Come out with your hands up."

Odds were that Clay had no weapon, but he wasn't taking chances. More rustling ensued, and Dylan held his gun steady, aimed and ready to fire. From the thicket, a doe emerged, terrified and snorting a warning. She thundered past him and disappeared again into the woods, her hooves pounding the peat. He slowly holstered his weapon, wondering which of them had suffered the greater scare at the unexpected encounter.

He was at a distinct disadvantage here. Clay knew this swamp better than him.

"WHICH WAY DO you think Clay's heading?" Bailey asked Greg as she hung up her cell phone. "If he keeps straight he's headed to the Lily Pad prairie."

Greg hustled up beside her, panting. "I can't believe he ran."

"Which direction do you think he's going?" she asked again.

"He might take the green trail and head on home. His place is only three miles in that direction, off of Blankenship Road."

She thought fast. "I can cut him off at the mouth of the trail. He's gotta cross it to get back home."

"Shouldn't we wait on the cops to chase him down?"

"That'll take too long. Just give me the keys to your fastest boat."

Greg shook his head and turned to run back to the dock. "I'm going with you. Hurry."

Alma, Greg's wife, hurried out of the building and caught up to them as they ran across the pier. "Greg? What's going on? Something wrong?"

Quickly, Bailey began untying the rope as Greg jumped in the boat.

"It's okay," he assured Alma. "Cops will be arriving shortly. Tell them Bailey and I are headed to the egret prairie."

"But—"

Greg started the motor, cutting off Alma's protest, and Bailey hopped on board. Greg revved the engine and they sped out of the small marina, for once careless of the wake breaking over the old platform dock boards. Her former boss pushed the small boat to its maximum speed and they busted through the narrow Tater Rake Run Trail heavily lined with hoorah bushes and ty ty shrubs, then navigated between islands thick with maidencane and rose pogonia.

Lazy alligators slowly slithered from the banks as they espied the racing boat. They were more frightened of humans than vice versa.

The first water prairie they sludged through was populated with batteries of floating peat abloom with pitcher plants, and the copper reeds of broomsedge. Bailey kept her eyes peeled along the banks, hoping for signs of human movement, but nothing appeared out of the ordinary. Greg channeled them through another short, narrow water trail and then abruptly shut off the boat engine.

"If he was headin' home, Clay can't run further than this point. Water's too deep and too wide. But could be he has a small boat or canoe cached 'round here. A few days last month he came to work by boat because his car was broken."

They both fixed their gaze on the shoreline, eyes and ears straining for signs of life as Greg slowly navigated the boat parallel to the bank.

"Can't believe Clay would hunt down those women," Greg said at last. "But running off like he did sure makes him look guilty."

"I wouldn't put anything past the man," she answered sharply.

"Just because Clay is Edgar's brother doesn't mean he's cut from the same cloth."

She kept her lips fused into a tight line, refusing to give voice to the memories. Did Clay even remember her? Or was she some throwaway kid that he'd seen mistreated and then immediately wiped from his consciousness? She picked up the binoculars Greg always kept in the seat compartment and trained them on the shore. Minutes later, she discerned the faint outline of an old, dented johnboat leaning against a cypress tree.

"Bingo," she said, pointing to the tree. "Found his boat. Let's land here."

They pulled up to the bank, their boat landing with a soft thud. Greg handed her the rope they used to tie up the boat, picked up an oar he kept stored for potential motor malfunctions and gripped it tightly. "In case I need a weapon," he told her. "But I have a good relationship with Clay. Shouldn't be necessary to use force to subdue him if he comes our way."

"You know what we could do?" she said, thinking aloud. "If we take Clay's boat, then we might not need to fight him at all. He'll see he can't escape and he'll give himself up."

"Always knew you were a smart girl," Greg said with a chuckle.

She shrugged dismissively. "You'd have thought of it, too, eventually."

But his praise warmed her. Her former boss had a master's degree in biology and knew the species of every plant in the swamp as well as the behavior patterns of every bird, reptile and wildlife animal that called this lonely place home. His wisdom and kindness had inspired her life's path as a forest ranger.

Together, they hauled Clay's boat from the bank. Greg waded further into the water and began tying Clay's boat to their skiff.

Out of nowhere, a loud rustling filled the air and she went still, unsure if it was a deer or a man. Crashing footfalls blasted from the wood's dark interior and then Clay stumbled forward. His eyes were wild and hunted as he blinked, assessing this new danger.

"Give it up, Clay," Greg called out, the rope still in his hands where he was yoking the two boats together.

Clay bent over double, one hand clutching his stomach, the other anchored on a knee. His panting was loud and labored. From behind, Dylan crashed through the woods. Clay's posture slumped a bit further, as though conceding defeat at being covered front and back. Still, his eyes focused on her and, oddly, seemed to burn into hers. It'd been so long ago that he'd dismissed his brother's treatment of her with nothing but a smirk. But did he recognize her now?

His head raised, and he grunted an acknowledgment. "I remember you. Bonnie? Brenda? Always were trouble."

Bailey gave a quick tap to the crow feather nestled at

her breastbone. Lulu's custom talisman always provided the needed boost of strength for any situation.

Without warning, Clay pulled a slapjack from his pants pocket. She'd seen that weapon once before when Edgar and Clay had had a drunken fight one evening. The black leather baton was about eight inches in length and filled with buckshot. Her eyes fixated on the slapjack and her vision tunneled. A splash sounded behind her; Greg had slipped and fallen into the water.

Clay charged forward. A mad bull, intent on his target.

Her mind swiftly calculated the odds of help. Greg still splashed in the water, evidently trying to regain his footing. Dylan shouted something, but she couldn't say what, only that he'd never get to her in time to prevent an attack.

She was on her own.

Clay might hurt her, but she wasn't going down without getting in a few licks of her own.

She'd show him that she was no longer a silent, passive victim.

She'd fight for that lost girl who'd taken so much at the hands of her foster father.

And she'd prove to herself that no man could mistreat her and not suffer a consequence.

The air around her stirred with Clay's charge. Instead of running away, Bailey swiftly bent forward and moved sideways, ramming his rib cage. A satisfying grunt of pain escaped his lips before he grabbed her arm and they both fell to the ground. The impact knocked loose his bruising grip. Quickly she rolled over, scrambling to her feet.

Clay was a second ahead of her. He loomed above, blocking the sun, the slapjack held high in his right hand. With a *whoosh*, it descended. Bailey lunged to the right, trying to escape its inevitable impact, but its leaded weight crashed against her left shoulder. Fire welted along her flesh and her eyes went teary from pain. Her traitorous knees turned to jelly, and she crumbled. Another whir from above and she knew what was coming. Before the blow landed, Bailey grabbed Clay's right calf and pulled with all her might, praying to knock him off balance.

The second strike landed on her right hip and a kaleidoscope of color burst behind her eyes, blinding her. But she felt the vibration of the wet peat as Clay landed beside her, cursing. She kicked at him as two male voices barked at one another from somewhere above. Help had at last arrived.

She blinked through the pain and watched as Greg struggled to hold Clay's kicking feet while Dylan grappled with Clay's arms and shoulders. Together, the two managed to roll Clay onto his belly. Dylan slapped on handcuffs, the metal clicking loud and reassuring her of her safety. Greg, ever resourceful, tied Clay's feet together with his boat rope.

Once the cuffs were secured, Dylan darted her a wild glance. "How bad are you hurt, Bailey? Any broken bones?"

She slowly sat up and shook her head to clear out the ringing. "Don't…" She inhaled sharply at the stinging pain in her shoulder and hip. "…don't think so."

Greg's arm wrapped around her. "Think you can stand? If not, I'll carry you to the boat."

No. She wouldn't give Clay the satisfaction of seeing her incapacitated. "I've got this," she protested. "Just lend me a hand."

Gritting her teeth, she stood and glared down at Clay, who writhed and cursed, even trussed like a chicken for Sunday dinner.

Dylan gave her a somber nod before he returned his attention to the suspect. "You're under arrest," he began.

Her lips grimly curled at the corners. Squaring off with two Slacombs in one day was tough on a woman, but she'd survived. She dropped to one knee beside the still-squirming Clay and whispered in his ear, "Who's laughing now?"

Chapter Ten

"I'm okay," Bailey kept insisting to Dylan, Evan, Sheriff Chesser and the mélange of cops and federal agents when they'd returned to the sheriff station. "Really. It was only a couple of hits from a slapjack. I don't need to go home and take it easy."

But they insisted, and she reluctantly gave in after Dylan promised to drop by her cabin in the evening to update her on the investigation. Driving home, she felt the pain in her shoulder and hip deepen, and she gripped the steering wheel to steady her body's sudden tremors. She hadn't counted on this delayed onslaught of nerves. Her teeth chattered, and as though her car was on autopilot, she was driving down her road with no clear memory of navigating.

Her mind played another trick on her as, without a conscious plan of action, she sped past her own cabin and pulled into Lulu's dirt driveway. The blue pickup parked by the side of Lulu's place took her by surprise. Holt was back in town. She threw her car in Reverse to leave, not wanting to interrupt their time together.

The front door banged open and Lulu emerged onto the porch, beckoning her to come inside. Bailey stuck her head out the window and waved. "That's okay. Didn't know you had company. I'll see ya later."

"Don't you dare run off." Lulu hurried toward the car, her face drawn with concern. "Heard 'bout what happened with that Slacomb boy. How bad you hurt?"

Should have known this morning's events would have spread all over town. "I'm fine," she answered, for what seemed like the hundredth time today.

"I got just the thing for you. Come on in."

"But Holt's here—"

"So what?"

"I don't want to intrude."

Lulu scowled and pivoted toward the porch, expecting Bailey to follow.

She did. Not because she felt up to a social call, but because if she didn't visit, Lulu would merely show up at her cabin and demand entrance. Might as well get this over with. After all, it was her own fault for coming over in the first place.

Inside, Holt stood and strode over, his weathered face echoing Lulu's concern. He held out a hand and she shook it. "How bad did that man hurt you, darlin'?"

"I'm fine." She repeated the words by rote.

Lulu pointed at the couch and Bailey sat, almost sighing at the relief of taking the weight off her shaky legs. Holt brought her a glass of iced tea and she swallowed a long draft. Lulu hovered over the couch, holding a small tin container.

"Where'd he strike you? This'll take the sting right out," she promised, scooping a bit of yellow salve on her index finger.

The room filled with the cooling scent of peppermint and some earthy smell Bailey couldn't identify. "I can put it on at home," she said.

"Where?" Lulu asked, ignoring her protest.

Bailey sighed and pushed aside a couple of inches of her uniform blouse. "Left shoulder and neck."

She closed her eyes and tried not to wince at Lulu's touch. The salve stung for a second, and then the cooling began to numb the sting.

"What's in this magic elixir?"

"A large dose of peppermint mixed with castor oil and beeswax from my own hives. I also put in Saint-John's-wort and Solomon's seal for speedy healing."

"It's awesome. Thanks."

"Anywhere else you need it?"

Bailey cast a significant nod at Holt. "I'll, um, take care of that at home."

"I'll leave the room," he quickly volunteered, making a move toward the hall.

"No, don't. I'm going home." Lulu's mouth opened to protest, but Bailey spoke quickly. "I just want to lie down and rest," she lied. Her friend couldn't argue with that sentiment.

"Humph." Lulu gave her a squinty I-don't-trust-you side-glance. "At least let me take care of your talisman. Hand me your necklace."

Bailey pulled the leather cord over her neck and placed it in Lulu's palm, already knowing the brief ceremony her friend wanted to perform. This was at least the third time she'd had to cleanse the bad juju and replace the crow feather. Feathers didn't hold up well against sweaty skin during the humid Georgia summers.

Lulu retrieved a new crow feather from her desk drawer, then lit a sage smudge stick. The acrid-sweet smoke wisped around the new plume while Lulu mumbled a quick prayer.

"I'll bury the old one," Holt offered. Although only one-sixteenth Native American, he was well versed in

their customs and held the old ways in respect. He un-
hooked it from the leather cord and exited the back door.

Finished with the blessing, Lulu took the necklace to
the sink and rinsed water over the turquoise beads and
obsidian to purify them. "That should do it," she pro-
nounced, returning the talisman to Bailey.

The stones lay heavy and smooth in her hand, the new
feather tickling her palm. Bailey wasn't convinced that
the ritual was necessary, but she couldn't deny that the
necklace provided her comfort and strength. The talisman helped, and she wasn't messing with what worked.

"Thank you," she murmured. "I'll be on my way. Tell
Holt thanks, too. When did he get back in town?"

"Got back this morning from an expedition in Maggie Valley, North Carolina. Says he doesn't have another
one booked for nearly a month."

"Good." Lulu would never admit it, but Bailey guessed
her existence was often a lonely one. She enjoyed working with her beehives and gardening but had little interaction with people.

Driving home, niggling worries scrabbled through her
mind. She wasn't lonely like Lulu, was she? After all,
she had her job and coworkers.

*What about friends? What about family? What about
a lover?*

Not her fault she had no family—and Lulu was her
best friend. Okay, her only friend. Everybody else was
merely an acquaintance.

And a lover? Dylan's face sprang into her consciousness, a handsome picture with kind, olive green eyes
and sandy hair that curled slightly at the ends. Maybe.
She couldn't deny she was attracted to him, even if he
was an Armstrong. With an effort, she shrugged off the

thought. Getting attacked and confronting two enemies in one day had rattled her, that's all.

All she wanted to do was take a couple of ibuprofen, get a bath and then apply Lulu's salve on her injuries. But when she got home, she groaned at the sight of the park management vehicle in her driveway.

Evan exited his car and watched as she parked her vehicle and then approached. She lifted her chin and painted on a breezy smile. "Hi, Evan. What brings you here?"

"Came to check on you."

"I'm fine," she said once again.

"It's just the two of us now."

The intensity in his eyes made her uncomfortable, especially when he stepped in a little closer.

"You can tell me if you're hurting."

She opened her mouth to deny it, then snapped it shut. Once she told Evan what he wanted to hear, he'd leave. "Okay, it stings a little. But it's not like I've got broken bones or anything."

"You're always so brave." Evan laid a hand on her shoulder. The weight on her tender flesh sent pain shooting through her arm. She hissed in pain.

"Sorry, I forgot that's where you're hurt."

Evan closed the distance between them, pulled her to his chest and patted her between her shoulder blades.

Surely he wasn't putting a move on her—was he? It must be her imagination.

"If you don't mind, I'm going inside now to rest. Been a crazy day."

"Poor Bailey." He pulled back and looked at her with an intense gleam in his eyes. "Let me take care of you."

"I don't need taking care of," she replied tartly. "See you tomorrow morning, Evan."

With that, she spun on her heels and stepped away, determined to shake off the unwanted advance.

"Wait." His hand grabbed her elbow.

"That's enough, Evan. I'm going inside. Alone."

"But I only want to—"

"The lady said *that's enough*," a male voice boomed.

She swore she'd never seen a more welcome sight than Dylan's stern face as he stared down her boss.

Evan let her go and raised his hands, palms up. An aw-shucks expression crossed his face. "It's not what you think. I only came by to see how Bailey's doing." He turned to her, his eyes oddly pleading. "Isn't that right, Bailey?"

Confusion knotted her brow. Maybe she'd read something into their exchange that wasn't there. They'd worked together for years without so much as an inappropriate comment passing his lips. For her part, she'd regarded him as something of a father figure. Not that she'd ever had a role model for how a normal father-daughter relationship really worked. Her biological father had never been in the picture and Edgar Slacomb had surely demonstrated the worst possible example of fatherhood.

She was spared answering Evan when Dylan spoke up. "You've expressed your concern and seen that she's fine. Best be on your way, then, Mr. Johnson," he said coolly.

"Yes, yes, of course." Evan shuffled toward his car and waved casually. "Glad you're okay, Bailey."

The speed with which he started his car and backed out of her driveway was almost comical. She'd have laughed if she didn't dread the inevitable awkwardness of their next encounter.

Dylan stood beside her, watching Evan as he drove out of sight. "I don't like that man," he said slowly.

"Evan's okay. I'm sure that—whatever *that* was—won't happen again."

"It better not."

"If it does, I'll put him quickly in his place."

"Promise?"

"Absolutely."

He nodded. "Are you really okay? It's been one heck of a day for you so far."

"If one more person asks me that…"

Dylan laughed as he walked to his car. "Got someone here who wants to say hello."

He bent inside the vehicle and emerged holding twenty pounds of squirming, tail-wagging canine.

"Ace!" She laughed, surprised at the burst of warmth that exploded in her chest as the dog yipped a happy reply. Then she spotted the bandage on his haunch. "Is he doing okay?"

"Vet says he is. Like you, I expect Ace is sick of people mooning over his injury. He wants out and about."

He set the dog on the ground and Ace scurried over, limping only slightly. Tentatively, she bent down and patted the top of his head.

"Now there's progress for you," Dylan said, his voice smug with satisfaction.

She looked up at him. "Doesn't mean I want him slobbering all over me."

"Of course." Dylan whistled, and Ace reluctantly hobbled to his side and sat, regarding her with a wistful cock of his head as his tail thumped the ground.

"It's blazing hot out here. Want to come inside?" she asked impulsively. Never mind that a minute ago she'd wanted nothing more than to be alone. Dylan seemed to have a positive, calming effect on her mood.

"Thought you'd never ask. Want me to leash Ace on your porch railing?"

Ace emitted a tiny high-pitched whimper, as though he understood their conversation and needed to voice his desire to stay with them. How could she refuse?

"He can come in, too. As long as he behaves."

They followed her onto the porch and she unlocked the door.

"You smell like—" he took a deep sniff "—Christmas candy," Dylan observed.

She laughed. "Lulu's special concoction for pain. It really does seem to take some of the sting out."

"Ah, right. Your friend down the road."

They entered the cabin and she led them to the kitchen, where she set Lulu's elixir on the table and then filled a bowl of water for Ace.

"Are you thirsty?"

"I wouldn't turn down a glass of water. Thanks."

She grabbed two water bottles from the fridge and they sat at the table side by side. "What's happening with Clay Slacomb?"

"For now, he's being held for assaulting an officer."

"How long can you keep him locked up on that charge?"

"A few days at least. Long enough to give us time to dig a little more and see if any forensic evidence shows up to pin him to these crimes."

She picked at the plastic wrapping on her bottle. "I can't stop thinking about Amy Holley. Wondering if she's still alive. If she's in pain. She must be so scared."

"We'll find her, or…" He abruptly closed his mouth.

"Or she might meet the same fate as her sister?" Bailey supplied.

"We don't know for sure that her sister is dead.

There's a large force out searching the entire Okefenokee. They've even got the heat-seeking helicopter coming in the morning. Everything that can be done is being done."

She nodded and gazed out the window at the thick copse of trees that stretched as far as the eye could see. The swamp was vast and there were most likely areas of it that no one had ever roamed. A man—or woman—could easily get lost and stay lost in that vastness.

Ace, curled up on her kitchen rug, snored noisily, snapping her back to the present moment. Bailey squared her shoulders. "What's our next step? Where do we go from here?"

"You tell me. So far, your hunches have been spot-on. Without you, we'd still be nowhere in this investigation."

She bit her lip, desperately trying to decide what search location might prove fruitful. "All that comes to mind at the moment is Chesser Island, although I have to admit it's a stretch. Too public. Our guy would be extremely brazen to use the Chesser homestead to hold his victim. We do tours through it at least twice a week. Not to mention that the island now has a well-traveled road built to it. Tourists drive out there all the time on the way to the wildlife boardwalk and observation tower."

"I don't remember there being any mounds on that property, though, so it's not like the other sites we searched."

"True. But there's an old corncob shed and a defunct turpentine still at the back of the property. In their own way, you could argue that they're shrines to a way of life that no longer exists, an homage to early settlers of the swamp."

"We have nothing to lose by trying," Dylan pointed out.

"Should we go now?" Bailey glanced at the clock on

the kitchen wall and half rose from her chair. "Still plenty of daylight left if we hurry."

"Heck, no."

Dylan laid a hand on her arm and her skin tingled once again—this time with warmth. Nothing like the creepy feel of Evan's touch.

Dylan's fingers traveled down her arm until he found her hand and clasped it within his own. "We've both been through the wringer today. And we both know that wherever Amy is, we won't find her curled up in bed at the Chesser homestead. If she was there, she'd have been found by now."

She couldn't argue with his logic.

"Best thing we can do is chill out, get a good night's rest this evening and then meet at dawn to start searching again."

He picked up the tin of salve and experimentally sniffed. "Yep. Makes me think of candy canes hanging on a Christmas tree."

"You should smell some of her other herbal concoctions." Bailey chuckled. "Nothing pleasant about them at all. Especially the tinctures she wants you to drink."

Dylan scooped a dollop and then brushed her hair back. "I see where he struck you."

He lightly applied more of the cooling salve and it helped numb the welt's heat, although it did set off a warmth in her core that had nothing to do with this morning's attack and everything to do with Dylan. He undid the first button of her shirt and the feel of his hands so near her breasts set her heart pounding. He lifted her necklace, observing her collection of talismans before slanting her a hooded glance. "Beautiful," he murmured.

Bailey wasn't sure if he was referring to her or the necklace, so she didn't respond.

His fingers slid down the rest of the welt, and then he ever-so-slowly rebuttoned her shirt.

"Thanks," she croaked.

His voice was equally as gruff. "I read the incident report. He also struck you on the hip."

"Yes, well. Never mind that. I'll take care of it myself."

"Why don't you let me help you?" He breathed the question into her ear, sending a shiver of passion that shot straight to her core and made her thighs tightly squeeze together. It was obvious he wanted more than to merely soothe the throbbing welt inflicted by the slapjack.

Why not? At the moment, she couldn't muster a single objection. It'd been a heck of a day, so why shouldn't she give in to her desire? He wanted her, too; she could tell by the smolder in his eyes and the palpable charge that now arced between them. Initially she'd resented him because of who his father was and how he'd betrayed her. But she'd put the past behind her. She'd proven it today by facing the Slacomb brothers and emerging relatively unscathed.

That initial tension had morphed into an awareness, then an attraction. An attraction that she could no longer deny.

Bailey stood, picked up the salve and took Dylan's hand. He scrabbled to his feet, olive eyes darkening and glowing, fierce with need. She led him down the hallway and into her small bedroom, their hands still joined. She released his hand and slowly slipped out of her shirt and shorts, her skin tingling as he watched her with hawkish concentration. Easing onto the bed, she held out the tin to Dylan.

He sat beside her, and his hands trembled slightly as he unscrewed the top. That slight hint of his nervousness eradicated her own. Whatever was between them, Dylan did not take it lightly, and she found the knowledge reassuring. Bailey lay on her side and drew down the edge of her lace panties, exposing the welt on her hip. With bated breath, she awaited his touch.

His fingers slid along the curve of her hip, and she marveled at the gentleness of his touch as he skimmed her injury with the salve. The stinging numbed instantly, and she promptly forgot all about it, consumed only with the fire that roared to life at his touch.

The edge of her panties eased down her sensitive skin as he finished applying the salve. Then he carefully replaced her panties over the injury. She closed her eyes and anticipated what she hoped was coming next.

Instead of his whispered murmurs of seduction, all she heard was the thump of the tin can on her nightstand and the gasp that burst through his lips.

"What the heck?" he asked loudly, breaking the seductive mood.

Alarmed, she rolled over and faced him. "What's wrong?"

His hand found the inside of her right thigh, and his fingers grazed the scars that ran in half-moon circles from midthigh to her knees.

"Childhood accident," she muttered, pushing his hand away. "Forget about it."

"Accident, heck. Those are bite marks."

"And now you know why dogs freak me out," she said, striving for a light, casual tone. "I was attacked once."

His face looked incredulous, outrage shining in his eyes and a hard set to his jaw. "By what? A pack of wild pit bulls?"

"Dobermans, actually. Can you just let it go? I don't want to talk about that right now."

Understanding gleamed in his eyes. "Edgar Slacomb's Dobermans?"

"Yes."

"How did it happen?"

She bit her lip and shrugged, as though the old injury was of no consequence. "Doesn't matter."

"The heck it doesn't." He wrapped her right hand in both of his own and squeezed—an offering of sympathy and reassurance. "I want to know," he urged softly. "I want to know everything about you."

No one had ever said that to her before. Other men had noticed her scars while in bed and had offered a fleeting sympathy before moving on to have sex, but none had taken the time to question her further.

Her eyes teared up—not from a painful memory, but from Dylan's caring.

"I was sixteen," she said. "Fed up with my foster family and desperate to escape. So one night when I'd had enough, I snuck out of the house with an overnight bag stuffed with everything I owned in the world." She sat up in bed, tucking a pillow behind her as she leaned against the headboard.

"I'd squirreled away a bit of cash from working at Greg's place, whatever Edgar didn't manage to steal from my paycheck, and I knew the lay of the land. I thought it'd be enough to get away, but..." She hesitated, remembering what it'd felt like to flee in the darkness. A mixture of fear and excitement as adrenaline had flooded every cell of her body and freedom seemed within her grasp. She'd imagined herself invincible. Strong, smart and daring.

But Edgar had been older and more clever.

The dogs circled the edge of his property at night,

and although she'd waited until they were asleep, they'd roused at her quiet movement as she'd fled to the woods. Even now, the memory of their feverish barking set her heart pumping in overdrive.

"Edgar's dogs chased you down," Dylan said flatly. His eyes squeezed shut as he took in her story.

The dogs had circled her, snapping their jaws and baring their fangs. A few lunged from time to time, nipping and tearing her jeans. But their aggression had been contained until Edgar arrived on the scene, his face a mask of fury. He'd sent away the pack, save the alpha. *Sic her*, Edgar had screamed.

"Even after being cornered, I didn't believe they'd hurt me. Edgar had them well trained to only attack on command."

"But they did, anyway."

"After being ordered to—yes."

"Edgar ordered them to attack you?" Dylan asked slowly, his words weighted with anger.

"Only one of them. If the whole pack had attacked, I don't think I'd have lived through it."

Dylan didn't speak for several heartbeats, then stood and paced the room, his body taut with outrage. "Unbelievable. I'll make Slacomb pay for that. I promise you, Bailey."

"It's over," she said quietly. "It hurt, but I survived. Can we drop this now, please?"

Indecision warred on his face. He clearly didn't want to let the matter drop, but he didn't want to upset her any more, either.

"For now," he agreed, returning to sit on her bed. He cupped her face in his hands. "I'm sorry this happened to you."

"Thanks, but I don't want your pity. It was a long time ago. Can we just concentrate on us now?" she asked.

He shook his head, as though to clear it of the horror of what she'd shared.

"Just so you know, I think you're an amazing woman. Strong, courageous and resourceful. You survived trauma and refused to let it stop you from pursuing a challenging career and then working with me to catch a killer."

It was probably the nicest compliment she'd ever received. She blinked back tears at the warm words and the tender glow in his eyes. Instead of viewing her fear of dogs as a sign of weakness, he chose to focus on her determination to help other victims.

"Thank you," she breathed. She hated anyone seeing this vulnerable side of her, but Dylan had made her feel safe and hadn't belittled her fear. Her estimation of his character grew. He was not his father. He was his own man. One she wanted to know intimately.

Bailey tilted her chin up and whispered, "You're a little overdressed for what I have in mind." Her hands began to unbutton the front of his uniform shirt. At his sharp intake of breath, a smile curled her lips.

Evidently she wasn't moving fast enough for Dylan, and he quickly finished unbuttoning the rest of his shirt. "Are you sure about this?" he asked, his voice gruff.

"I've never been more sure."

In one fell swoop, he pulled the shirt off.

Bailey ran her fingers through the curly hair on his chest and then frowned at the bruise a mere three inches above his heart. Clay Slacomb's knuckles had left an imprint from this morning's tussle.

"You're hurt, too."

"It's minor."

His lips pressed against hers, tender and exploratory

at first, and then deepening with passion. All thoughts of the Slacombs and their brutality were cleansed by the searing heat of desire. Her pulse quickened and heat spread through her like fever. The scent of his amber aftershave intoxicated her further.

Dylan drew her into his arms, and she laid her head against his chest, feeling the strong, steady hammer of his heart against the side of her face. She traced the fingers of her right hand down the sinewy muscle of his left arm and when she reached his calloused palm, he clasped her small hand in his and squeezed, offering reassurance.

His hands then roamed her back, exploring and leaving behind a trail of fire wherever he touched her. She ached for him to be inside her, and her hands did their own exploring. His body was splendid—strong, hard and smooth. A perfect complement to her soft curves.

With no embarrassment, she rose and pulled off all her clothes. His eyes glowed appreciatively as she stood naked before him. Quickly, he shed the rest of his clothes. He held out his hand to her and she took it, allowing him to draw her close, bare skin to bare skin.

And as he claimed her, she responded with everything she had—mind, body and soul aligned with Dylan. If only she could contain this magic, store it up and tuck it away like a treasure to be relived forever—because she'd never experienced anything like it before and doubted she ever would again once this case was over and they returned to their separate lives.

Chapter Eleven

Dylan fought hard not to keep stealing glances at Bailey next to him in the vehicle. Memories of last night's lovemaking kept flitting through his mind—the sound and feel and smell and taste of her. He wished they could have stayed in bed forever.

He tried to squash a grin as he remembered that sometime during the night while they slumbered, Ace had crawled to the foot of the bed and gone to sleep. At a particularly loud doggy snore, Bailey had startled awake and glared at the pooch. But she hadn't kicked Ace to the curb, and Dylan viewed it as a real sign of progress.

His amusement faded as he remembered why Bailey feared dogs. Someday, somehow, Edgar Slacomb would pay for his cruelty to Bailey. He'd never, ever allow anyone to mistreat her again.

The worst of the late-afternoon heat had passed. In spite of their plans to search the island at first light, they'd been called into Chesser's office to be updated on the latest developments and to map out a new plan of action.

Evan had acted overly polite and stiff at the meeting, evidently realizing he'd overstepped his bounds yesterday. As much as possible, he'd avoided speaking directly to either of them—and that suited Dylan just fine.

He and Bailey had submitted their proposal to search

the Chesser homestead and then spend the night there if they found any promising leads. It was a long shot, but they hoped the killer might return to his crime scene or to check on a buried trophy. Evan's eyes had twitched at the mention of them sharing an all-night stakeout, but he'd clamped his jaw shut and offered no objection. Sheriff Chesser had agreed to their plan, cautioning that they were to inform him immediately if they found any leads.

"They haven't been able to crack Clay at all yet," Bailey said with a sigh, breaking into Dylan's thoughts as he drove. "If he is guilty, do you think he'll ever confess?"

"They usually sing at some point to cut a deal with the prosecution. Or, better yet, Clay might boast about his crimes to a cell mate who'll turn snitch to cut his own deal."

"What's your gut telling you about Clay?" she asked. "Do you think he has anything to do with the missing kayakers or Lisa Shaw?"

"I have my doubts. What about you?"

She let out a dispirited sigh. "I thought he was guilty at first, but now I'm not so sure."

"All we can do is keep searching the swamp while Clay's being interrogated." He tried to renew her hope. "A break will come in the case soon enough."

He pulled his car into a copse of trees twenty yards past the parking lot and made sure it was well hidden from view. They unloaded their metal detectors before walking the short distance through a well-worn trail to reach the Chesser homestead. Dylan carried Ace in the crook of his free arm, not wanting to unnecessarily tire him in the search. His boss had suggested using a different dog for the day, but Dylan had declined. Bailey wouldn't be comfortable with another canine.

Soon they reached the clearing, and he set Ace on the ground.

The place didn't have an island vibe at all. At nearly six hundred acres, the land had been joined to a paved park road and was easily accessible to the public. The last tour of the day was in progress as they reached the neat, raked property—so groomed by the early settlers to easily spot venomous snakes.

"...settled in 1858," they heard the guide explain. "The rugged Chessers hunted and trapped game and grew what they could in the sandy soil. Twice a year they went to town for salt, sugar, flour and gunpowder."

"Bor*ing*," one of the teenage tourists sang out. He turned to his parents and rolled his eyes. "I'd hate to be stuck here in the boonies like they were."

Privately, Dylan agreed with the teenager. Not much to do back then except work and suffer the heat and lack of indoor plumbing.

The guide spotted them and waved a hand, strolling over from the porch. "Mr. Johnson called ahead to say you were coming. I was just finishing up."

"No hurry," Bailey assured her. She patted the front pocket of her shorts. "I've got the key to lock up if you want to go ahead and leave."

They watched as the tourists, and a minute later the guide, exited the homestead and drove away. Ace began experimentally sniffing the ground.

"Want to search the property first?" he suggested.

"I'll take the corncob shed while you take the turpentine still."

They split paths and Dylan set to work, arcing the detector over the old wooden structure. It was slow, tedious work and he knew the odds were low they'd find any relic here. At least it gave him another opportunity to work with Bailey, and he looked forward to spending the night here with her—primitive and uncomfortable as it might prove.

And to think she'd rubbed him the wrong way in the beginning. Instead of proving an unwelcome hindrance that had been foisted upon him, Bailey had provided the crucial break in this case. It certainly hadn't been him or anyone in the sheriff's office.

In the privacy of the old still, Dylan felt his face and neck burn in humiliation. In the future, he'd be more open to input from others outside of an official investigation. Lesson learned.

Methodically, he covered every inch of ground. Distilling turpentine from pine tree bark had been a dangerous, messy business. He couldn't imagine how they'd endured the steam from the boiling water on top of the hot, humid climate.

"Dylan! Come quick!"

Was Bailey hurt or in danger? He flung the detector to the ground and ran next door to the shed.

The interior smelled pungent and he squinted his eyes at the sudden darkness. Ace barked and ran in circles around Bailey. Wordlessly, she held out her gloved hand. A gold charm nestled in her palm, and he donned his own gloves before picking up the piece and examining it.

The claddagh. Two hands, representing friendship, clasped a heart, symbolizing love, which was surmounted by a crown, a sign of loyalty.

"Mary Thornton has a claddagh," Bailey said tightly. "Has to be hers."

Rather, Mary *had* one—past tense. Bailey looked up from the charm, her eyes wide and full of pain. Without him saying a word, she knew what this meant as well.

Mary was most likely dead.

He took the claddagh from her hand, bagged it and glanced around the coffin-like interior of the shed. "Where did you find it?"

"Far right corner, buried only an inch under the sand." She showed him her cell phone. "I took a picture before I picked it up."

"Her body might be buried nearby, just like the other body wasn't far from the ring. I'll notify the sheriff."

"Wait." Her hand stayed his arm when he reached for his two-way radio. "Let's think about this a minute."

He raised a brow. "Why? We need to get the cadaver dogs out here."

"But if we don't tell anyone, we have a chance to find the killer tonight. If you call Chesser they'll set out flood-lights and have dogs and search personnel crawling over every inch of this place. The killer will never return."

"We could still stake out the homestead another night. He might return for his trophy."

"No, it'd be too risky for him. News of Mary's recovered body will be all over the news by morning."

"The likelihood of him returning tonight is slim," he argued.

"But it's our best chance. Our only chance. It's tonight or never."

The idea was tempting. He wanted nothing more than to catch the killer in an act that any jury would buy as evidence of his guilt. But protocol was protocol. "Let me present that argument to my boss."

"No." She shook her head emphatically. "He'll never go along with the plan and you know it. We can say we found the claddagh the next morning. Chesser will be none the wiser."

He'd never lied to his boss before and the idea didn't

sit well with him. Still, the possibility of catching the killer, no matter how remote, was too tempting to pass up.

Bailey seemed to sense him relenting. "Please. Our best hope of finding Amy alive is to find her abductor straightaway. Her time might be running out, if it hasn't already."

He drew a deep breath and took the plunge. "Where's the rake? If we don't want the killer to know we're here, we'll need to cover our tracks, especially Ace's paw prints."

"Thank you," she breathed. "The rake's on the back porch. I'll run and get it."

Ace trotted out behind Bailey and he stood alone, arms folded. Prickles of unease stabbed his gut. This hiding space was so brazen. Their killer thought himself more clever than the law enforcement officers searching for clues. What if… Dylan sucked in his breath. What if the killer was so bold because he *was* one of the cops?

Bailey returned with the rake, and he spun around as she entered the shed. His disturbing thoughts must have shown on his face.

"What is it?" she asked. "Having a change of heart?"

"No, just speculating if the killer is one of us—a police officer, that is."

"I've wondered the same thing. All the more reason to keep this discovery to ourselves until morning."

"Evan Johnson always seems to be around," he noted, thinking aloud.

Bailey blinked and then shook her head. "No way. I'd suspect *your* boss before I would mine."

"Chesser?" he said in surprise. "Never. I've known him all my life. He and my dad were good friends. The guy's straight-up decent. On the other hand, Evan pulled a creepy move yesterday hitting on you."

"It was out of character for him," she argued. "The only time he's ever stepped over a line. Maybe I misread his intentions."

"Get real. You don't really believe that, do you? Let's put his advance to the side for the moment and look at the facts. He could well be the killer. Johnson has an intimate knowledge of this swamp and access to everything in the park."

"By your logic, Sheriff Chesser looks just as guilty. He has the same familiarity of the swamp and freedom to access anything within the park. Plus, this homestead is special to him—it belonged to his family. Speaking of which, the Chesser patriarch only ran to the Okefenokee and settled here to evade a murder charge."

"He was innocent, and you know it. It was merely a fight that turned tragic. Years later, a witness came forward and defended him."

Bailey sighed. "I don't want to argue. On the off chance it's either of our bosses, that's even more reason not to report our finding tonight. Agreed?"

He weighed the pros and cons before tersely nodding his head. "Agreed."

"Good. Go on outside with Ace and I'll sweep over our footprints in the sand."

"I'll give the house a preliminary look through." Dylan retrieved his metal detector from the still and made his way to the porch. He whistled for Ace, and the dog reluctantly left Bailey's side.

"Traitor," he mumbled under his breath. The beagle had taken a shine to his newest partner.

Dylan figured he might as well take a quick scan around the homestead's perimeter before starting inside. But neither Ace, nor the metal detector, nor his own eyes picked up anything unusual. In the homestead he began his search in the common room and then proceeded in a U-shaped pattern. Thankfully, the interior was sparse—small beds with iron headboards and quilts, a few antique photos on the wall and tools near the back of the structure.

Footsteps stomped up the porch steps. "I forgot about the smoke shed out back," she called out. "Be back in a few minutes."

"Wait. I'll go with you." Dylan temporarily abandoned his search. Plenty of time for more of that before it grew dark.

"That's not necessary," she said as he joined her at the front.

"I insist."

They walked side by side, Ace scurrying along, nose to the ground. Only Bailey carried a metal detector to search the small smokehouse.

"Where is it? I don't recall ever seeing it before."

"It's a good thirty yards behind the house. We stopped maintaining a path out there and keeping up the building. It's just another empty, dilapidated structure. A wonder it didn't burn to the ground in 2011."

The great fire of 2011 had raged through almost three-quarters of Okefenokee. Burned bark remained on many of the surviving trees and bore testimony to the devastation. But it hadn't been the first severe fire in the swamp's 6,500-year existence, and it wouldn't be the last. Incredibly, the marshland forest always regenerated and endured.

Saw palmetto and other shrubs encroached on the almost-forgotten path, and they proceeded single file until the small leaning shed was suddenly before them. Bailey went straight to the door and started inside.

At a swish of movement from above, Dylan glanced

up, expecting to find a startled bird. But it was no bird. In fact, it was no bird or animal, or anything found in nature. The object missiling down toward Bailey was a homemade contraption—a large rock encased with rope and metal spikes protruding in every direction. It hung high on a nearby tree branch that must have been loaded with a trip-wire trigger.

The spiked rock hurtled with frightening speed. Its trajectory would blindside Bailey in her head and neck area. His mouth opened to scream, but there was no time for even that verbal warning. Another two seconds and the sharp spikes would pierce her unprotected, unsuspecting face. The blow could prove lethal.

Dylan lunged, desperate to save her. He propelled forward, watched as the stirring and hissing of air finally warned Bailey of danger and she looked up to determine its cause—a second too late for her to register the danger and respond.

He had to reach her. His arms grabbed at the empty space between them and then, finally, he felt her, latching on for dear life as they toppled to the sandy soil just in time to miss the spiked rock that swung toward them.

"What the heck was that?" Bailey asked in a whoosh of breath.

The rock crested a few yards upward, and then the pendulum swung toward them again. "Stay down," he cautioned.

Dylan rolled on his left side and immediately withdrew his sidearm, scanning the darkness between the trees. Was the killer still out there? Waiting and watching?

Logic told him no one lurked nearby unseen and unheard—that the purpose of the booby trap was to scare off trespassers when he wasn't around to guard the area.

"Another body might be nearby," Bailey whispered. "Either that, or Amy could be imprisoned not far from here."

"We have no proof, but that's my guess as well. Such an extreme measure is the mark of a dangerous person."

"Don't call for backup," she urged. "If he was close, he'd have already shot us. If you call, we've lost our chance to catch him unawares."

"I'm not calling," he assured her. "I want to get that bastard tonight as much as you do."

"What should we do about the booby trap? Tie it back up? If he sees it down, he'll guess the area's been compromised."

"At this point, I want him to know we're closing in. If we're lucky, he'll panic and make a stupid mistake. May I borrow your knife?"

"I've got this." Bailey took out her knife and made quick work of cutting the rope and freeing the attached weapon.

"Let's make a run for the cabin," he suggested. "I've already been in there. It's safe. We can search the shed in the morning."

They rose to their feet and he took out his gun again. "Stay close to me so that I'm free to shoot if needed. Stay close to me," he cautioned.

And then they were running. Despite that, it seemed to take twice as long on the return trip as it had on the initial foray. At the end of the trail, he held out an arm, stopping her from advancing into the clearing.

Dusk had soundlessly slipped into the wilderness, sprinkling long, distorted shadows in its wake. Birds loudly chirped as they flitted from tree to tree, seeking lofty asylum for their nightly rest. Nothing appeared out of the ordinary.

"Ready to make a quick break for the back door?" he asked.

"Ready."

Gun still drawn and at the ready, he burst from the tree line. Once Bailey ran past him, he dropped in behind her, shielding her as best he could. They tumbled inside, breathing hard.

"Stay down and away from the windows while I lock the front door."

Quickly, he slid the lock into place and did a quick walk-through of the rooms, thankful for the sparseness of the homestead. There were no closets to hide in, and the quilts were neatly tucked into the bottom of every mattress.

They were alone.

As though of one mind, they each sank to the floor and leaned their backs against a wall, catching their breaths. Dylan holstered his gun.

Bailey ran a trembling hand through her hair. "Thank you. If you hadn't been there, I could have been killed."

And if she'd been by herself and survived, the killer would have found her before anyone else. Alone and defenseless, she'd have been easy prey as his next victim.

At a sudden clap of thunder, they both scrambled to their feet. "Just a summer storm rumbling in the distance," he said. He took her hand and squeezed it. "Sure you want to stay the night? If we do, we'll both need to be alert and on the lookout every second."

"Positive," she assured him. "I'm up for it. My insomnia can once again prove useful. It's no big deal for me to stay awake."

Confusion furrowed his brow. "I didn't know you struggled with insomnia. And what do you mean by it can help you *again*?"

"Forget it."

"No. Tell me, Bailey. Like I've said, I want to know everything about you."

"Just that…staying awake, or sleeping really light, keeps you alert for danger."

"What danger?" Sudden realization lit his mind. "Are you talking about your foster father?"

A grim smile tugged the edges of her mouth. "Never knew when a ticking time bomb like him would explode. I learned to stay prepared."

Anger rushed through him anew at the idea of Bailey being subjected to the likes of Edgar Slacomb. When this was over… "He'll pay for what he did to you," Dylan vowed. "And whoever you went to for help that ignored you."

He pulled her tightly against his chest, wishing like heck he could have protected her back then.

"Be careful what you wish for," she whispered in his ear.

He held her at arm's length. "What's that supposed to mean?"

"Never mind. I shouldn't have said anything." She shrugged out of his arms. "Shouldn't we each take a position by the windows to keep watch? We're on a stake-out. Remember?"

"The sooner you tell me who dropped the ball on helping you back then, the sooner we can do our job."

"Let it go."

"Tell me his name."

They eyed one another warily in the weight of the darkness, thunder rumbling ominously in the distance. Uneasiness danced under his veins. Whoever it was, Dylan had a feeling he wasn't going to like her answer.

"If you insist. The man I placed all my hope and trust in all those years ago was your father. Officer Dylan Armstrong Senior."

Chapter Twelve

The slash of incredulity and pain on Dylan's face made Bailey wish she could take back the words. It wasn't Dylan's fault that his dad was such a jerk. "It doesn't matter now," she hastened to add. "Ancient history."

"You're mistaken," he said at last, his voice harsh. "Dad would never stand by and let an innocent child suffer."

Her own anger, always on a slow simmer when she recalled the past, came bubbling to the surface. If Armstrong Senior had only made one little phone call, or filed an official report, she'd have been spared two more years of misery. Was that little bit of effort on his part too much trouble? It would have taken such a small part of his day to investigate the matter and have her removed from the foster family. But he'd done nothing.

"All I can tell you is that I went to your father and told him what was happening in that house. He said he'd get in contact with my social worker and take care of it immediately. So I went home and waited. And waited. Nothing ever came of it."

"No way. He—"

"Actually, I take that back. Something *did* happen. Edgar found out that I'd tried to turn him in and the situation got worse."

"How did he find out?"

"He never said. I certainly didn't tell him. Only two people knew of that conversation. Me." She paused a heartbeat. "And your dad."

"I'm going to get to the bottom of this," Dylan assured her. "Because my dad was one of the kindest people you'd ever want to meet."

"Was?" she asked uncertainly, immediately noticing his use of the past tense.

"He died over a decade ago."

Now she *really* wished she'd kept her mouth shut about the whole thing. If she'd known the senior Armstrong was dead she wouldn't have spoken ill of the man. Not to his son, anyway.

"Um, sorry, Dylan. Forget I said anything." She pointed at the windows. "Guess we should get to work. Right?"

Without waiting for a reply, she strode to the front window and pulled the homespun cotton curtain back an inch. Ace settled at her feet, resting his head on top of her shoes.

More blackness had descended over the swamp, and from far off, lightning slashed the inky sky. Every flash created a strobe-like effect that lit the landscape for a split second before it pitched dark again.

All the better to catch a killer.

Between the lightning and a nearby parking lot light up the road, she'd be able to detect anyone moving around the homestead. And Dylan had her back—in more ways than one. Funny how strange life could be. She'd gone all in trusting the son of the man she hated almost as much as Edgar Slacomb.

Should she tell Dylan? He might be in no mood to hear that she trusted him in spite of his father. She glanced over her shoulder where Dylan's long, lean body was silhouetted against the back window. She swallowed hard, remembering the feel of lying against that naked body, of his touch and his kisses that'd kept her up most of the night—in the best way possible, of course.

"See anything?" she called out softly.

"No."

Was he angry with her? Sulking perhaps? She tried again. "What's our game plan if we see somebody?"

"Tell me if you do. I'll call for backup before I leave the cabin to investigate."

"I'll go with you," she volunteered.

"You may be on loan to the sheriff's office for this investigation, but you're no cop. Don't even think about leaving the homestead if I venture out."

Ouch. He was definitely upset about her revelation. "Don't be angry, Dylan," she said softly. "If I'd known your father was dead, I wouldn't have told you."

He waited so long to answer that she thought he'd spend the rest of the night ignoring her. She kept her gaze focused on the front yard, a ball of misery knotting her gut.

"Don't ever apologize for speaking the truth," he said at last. "Or, rather, the truth as you see it. But I know my dad. He wouldn't have ignored a cry for help. There must be some logical explanation and I'll find out why."

"Fine with me." Her fingers curled tightly on the window ledge. Let him have his delusions on that score. She'd never bring up the subject again. The past had hurt her enough without it ruining her future as well. But would this issue always remain between them? She definitely wanted Dylan to be a part of her future.

That scared her more than whatever might be lurking in the darkness. Could she completely let go of her resentment toward his beloved father?

This case would be wrapping up soon, possibly even tonight. She didn't want it to end on a low note with Dylan. Silence slid between them again, but this time it was comfortable and not the previous tension-filled quiet.

Bailey concentrated on observing the dark edges that shadowed the small pool of available light, searching for any shift of light or movement. From the half-opened window, she listened to the high-pitched buzzing of myriad insects and the low thrumming of frogs, the night orchestra of the swamp. Her legs grew heavy, so she pulled a wooden chair close to the window and sat. At least until its hard surface became unbearable and she stood again to shake out her legs.

"Want to switch sides? Break up the monotony a bit?" Dylan offered.

"Might as well."

Without explanation, Dylan left the room, and then she heard a loud scraping of metal against the old wooden floorboards. He emerged in the common room, dragging a single-wide bed by its iron headboard.

"This'll be more comfortable than your chair," he said, sliding the bed under the rear window frame.

Gratefully, she sank onto the mattress. It was bumpy and hard, but infinitely better than the wooden chair.

"Heavenly," she said, shooting him a grateful smile.

He planted an unexpected, hot kiss on the top of her scalp before moving to the front window and settling in.

Smiling in bemusement, Bailey focused her attention on the backyard. The view here was much darker than the front. All she could make out was a subtle shift between the raked Chesser property and the looming tree line a good twenty yards away. The sliver of moonlight through the clouds was little help.

Another strobe of lightning flashed, illuminating the landscape in a brief, quick burst. A slight fluctuation of darkness darted at the right edge of the property. What was that? Bailey's heartbeat accelerated as she focused on the spot, waiting for another flash of lightning. She stared so hard and so long her eyes dried uncomfortably, but she had to be ready for the next bolt or she'd blink and miss the opportunity.

Lightning flashed again, but this time she spotted nothing unusual. A false alarm then. No point in having Dylan investigate. Thunder rumbled seconds later—the storm was moving closer. Leaves rustled in a sudden wind gust, and she smelled the scent of rain only seconds before it pounded the tin roof, a staccato percussion that drowned out all other sound. Rain splattered the window ledge, and she reluctantly closed the window. A shuffle and click from behind and she realized Dylan had done the same.

"So much for hearing anyone moving around out there," she quipped.

"This'll pass soon enough."

And well she knew it. These sudden Southern storms were violent—but often brief. "At least we have cover."

The pounding rain continued, lending a cozy atmosphere to the homestead where they were sheltered. Then she ruined the peaceful interlude, imagining Amy Holley alone in some damp hovel while the rain beat down and wondering when her abductor would return—when he'd kill her as he'd done to her sister. Did Amy imagine each day would be her last? Perhaps, at this point, the woman welcomed death.

The rain stopped as suddenly as it had begun, and

she cracked the window, gulping in the soaked air. Time flowed effortlessly by, seconds, then minutes, then hours. Bailey's eyelids felt as though they lifted one-pound weights. She rubbed at the grittiness in her eyes, closed them a moment, and opened them again.

Blue eyes speared her with glittering hatred, only inches from her face—the window pane a fragile barrier between her and madness. Rain blurred his features, which only served to highlight the burning eyes. A scream tore through the cabin—her own, she realized belatedly. Ace growled and began barking.

Dylan was at her side. "Where is he?"

She lifted a finger to point, but only darkness pooled before them. "He—he was right here in front of the window a moment ago."

Dylan raced to the door and jerked it open. Ace shot outside and ran toward the woods. Dylan raised his gun and shot into the air. "Halt! Police officer."

She hurried to his side, peering over his shoulder. "Do you see anyone?"

"No. Get the flashlight." She picked it up from the table where he'd placed it earlier and turned it on, directing the beam along the back wall of the house.

There was no one.

Had she imagined the face? Perhaps she'd fallen asleep for an instant and had awakened from a nightmare.

"Maybe I imagined it," she said sheepishly.

"No. Ace saw or heard something, too. I'm going to try and follow. Lock yourself inside."

He ignored her protest, slipping into the night. She couldn't see him; she only heard his footsteps running across the yard. Bailey hurried back inside and grabbed the other flashlight. She stepped outside, aiming the elliptical beam at the tree line, but Dylan had disappeared.

Damn it, she must have fallen asleep for the intruder to have managed to walk almost right up on her before she spotted him. If anything happened to Dylan, the fault would fall on her own shoulders.

At the back wall, she aimed the flashlight by the window and found footprints right under the sill. Someone *had* stood there. He knew her now, had seen her up close. He probably knew who she was from the first time she'd spotted him leaving the church, if it was the same man. Yet she still didn't know who he was.

Think, Bailey. What did you see at the window?

The eyes had magnetized her, commanding her complete attention. But what about the rest of his face? His hair? She replayed his image, but all she conjured were the crazy eyes and wet hair plastered on his skull.

Bailey stood on the steps, waiting. She withdrew her knife and wished like heck it was a gun. Where was Dylan? What was taking so long? She'd give him five minutes. If he hadn't returned, she'd call for backup.

A shout emanated from somewhere in the marsh. Dylan calling for Ace. Relief swooshed through her body. He was safe, at least at this moment. The air shifted from black to gray, the rising sun a sickly whisper of light in the east.

Ace broke through the underbrush, and she could swear he wore a look of frustration on his normally cheerful face. He wanted a piece of the guy he'd chased. Badly. Any other night, he might have caught his prey, but his injury had slowed him down too much. Again, this was entirely her fault. Dylan hadn't brought along a fresh, different tracking dog out of consideration for her fear.

Seconds later, Dylan strode through the woods and walked toward her.

"Did you see him?" she called out.

"Not a thing. I heard rustling ahead of me, but never saw anyone. Could have been a deer for all I know."

Her shoulders sagged in defeat. "I'm sorry."

"For what?"

"Everything. For not wanting backup this evening, for falling asleep, for having a dog with us who isn't at full running capacity."

"Whoa, there. Stop beating yourself up. I went along with the decision not to call last night. Remember?"

"But we were so close," she said with a groan. "He was right here, and I let him get away. Now we've got nothing."

"I wouldn't say that." He shone his flashlight by the wall. "We've got footprints. That's a start. We'll make casts of them. Should provide us with general information about his size."

"Big whoop. You're just trying to make me feel better."

He came to where she stood and took a seat on the porch step. "Might as well sit a spell and watch the sunrise," he said, pointing to the empty space beside him. "Our guy won't venture back here anytime soon. I'll call the office shortly to report our findings and tell them they'll need to bring dogs with them."

Cadaver dogs to perhaps find Mary Thornton's body. She dropped down onto the wooden step, and Ace plopped at her feet, still panting from his recent exertion. They sat together, silently watching as the gray brightened in slow degrees and the rising sun's rays cast a coral glow on the clouds.

An owl hooted and the hairs on her arms rose.

"An owl's bad luck," she commented, absently fiddling with her necklace. "Some Native Americans believe they foretell death. I have a bad feeling about all this. Like the killer has unfinished business and there'll be more victims."

"Superstitions. Your friend's been filling your head with too many old tales."

"Maybe. But Lulu can be downright uncanny about signs. She sometimes predicts local news headlines before they're even reported."

"Coincidence," he said firmly. He nudged her shoulder playfully. "Next thing I know you'll be claiming to believe in the existence of the South Georgia Pig Man and the Skunk Ape."

"Who knows what lurks out there?" she said, attempting a laugh. "I've seen some pretty eerie things like balls of fire that glow—"

"Swamp gas."

Bailey cast him an enigmatic smile. His pragmatism didn't rankle. She had her own beliefs and he had his. She'd spent so much time alone in the wilderness that she could appreciate its mystery. At times, she'd sensed the ghosts of Native Americans striding through the land, had vividly imagined them as well as the desperate plight of slaves on the run, plus a host of other frantic people seeking to meld into the Okefenokee and become invisible to the rest of the world.

"Guess I'll head on inside and radio my boss," Dylan said, rising to his feet. "It will be light enough soon for forensics to sweep the area and others can begin searching."

"Join you in a minute," she answered, wanting a minute alone to sort her thoughts. The land spread before her, vast and unspoiled. Untamed. A morning mist blurred the sharp edges of the cypress and pine. In the muted black-and-green panorama, a white bird exploded from the underbrush, fluttering like an omen. She'd have to ask Lulu what it meant.

Bailey had a hunch it wouldn't be anything of a cheery nature.

Chapter Thirteen

It didn't take the cadaver dogs long.

The woods beyond the homestead echoed with the sounds of their barks and officers shouting harsh commands.

"They've found another one," Jeff commented beside him.

Dylan had expected as much, yet the commotion twisted his gut. "It's my guess it will be Mary Thornton's body," he said. "We found jewelry last night—I mean this morning—that may have belonged to her."

Jeff darted him a sharp side-glance. "Better get your timing straight when you speak to the boss. If you found it last night, you should have reported it immediately."

"Right. Of course, I would have called earlier," Dylan deadpanned.

"Whatever you say." His old friend wasn't fooled. Jeff's gaze drifted to where Bailey and Evan stood off to the side. "The body y'all found on Billy's Island has been positively identified."

"Who?"

"Lisa Shaw."

He wasn't surprised. Dylan continued to stare at Bailey and Evan. From the set of their faces, the conversation looked intense. He hoped Bailey held firm to their story that they'd found the claddagh early this morning. Once again, Ace tried to wander off in Bailey's direction, but Dylan snapped his fingers for him to heel.

"What's going on between you and Ranger Covington?" Jeff asked.

"Nothing," he protested. Perhaps too vehemently. He lowered his voice and spoke more calmly. "We're working a case together. Period."

"Uh-huh. Be careful, that's all I'm saying."

Was it that obvious he had feelings for Bailey? "Point taken," he said stiffly.

Jeff clapped his shoulder. "I've known you too long. Probably no one else has caught wind. Not yet, anyway."

Time to change the subject. "What do you know about Evan Johnson?" Dylan asked his friend.

"The park manager? Not much really. He goes to the same church as my parents, so they'd know him better than me. I'll tap them. Why? You think he has something to do with the murders?"

Dylan wasn't ready to voice his suspicions, not even to Jeff. His annoyance with the man's advances to Bailey could well be coloring his perception of Evan's character.

"The man's probably above reproach. Let's just say that anyone with knowledge and opportunity should be closely looked at."

"Agreed."

"Did you ever get a chance to see if Bailey—er, Ranger Covington—had any mention in our records?"

"I poked around. There's nothing. Should there be?"

"If there was, it would have been over a decade ago. How far back do we keep paper files?"

"We don't. Old records are on microfilm in the government storage facility near Folkston." Jeff's forehead creased in concern. "What's going on, Dylan? You've been awful cryptic lately. I'll grant that your ranger is one hot chick, but don't be stupid. If she's trouble, better put it all out in the open. Think of your career."

"It's nothing that *she's* done wrong. It's what's been done against her, or rather, something that wasn't done for her. It's complicated." Dylan wouldn't betray Bailey's trust by spilling secrets, not even to his best friend.

Four officers, two on each side, carried a body bag into the backyard, where a forensics vehicle awaited it for transport to their lab. A respectful hush fell over the crowd of men and women until the car pulled out with its gruesome cargo.

Dylan caught Bailey's eyes. Dark circles stood out on her pale face and she hugged her arms tightly around her body. Witnessing a body recovered from a crime scene wasn't easy for anyone, least of all a civilian. That, coupled with lack of sleep, was obviously affecting her mentally and physically. Too often, he forgot that she was a civilian. Bailey was so good at providing leads and so determined in seeking justice that it was easy to forget this wasn't her everyday job.

He scooped Ace up and handed him to Jeff. "Take care of the little guy. He's had a long night, too."

"But—"

"Later, Jeff," he said, stepping in Bailey's direction and leaving the squirming pup in his friend's hands.

He didn't make it three steps before Sheriff Chesser intercepted him. "Anything you're not telling me? You and Ranger Covington sure got a lot accomplished in the first light of dawn—found the jewelry, cut down a trip wire and spotted footprints by the homestead back wall."

"Busy morning," he cryptically agreed.

Chesser narrowed his eyes, hands on his hips. "Odd how evidence keeps turning up whenever Ranger Covington's around. She seems to have a real knack for find-ing things in the most obscure areas."

"She'd have made an excellent detective," Dylan said, pretending not to catch the sheriff's drift. "Too bad her calling was in forestry and not law enforcement."

"Even odder that only she's seen the suspected killer."

Dylan's voice grew sharp. "What are you saying?"

"If we hadn't found the remains of two women, I'd have said she was leading us on a merry chase."

"The bodies say otherwise."

"Which leads me to wonder how deep her involve-ment really is. Could she possibly be in league with the killer?" Chesser's eyes roamed to where Bailey and Evan continued their animated discussion.

"That's ridiculous," he said. Heat flushed the back of his neck and face. "If you want to cast suspicion on Evan Johnson, welcome to the club. But Bailey Covington? No way. Why would she cover for him if he's a killer?"

"Love—or lust—is a powerful motivator. I've seen the way Johnson looks at her when he thinks no one's watching. I mean, look at them even now. Their conver-sation looks too intense, not professional in the least."

"That's probably because Johnson is putting another unwanted move on her."

"Another one?"

"This wouldn't be the first time. I better head over and check it out."

"So now you're playing her protector, are you?"

"She's a colleague," he said tightly.

Bailey happened to break her gaze with Johnson and their eyes met. She quirked a brow as though to ask if everything was okay on his end. He gave a curt nod be-fore giving the sheriff his full attention again.

"Make sure your relationship with Covington stays

professional," Chesser warned him. "Keep your eyes open and remember this conversation. If I get wind of any hanky-panky, you'll be stuck at a desk the rest of your career. Understood?"

He wanted nothing more than to tell his boss where to go, but he couldn't risk getting pulled from the case. "Yes, sir. Are we done here?"

"We are."

Dylan quickly made his way to Bailey and Evan Johnson, conscious of Chesser watching every step he took.

"Done filling your boss in on our findings?" he asked Bailey while holding Johnson's gaze, not bothering to address him directly or extend any courtesy. Johnson had lost his respect.

"I am. Just need to report to headquarters and fill out paperwork." She nodded toward Johnson. "I'll be at the office shortly."

He followed Bailey and they made their way across the homestead.

"I imagine you have even more reports to fill out than I do," she said. "Going to be a long day for both of us. Everything okay with your boss?"

"I was going to ask you the same thing. You and Johnson looked...engrossed."

Bailey crinkled her nose. "He's upset with all the negative publicity."

"Chesser mentioned that the annual astronomy night was canceled for this evening. I know staff has put in a lot of time to arrange for teachers to speak to the public about the stars but they really had no choice, big event or not."

"Not to mention all the telescopes we've already arranged to bring in for everyone," Bailey said. "Speaking of your boss, y'all seemed to be having your own intense conversation."

"He's in a tight spot, too. Between the press and the feds coming in and assuming control of the case—"

"The FBI's in charge now?" She stopped in her tracks and regarded him with wide eyes.

"Yeah, multiple bodies will do it."

"What about us? Will we continue working together?"

From the corner of his eye, Dylan spotted several people glancing their way. He needed to remember that they were both going to be closely scrutinized from here on out.

"Honestly, I can't say for sure." He cocked his head to the side. "Let's keep walking. We seem to have an audience."

Once they hit the sandy path to the parking lot, he turned to her. "You may not have noticed, but we're being watched."

"But why? We're the only ones who've made any kind of break in the investigation."

"Exactly."

At her quizzical scowl, he shrugged and tried to explain. "Cops are a suspicious bunch. Too many breaks or leads and they wonder if the person or persons providing them have their own agenda."

"They think we had something to do with those poor women?" Her voice was loud, and he feared it might carry to the others.

"Let's talk about it in my car."

"But what about Ace? What about all our things? We can't just leave them—"

He laid a hand on her arm and gently pulled her forward. "I'll have Jeff take care of everything. We have a long afternoon ahead. I don't know about you, but I'll be ready to crash after the administrative work is finished. Tomorrow, we'll figure out where we go from here."

"Makes sense," she agreed. "But I'd hate to be bumped off the case when everything's finally heating up."

"Hadn't we run out of options, anyway? There aren't any other places in the swamp with standing structures located near a shrine of some sort."

"Not that I can think of," she admitted, running a hand through her chestnut hair. "But I can't give up trying. I'll rack my brain and see if I can come up with another location to check."

"Theoretically, Clay Slacomb could still be our guy. Whoever came by the cabin might be a Peeping Tom or something. I know the odds of that are slim, but it's something everyone will keep in mind."

"They can think what they want, but I no longer believe either of the Slacombs is guilty. I didn't recognize that man at the window."

They slipped into his car, and he started the engine, willing the air-conditioning to quickly kick in. He leaned back in the seat and Bailey did the same. Cold air blasted through the vents and cooled his clammy face and forearms.

"Heaven," he said after a minute. "I could probably doze off right here, right now."

"Me, too," she admitted, flashing him a wan smile. "Matter of fact, the AC's made me so mellow I can't even muster the energy to stay angry at Sheriff Chesser."

"What do you mean?"

"That's who you were talking to before me. So if anyone's raised suspicions about us, or me, it's your boss."

"He's a stickler for protocol and jaded from years on the job."

"Ha. Maybe he should cast aspersions on his own self.

He has knowledge and opportunity. Heck, his family is connected to the Chesser homestead where a body's been found."

"Hmm," he answered noncommittally, pulling out of the parking lot and entering the main road. It felt good to be behind the wheel and return to some degree of normalcy. "How about some coffee?"

"Do you even need to ask?"

He took her hand and brought it to his mouth, bestowing a quick kiss on her knuckles. "No matter what happens with our jobs, I still want to see you, Bailey."

His breath caught when she didn't answer straightaway. "Bailey?" he asked huskily.

She closed her eyes and leaned her head back. "I'd like that," she said, so softly he almost didn't hear it.

His shoulders slumped with a release of tension he hadn't even known he carried.

His phone vibrated in his pocket, an urgent, angry command to pick it up. Dylan fished it out and pressed a button. "Armstrong here."

"There's been another missing person reported," Sheriff Chesser barked without preamble. "Forget the reports and turn around. We need you back. Both of you."

Energy spiked his tired muscles and he did a swift U-turn as he flipped on his siren. All thoughts of a quiet afternoon sipping coffee and writing reports fled out the window.

A sea of strobing blue lights approached as a convoy of state trooper vehicles sped by his car.

"What in the world's happened?" Bailey asked. "Did they find another body buried on the property?"

"A new person's been reported missing. I don't know the details yet."

"And here I thought we'd scared the killer into hiding. I was so sure we were close to capturing him before someone else got hurt."

"Ditto. Never can tell about these kinds of cases though."

"I'm assuming Clay Slacomb's definitely off the suspect list now. Unless he managed to escape from county lockup?"

"No. Chesser would have told me if that's the case."

The minute he stopped in the parking lot, they both raced down to the homestead, where they found Chesser, Johnson and a few FBI agents stood at the picnic table by the edge of the property. The place was crawling with law enforcement officers and dogs. Between the sirens, officers barking orders and the buzzing of two-way radios, Dylan's ears rang. At the picnic table, a large map of the Okefenokee wildlife refuge lay open. Black X's marked the spots where bodies were found and the trophy pieces located.

"Who's missing?" Dylan asked as he took a seat.

"A woman named Janet Blackwell. Husband called because she never returned from her all-night factory shift in Beulah. We're searching all roads between there and her home in Folkston. Jeff and a couple of feds are going to speak with the husband." Chesser turned to Bailey. "Any ideas on where we might narrow our search?"

Indignation burned in Dylan's gut. First Chesser threw aspersions against Bailey for her hunches and now he wanted her help?

Bailey shook her head. "Honestly, no. But let me think." She scanned the map, running a hand through her hair. "There's a couple sheds on Gannet Lake and over by Buzzard's Roost. Could be there are mounds around there, too, but I don't recall. What about you, Evan? Do you remember?"

"I'm not sure either."

Dylan wanted to snort. Some help her boss was.

Bailey turned back to Chesser with a shrug. "Sorry I can't help more this time."

The sheriff gave a curt nod. "Thought it was worth a shot to ask."

"If you're through with us?" Evan asked. "Ranger Covington needs to file a report on all this."

Chesser waved a dismissive hand at Evan and Bailey. "Y'all are free to go. You, too, Armstrong. We've got more than enough officers to start the new search."

"I'd rather stay and join in. If you don't mind, sir."

Now that Bailey had planted a seed of suspicion about the sheriff, he wouldn't feel right unless he kept an eye on how Chesser handled this latest development.

A woman's life depended on it.

Chapter Fourteen

Bailey emailed her report to Evan, leaned back in her chair and gazed out the kitchen window of her cabin. The first hint of dusk smudged the sky. She should be tired but a second wind, largely the result of several cups of coffee, energized her body, so she stood and paced. What was the latest news on the missing woman? So far, she'd refrained from calling Dylan to check, but now curiosity overrode concern of interrupting his work.

She sent him a text and then carried her phone to the porch. For her, the best remedy for restlessness was quiet time outside. Much as she wanted to enjoy the respite, her mind kept circling back to the missing women. Was Amy still alive after all this time? Every day that passed, the hope of finding her grew smaller. And if the killer had captured another woman, it might mean Amy was dead and he craved a new victim to replace the old.

A police car rumbled down her road—way too early for the sporadic drive-by patrol of her cabin. A flutter of unease danced inside her chest until she saw it was Dylan. He pulled into the driveway and held up his phone as he exited his car. "Just got your text."

"You didn't have to come see me in person to answer it," she teased.

"Maybe I needed an excuse to see you." He plopped down beside her and pressed a quick, hot kiss on her lips.

"Any news?"

"Nothing definite, but we discovered that Mrs. Blackwell is having an affair with a coworker. Who also happens to be AWOL. Chances are pretty good that we'll find they've run off together. Troopers put out an APB on the guy's car, so I'm hoping this is wrapped up soon."

She closed her eyes and released a quick breath. If the killer hadn't struck again, it might bode well for Amy. *Hang in there, Amy.* She leaned in to Dylan as he threw an arm over her shoulder and gave her a brief hug.

"I still don't know where to search in the morning," she admitted. "Before I waste anyone's time, I thought I'd go out on my own and poke around Buzzard's Roost and Gannet Lake."

"We'll go together. Your guess is as good as anybody's at this point."

"Not sure your boss will like the idea."

"Speaking of which… We need to be careful about our, uh, relationship. Chesser warned me to keep it professional."

"So did Evan." She looked up at him. "I hope this new directive doesn't mean you won't spend tonight with me."

His eyes darkened to a deep green and he leaned his forehead against hers. "I'd like nothing better, but it won't do for my vehicle to be spotted by whatever officer patrols here tonight." He straightened with a sigh of regret. "Besides, you must be worn out. You need uninterrupted sleep."

She'd much rather have Dylan's lovemaking interrupting that sleep, but she kept the thought to herself.

"I am concerned about you, though. That man last night got a really good close-up of your face. And given the fact someone already tried to burn down your cabin—well, you see why I'm worried."

"I'm not too thrilled with the idea of being alone, either," she admitted.

"Why don't you stay with your friend down the road?"

Bailey glanced over at Lulu's empty driveway. "She's not even home. Holt's in town so she might be staying at his place."

"Holt's her boyfriend?"

"Yeah. Holt Rucker. His job keeps him on the road a good bit. I don't want to be a third wheel there."

"Why don't you call her? If she's not going to be home, you could sleep at her house. Our guy won't know to check there."

Bailey hesitated. It went against the grain to ask a favor from anyone, but this was Lulu after all. Her friend wouldn't mind a bit. "Okay."

"Go ahead and call her. I can let the patrol officer know where you'll be, and I'll leave here reassured you'll be okay."

She called Lulu, and her friend answered almost at once. Bailey asked about spending the night, and Lulu immediately agreed.

"But I have an even better idea," Lulu said. "Holt's hitting the road shortly. Got a last-minute gig in Maggie Valley when the scheduled guide canceled. Why don't you spend the night over here with me at his place? Would be safer for both of us than my cabin."

Guilt pinged Bailey's gut. She hadn't even considered that her request would put Lulu in possible danger. "Of course. Text me his address and I'll be on my way."

"What's up?" Dylan asked as soon as she ended the call.

"Change of plans. I'm staying at her boyfriend's place tonight. Which should be even safer."

"Perfect." Dylan tapped on his phone and paused, fingers at the ready. "What's that address?"

Sighing, she reopened her phone and saw Lulu had already texted, so she read the address aloud. He was being overprotective, but it'd be easier to provide the information than get in an argument.

Dylan left shortly afterward, first planting another quick, hot kiss on her lips. Bemused, she packed an overnight bag and headed out. The rhythmic whir of car tires on the blacktop road lulled her into drowsiness. Her second wind had definitely fled. At least Lulu would understand her exhaustion and wouldn't expect to be entertained.

At the first fork in the road, she veered left as the GPS instructed. Ah, she knew this road well. It was the back way to Edgar Slacomb's house. Just her luck if Holt Rucker turned out to be the man's neighbor and best friend. If Edgar was over there, she'd drive right on by the house and make up an excuse to Lulu for not showing up as planned. She'd much rather spring for a motel room in the nearest city than suffer Edgar's company for one minute. No doubt he'd prefer to avoid her, too.

The road narrowed and made a sharp curve to the right, and then sand replaced asphalt. According to her GPS, she had another quarter mile to go. She steeled herself for some messy, primitive cabin but was pleasantly surprised when she arrived at a neat ranch house with a well-tended vegetable garden on one side. Lulu stepped onto the porch and waved.

Two cars were parked in the curved drive—so Holt hadn't yet left.

"Any trouble finding this place?" Lulu called from the front porch.

"Nope. GPS is the best invention ever." In Bailey's directionally challenged mind, it even topped man's landing on the moon. She lifted her overnight bag from the passenger side and strode to the porch.

"Nice garden," she commented.

"Holt takes a lot of pride in it. When he's gone, I come out here and keep it watered for him. We've got corn, tomatoes, zucchini, cucumbers—all the essentials. Plus, I planted an herb patch. Once I made him a salad with fresh oregano and basil, he was hooked on herbs. Come on out and I'll show it to you."

Bailey dropped her bag on the porch swing and followed Lulu. She wasn't much into gardening, but her friend took pride in it. Dutifully, she went with Lulu down the rows, oohing over the size of the tomatoes. Not far from the garden, several bags of fertilizer and lime were stacked against the side of a potting shed.

She yawned and stretched her hands high in the air.

"Sorry, I'm rambling on and you're tired," Lulu said, coming to an abrupt halt. "Let's go inside. I saved you some leftovers from dinner. Barbecue ribs and mashed potatoes."

They drifted toward the house.

"When's Holt leaving?" She hated being a third wheel.

"Soon. He's packing his bags now. Ah, there he is."

Holt passed by them carrying a suitcase and several pressed uniforms in a plastic bag slung over one shoulder. Bailey glanced at the patch on one of the shirts, noting the words Southern Expeditions embroidered in a circle around a tree emblem.

"Evening, Bailey," he said. "Enjoy your stay. I'm a bachelor, but I generally keep things tidy 'round here."

"Your home's lovely," she assured him. "Thanks for letting me come over at the last minute."

"No trouble at all. Lulu will take good care of you.

She told me you've had a rough week. I was sad to hear they'd found the body of one of them missing women." He paused on the steps and set down the suitcase. "Making any progress on that case?"

"A little, but I can't discuss the details."

"I understand. I read about Clay Slacomb's arrest but since another person went missing today, looks like y'all locked up the wrong man."

"Maybe. Maybe not."

Holt flashed a rueful grin. "I see I won't get any inside scoop from you."

"I bet that latest woman, Janet, turns up by morning," Lulu said.

Bailey whirled to face her. "How did you— I mean, what makes you say that?"

"Woman's intuition. They showed a photo of her on the TV, a pretty little woman, and then later reported that a coworker—a *male* coworker—had also gone missing. Easy to put two and two together."

"Then I say there's a good possibility Clay Slacomb is the killer," Holt said. "Everyone knows them Slacombs are nothing but trouble."

Bailey didn't rise to the bait and pointedly didn't respond.

"How about a cup of coffee before you hit the road?" Lulu asked him. "Long drive ahead."

"Sure thing. Be right there."

Holt continued to his car and Bailey picked up her overnight bag and followed Lulu inside. The decor was minimalistic, but cozy—all leather furniture and a slightly scarred coffee table and end tables.

"Nice place," she commented, tossing her bag on the sofa and following Lulu to the kitchen.

Pine cabinets and flooring glowed amber under the

kitchen light, and the room smelled of tangy, sweet barbecue sauce.

"Here's a plate." Lulu pointed to a drawer by the sink. "Utensils in there. Want some iced tea?"

"Yes, thanks."

She loaded her plate with food and took a seat at the table, her gaze drifting to the garden. Unease snaked down her spine for no good reason.

Lulu set the iced tea on the table and then sat across from her. A fading ray of sunlight lit the gold chain around her neck and the cross pendant that dangled on her olive skin.

Bailey stared at the pendant—transfixed.

"Something wrong?" Lulu asked.

"That's a pretty necklace. But what happened to the turquoise and copper one you always wear?"

Lulu lifted a hand, her fingers caressing the golden charm. "Holt got me this."

"When?" Bailey's voice was sharp, shredding the short distance between them.

Lulu's hand abruptly dropped. "Weeks ago. Why? What's your problem?"

"Nothing. Never mind." She was being ridiculous, making a federal case over a stupid necklace. This case was working a number on her.

Holt's boots clomped across the den and her heart inexplicably pounded inside her chest.

"Reckon I'll take that coffee to go, Lulu. The sooner I hit the road, the more shut-eye I'll catch before the job."

Lulu immediately rose to fix his drink, and Holt turned to her, his blue eyes probing and intense. Had he overheard their conversation? And what would it matter if he did? All she'd asked was when he'd given the necklace to Lulu.

She couldn't look away from those blue eyes. A cabinet door opened and closed, and from her peripheral vision, she observed Lulu pouring coffee into a thermos. Perfectly normal, everyday kind of sounds. But Bailey's skin tingled, and her ears whirred a warning that something was...*off.*

Way, way off.

"Here ya go," Lulu said, thrusting the thermos into Holt's hands.

Holt smiled at Bailey. A curve of the lips that had nothing to do with amusement. His eyes were hard and cold.

Had they been the mad, mad blue eyes that had glared at her last night in the rain? Or was she the crazy one in the room?

Holt jerked his gaze from her to Lulu. "Walk me to my car?" he asked.

The couple left the kitchen, *clomp clomp clomp,* through the den, then the screen door banged shut—loud as a shotgun blast in the middle of a quiet forest. And there she sat, mired in suspicion as her mind flickered with ominous images:

The round patch on his uniform embroidered with a tree—which reminded her of the drawing on the wooden flooring at Floyd's Island. *Click.*

Holt's acceptance and reverence of Lulu's relics the night he'd buried the old crow feather from her necklace. *Click.*

His intimate knowledge of the swamp. *Click.*

The cross pendant, same as the one missing from Amy, that he gave Lulu. *Click.*

A schedule and job where he came and went with no one questioning his movements. *Click, click, click, click* and *click.*

But did it all add up to a guilty man?

With shaky legs, Bailey rose from the table and peered out the kitchen window, watching as Lulu and Holt talked. The voices were low enough so that even with the open window, she couldn't make out the words.

Everything her brain fired off was so circumstantial, so flimsy—except for the necklace. Somehow, she had to convince Lulu to give her Holt's gift and let the cops check it out.

She watched as at the car, Holt suddenly pulled Lulu into an embrace and they began to kiss. Bailey stepped away from the window and paced the room, trying to think of a reason to give Lulu for such an odd request. She couldn't outright accuse her boyfriend of anything. How insulting would that be? Lulu was a good friend, and asking for the necklace could ruin that friendship forever.

Think. There has to be a way.

A car engine started, and she returned to peer out the window. Holt's car puttered down the drive and out of sight. The wild beating of her heart slowed. At least he was gone. She'd sit down with Lulu and think of something. If she couldn't come up with an excuse, the truth would have to suffice.

Lulu returned to the kitchen, her face as calm and inscrutable as ever. "Let me refresh your drink. I made an herbal tea I think you'll like. It's got kava kava in it, which'll help you unwind. You seem a little tense tonight."

She didn't need tea. She needed that necklace. Bailey watched as Lulu boiled water and then poured it over crushed herbs before returning to the table and placing it in front of her. "Drink up and let's talk."

The boiled sludge didn't look terribly inviting. Grudgingly she took a small sip. Her mouth puckered. "Ugh. It's so bitter."

Wordlessly, Lulu got up and returned with a packet of sugar and a spoon. "This'll help."

Bailey stirred the tea and tried again. "Better. Look." She cleared her throat and plunged in. "Lulu, we have to talk. There's no easy way to broach this, so I'll just come right out and—"

"Finish your drink first. You sound distressed and this will help you relax."

She lifted the mug and scalding tea slushed over the brim. Why were her hands shaking so bad? Lulu would probably laugh at her strange request and hand over the necklace. If her friend got upset, she'd just get in her car and leave. Plenty of good motels down the road in Waycross. Bailey sipped until the mug was half empty and then set it down on the counter.

Or rather—she tried to. Her fingers and mouth were strangely numb. The mug wobbled in her hand, and Lulu steadied the trembling with a steady hold on her wrist.

"You haven't finished yet," she said.

Her friend's face distorted, as though she were looking at Lulu's face at the bottom of a pool of water. Something was wrong. A calm, inner voice that she remembered from long ago kicked in—the voice that guided her at the worst moments in foster care. It was clear as an unflawed diamond and spoke with an authority that brooked immediate action.

You're in danger. Do not drink another drop. Do not mention the necklace.

Bailey snapped her wrist. The mug fell on the table and then rolled onto the floor, breaking into shards that seemed to explode in slow motion. Black-green liquid sloshed on the table and spilled onto her shorts. "Oops," she said, as though it'd been an accident. "Sorry about that. I'll clean it up."

"I've got it."

They both stood, and Bailey forced a shaky laugh. "I'm wet. I better go change clothes."

"How are you feeling?" Lulu leaned forward, scrutinizing her face. "You look a little shaky."

She stepped back and fought to not betray her growing uneasiness. "I'm fine. Back in a minute."

Her legs were wobbly, but she stumbled forward and picked her overnight bag up off the sofa. She waved at Lulu and headed for the hallway, a fake, goofy grin plastered on her face. "Which room am I in?"

"Last one to the left."

She felt Lulu's eyes on her as she made it down the hallway and into the bedroom. Heart thudding, she locked the door behind her and leaned against it. *Deep breaths. Get it together and then scope out the area.*

The sparse room contained a double bed covered with a plaid comforter, a nightstand and one small dresser. More importantly—blessedly—it had a window on the back wall. Bailey flipped on the light switch and ripped into her bag, flinging clothes everywhere. Where the heck was her cell phone and car keys? She must have set them on the coffee table when she'd come in. She leaned her ear against the door.

A murmur came from the den. Lulu was on the phone. Talking with Holt perhaps? Ever so slowly, she eased open the door.

Lulu stood in front of the sofa, staring at her hand—which clutched Bailey's keys. Bailey stifled a groan. Those keys were her only means for a quick, certain escape. Only Lulu's profile was visible, and it shook her that the woman was so unemotional.

"I told you. She's out of it. I slipped something in her tea."

She spoke with a flatness that nonplussed Bailey more than if Lulu had ranted like a crazed psychopath thwarted from getting her way. Until ten minutes ago, she'd trusted this woman with her life. Her mind spun like a Ferris wheel on speed, until her inner voice nixed the buzzing in her ears.

So, she betrayed you. Deal with that fact later.

"Go ahead and circle on back," she heard Lulu say.

Get out now!

Quickly, Bailey shut the bedroom door and clicked the lock shut. That might buy her a precious minute to escape. She fled to the window and tried to lift the sash. It held tight. From a distance, footsteps started down the hallway. She pushed against the window with every scrap of her energy and it squeaked partially open with a begrudging protest.

The footfalls grew closer.

No time to fiddle with the screen fastenings. She kicked out the screen and then plunged forward head-first. Her hips strained in the tight opening and she dangled from the window, half in and half out. A sharp rap sounded at the locked door.

"Bailey? You all right? What's going on in there?"

The doorknob violently rattled.

Chapter Fifteen

Bailey hit the ground on her right side with a hard thump. A combination of fear, fresh air and pain helped sober her from the worst effects of whatever Lulu had added to her drink. Yet when she stood on shaky legs, a bit of brain fog remained.

A splintering crash rent the air behind her. Lulu was kicking in the door and, from the sound of it, was about to burst into the room. Cursing herself one last time for not keeping her car keys and phone in her pocket, Bailey fled to the woods. There was no other option.

Her legs stumbled forward as though they were made of lead, her brain and muscles not quite connecting. A dangerous whirring buzzed through her brain and she bit her lip hard, concentrating on the pain to keep from passing out.

The full moon beamed on her like a spotlight as she ran to the trees.

"Bailey! Get back here! Why are you running?"

Lulu's screams felt like claws gouging down her back. It was only when Bailey slipped into the shadows of the woods that she dared to look behind her.

Lulu stood at the window, her long black hair streaming in the wind and dark eyes burning like hot ash—

like a witch from a childhood nightmare—and then she disappeared.

She's coming for me.

Blindly, Bailey moved forward a few feet. Her foot hit an exposed root and she tripped in the darkness. *Oomph.* Her forehead bumped against the rough, solid bark of a tree and the rest of her body shortly followed.

"Damn it," she cried, slapping a hand on her bleeding forehead.

Even with the full moon, the air was dark and thick. Bailey blinked, willing her eyes to adjust.

A door slammed from behind her, and she was still close enough to the house to make out the sound of Lulu running across the wooden porch.

Again, she started forward, her hands out in front of her to prevent running into another obstacle. Every step was methodical as she tested the ground an instant before each footfall.

She was getting nowhere fast.

"Baaay-leee! Where are you?"

An unexpected beam of illumination burst through the night, and it took Bailey a moment to realize Lulu was directing a flashlight into the woods. Soon, she'd be revealed like a possum stuck in the headlights—easy prey for Lulu and Holt. An effortless night's hunt for the killers.

She turned back in the direction of Holt's yard in time to see Lulu tuck a gun in the waistband of her pants. The lady meant business.

"I think there's been a misunderstanding," Lulu shouted. "Come back and let's talk."

Like heck. She may have been a blind fool all these years when it came to the true nature of her former friend, and she might still be a tad slow from Lulu's drug, but she wasn't an idiot. Bailey picked up her pace, frantic to put more distance between them. Leaves crunched underfoot, sounding as loud as firecrackers in the stillness. But she couldn't worry about the noise. Her focus was on moving forward as quickly as possible, careful not to fall and risk hurting an ankle or knocking herself out with another head injury.

An elliptical beam of light fractured through the shrubs and foliage, less than six feet to her right. Bailey sucked in her breath, and then took advantage of the sudden illumination to run forward several feet, stopping when the light arced away.

It happened twice more. The light illuminated a path for several precious seconds and then she'd dart forward, stopping and leaning her back against a tree when the beam moved on. Her eyes darted upward to the silver tops of the tree limbs etched against the moon. Maybe she should climb. Would Lulu think to shine the flashlight upward?

Bailey decided against it. She imagined herself being cornered while Lulu and Holt stood below, waiting with knives. Or they could shoot, picking her off like a bird.

So on she went. Sandy soil gave way to damp peat and the ground grew more wet as she forged ahead, her sneakers glopping in the mud. The tracks would make it easier for the killers to hunt her, but it couldn't be helped. Her legs grew weak with exhaustion and her stomach rumbled. She leaned against a tree and retched. Immediately, her stomach settled down, happy to have expelled whatever toxin she'd ingested in the tea. That over, Bailey continued forward, perhaps in circles as far as she knew.

Abruptly, the darkness lightened several degrees and she scanned a small clearing ahead. An old barn and a deserted, rusty tractor stood silhouetted at the far side of the open land. A bolt of recognition shot up her spine. She *knew* this place. Edgar Slacomb's house was less than a quarter mile to the east. Somehow, it brought a modicum of comfort to get her bearings.

Now what? She'd never make it to the barn undetected without the cover of trees and underbrush. She bent over double, panting hard and nursing a stitch in her side.

Lulu had gone off on a tangent, drifting further away, but the flashlight beam must have picked up her muddy footprints because she reversed direction and headed unerringly toward her.

She had maybe five minutes. Even if she made it to the barn, circling around the clearing using the cover of trees, Lulu would no doubt search the barn when she spotted it. *Think.* How could she cover her tracks? The image of a ditch formed in her memory, and she recalled one was located close by. Last night's rain had probably filled it with water. If she found it, she could run in the water, obliterating her footsteps.

It shaved at least two minutes of her precious time, but she located it and ran, water sloshing up to her knees. The trampling of leaves drew ever closer. Time was up.

Bailey dropped to the side of the narrow ditch, covering her body with mud, leaves and pine needles. Playing possum was her best bet. The wet peat absorbed her body like quicksand, which terrified and relieved her all at once. She lay absolutely still and tried to muffle her labored breathing, which sounded loud as a hurricane to her ears. A mosquito buzzed by her nose and she squinted her eyes closed, resisting the impulse to swat it away.

Twigs snapped, and bushes and low-lying tree limbs slapped against a moving object.

"Where'd she go?" Lulu grumbled, the flashlight beam

casting a merciless light not ten yards from where she lay hidden.

Lulu tried to draw her out again. "I know you're nearby. Heard the water sloshing as you ran. Holt's not here, Bailey. Everything'll be all right. Come on out now. You know I won't hurt you."

Bailey didn't believe a word.

Loud sighs and muttered cursing ensued. Too late, she wished she'd confronted Lulu instead of running to the bedroom. She was younger and in better shape than Lulu and could have easily beat her in a fight. Clearly, the spiked tea had muddled her mind. And now it was too late. She couldn't out-muscle a gun.

"Damn it, girl," Lulu spat out. "You'd rather deal with me than Holt. I can promise you that."

A bit of mud seeped into Bailey's nose and a sneeze began to tickle. She gritted her teeth, fighting the urge. At last, the tickling stopped, and she breathed easier.

"Ahhh, that's more like it."

Slowly, Bailey turned toward the sound of Lulu's muttering. The woman eased down on the ground and sat back against a tree, the gun resting in her lap. Lulu killed the flashlight.

"If you strike out now in the dark, I'll hear you," she said in an almost cheerful voice. "Stay in your hidey-hole then. At first light of dawn, I'll be here waiting for you. And I *will* find you."

Bailey shivered in the slime, contemplating her options. No one would miss her tonight. Dylan thought she was safe spending the night with a trusted friend. By the time he tried to contact her in the morning and grew alarmed, it would be too late.

Dylan. What she wouldn't give to see him right now, to wrap her arms around him and lay her head against his broad chest and feel like everything was going to be all right, that she was safe and protected.

"Holt's my man, Bailey," Lulu continued in the same casual, conversational tone. "I'd do anything for him. Anything. I was dying living alone. I'm not some cold fish like you who doesn't care if she has a man or not."

Dying of loneliness? She'd never known, had always assumed Lulu was perfectly content with her solitary life, just as she had been with hers. Or rather, she'd thought she didn't want anyone. But Dylan had come into her life and proved her wrong on that count. She hadn't even realized how much she'd come to care for him until now.

"Sure, Holt's got his flaws. He likes to grab them young women and have his way. 'Course he has to kill them later or they'll identify him, ya see?"

Chills raced over every inch of her muddy body. Bailey kept her silence and wished Lulu would do the same. She didn't want to hear any more of the craziness.

A rustling erupted from somewhere behind Lulu and Bailey stifled her impulse to cry out.

Lulu scrambled to her feet. "Holt? That you?"

A doe and her fawn emerged and then gave a startled whistle before running back in the direction they'd come. Her heart slowed its wild beat. It wasn't Holt—not this time. But he'd be here eventually.

Lulu chuckled and resumed her spot leaning against a tree. As though reading Bailey's mind, she said, "Oh, you'll never escape Holt, hon. He's already disabled your car. I suspect he's hiding out somewhere near the house, figuring you'll come back and try to drive off or call for help. He'll keep an eye on the main road, too. He's almost as good at tracking as I am. If I don't return with you by dawn, he'll swing by here and help me handle this situation."

She chuckled again. "Seems I'm as forgetful as you when it comes to keeping up with my cell phone. If I had it, I could call, and he'd be here in minutes. Way I figure, he might get tired of waiting for you to show up at his place and start tracking. He could pop by anytime."

As if she wasn't in enough danger. Bailey reasoned that she had two choices. Wait for dawn and hope to catch Lulu unawares as she stepped close to her hiding place, or make a mad dash at her now. The disadvantage with option one was that Holt might show up and she'd be outnumbered and unable to take them both down. But the second option? There was a high probability that Lulu would shoot her before she could tackle her to the ground.

Lulu gave a loud yawn, stretching her legs out in front of her.

Which made Bailey realize she had a third option. Wait it out a bit longer. If luck was on her side, Lulu would fall asleep. She'd sneak up on her, get the gun and…shoot her? Could she really shoot another person? Bailey gritted her teeth. Whatever it took to escape alive, that's what she'd have to do.

Mind made up, she bided her time, thankful that Lulu had grown tired of being chatty. Instead, the woman moaned out a few more yawns.

I'll count to one hundred, Bailey decided. Whether Lulu was asleep or not, she'd make her move for freedom. Lying in the wet peat in a coffin-sized ditch, waiting for Holt to arrive, had become unbearable. Better to face a fatal shot in the chest than to be captured by Holt and endure a slower death.

…forty-eight, forty-nine, she silently counted. A snore rumbled nearby. Had her luck turned? Or was Lulu trying to fake her out? She'd find out soon enough. Bailey

resumed counting, slow and deliberate, eyes and ears attuned to the pulse of the forest at night.

…*ninety-eight, ninety-nine*… Her breath grew shallow and her heartbeat accelerated…*one hundred*.

Eyes focused on Lulu, Bailey shifted slightly in the mud. She couldn't see Lulu's face in the darkness to tell if her eyes were even closed, but her head lolled to one side, her arms out to the side, palms up, and the revolver lay in her lap.

Mud trickled and splashed in the ditch as Bailey moved, but Lulu didn't react. Bailey strove for patience even as she longed to hurtle herself straight at Lulu. The closer she came to her enemy, the better her chances of taking her down.

She struggled to her knees, waited, then rose to her feet. A suctioning noise escaped as she lifted a foot. Still no movement from Lulu. Slowly, slowly, inch by inch, Bailey emerged from the ditch and made her way over. So very close now. Close enough to see Lulu's face. Her eyes were closed. Bailey crouched, advancing. A few more steps and she'd snatch the gun.

Whoo-whoo, an owl hooted from a nearby tree, and she nearly screamed. *Damn*.

Lulu awakened with a jerk and rose to her knees, wildly searching for the source of the disturbance. The owl took off from a nearby perch, wings flapping in raucous commotion. Lulu's gaze dropped down, and as though sensing a presence, she faced Bailey.

Their eyes met.

Lulu's mouth widened, and she gasped, no doubt astounded given Bailey's mud-saturated state. Bailey imagined she appeared cartoonish, a monstrous swamp creature arisen from the bowels of the earth. The moment of shock was the one break Bailey had been praying for. She spotted the revolver lying only inches from Lulu's right hand, and then she lunged at the kneeling woman, throwing all her weight against her solid bulk.

The back of Lulu's head hit the tree—hard, with a dull thump that Bailey hoped would knock her out cold. But she only grunted before clamping her strong hands on Bailey's arms and squeezing with enough force that Bailey cried out in pain. Lulu might be thirty years her senior, but she was as strong as hate mixed with vinegar.

Bailey kneed her in the stomach and managed to kick the revolver several feet away. The grip on her arms loosened and Lulu groaned.

"Stop," she pleaded. "Please."

Bailey backed off, breathing heavily as Lulu gasped for breath and struggled to her knees.

"How could you?" Bailey asked in a thin voice. "How could you be with a killer? He's a monster."

Lulu's eyes gleamed with fury at the insult to Holt. "Don't you dare judge me."

Bailey stared, mesmerized. This woman was a stranger, one she'd never truly known until this moment. Hard to believe that she was the same person who'd fixed her dinners and chatted as they kept each other company many a long evening.

Lulu gathered her energy and made a sudden leap at the pistol gleaming in the moonlight.

That was what Bailey got for showing a moment of weakness. Mercy repaid by yet another attempt.

Bailey jumped on top of the woman and pinned her arm back. Lulu bucked and twisted beneath her like a wild animal—spitting and hissing. They rolled on the ground, kicking and punching. Lulu had difficulty maintaining a grasp on her mud-slimed body. The woman's hands slipped and fell away at every attempt to gain purchase.

At least Bailey had that going for her. With every roll, Bailey's eyes sought the gun; it was her focal point in the mad moonlit dance. If she could just reach it...

She slid from Lulu's grasp and inched her body to the right, her fingers hitting the gun's cold metal barrel. Another inch...there, she had it. Her fingers curled around the barrel and she slid it closer to her body. But she needed to distract Lulu before raising the weapon.

"It's Holt," she croaked, affixing her gaze just past Lulu's left shoulder.

Lulu's eyes narrowed with suspicion, but she looked back over her shoulder into the gaping darkness.

There would be no mercy this time. Bailey swung the pistol as hard as she could, making contact with Lulu's right temple. With a thud, the woman's stout torso crumbled and fell upon her. Bailey quickly rolled away from the dead weight and stood over Lulu, holding the gun and aiming it at her with steady hands.

Lulu lay motionless.

"Playing possum?" Bailey asked. Her voice was hard and gravelly, unrecognizable even to herself. She slowly inched to Lulu's side, never lowering the gun. A stream of blood ran in rivulets down the right side of the woman's face.

Tentatively, she kicked at her hip, rolling Lulu onto her back. Still no movement from the prone, inert body. Bailey couldn't bring herself to believe she was out for good. She laid a wet sneaker on Lulu's stomach, gradually shifting the full weight of her body in her gut. When Lulu didn't move, Bailey nodded in satisfaction. No one could fake it that well.

She stepped away from the body and tucked the gun

in the waistband of her shorts. Might come in handy before the night was over. If Lulu or Holt caught up to her, she'd have no hesitation shooting to kill.

Bailey tugged the leather cord off her neck and flung the crow feather necklace at the motionless Lulu. "Keep your talismans."

She glanced around, formulating a new course of action. If Edgar were a halfway decent human being, she could arrive at his house in fifteen minutes and ask him to phone the police. The next neighbor was another mile or two down the road, but that was her best option. She'd rather opt for the kindness of strangers than Edgar.

Which meant she had a long walk in front of her. Bailey moved her exhausted, wooden legs forward. The main road was up past the barn. She'd stay to the forest alongside the road, keeping cover in case Holt drove along searching for her. Decision made, she cast one last look at Lulu and then shoved off. When all this was over, she'd soak at least an hour in a hot bath and then sleep like a baby. The thought of warm water caressing her skin gave Bailey strength. She could even smell the clean scent of soap and shampoo as it washed away every last trace of mud and slime.

Vines, thorns and palmetto leaves shredded her legs and arms, while mosquitoes nipped everywhere. But Bailey kept plodding along, even when she wanted nothing more than to curl into a ball and bed down in pine needles like a fawn.

Maybe just one little rest. A few moments to recoup her energy. She leaned against a cypress and sagged into its support.

From afar, a pack of dogs howled and barked. Instantly she stiffened, alert as a hunted animal. Edgar's dogs. She whirled in a circle, trying to determine from what direc-

tion they were coming. Hadn't Dylan told Edgar to keep
them contained? They clearly were not. Her skin crawled
as she remembered the last attack when she was a teenager, the terror as the alpha had bitten her, his canine
teeth sinking into her hip and remaining there, burning
like hot metal spikes, while the others circled her body,
growling and snapping their bared fangs. She'd expected
a savage death, her flesh shredded to a bloody pulp. But
the other dogs hadn't joined in as they awaited Edgar's
command when he'd found her.

You have a gun this time. Use it.

She didn't even know how many bullets were loaded.
Would it be enough? By the time the dogs were close
enough for her to shoot, it might well be too late.

She needed higher ground. Bailey eyed the trees, seeking one suitable for climbing. All the while, the Dobermans howled in a frenzy of bloodlust. They were closer
now. Desperately she located a live oak with low-lying
branches and began to climb.

The first dog rounded the copse of trees, black fur
blending into the night and accenting his white fangs.
Others followed, and within seconds the whole gang
had arrived. Did they remember her? Bailey desperately
grasped the next branch, pulling her body up in small
spurts. Another branch, another foot upward to safety.

But she wasn't fast enough. Teeth bore into her right
ankle. She screamed and tried to kick at the dog with her
other foot, but he was impervious to her attempts, only
seeming to dig his fangs in further, tugging her body
down. She hung from a branch, flailing in panic.

"Edgar! Stop them." Was he even with his animals?
Usually he was, awake at the first bark of trouble.

Her palms were slick with sweat as she tried not to
lose her grip. There was no way to fish the gun from her

waistband and maintain her hold on the limb with her free hand. Her arms reached the breaking point and lost the tug-of-war battle. The fall was short, but the dogs were on her in an instant. The growls were everywhere, so menacing and close she felt their vibration seep into her flesh, shaking her to the core.

For the second time in her life, she lay trapped as they kept her pinned to the ground. Hot saliva slobbered her neck, fangs grazing her throat. One wrong move, and that steel jaw would tighten, crushing her airway.

She was trapped.

Chapter Sixteen

The streets were deserted as Dylan slipped the key into the warehouse lock. Since he was too wound up to sleep, he might as well investigate the small matter that niggled at the back of his mind.

Sure enough, Janet Blackwell and her lover had been found at a motel in Atlanta, running away to start a new life by ditching their spouses. Would have saved law enforcement time and money if they'd bothered to tell someone their plans. At least that was one less matter to distract them from their search for a serial killer. And it also left him free to check old police records.

His father would never have ignored a child being mistreated, and Dylan meant to prove it—to himself as much as Bailey. He eyed the stacks of cardboard boxes as he stepped into the warehouse and sighed. Jeff had done him a huge favor today and checked the microfilm documents. None of his father's old case notes had been filmed yet, which meant the original paper copies were still in here. Somewhere.

He went to the nearest stack and discovered they were all neatly labeled by date. That would make his quest much more manageable. Working backward, he found the boxes that would have been the year Bailey was sixteen and went to see his father.

Dylan sat on the concrete floor and opened the box that he hoped would have answers. It didn't take long to find the file for Armstrong, Sr. He flipped through the papers and his heart pinched at the few handwritten notes accompanying various incident reports. He ran his fingers along the faded script and felt unexpectedly connected to his dad. Near the end of the file in one of the last reports, he found what he'd come for.

February 10, 16-year-old Bailey Covington…alleged abuse… Social Services to be notified. Matter forwarded to Police Chief Alex Liverette of Enigma Township who has jurisdiction. Follow up in two weeks…ensure matter is investigated.

That date had been only a week before Dad had had a heart attack. He'd had emergency triple bypass surgery and had been recuperating in ICU for three weeks before contracting pneumonia. Just as they'd thought Dad was going to survive the ordeal, he died. That certainly explained his lack of a follow-up to the complaint, but why had the chief never resolved it?

He frowned, remembered that Chief Liverette had been convicted in a huge corruption scandal about three years after this incident. But that didn't have anything to do with Bailey. Her complaint of alleged abuse should have at least been forwarded to Social Services. Maybe beside being corrupt, Chief Liverette had been incompetent as well—or a friend of Edgar Slacomb.

Even though this exonerated his father, as he'd known it would, Dylan vowed to get the full story. The case had been out of his father's jurisdiction. Bailey must have gone to his dad, mistrustful of Chief Liverette. Hopefully, Liverette was still in prison and he could interview the guy. Either Liverette had dropped the ball, or he'd deliberately buried the abuse allegation. Dylan took a photo of the notes with his phone and then shoved to his feet. Bailey might not care who'd been at fault and why—it wouldn't change what she'd been through—but at least she wouldn't harbor ill will anymore against his family.

Although it was late, Dylan texted her. You up? Wanted to make sure you're okay. Once the message was sent, he exited the warehouse after locking up. The streets remained deserted and he drove slowly, feeling restless. He double-checked his phone—still no word from Bailey. She must be asleep. Apparently, everyone in Folkston was sleeping but him.

He'd swing by where she was staying. A quick drive-by to make sure all was in order. All he cared about was her safety. Once he'd determined nothing looked amiss, he'd finally be able to sleep. Dylan met his rueful smile in the car's dashboard mirror. *Oh, heck.* Bailey had totally captured his heart.

Chapter Seventeen

Dog stink permeated her nose and lungs with every shallow breath. It even seemed to seep into her very pores. Bailey imagined the scent would remain with her forever—that is, if she made it through the night. Had she escaped Lulu and evaded Holt only to land right back in her worst childhood nightmare? She cursed fate, willing her anger to override the terror.

Did she even want Edgar to find her this time? If nothing else, having the dogs around her would dissuade Holt from snatching her up. If Edgar didn't come, she could lie here the rest of the night until Dylan realized she was in trouble and a search team was called out.

But that was hours and hours away. The thought of breathing in the dogs' hot, panting breaths and listening to their growls for that length of time consumed her with a familiar panic. She'd rather face an armed Holt than this. Anything but this.

Pinned in by the dogs, on the ground, she kept her eyes scrunched closed to avoid the sight of their snipping fangs and their glaring eyes. If she was to be eaten alive, she'd rather not see the gruesome bloodbath. The gun was cold and hard against her hip, but if she moved to get it, the dogs might go into a frenzy. Too risky.

The unmistakable click of a bullet being pumped into

a shotgun chamber rang out. Her eyes popped open. The crunch of footsteps approached.

"Who's out there?" a gruff voice called out. "You're on my property."

Edgar. She'd recognize that voice anywhere. Bailey didn't answer, afraid the dogs' taut eagerness to attack would tip over the edge if she made any noise. Her throat closed so tightly that Bailey wasn't even sure she was capable of speech.

He was near her now. The ground vibrated with the weight of his steps. The dogs peered up at their master, awaiting his command. His shadow loomed over her body, blocking the moonlight. Edgar blinked down at her, shotgun aimed at her chest, then chuckled.

"That you, Bailey? Damn. You been crawling around in a mud pond? You don't look good."

Her throat worked, but no sound emerged.

"Cat got your tongue?" he asked. "Never thought to find you pinned down like this again." He leaned the shotgun barrel against his shoulder, now that he realized the intruder was no threat to him. "No, sir. Not since the last time you ran from me."

Bailey found her voice. "Call. Them. Off."

"Why should I? What you doin' on my land? Spying on me?"

"I've got better things to do."

He tilted his head back and laughed. "Think you're some big shot now, coming around here and telling tales on me to that cop you were with. Didn't do you no good last time when you tried it, and it won't do you no good now."

She challenged him. "You sure about that?"

A flicker of unease crossed his face. "You threatening me?"

"Call off your dogs and we'll talk."

Edgar rubbed the back of his neck and scowled, evidently weighing the pros and cons of having the Dobermans feast on her flesh. At last, he pointed at the dogs and growled, "Get back, ya hear?"

They whined in protest, but Edgar lifted a leg as if to soccer kick them into kingdom come, and they begrudgingly complied. Instantly Bailey scrambled to her feet, wincing as her right ankle bore her weight. "One of them bit me," she spat out.

"You were trespassin'. You're lucky they didn't tear you to pieces."

Bailey gritted her teeth together to keep him from seeing her tremble. She had to deal with Edgar from a position of strength and not let him believe he had total control.

"And what if they did kill me? You think you'd get away with murder after a cop warned you to keep them locked up?"

His chin rose and his eyes almost squinted shut. All signs he was very close to losing his temper. "Why are you here?"

There was no reason to lie. "I found out your neighbor, Holt Rucker, is a killer. I'm on the run from him."

"Holt? A killer?" Edgar's voice rose to a squeak. "You're joking, right?"

"Do you see me laughing? He's somewhere out here looking for me. Thanks to all the yapping of your stupid dogs, he might be really close."

"Holt? You out there?" Edgar called out in a singsong voice, mocking her explanation. "Olly olly oxen free!"

"Shut up!"

His face hardened. "Get off my land and stay off." He gestured to the dogs. "Let's get on home, boys."

Edgar turned his back on her and walked away. She blinked in surprise at his sudden departure. "Wait!"

He kept walking.

Bailey limped along after him. "Stop! You can't just leave me alone out here. I need your help."

"Ain't no law says I got to help you," he called over his shoulder, picking up his pace to a brisk trot, the Dobermans racing in front of him, eager to be home.

She struggled to walk with her injured right ankle. "But…but…"

On he walked. It was useless. The man had no mercy in him. Never did and never would. She was on her own.

Anger roiled through her body. She grasped the gun's handle and pulled it out of her waistband, then raised her arm and pointed at the man who'd caused her so much grief. Revenge was only a click away.

Her finger trembled on the trigger.

Edgar disappeared into the dark and the anger left her as swiftly as it had flared. She lowered her arm and shook at what she'd even dared contemplate.

Bailey hugged her muddy arms to her chest and glanced around, certain that Holt was nearby, ready to grab her and force her into a black oblivion. She'd be like Mary and Amy and Lisa and who knew how many others, never to be seen or heard from again.

Keep walking. Get to the road and keep the gun at your side, that calm, inner voice advised. She inhaled deeply to get her bearings and determine which direction to go. Best to follow the narrow trail toward Edgar's and then veer to the left at the next clearing. Bailey set off, hoping she was heading in the right direction. The pain in her ankle slowed her down, but she kept going forward.

Only minutes into the journey, the back of her neck suddenly prickled, and she whirled around. A large column of black stood only six feet behind her. The figure moved, breaking up the pattern. She discerned a length of the darkness breaking away and rising upward.

An arm.

Holding a gun.

Pointed at her.

"Drop your weapon!" he shouted.

She did. No way to use it before he could fire a round at her first.

Bailey's mouth went dry and she instinctively stretched out her arms, throwing her hands in front of her face. As if that would ward off a bullet.

The column moved toward her until Holt's gaunt face appeared, the pale blue eyes as piercing as the night they'd materialized mere inches from her face in the homestead window. The sort of gleam that only the truly insane sported. A potpourri of paranoia, rage and a coldness that resulted from a total lack of human warmth.

Pleading for mercy would be pointless. As would running. She could only hope to appeal to whatever remained of his rational mind.

"Don't shoot me, Holt. There's a witness nearby."

Holt stepped closer, his gun still pointed at her torso. "Slacomb? He's gone. I heard you pleading with him. You'll get no help from that quarter."

Never removing his eyes from her, he used his foot to slide her weapon closer to him. "Never cared for the man or his dogs, but tonight all the commotion made you easy to find. I owe him one."

Those two should get along famously, she thought. Both cold, vicious and with no regard for life.

"Why?" she whispered. "Why are you doing this? What have you done to the others?"

"Never mind that." His voice was hard and his motions fast as bullets as he picked up the gun and tucked it in his waistband. "What'd you do to Lulu?"

She didn't want to add fuel to his temper's fire. "Nothing," she lied. "I gave her the slip. Not that it did me any good."

He was on her in a flash, grabbing a fistful of her hair and sticking the gun's nozzle into her burning scalp. "No games. Where is she?"

"At least…" she hissed in oxygen through the searing pain "…a mile back. I—I can show you." Tears streamed down her face, and although she knew it was pointless, she added, "Please."

The grip loosened, but Holt's eyes were no less menacing. "If you've hurt her—"

"No. No. I couldn't hurt a friend." Lies were easy when they bought you precious time to live, and to plan your next move to keep on living.

"Where?" he demanded.

"I'll show you." There. She could spend hours leading him on a wild-goose chase. Would it be enough time? How much longer until morning broke and Dylan tried to contact her?

"Just tell me."

"It's not far from the barn. I can't say exactly."

"Get moving, then."

His hand circled her upper arm, bruising and merciless. "Don't try and run away," he warned. "I'll find you. No matter what. I'll always find you." He let go and pushed her forward. Light exploded, illuminating the path ahead. With one hand he held the flashlight, and with the other, he kept the gun digging into her lower spine. "Go," he ordered.

Bailey obeyed, her mind racing as each step brought her closer to the barn. Should she claim to be lost? Or should she eventually take him to Lulu? When Holt spotted her body, perhaps he'd be distracted by grief and she could grab one of the guns or run away.

"How'd you get away from her?" Holt asked as they pressed ever forward.

"I'm decades younger. I have better eyesight and can outrun her."

"Liar. How'd you get her gun, then?"

He had her there. The beam of light wavered in front of her as he drew his arm back and lifted it as though to strike.

"Okay, okay. I'll tell you the truth."

Holt lowered his hand. "Keep walking and talking."

"I realized she'd slipped something in my drink. I went to the back bedroom and heard her on the phone with you." Even now the horror of that moment knifed her gut. "I opened the window and ran away. She followed me."

She tripped on a root and lost her footing. Holt grabbed her hair again and pulled her up. She couldn't stop the scream of pain. He loosened his hold. "Go on. Walk and talk. Remember?"

"Th-then she caught up with me. We got in a tussle. I wrestled the gun from her and hit her in the head with it. I don't know how badly she's hurt." No need to mention that she'd left Lulu unconscious. "Then I just ran."

"You better not have shot her," Holt rasped. "If you did, you'll suffer extra."

Had Lulu survived the blow to the head? Her only hope might be that the head injury had slammed some sense into her former friend's mind. That Lulu would magically return to the person Bailey once thought she was.

But there was no magic. Only this slow, steady midnight progression toward the barn and certain death.

By the thin glow of the flashlight came the outline of the old barn. Bailey's legs felt heavy at the sight and she abruptly halted.

"Get moving," he said. The guttural command screamed near her ears. It ricocheted inside her mind like bullets.

"No. If you're going to kill me, do it now." She'd rather get a quick bullet than whatever torture Holt had in mind.

Her knees trembled, and she gulped in humid air that was sticky and heavy and cloying. She prayed Dylan wouldn't be the person who found her body. Bailey sank to her knees and stared at the full moon, wondering how many seconds she had left to live. She thought of Dylan and the tender way he kissed her, the way he had moaned in her arms the night they'd spent together.

And now it was all over. One night—no more chances to repeat that magic. But she had no regrets, only a deep thankfulness he'd come into her life, no matter if it was only to be for a short time. Because at last, she knew what it meant to love a man. To utterly and completely trust him and want to be with him the rest of her life.

"Get up. You ain't getting off so easy." Holt kicked the middle of her back with his heavy boot and she fell onto her face. Her teeth cut into her upper lip and she tasted blood mixed with mud.

"You've caused me too much trouble already."

Bailey rose to her feet and kept walking. What did it matter if he beat her to death here or in the barn? Both choices ended with the same result.

"Why have you hurt so many people?" she asked, trying to make sense of what was happening to her and what had befallen the other victims.

"Because I can."

It was as simple and awful as that.

Bailey plunged into the barn and the darkness deepened. Only a few slats of moonbeams shone through openings in the rotting wood. Holt jerked her by the arm, pulling her next to a rusted farm machine that looked like it hadn't been used for at least a decade.

"Don't move," he warned.

The flashlight fell to the ground, and from his back pants pocket he pulled out two small orbs of silver that glistened.

Handcuffs, she realized with horror. *Heck, no. Run!*

Bailey twisted to the side and tried to skirt around Holt. He grabbed her forearms and pushed her against the rusted metal. This was her only chance. Once he got those cuffs on her, she was a dead woman.

She kicked at his shins and groin, fighting as wild and desperate as a cornered animal. One blow landed and Holt groaned and bent over double, placing his hands on his thighs. She darted past him and ran for the door. Freedom was only a foot away when Holt tackled her from behind and she fell face-first.

A scream echoed in the barn. Had that been her?

Hands clamped over her injured right ankle and dragged her back to the tractor. Bailey squirmed and kicked, landing a few blows to his legs. Holt didn't even seem to notice, as though she were as harmless as a gnat.

"No!" She screamed until her throat was raw. But who was out there to hear her cry for help? Edgar? He wouldn't lift a finger to save her. He'd already made that clear.

She continued kicking and screaming—even after she heard the metal gears of the cuff grind around one wrist. Metal slammed against metal—a death knell. The fight drained from her.

Holt's lips twisted into a mockery of a smile. "Scream

all you want. It'll do no good." He cocked his head toward the back corner of the barn. "Just ask Amy."

Amy? Bailey whipped her head around, seeking the other woman. "She's alive? In here?"

"Barely."

Holt's fingers dug in her chin and he forced her head around. Those crazy blue eyes were only inches from her face. "I'm going to find Lulu. And she better not be dead, or you'll pay dearly."

He picked the flashlight up off the floor and flicked its beam to the back corner. "Say hello to your new neighbor, Amy."

Bailey inhaled sharply when the light pinpointed a woman whose hands and feet were bound with rope. A number of bruises and patches of dried blood were scattered over her naked body.

Amy Holley didn't so much as whimper.

Holt laughed, the sight of her suffering seeming to lift his dour spirits. "See you ladies in a bit."

The minute he faded from sight, Bailey breathed a tiny bit easier. She tugged at the cuffs, which didn't loosen an inch.

Her mind flooded with a darkness that matched the night. This wasn't her first time being bound. Not by a long shot. It had been Edgar's favorite means to discipline her, to break her spirit and bend her to his will. Somehow she'd found the strength to escape him, refusing to become a shadow of woman like his wife, Millie.

Don't panic. Don't accept this fate.

Bailey fought through the panic and despair. "Amy?" she called out. "Everyone's been looking for you. How badly are you hurt?"

"I wish I was dead."

The sound of Amy's voice, so flat and void of hope,

pinched Bailey's heart. She had to find a way to get them out of this prison. Amy needed her.

"We're going to get out of here," she assured Amy. "I promise."

Bailey forced her breathing back to normal and searched rationally for ideas. She'd seen plenty of internet videos recently on how to escape zip-tie bindings, but these were actual cuffs.

Holt had used a tiny key to lock the cuffs. Stood to reason that if she had a sharp piece of metal, she could jimmy the lock. But where? With her free hand, she patted down her pockets, nothing there, then glanced at her muddy sneakers. Nothing there, either. She wore no barrettes and had never bothered with bobby pins, not even when her hair was long enough for a ponytail.

She swallowed down a lump of fear. She carried nothing of use, which meant she had to find a piece of metal, or a sliver of something sharp nearby. Her eyes cast around the barn littered with abandoned farm equipment. But all the machinery within her reach was big and clunky—entirely useless for lock picking. She glided one foot, and then another, covering the ground in a semicircle—like a trapped ballerina.

Her shins connected with something solid. Something long and wooden. A hollowed trough, she realized. There were several rows of them. This place must have once been a pig farm. She groaned, kicking the trough until the bottoms of her feet blistered. The rotten wood easily cracked and splintered, the shards nesting by her feet. Though long and sharp, they were entirely too fragile for her purpose.

She swiped at them with the sides of her feet, cursing under her breath, willing the anger to provide strength. Anything was preferable to despair. The shards scattered, and in the remaining debris something glittered. She peered closely until recognition dawned.

It was a nail. A long, thin nail.

"Yes!" She raised her free fist and pumped the stale, humid air. "Amy, we're in luck."

Amy whimpered. Bailey twisted to face her, but could only see her pale, naked body hunkered into a tight ball. The woman must be so traumatized that hope had long since fled.

"Hang in there, Amy," she said softly.

Bailey returned her focus to the nail, even more determined to shed her handcuffs. Time was ticking away at an alarming rate. She stretched a leg, pointed her toes and reached for the nail. It brushed the tip of her sneakers—just out of reach. Bailey leaned forward another inch, crying out as the cuffs cut into her wrist. And she was still too short to pull it into reach.

There had to be a way.

Bailey kicked off her sneakers and grasped one of the broken wood pieces between her toes. Carefully, she again strained forward and brushed the nail toward her with her improvised, primitive tool. It took several attempts, but she managed to grasp the nail between her toes and lift it to her free hand.

She wanted to weep with victory. Still, the hardest part was yet to come. She had zero experience picking a lock, but survival was a powerful motivator. Fumbling, she inserted the rusted point of the nail into the keyhole and wiggled it. Nothing.

"Come on, come on," she muttered, trying it over and over.

A click pinged in the still darkness. The lock mechanism surrendered its hold.

"It worked!" she shouted, tears of joy and relief wet-ting her face. She flung the handcuffs away. They thudded against a wall and dropped out of sight. Quickly she slipped back on her sneakers and ran to the back of the barn.

Amy's shoulders rose all the way to her ears, and she lifted both bound hands in front of her face.

Bailey slowed to a walk, holding out her hand. "It's okay, Amy," she said gently. "I'm not going to hurt you."

She crouched in front of the huddled woman, wanting to reassure her and not make any sudden moves, while at the same time looking over her shoulder, expecting Holt to return at any moment.

"Let's get out of this place." She touched Amy's hands, gently lowering them from her face. "First I'll untie you, okay?"

At Amy's reluctant nod, Bailey set to work. The rope binding was tight, but she soon had it loosened. Amy gasped and moaned as the rope slid against her abrasions. "Sorry, hon. Stretch out your feet now," Bailey instructed. "We're almost there."

Amy untucked her legs and Bailey pulled at the binding, keeping eyes and ears on alert for Holt. At last she had the ropes off.

"Can you stand?" she asked.

Amy bit her lip and nodded. She rose halfway up on her legs, wobbly as a newborn fawn.

Bailey slipped an arm under Amy's shoulders. "Lean against me. I've got you. Let's walk now and get the heck away."

Amy's eyes filled with tears and something new—hope. "Thank you," she said simply.

Slowly they made their way to the barn door. Bailey strove for patience, but despite her outward calm and optimism for Amy, her stomach churned, and her mind screamed for her to run as fast as possible from the danger.

At the door, Bailey peered out, checking to see if the coast was clear. She didn't see anyone, but she was sure that Holt had a hidden camera mounted nearby, just as he had at the old church where he'd temporarily kept his victims. The killer closely monitored his makeshift prisons in case of an escape or an intruder, always managing to keep a step ahead of being discovered.

"We're good, but we need to hurry," she said, pulling Amy out and urging her to move faster. Between her injured ankle and Amy's overall weakness, progress was slow. Somehow, they had to make it to the road and flag down the first driver for help.

She breathed a little easier once they made it out of the clearing and into the cover of trees—but they were never going to make it to the road in time to be saved. Not at this pace.

What to do? She couldn't just abandon Amy to be caught yet again by Holt. Or, just as bad, attacked by Edgar's dogs.

You have to save yourself first to save Amy.

Bailey drew to a stop. "It's at least another two miles to the road. I'm going to have to make a run for it."

Amy stared at her with huge eyes, and the slight glimmer of hope that had flared in them died. Her fingers dug into Bailey's arm. "Don't leave me," she begged. "He'll find me. Please!"

"I'll come back for you. I promise." Bailey disengaged from Amy's grasp. "I'll find you a hiding place and then I'll come back with the cops. This is our best chance. You're going to be okay, Amy. Just hold out a little longer."

Bailey scanned the area, spotting an oak that would

do. She tugged on Amy's arm, urging her toward the tree. "I don't want to scare you even more, but there's a pack of vicious dogs roaming out here. You'll be safer up in a tree."

"Dogs?" She fearfully glanced around.

Bailey pointed at the tree. "They won't hurt you up there."

It took more persuading and strength she didn't know she had in reserve before Bailey, using a combination of her pulling and Amy climbing as best she could, got Amy safely ensconced in the uppermost branches of the tree.

"I'll be back soon. Shh," she whispered, placing a finger in front of her pursed lips.

Amy nodded and laid her head to rest on a limb, arms and legs bracketing its thickness.

Bailey scrambled down the tree and hit the ground running—as fast as she could with an injured ankle. Trees and thick underbrush loomed, preventing a quick escape. Finally, what seemed like hours later, she saw lights flicker from the road, strobing through the woods a few seconds before disappearing. Headlights. Relief whooshed through her lungs. She was so very close now.

Twigs snapped, and leaves rustled from behind. *Not now! Please. Not when I'm almost home free. Not with Amy depending on me for her life.* Bailey upped her speed, her heart jackhammering against her ribs.

Just a little farther to go.

Chapter Eighteen

A truck slowly approached, blinding Dylan with bright headlight beams. What was it doing on this lonesome road way past midnight? Judging from the truck's über-slow speed, he guessed the person was returning home from a night of drinking at a bar, inebriated and driving at a snail's pace to keep from running off the road. Dylan frowned, wishing he were in his cop car so he could pull the driver over.

"Your destination is on the right," came the disembodied voice of the GPS.

Dylan pushed down on his brake, easing his car to the side of the road. Bailey's car was in the driveway as well as a light blue sedan he recognized as belonging to her neighbor, Lulu. The tidy home was dark, and he had no reason to doubt both women were ensconced inside, sound asleep and in no danger.

The other truck rambled alongside him and he caught a fleeting glimpse of a gray-haired man staring out his window, his eyes piercing and glaring at him with suspicion, before he picked up speed and passed. Why that look? Dylan shrugged it off as he continued down the road. Maybe the fellow lived nearby and thought Dylan was the suspicious-looking one by pulling off the street and staring at his neighbor's house.

There was no cause for alarm, yet he shifted uneasily in his seat. Bailey might be annoyed but he wouldn't rest easy until he heard her voice. He picked up his cell phone and called her.

It rang five times before switching to voice mail. He flung the phone on the empty seat beside him. Ridiculous or not, he had to know she was okay. He grabbed the steering wheel and started to make a U-turn when a movement from the woods caught his eye.

A mud-covered figure stumbled from the tree line, waving its arms and limping toward his vehicle. Dylan strained his eyes to see into the darkness, then doubted the image he thought appeared before him. He was sleep-deprived and worried about Bailey, a volatile cocktail of emotions that caused his eyes to play tricks on him.

But no, he wasn't seeing things. The person drifted closer and he got a good luck at their face. Beneath the filth and blood crusting the mouth and chin, he'd recognize her no matter what.

"Bailey!" Dylan jumped out of the car. "What the heck—"

She threw herself onto him, and he felt her entire body trembling against his. A deep relief welled inside him. She was alive and here in his arms.

"We've got to get in the car," she said before he could question her. She withdrew from his arms and cast a fearful glance over her shoulder. "Holt's behind me."

"Holt Rucker? What's he got—"

"He's the killer," she said, limping to the passenger side and opening the door. "You've got to radio for backup. Amy's still back there."

For a moment, he stood rooted on the blacktop, his thoughts spinning and disjointed. A killer had been chasing Bailey through the woods, Amy was alive, Bailey was hurt and they were in danger.

Dylan sprinted back to his vehicle and called the emergency dispatcher, quickly explaining the situation and his location and requesting helicopter assistance. With their thermal imaging detectors, a chopper had the best chance of pinpointing Holt and Amy's whereabouts. He wanted to end this as quickly as possible and get Amy to safety. A sudden thought occurred. "What about your friend, Lulu? Is she also out there in the woods?"

A headlight pierced the darkness behind them. Dylan turned and narrowed his eyes, adjusting to the light's glare. It was the vehicle he'd spotted earlier. "Does Holt Rucker drive a blue truck?"

Bailey whipped her head around. "Yes. Is that him behind us?"

"That or someone's borrowed his vehicle. Buckle up and keep your head down below the window," he ordered, jerking the car around 180 degrees. He withdrew his gun and released the safety.

He was almost upon the truck when the driver rolled down his window. The long barrel of a shotgun extended, aimed smack dab at Dylan. He crouched below the dashboard, placing a hand on Bailey's shoulder to make sure she stayed down.

A second later, pellets exploded through the front windshield and shards of glass rained down on them.

Their vehicles were almost side by side now. Dylan rose up and shot at the driver. Damn it, he missed. Another shotgun blast and pain exploded in his left shoulder. He felt himself sinking, his world going to black. Only one thought formed in his quickly hazing mind. Bailey had gone through unspeakable trauma tonight, had outwitted Holt in the woods and made it to the road, only to have Dylan gunned down and be recaptured again—all when he was supposed to save her.

"Dylan!" He could tell she was screaming by the frantic edge to her voice—but it sounded as though she were far, far away. Strong hands shoved him to the passenger side, and her body slid over his and then took his place behind the wheel. His car lurched forward, and they were hurtling away into the darkness. He swallowed down the pain, took off his shirt and pressed it against the bloody wound. It hurt, but the pain braced him, and he sat up straight. Lucky for him, the damage was on his left shoulder instead of his right.

Bailey had taken command of the car, her foot bearing down hard on the accelerator. Through the side mirror he saw Holt still in pursuit and closing in. A roar sounded in the sky, lasting too long to be thunder. A blinding beam speared downward.

A rescue helicopter had arrived.

Police sirens also closed in from both directions, their blue lights flashing. The cop car behind Holt was rapidly gaining on him.

"Looks like he's the one trapped now," Bailey said with satisfaction as the blue truck screeched to a stop.

To his left was the great Okefenokee swamp, teeming with alligators, and to his right the woods.

The truck made a sudden lurch to the right.

"He's going to make a run through the woods. Let me drive."

Bailey shook her head, sharply turning his vehicle around and taking it off-road. "I've got this." They bounced along the sandy soil, other cops following their lead. The helicopter hovered overhead, clearly spotlighting Holt as he exited his truck, still carrying the shotgun.

He grabbed Bailey's arm as she opened her door. "You're not going out there."

"But—"

"No way."

Other officers got out of their vehicles. They commanded Holt to surrender and finally, realizing there was no escape, he threw down his weapon. Cops swarmed him.

"It's over now," he reassured Bailey. "We've got the guy. Thanks to you."

"But Amy's still out there. I have to show you where she's hidden."

"The helicopters will spot her."

"You don't understand. She's traumatized. I want to be there when she's found. I told her I'd return, and she trusts me."

Dylan nodded. All he wanted was to take Bailey home and keep her safe, to comfort her after the trauma of the night. To feel her heartbeat thumping against him. But he understood her need to help Amy. "Okay, but we go together."

They got out of his vehicle and found Sheriff Chesser, quickly explaining the situation and roughly where to direct the helicopters to find Amy. He nodded his assent, insisting that backup escort them to the site.

It didn't take them long to spot Amy. The helicopters had arrived first, and their lights flashed down on an emaciated woman who cowered in the treetop, clinging to a limb as though drowning in the storm of sudden light, wind and sound.

"Amy!" Bailey jumped up and down, waving her arms, but Amy's gaze was locked on the helicopter above, and Dylan doubted the woman could hear Bailey over the chopper motor.

Bailey started up the tree and he followed, hoping Amy would allow him to carry her down to safety. The wound on his left shoulder throbbed, but not enough to incapacitate him. Ambulances with EMTs were on standby in the clearing, waiting to take her to a hospital.

Bailey reached her first and leaned over Amy, cautiously touching her shoulder. The woman recoiled with a scream.

"Amy, it's me, Bailey. Remember? I told you I'd be back."

Amy's wide eyes flickered with terror before understanding dawned. She nodded, and Bailey took her hand, giving it a squeeze. "Time to come down now."

With great care, Amy sat up and then froze when she saw Dylan.

"This is my friend, Dylan," Bailey explained. "He's going to help you down if you need it."

Amy held out her hand to him and he clasped it, relieved she'd so easily accepted his presence. "I'll carry you. It'll be easier," he shouted over the chopper noise.

Bailey sidled out of his way and he scooped Amy in his arms, wincing at the throb in his left shoulder as he shifted her body weight onto his good arm. He marveled that an adult could weigh so little. Skeletal bones poked close to the surface of her skin.

When they reached the ground, Sheriff Chesser was already there, concern suffusing his face. He quickly wrapped a blanket around Amy. "I'll radio EMS to bring a stretcher out here. How's she doing?" He leaned in closer. "Ma'am, we're taking you to a hospital. We'll get a statement from you after you've been admitted and treated."

Amy ignored him and searched around frantically. "Bailey?"

She stepped closer to them. "I'm here."

Amy grasped her hand. "Stay with me."

"I'll stay by your side as long as you need me," Bailey reassured her.

Dylan's heart pinched at the exchange. It was only thanks to Bailey that this woman was still alive. Bailey was incredible—smart, compassionate and beautiful. A woman you'd be honored to have on your side in any situation.

And to think he'd come so close to losing her. Holt could easily have killed her tonight. A shudder ran down his back at the very thought of never seeing Bailey again, never having a chance to tell her how he felt, how he wanted her to be a part of his future.

He cleared his throat. "EMTs are taking too long. I'll carry Amy to the clearing."

Chesser spoke beside him. "Bailey—Dylan—you both need to have your injuries checked out, too."

The helicopter followed them, providing light as bright as an afternoon sun as they made their way slowly through the brush. How had Bailey navigated out here in the darkness with a killer on her heels? He was sure he'd have nightmares about this the rest of his life.

They burst into the clearing, by now awash with blue and red lights from over a dozen cop cars and ambulances. He rushed to the nearest ambulance, where an EMT met him and took over. Amy appeared bewildered at all the commotion and kept a tight grip on Bailey's hand.

"Don't leave me," she again pleaded with Bailey as they loaded the stretcher on the ambulance.

"I'm staying with you."

Bailey glanced up at him. "Are you coming with us? Your shoulder needs to be examined."

"I'll catch a ride with Chesser." The fewer people and less noise around Amy, the less her emotional distress.

"See you at the hospital later?" she asked.

He nodded, and the tightness in his throat spread to his chest. He had to tell Bailey how he felt about her. Now.

"Bailey, I—I…" His throat closed, and the words clogged deep inside.

Her eyes grew tender and a soft smile tugged the edges of her lips. "I know you care about me."

He found his voice and grasped her hand. "Care about you? That doesn't begin to express it. When I thought Holt might have killed you, my heart almost stopped beating. I was afraid I'd never get a chance to tell you that…" he swallowed hard past the lump in his throat "…that I'm in love with you, Bailey Covington. Day one, I was intrigued the moment you glared at me when I pulled you over on the ATV."

Her eyes misted as she softly chuckled. "I can't say I felt the same when you pulled me over, but through all this, I finally realized I could trust you with my life and my heart. I love you, too, Dylan."

An EMT interrupted with a stern command, "Time to go." Reluctantly, he released Bailey's hand. The EMT ushered him out, shutting the door of the ambulance. He watched as it sped out of the clearing, feeling like it was driving off with all the light and warmth of his world.

An arm clamped around his uninjured shoulder. "Ranger Covington's an amazing woman," Sheriff Chesser said. "She's going to be fine."

Epilogue

Pain exploded in her right thumb and Bailey dropped the hammer. "Damn it," she growled, shaking out her hand. This wasn't even her first mishap today.

Ace climbed into her lap, trying to slather her face with his tongue.

Absently, she rubbed behind his ears as she surveyed the doghouse she was building. Something was amiss. It tilted to the side and there were gaps in the slats. She gazed down at the directions, wondering how she'd gone so wrong.

A car pulled into the driveway and she moaned. She'd been so wrapped up with this project that time had slipped away. She and Dylan had made plans to picnic with his sister, Janie, and her daughter this afternoon. To Bailey's surprise, she enjoyed these outings with his loud, boisterous family. She'd lived a solitary existence for way too many years.

Dylan approached from the side of her cabin and, as always, her heart did a funny little thump. She'd quickly gotten over her aversion to the Armstrong name, especially when he explained that his father had really tried to help her when she'd reached out to him as a teenager. It was just rotten luck that the abuse hadn't been committed in his jurisdiction and that the neighboring cop had been friends with Edgar.

Ace barked a greeting and ran to Dylan as she scrambled to her feet. He picked up Ace and ambled her way, tilting his head as he surveyed her handiwork.

She held up a hand. "Don't say it. Things went horribly astray at some point in the construction."

"If you want me to—"

"Nope. I'll figure it out."

He shrugged. "Don't know why you're wasting time building a doghouse. Ace stays inside with you all the time. I'd say he's fully enjoying his retirement from police searches."

"I worry about him when I'm at work. A dog needs to enjoy sunshine and run free, not be cooped up inside. I'm thinking my next project is to fence the backyard and then—" She broke off at the amusement in his eyes.

"This rascal has got you hooked around his little paws," he said with a laugh. "I'm jealous."

She laughed with him. Dylan had no reason to be jealous, as he well knew. Ever since Holt's arrest six weeks ago, they'd been almost inseparable, spending practically every night together either at his place or her cabin.

Dylan set Ace on the ground and his expression turned serious.

"What's up?" she asked at once.

"I'm going by Edgar Slacomb's place."

Her good mood soured at the man's name. "Why?"

"I have a bone to pick with him. And something needs to be done about those dogs. They're a danger to the community."

"He refuses to keep them penned."

"Exactly. Anyway, it occurred to me you might want to come along. Confront him for leaving you alone and injured in the woods while you were being hunted." Dylan's voice shook with anger and his whole body grew tight.

"Easy," she cautioned. "Maybe Jeff or another officer should handle this. Someone with no emotional investment."

"No, I'm going," he insisted. "I need to do this."

She drew a deep breath. "I think I do, too."

"You sure?" His olive green eyes bore into her, alight with concern.

"Yes. Let's do it now, before Janie's picnic."

He nodded, and they walked to the front of her cabin. Ace ran ahead to Dylan's car, anticipating an outing.

"Oh, no, you don't, little fellow. Those Dobermans would make mincemeat of you." She scooped him up and left him in the cabin before rejoining Dylan. As usual, her gaze flickered to Lulu's empty cabin.

She hadn't killed her former friend that night. Lulu had suffered a concussion and had been treated, right before the police had arrested her for accessory to murder and locked her up in the Charlton County jail to await trial. Holt Rucker, deemed more of a security threat and escape risk, was waiting in a maximum-security facility.

The sight of Lulu's cabin churned her gut as she remembered the betrayal. It didn't make sense, and Bailey recognized it never would. Not even if she lived to be a hundred. She'd tried to look back; had there been signs she'd missed along the way?

But no. No, there were not. She had no idea her friend was so lonely and desperate she'd go along with murder to keep a boyfriend who was in and out of her life. Maybe Bailey had projected her own feelings onto Lulu, assuming her own contentment with solitude was the same for the older woman. That seemed so long ago. She'd never want to go back to a such a solitary existence. With Dylan by her side, life was much richer and enjoyable. Sharing time with him was her greatest happiness.

Bailey shook off the thoughts of Lulu and climbed into Dylan's car. He shot her an understanding sideways glance.

"Maybe you should think about moving," he suggested.

"Maybe one day. We'll see."

They sped down the familiar roads to the Slacomb house, but this time it barely bothered her. She'd survived that night, no thanks to him, and if she could get through that, she could handle anything.

Dylan pulled up to the house. The mechanic garage was closed and there were no signs of any dogs, but as they exited the vehicle and walked to the front door, the barking began, somewhere near the back of the house.

Bailey gripped the canister of mace in her hands. She'd made a concession that a few dogs, like Ace, were okay—but these Dobermans were an altogether different matter.

Dylan knocked on the door and Millie opened it.

"Where are the dogs?" Dylan asked at once.

"Got 'em penned 'round back. They can't hurt you."

"Penned?" Bailey blurted. She'd never imagined Edgar would agree to that.

"Yes. Want me to show you?"

"I'd like to confirm they're no longer a menace," Dylan said.

They trooped around back. Sure enough, a large area of the yard was now fenced in chain link. The Dobermans rushed the barricade, barking and snarling.

"How did you get Edgar to agree to this?" she asked Millie. "And where is he? I have a few things I'd like to say to him."

Millie faced her, and Bailey noticed a fading yellow

bruise on her left eye. "He's gone. Been gone over a week now."

Dylan gave a satisfied nod. "Glad to see he's being sensible about those dogs. Tell him I'd like to speak with him when he gets back."

Dylan's phone rang, and he fished it out of his pocket. "Excuse me," he said, stepping away to take the call.

Bailey shifted awkwardly. "Are you okay?" she finally asked.

"Better than I've been in years."

Bailey regarded her closely. Something *was* different about Millie—a certain ease and quiet confidence she'd never seen with her former foster mother.

Millie wet her thin lips. "I'm sorry about…you know… everything in the past. I hope you can forgive me."

Bailey drew a deep breath, recalling the many times Millie had turned her head and done nothing to stop the abuse. She'd bet this woman had been a victim, too. "I'm willing to let it go," she said slowly. "Edgar's a different story, though."

"Don't worry about Edgar." A new conviction rang in Millie's voice. "Neither of us will ever be seeing him again."

"We're both better off without him," Bailey said with a nod.

Their eyes locked another moment before Dylan returned, stuffing his phone in his pocket. "Ready to go?" he asked.

"Ready."

She turned on her heel and took his hand as they walked back to his car. *Ready.* She'd never been more ready to leave the past behind, especially now that he was in her life. As though sensing her feelings, Dylan brushed a quick kiss on her forehead. "You never have to come back to this place," he said.

"I don't plan on it." Impulsively, she wrapped her arms around his neck and kissed him.

He laughed and hugged her close. "What brought this on?"

"I'm just happy. Truly happy. Because of you."

Dylan cupped her chin in his hands. "I always want to make you feel this way. Always," he vowed, his voice husky.

Always. Yes, it was what she wanted as well. She kissed him—a long, long kiss full of promise and hope for their future. Together.

* * * * *

DEADLY COLTON
SEARCH

ADDISON FOX

For my fellow authors in The Coltons of Mustang Valley continuity. It's been a pleasure writing this with all of you!

And most of all to our fearless leader, Carly Silver. She understands the importance of uniform color, proper names of Mustang Valley watering holes and the exact position of town landmarks to ensure we all stay on track. I know I speak for us all when I say we <3 you with the affection and gratitude of a million Corgi photos.

Prologue

Nova Ellis lay in misery on the small leather couch in her boyfriend's office and prayed for death. Anything—the horror of a firing squad, the terror of being snared in a noose, even contracting some flesh-eating bacteria—had to be better than this.

Roiling waves of nausea that suggested she'd somehow gone from the rock-solid streets of New York City to the high seas of the Atlantic mere hours before a hurricane hit assaulted her system with ruthless abandon. At the mere thought of a wavy ocean her stomach rolled once more and Nova held tight to the couch, praying she'd be allowed to keep what little was left in her stomach.

Like its lining.

Because that was all that was left, and after the past three weeks of abject afternoon sickness she was even starting to wonder about that.

It was her fault. Realistically, she knew that. The bagel smothered in whitefish salad she'd inhaled that morning had tasted great at the time but the fish had had its revenge. So had the tapioca pudding she'd snagged at the deli on her walk over to Ferdy's office. And the small bag of gummy bears she'd dug out of the bottom of her purse—shocked and *grateful* when she'd found that prize—had been the last thing to seal her fate. She'd even eaten the lime-flavored ones, something she'd avoided her entire life.

Who even liked lime?

Why did they even *make* lime?

That hateful flavor she should have avoided, as lime-flavored whitefish made a rather unpleasant combination when one couldn't keep anything down.

She closed her eyes, willing the dancing images of gummy bears and bagels out of her head and vowing that all she needed was a few more minutes. She'd come to tell Ferdy the good news of her pregnancy and she wanted to look nice when she told him.

She wanted him to be as excited as she was.

Even if the small voice that kept whispering he wasn't going to be excited seemed to be winning as of late.

Oh, sure, it wasn't the most ideal time. They'd only been dating a few months but their relationship had been a whirlwind from the start, and she knew he was looking toward having a family of his own. He'd told her as much on their first date. He wasn't a man trying to play games or keep diving into the dating pool.

He wanted a future and he was seeking a woman who wanted the same.

They'd talked about everything that first night. Their love of music and movies, their dreams and aspirations, and their equally challenging childhoods—his with parents who couldn't seem to make up their minds between overbearing and absent, and hers with a mother whose idea of encouragement and support was shopping on the Champs-élysées to solve any problem.

Ferdy had seemed to understand and she'd been so happy to find that in her significant other. Even if he hadn't shown the same understanding since then, his own behavior oddly like that of the father he spoke of with disdain. He seemed to be overbearing or absent far too often.

But could she blame him? He had a busy job and was often out for days at a time working on real estate deals. And it wasn't like she'd been totally honest with him, either. It wasn't a complete lie that her father had died, but it wasn't totally true, either.

The dead man she'd always called "Dad" wasn't actually her real father. She'd spent most of her life believing Paul Ellis was her father and her mother's deathbed confession—that Allegra Ellis had gone out and found a more attractive man after her ill-fated relationship with another had resulted in the pregnancy with Nova—couldn't change that.

Even if it had changed *everything*.

But no, she wouldn't give in to that line of thinking. There might be some man named Colton all the way out in Arizona who was her biological father, but he hadn't been her real father. Hadn't been the person who'd raised her. Her mother might have believed she was getting her revenge on the man by never telling him that she was pregnant, but Nova couldn't see how. Now that she was pregnant with a child of her own, she understood the difference.

A door opened in Ferdy's outer office and she mustered up a wan smile to herself, thinking of his face when she told him. She'd settled on surprising him in his office, taking some strange comfort in her mind's eye that there would be others nearby. Of course, because he'd be so excited he'd want to share his joy.

Of course it would be excitement.

His dark brown eyes would crinkle at the corners,

before his strong lips pursed in thought. He was always like that, considering the world around him before he let his emotions come through.

Before his dazzling, bright white smile would take over his face and he'd pull her close in happiness at the news he was going to be a father.

She struggled to sit up, desperate for the sweet image in her mind to will away the nausea that still had her stomach quaking. Slowing her movements, she gingerly laid her head back against the thick leather cushions.

Just a few more minutes with her eyes closed… That was all she needed.

Nova had no idea how long she'd been out, drifting on the blessed wings of sleep, when she heard a heavy crash from the outer office. Was that a glass? One of the pretty crystal tumblers Ferdy kept on his credenza?

"Come the hell on, Ferd. I expected that shipment three days ago!"

"Port's on lockdown, Gino. My contacts there can't do nothing about it."

Eyes popping open, Nova struggled to sit up. She didn't know all the ins and outs of Ferdy's business but she knew enough to know that something wasn't right. He worked in real estate, not shipping. And she'd never heard that terse tone in his voice before.

It was…nasty, somehow. Dark.

An involuntary shiver ran down her spine, the blessed cool of the room she'd reveled in a few minutes earlier suddenly making her skin clammy.

"My business partners and I trusted you with that shipment!"

"And I'm telling you I can't do a damn thing until the Feds ease up their sniffing around the docks. It was bad luck all around the Russians lost that shipment a few weeks back. Got the Feds on high alert, especially after they found a thousand kilos of smack nestled inside all those cheap nesting doll souvenirs."

The nausea that had coated her stomach like battery acid changed in that moment. The roiling upset was still there, but something had changed. Fear coated her tongue, leaving a bitter, metallic taste behind that had nothing to do with lime-flavored gummies.

Ferdy was a real estate developer. Yet from the sounds of it, he knew how shipments came in and out of port and which ones held drugs or other illicit substances.

Scrambling off the couch, she grabbed her purse and ran to the private bathroom off the side of his office. When he came in she'd claim she'd gotten sick off her lunch and had been huddled in there feeling miserable. For the first time since arriving twenty minutes ago, she was grateful for her pasty white visage and bloodshot eyes.

She just might convince him she had food poisoning.

And if he thought she'd been in the bathroom he wouldn't know what she'd heard through the door.

It would buy her some time to figure out what to do. And would give her a small window to plan her next step.

The door to his office clicked open and she heard voices grow louder as Ferdy walked into the room with the man he'd been talking to. Nova was tempted to peek through a crack in the door but she stayed where she was, convinced things would go easier if she was discovered huddled over the toilet instead of watching through the door.

Thick footsteps traversed the outer office, moving around as the conversation continued. More talk of shipments and an "expected delivery" and estimates of when issues at the port would calm down.

Each word more damning than the last.

And each syllable like a bullet to the chest, convincing her that the man she'd believed herself in love with—the man whose baby she carried even now—was a liar and a cheat.

And a drug dealer.

Good Lord, who had she taken up with?

She laid a protective hand over her stomach, suddenly grateful she hadn't had a chance to share her news of the baby.

Once again, footsteps came perilously close to the bathroom door before the shrill ring of a cell phone filtered through the partially closed door.

"Adler," Ferdy snapped out.

Nova heard a few mumbled yeses, noes and even a "not my fault," before she heard the distinct sound of his phone hitting the glass top of his desk. The string of curses that followed suggested the call hadn't gone as planned, but it was the added taunt from the other faceless voice she'd heard that had her wincing.

"Told you the boss wasn't going to be happy."

After another muttered curse, Ferdy's voice came loud and clear through the door. "Looks like it's our lucky day. Bastard wants to see both of us. Now."

Those thick footfalls vanished nearly as quickly as they'd come, the door to his inner office slamming closed. Nova counted to a thousand, willing herself to stay right beside the toilet. It was her only defense in the event Ferdy came back and the only way she could brazen her way through a confrontation if he questioned what she might have heard.

Picking herself up off the marble tile, she reached

for her purse and slung it over her shoulder. She forced herself to walk back out of the office with the same calm she'd walked in with, and offered a silent prayer of thanks as she passed his secretary's desk. The woman had been out for lunch when Nova had arrived and was still gone.

Small miracles.

Pieces of a heavy crystal tumbler lay in a pile on the floor beside the credenza, further reinforcement of all she'd heard.

She kept her walk steady and easy, breezy even, as she walked to the elevator and on down to the lobby. Her purse swung from her fingertips as if she had nothing to lose.

As if her entire world hadn't just cratered.

It was only when she was outside once more, the fresh air blowing in her face, that Nova made her decision.

Whatever Ferdy was into, sticking around and trying to get to the bottom of it with him wasn't going to end well. If it hadn't been for the baby she might have tried it. Might have given him the slightest benefit of the doubt and brazened her way through a conversation, but not anymore. She had a child to look out for.

With that sole thought pounding through her mind, Nova made her decision.

And ran.

Chapter One

Five months later
Mustang Valley, Arizona

Nikolas Slater rubbed the bridge of his nose as he reread his contract with Selina Barnes Colton. The woman had a temperament that would make a rattler turn tail and slither away, yet that hadn't stopped him from making a deal with the she-devil.

Which meant he was either really good or miserably foolish.

He preferred smart over fool any day but knew that, in order to stay afloat, a PI with an expensive set of services needed to take the big fish when they knocked on his door.

And Selina Barnes Colton was a big fish.

Coldly beautiful, the second—and now *ex*—wife of Payne Colton was a piece of work. And while she might be seriously high maintenance, she wasn't asking anything out of line.

Besides, the ink was well and dry on the contract and he'd already cashed Selina's up-front payment, so really, he had nothing to worry about. Something he kept reminding himself of even as he went over the agreed-to work and considered how he was going to approach the case.

Things did not look good for Ace Colton. The man had had a solid, upstanding reputation, but recent events had seriously tarnished it. A gun discovered in his apartment—one definitively proven as the one used on his father—was bad enough. The fact the man fled when the cops went to charge him was just bad news all around.

And then Selina had come calling.

Selina had hired him to prove that Ace Colton had shot his father, former oil exec Payne Colton, in cold blood. While it was a handy story and one that had kept Mustang Valley talking since the January shooting, something didn't fully play for Nikolas. Even if it had played for the local press like a well-tuned piano. The golden boy. The powerful father. And a family name that had plenty of notoriety. Hell, a distant cousin of Payne's had served as president.

Nikolas suspected the recent escapades of the Arizona branch weren't finding too much favor with such illustrious relatives, no matter how distant, but they didn't call certain branches of families black sheep for nothing.

Even now, Payne remained in a coma over at Mustang Valley General Hospital, the victim of a gunshot wound late one night in his office at Colton Oil. A situation that had kept the local press busy for nearly nine months and that ebbed and flowed in and out of the national news, as well. While they might no longer be husband and wife, Selina was still a bigwig at Colton Oil. And while it wasn't a secret she carried no soft feelings for Old Man Colton, she was also clearly not interested in losing her cash cow.

Despite the cynicism, Nikolas had played various angles in his mind. Was it so hard to believe she wanted to do right by him as well as the company? Or that she wanted a guilty man caught, especially if the whispers were true and it was Payne's oldest son, Ace, who had done the deed?

Maybe yes, maybe no.

Nikolas kept his ear to the ground and he knew there was more going on than even what Selina had briefed him on. The entire town had discovered over the past few months that Ace Colton wasn't actually Payne's son. Selina had confirmed that by showing him the result of a DNA test. The Mustang Valley rumor mill was working overtime, fixated on the notion that Ace had been switched at birth. If it was true, it gave Ace a possible motive for murdering the man who wasn't really his father, after having been ousted as the CEO of Colton Oil when it was proven that he wasn't really a Colton.

Add on the fact that Selina's desire to find Payne's shooter didn't seem fully altruistic—especially since she already had a candidate in mind—and Nikolas knew to watch his back. He might not have a particularly large reserve of restraint in the face of a beautiful woman seeking his professional help but he did have standards. Which meant he needed to stay focused and keep his nose clean.

And do whatever he could to determine who had put Payne Colton in his or her crosshairs.

In the meantime, he'd given Selina his agreement to work the case. The long-term success of Colton Oil depended on happy stockholders and a healthy leadership. If Payne didn't recover and the investment community caught wind of so much drama at the top, the stock prices would fall and all the Mustang Valley Coltons would suffer. As PR director for Colton Oil, Selina had the job of making sure that wind never swirled above a whisper. And Payne's daughter Marlowe, the current CEO, had managed to keep a firm finger in the dam, despite her own danger earlier in the year and the arrival of her new baby.

Even with the effort, there were cracks.

And it was his job to find answers before they split wide open.

NOVA WALKED THROUGH the main downtown thoroughfare of Mustang Valley and thought longingly of the breakfast bar she'd buried in her purse. She'd been trying to ration the food she had left, and the two boxes of breakfast bars she'd stumbled upon in a buy-one-get-one deal at a convenience store just over the line into Arizona had been too good to pass up. But she was always hungry now and the baby had her burning food like crazy. She was worried whatever passed as strawberry filling wasn't the healthiest approach to eating during pregnancy, but hadn't figured out any other choice.

She took some solace that it hadn't been like this the whole time. After the whole debacle in Ferdy's office, she'd run from New York, doing little more than grabbing a suitcase full of stuff from her apartment before she took off. Her mother's occasional notes of wisdom had come surprisingly handy and Nova was suddenly grateful she'd paid attention.

Her entire life her mother had always kept cash in the house. "Enough to pay a month's worth of bills" had always been the ever-eccentric Allegra Ellis's motto. Nova had often thought it an odd juxtaposition to a woman who'd willingly spend the same amount on a wild bender of a shopping trip, but some things stuck and she'd done her best to maintain that stash since going out on her own. It was only after she'd needed to go off the grid that she'd come to recognize the wisdom in her mother's teaching.

Between the five thousand she'd squirreled away and the odd jobs she'd taken at diners across the country, she'd gotten by. The diner owners she'd worked for hadn't cared that she was pregnant, only that she *could* work, and they'd been more than willing to feed her three square meals from the kitchen.

She'd been more diligent then, eating a proper balance of protein and fruit, keeping away from anything unhealthy and taking vitamins. Her first few weeks on the road she'd fallen love with the sticky buns on the counter in one of the diners where she'd worked and had quickly realized that there was no way she could fuel her growing baby on just sugar and carbs. So since then, she'd adhered to a strong eating regimen and even found ways to conserve gas in her car while walking around whatever town she'd worked in, getting some solid exercise in the process.

Even as kind as most everyone had been at all her stops along the way, she'd refused to stay anywhere for too long. The cell phone she'd stuffed in her bag had remained resolutely off and she'd finally given in and spent the money to get a burner phone in Iowa so she'd have some link to help if she needed it. Luckily, she hadn't needed it. Nor had she seen any sign of Ferdy or his colleagues, even as she'd kept careful watch every one of the one hundred and fifty days since she'd run.

Throughout that time, she'd questioned her initial panic. Would Ferdy really hurt her? Especially once he knew about the baby? Sure, he'd seemed different after that first date, a bit more hot-tempered and emotional than she'd expected. But wasn't that life? He had a big job and that meant big problems.

She'd nearly convinced herself to turn back about two weeks in, but something had ultimately held her back. That discussion of shipments and problems at the port sticking in her mind on an endless loop.

Ferdinand Adler was a real estate developer. Not a drug dealer. And yet…that exchange she'd overheard through the door suggested he was exactly that. Could she really expose her child to that?

So she'd stayed on the run. After a circuitous path out of New York, she'd headed straight for Tennessee before heading back north to Michigan, steadily weaving south and west from there. Somewhere deep inside of her, she'd known where she'd end up. The idea had nagged at her since her mother had shared the news of her real father's identity so many months ago.

But the search for Ace Colton—and her belief in his ability to help her—had grown deeper and more intense as she checked one state after another off her list.

She needed his help and she had to believe that he'd give it. And once safe, secure in the knowledge her child would be protected, she had to find a way to get word back to the authorities in New York.

Because there was no way Ferdy Adler was a good guy.

She'd finally given in and done an internet search at one of the towns she'd passed through. She'd noticed signs for the local library and had gone in to use the public computer terminals, curious to see if she'd find anything to help her understand the real personality of the man she'd believed herself in love with.

The man who had fathered her child.

What she'd found was full of suspicion and innuendo

and a few all-out accusations, and it all reinforced the suspected drug dealer angle. Several articles had comment sections underneath and the anonymous notes were not favorable. One mentioned he was "a real leg breaker," and another had flat out accused him of putting "laced dope" on the streets.

God, how could she have been so stupid?

Like, bone-deep stupid with a side of flighty airhead on the side. She knew better than to give her heart that easily. After all, what had she really known about Ferdinand Adler? Other than the good conversation they'd had on that very first date, his behavior after had been modestly kind at best. But oh boy, had he hooked her good.

She'd had a lot of time to think over the past months and one thing had become embarrassingly clear: Ferdy had played her like a fiddle. He'd somehow keyed into her deepest needs and desires on that very first date and had pushed and played every button she had from that moment on. Which didn't excuse her role in any of it, but it had given her a sense of how she'd found herself in such a raging mess.

And how she needed to protect herself—and her child—moving forward.

Although she hated coming to town feeling like she had her cup in hand, the idea to find her father had been a persistent flame since her mother had first told her of Ace Colton and their brief teenage love affair. The research she'd done on the man had turned up more than a few surprises, especially the notion that the man was suspected of trying to murder his own father and was recently ousted as the CEO of Colton Oil. There was also a blog post she'd read that gleefully shared "all the

Mustang Valley gossip" and said that the man wasn't even actually a Colton.

Was it possible?

Could the man whose blood flowed in her veins be that cold? That devoid of feeling or decency? And not at all the man her mother had told her about?

Even as she asked herself the question, images of the attractive, warm-eyed man she'd seen in photos didn't match the bill. Neither did the few memories her mother had shared with her.

Allegra Ellis and Ace Colton might have had an unintended consequence of their teenage romance while both on family vacations at a resort up in Montana, but from all her mother said he was a good person, even then. She'd spoken of his talk of his family and the warmth with which he spoke of his siblings, Ainsley and Grayson, his adoptive brother, Rafe, and his half siblings, Marlowe, Callum and Asher.

In her own way, Allegra had made it all sound so magical, and it was only as her story went on and on that she shared what Ace had told her on their last night together. While he hoped for a bond with his family, there were cracks in their relationships. His father's multiple marriages and the sheer number of siblings weren't quite as problem-free as it seemed. Yes, he loved them, but things weren't quite as easy as he'd made it all out to be.

And then he'd told Allegra the biggest secret of all. That he had a girlfriend back home. One he was likely being groomed to marry.

Although she was well past childhood, Nova had listened to her mother's story with a mix of shock and envy and, at the evidence of Ace's youthful choices, sadness. How much time had been lost?

And what would her life have been like if he and her mother hadn't been inexperienced teenagers?

Questions that had no bearing on her current reality.

Allegra had talked of other things, as well, all more evidence that the fleeting days she'd spent with Ace had meant so much to her. Ace's future at Colton Oil and his love for the family home in Mustang Valley, Arizona: Rattlesnake Ridge Ranch. Allegra had smiled as she'd spoken of it, her desire to have had a chance to see it— the "Triple R," she'd said with a smile—had been clear.

Nova shook her head, willing those memories to offer more clues about her father than the latest shocking headline in the Mustang Valley paper. Ace Colton had to be a *good* man.

She was betting her future on it.

Which, she well knew, flew totally in the face of the harsh lessons that had come from her relationship with Ferdy.

Her gaze caught on a wooden bench on the main thoroughfare through Mustang Valley and the image of that breakfast bar shimmered in her mind's eye once more. She was hungry and it was important to keep up her strength. And despite thinking of it all through her drive out to Arizona, she was no closer to understanding how to approach her real father.

Hey Dad, I'm here. The kid you never knew you had. Pregnant and alone and on the run from a possible criminal. Aren't you happy to meet me?

Shaking off the grim thoughts, she dug out that breakfast bar and opened it up, forcing herself to take small bites instead of devouring it in four like she really wanted to. It was all she had for a while and she'd better make it last. Plus, hadn't she read somewhere that eating slowly made you feel more full?

Doubting that was at all possible, she took a small bite anyway and chewed, thinking about the tiny human she carried inside.

She was going to be someone's mother.

In her more vulnerable moments the idea was scary beyond measure. In her quieter ones, like now, she considered what it all meant. Yes, she would be totally responsible for a defenseless human, but she'd also have a beautiful child to raise and watch him or her grow up.

Pride swelled within her at the thought and she laid a protective hand over her stomach. She could do this. If the past five months had taught her anything, it was that.

She was capable and not nearly as helpless as she'd allowed herself to believe in those alone and adrift days after her mother had died. And she refused to ever be that vulnerable again. She had two capable hands and wasn't afraid of work. Somehow she'd find a way.

If she found it with the support of her birth father, then she'd be thankful and grateful. And if he didn't want her and the baby in his life, she'd still be thankful and grateful she'd found out, and move them both on.

"Nothing but upside," she whispered down at her stomach. "Because we'll have each other."

The baby gave a swift kick, as if in agreement. Which was silly—it was most likely due to the sugar content in all that strawberry filling that had hit the baby's bloodstream—but Nova could allow herself the quiet moment to believe it was agreement, anyway.

A soft breeze whipped up, swirling the ends of her hair in the warm spring sun and Nova's gaze caught on a building across the street.

Nikolas Slater, Private Investigator.

Nova considered the sign and the tagline beneath

his name—Results. Period.—and wondered if this Mr. Slater might be able to help her. She had no money and no earthly idea if this man would even listen to her, but it couldn't hurt to talk to him. Who knew, he might take some pity on her and at least answer a few questions for free.

Maybe?

Besides, if he was a resident of Mustang Valley he might at least know about the town grapevine and any news traveling on it about her father.

The idea took shape and form, the breakfast bar forgotten in her hand.

Did she dare?

It was a leap to let someone in but this PI might be the answer to her prayers. At the very least he might have some pull in getting her an introduction to her father or a few answers to all the questions that had dogged her since she'd left New York.

The baby kicked again and, once more, Nova thought her little partner in crime was agreeing with her.

What was the harm in trying?

When that tiny kick came once again, Nova made her decision. Taking the last bite of the breakfast bar, she stood and dropped the wrapper in the trash.

And headed determinedly in the direction of Nikolas Slater, Private Investigator.

NIKOLAS RUBBED HIS stomach and ignored the heavy growl, promising himself he'd get some lunch after he finished running a few more names through his database. He was on a roll, and while he'd like nothing more than a steak sandwich from his favorite sub shop, he wanted to get a handle on the Colton project.

He'd already spent an hour hunting through the endless layers of information on the internet, surprised at how many articles had been written on Ace, his family and their elite position in Mustang Valley. The oldest child of Payne Colton, CEO of Colton Oil, and his first wife, Ace had been groomed to ascend to his father's place from an early age.

Although Selina had been cagey in what she shared, it hadn't taken much to put two and two together throughout the course of their conversation. She claimed her sole concern was catching Payne's attempted killer so that Colton Oil could continue to thrive.

She'd even—tearfully—suggested Ace had snapped and gone after "poor Payne."

What would it do to a man, if he'd believed he'd lost all that? All that position and prestige? And how much worse would it be if that loss also blended with the pain of discovering you weren't who you believed you were?

Nikolas imagined it, his own privileged upbringing winging through his mind. Only unlike Ace Colton, Nikolas hadn't run around with a whole pack of siblings. His mother, Clara Rivera Slater, had loved his father to distraction, but Guy Slater's playboy ways hadn't abated with marriage. He'd be a loving husband and father for a period of time, then something—or some-*one*—shiny would catch his eye and he'd become aloof and distant again. Nikolas had spent his youth living the cycle, watching his mother's happiness when his father was around and attentive, and then sad and lonely when he was all wrapped up elsewhere.

Whether by circumstance or a sadly determined effort, his mother hadn't ever had another child and Nikolas had found himself adrift five years ago when she'd died.

He loved her and had spent his life wanting to protect her. Wanted to prove to her that there was someone in her life she could depend on.

But it was five years later and no amount of money could fix that loss, or how it had put his entire life into perspective. A good living made life comfortable, but it didn't make life happy. And since his father's ongoing attitude once his dependable, loving wife had passed was that women only wanted you for your money, Nikolas had done his level best to focus on his job and off anything that carried an air of permanence.

Was he a coward? Nikolas wondered. Or had something simply broken in him the day his mother died?

Regardless of the answer, his dedication to his firm hadn't been entirely misplaced. He'd built something strong and solid on his own, with hard work, determination and the quicksilver tongue his mother said he'd been blessed with.

What she always added was that she wasn't sure if the gift had come from the good Lord above or the very devil. To which Nikolas had shot back with a quick wink and a grin that they'd both claim him depending on the day.

The swat she'd drop on his dark curls was never quite hard enough to bite, nor slight enough not to feel, and he smiled as the warm memory washed over him. Even now, he could feel her small palm lying against the back of his head after she gave him that playful pat, full of the affection that had always flowed easily between them.

A steady presence at odds with his father's flit-in-and-flit out approach.

A light buzz interrupted his thoughts, the front door to his office emitting the standard notice of a new arrival. Was Selina back to dish more dirt or make more demands about her former stepson?

Nikolas glanced one last time at the image of Ace Colton still sitting on his computer screen. Sure, the man looked formidable, but he hardly looked like a patricidal maniac.

Nikolas loved nothing more than a juicy case, but he had to admit, even if it was just to himself, that it was quite possible he'd bitten off too much with this one. Yes, the case was exciting, but he wasn't going to make up evidence or put a good man through the wringer.

On an inward sigh, Nikolas once more forced himself to look at the situation objectively. It was the same argument he'd made to himself earlier that week when he took the case. He'd been honest with Selina from the get-go that he would do the job and he'd stand by his findings about who shot Payne—whatever they were.

She'd agreed but he hadn't missed the skepticism in her eyes, as if she figured that the verdict would be a guilty one.

Which was her problem, not his.

Stepping out into his outer office, he'd already braced for round two with Selina when he found a different woman entirely. Small and petite, she had a mane of blond hair pulled back in a messy braid that was somehow enchanting for all its disarray. Pretty green eyes peered back at him from that small face and he felt something strangely protective kick in his gut, banishing all thoughts of food.

That protection shifted slightly—along with a subtle disappointment he couldn't quite define—as his gaze moved from her face to her small frame.

And the large, round, beach ball of a stomach that unmistakably announced her pregnancy.

"Can I help you?"

"Are you Mr. Slater?"

"Mr. Slater's my dad. Please call me Nikolas."

"Right. Nikolas." She clasped and unclasped her hands beneath that round belly, before glancing around. As if realizing she hadn't stepped fully inside, she finally did so, then turned to carefully close the door.

His intrigue grew apace with his curiosity. "And you are?" he finally asked.

"Oh. Sorry." She closed the rest of the distance between them, her hand out. "I'm Nova. Nova Ellis."

Although she shook with her right hand, she'd lifted her left to rest on the top of her belly and he couldn't help noticing there wasn't a wedding ring.

Or *any* ring, for that matter.

Which might be explained by her pregnancy weight, but somehow he didn't think so. There was no white line on her ring finger.

He let her hand drop, impressed by the solid handshake from such a small woman. No shy, retiring hothouse violet here. "How can I help you, Nova?"

"I'm looking for my father."

Not her baby's father. *Her* father. "I might be able to do something about that. When did he go missing?"

"I'm not sure."

"I thought you were looking for him."

"Well, I am. But I've never met him and he's never met me. He doesn't even know about me."

Realistically, there was little he could do for her. He'd give her the number for a national adoption organization and send her on her way. Which had him oddly disappointed their conversation was going to come to such a swift end.

"I've got a few people you can reach out to. I don't typically work on adoption cases but I do have some resources that can connect children with parents if both parties are willing."

"Sorry." She shook her head, a pretty little flush creeping up her neck. "I'm messing this up terribly." Her hand shot out to rest on his arm. "My mother knew who my father was. Before she died last year, she told me about their teenage fling. She never told him about me but she did tell me about him."

Nikolas gave her his broadest, most professional smile. This one was open-and-shut, and while he was strangely reluctant to send her on her way, he also had a sense that his fees were somehow out of her range. "If you have his name, reach out directly. There's no reason to pay for an investigator's services."

"Um. Well. I think maybe there is." Her gaze alighted on the small stack of the week's papers he kept on his waiting room coffee table. The latest story about Ace Colton was on the top, the headline screaming about the apparently guilty Colton heir, who had recently gone into hiding after the gun that had shot Payne was found in his apartment.

Some odd premonition skimmed over his nerve endings before seeming to rest on the back of his head, as warm as his mother's palm used to be.

In fact, he wasn't even all that surprised when Nova bent and picked up the paper, turning it so the headline faced him.

"Ace Colton is my father."

Chapter Two

Nova's words hung in the air between her and the cute private eye, seeming to expand and fill the space. She wasn't sure why she'd made such an impact, but something in the utterance of the words "Ace Colton" had stilled Nikolas Slater.

"Excuse me?" he asked, his hazel eyes growing darker by the moment.

Although she suspected there was some sort of confidentiality clause that protected all she might say to him if she were a client, she wasn't one. Nor did she have the funds to become one, she well knew. It would be worth confirming what she should—or shouldn't—say. "I can talk to you freely and confidentially, yes?"

He seemed to consider her for a moment and she figured that even if he did find a way to use the information she shared, she'd at least rest secure in the knowledge she'd tried to protect herself.

But she needed answers. And right now that need trumped what might happen later.

"Sure, I'm willing to do that for this conversation." That darkness cleared somewhat, even if that underlying sharpness she'd sensed in him hadn't faded one bit. In fact, he practically hummed in anticipation.

"You sure about that?"

"Yes, of course I am. Whatever you tell me is confidential."

Nova debated briefly with herself before she dived in. She'd already made the decision to come here; she might as well go all in. "I'm here because my mother told me that she had a relationship with Ace when they were both teenagers and I was the result. He'd already broken up with her, telling her he had commitments back in Arizona, and she never told him about me."

"Did she have any proof?"

"A few old photos and a couple of stories that she claimed would be something only the two of them would know."

"The Colton family is powerful." Nikolas pointed to the paper she'd dropped back onto the coffee table. "Even without his current situation, Ace Colton is a force in Mustang Valley. So's his family. Are you sure you want to pursue this?"

Whatever she'd expected on the long drive across the country, she'd never considered the idea that she *shouldn't* seek out her father. Or worse, that she'd be looked at as having ulterior motives if she did.

The hand she'd laid instinctively against her belly tightened as she imagined what she must look like. Young and pregnant.

Alone.

While she didn't want to risk telling anyone, even this stranger, about her relationship with Ferdy, she did suddenly have a sense of what she must look like. Despite Nikolas's kind eyes and willingness to listen to her, a cold sense of dread washed over Nova. "In spite of what you may think of me, I'm not here for his money."

"I didn't say you were." Nikolas scrubbed a hand over the dark stubble that coated his jaw and cheeks. She had a suspicion that he carried a perpetual five o'clock shadow, even with a daily shave, and found the look appealing. Dark and dangerous and, for reasons she couldn't define, protective.

There was something about the man that made her feel safe. After five months on the run, she hadn't realized just how badly she needed a few moments to feel that way.

"What I'm trying to say is that the Colton family wields a lot of power and has a lot of press attention. Do you want to wade into that? Especially in your—" he waved a hand "—condition."

Some small voice whispered that she should have been insulted by his words. But instead, there was something in the gesture that struck her as inordinately cute and she couldn't resist a moment of fun. "I'm not pregnant."

His eyebrows shot up nearly to his hairline, an "I'm sorry" already spilling out when Nova started laughing.

"It's just too fun to mess with people. Even if you deserved it because you didn't abide by the golden rule of pregnancy conversation."

He apparently didn't see the same humor as she did and the wariness in his gaze was evident. "Which is what?"

"Unless a woman tells you she's pregnant or you see the baby actually coming out of her uterus, all comments are off the table."

"Oh. Um."

She took pity and laid a hand on his arm once more. Just like the first time she'd touched him, she didn't miss the firm strength there. "I'm teasing you again.

It's totally clear that I'm pregnant. But you do bring up a good point about the Coltons. They've got a lot of attention right now and a long-lost kid—with a baby of her own on the way—might be a little much."

Since walking into Nikolas Slater's office, Nova had gotten the distinct impression that not much ruffled the man. So it was empowering to see that she'd shaken him a bit.

It was equally impressive to see him take the conversation back firmly in hand. "Why don't you come into my office and tell me your story? The whole story. We can game-plan from there."

"But you don't want my case."

"I don't *not* want your case. But *you* may not want me for your case."

Her gaze dropped to her stomach before heading back up to meet his. "I'm not exactly in a position to be picky right now."

"You may be once I tell you my side of things." He gestured toward his office. "Come on back and take a seat."

She followed him, taking in her surroundings as she walked back. The total office space was small, but he'd made the most of it. His cherrywood desk held minimal clutter—not much beyond his computer and large monitor, a few small files and a photo of what she guessed was his mother.

Interesting, Nova considered as she continued on around the room. No photos of a girlfriend or wife and family. In fact, very little personal detail at all.

Was he a neat freak?

Unbidden, an image of Ferdy's immaculate office came back to her. The cool, sleek furniture. The pink marble in the bathroom. Even the thick-cut glass decanter and glasses he'd kept in both his outer and inner office.

On a quick glance, she realized that not only did Nikolas Slater *not* have a credenza, but there wasn't a liquor tray anywhere in sight. Instead, he had three matched apothecary's cabinets along the far wall that he obviously used to keep his files. The old-fashioned touch was at odds with the modern computer and monitor, yet somehow it fit.

"Please," he gestured toward one of the seats opposite his desk.

She sat down, her perusal of the office and the ready comparisons to Ferdy still crowding her mind. The impulse that had her laughing in the outer office had fully faded, replaced with the same serious worry that had dogged her every single mile since leaving New York.

Was she really going to tell this man her most closely guarded secrets?

"This is what I needed to show you." Before she could question his intentions, Nikolas had his computer monitor turned around to show her the display.

A website had been minimized on the large screen with a digital note-taking program open. Her father's face filled the left side of the screen, dominating the top of an article.

But it was the easy-to-read file name in Nikolas's note-taking program that stopped her in her tracks.

Ace Colton Case. Task: Determine Guilt.

NIKOLAS HALF EXPECTED the woman to go running when she saw his screen, her messy braid flopping in her wake. He'd already imagined trying to chase a pregnant woman down the stairs in his building and out into the street, and wondered how big a show they'd put on for the lunch crowd out and about in downtown Mustang Valley.

Which made her next move that much more surprising.

Just like the way she'd teased him about her pregnancy, the intriguing Nova Ellis did the unexpected once again.

She flopped back in her chair, shaking her head. "This whole experience can*not* get more surreal."

"Excuse me?"

"I mean it. From the moment my mother mentioned the name Colton to me, it's been one ride after another on the crazy train."

"What crazy train?"

"The crazy that has become my life." She glanced down at her purse, settled on the guest chair beside her, her gaze focused on something only she could see.

Nikolas watched the play of emotions across her face, fascinated by both her expressiveness as well as how hard she still was to read.

Was she scared? Angry? Curious?

He'd sensed all three in a matter of moments, yet she'd still been able to laugh and make jokes. Had still been able to assess his points on the power of the Colton family in Mustang Valley and reshape her reasons for coming in to see him.

Who was this woman and how had she landed squarely in his life?

"Why don't we both start over? I can't really talk to you with any level of depth until you're a client."

Her face fell at that. "I'm sorry but I can't afford you."

It was what he'd expected—known, really, since she'd walked in—but he pressed on anyway. "I know that. And I'm willing to take on your case pro bono. On a trial basis."

"Trial basis? How? Or more to the point, why? You don't know me."

"And you don't know me. So we'll figure it out as we go along. But I do need your agreement to keep our conversation going. And I need to charge you something to make it official. Would a dollar work?"

She glanced down at her purse, seemingly considering his offer. Was there even a dollar in there? Nikolas wondered.

It was only when she lifted her gaze, a rueful smile at her lips, that he sensed another surprise coming. "Can I ask a favor first?"

"Sure."

"Do you by any chance have any food here? A small package of peanut butter crackers or pretzels?"

His gaze narrowed at that even as he was already reaching into his desk drawer. "As a matter of fact, I have both."

He handed her both packages, curious to see one more string of expressions cross her face.

Gratitude. Hunger. And unmistakable relief.

He'd deal with sharing stories first and then he was going to do something about the hunger. He didn't want to leave a pregnant woman hanging but the protein in the peanut butter would likely hold her for the half hour it would take to get her story. Then he'd get some real food into her and the baby.

Besides, he figured he'd need to earn a bit more of her trust to convince her to let him buy her lunch. And if she was hard up enough to gaze longingly at a bag of crackers he figured that would extend to a lack of hotel arrangements, too.

"Thanks. And thank you for the offer to work my case. We have a deal," she added hastily before tearing open the crackers. She took a dainty nibble off the first one. He nearly smiled at the restraint as he reached for a pack of his own.

"Like I said, client confidentiality. I do maintain it. But I can tell you I'm working on a case involving Ace Colton."

"What are you doing, exactly? Or what can you share?"

"I've been tasked to find any information on his guilt or innocence. And if I get lucky enough to stumble upon him, I'm to get him back into town if at all possible."

"Where is he?"

"No one knows. He wasn't supposed to leave Mustang Valley, but with the rumor mill working overtime it's hard to fault the guy for hightailing it out of here."

"Is he a criminal?"

"Not yet, but suspicions are rising."

"That he shot his father?" she asked him.

"Yes."

Nova pulled another cracker out of the sleeve, her expression thoughtful. "Thanks for telling me. And consider this question rhetorical, but why shoot his father? What is there to be gained?"

Quite a lot, actually. Nikolas briefly considered saying something to that end but held back. He did need to manage his confidentiality with Selina, and despite the rumors flooding the town, the family had been keeping Ace's status quiet.

So he shifted gears to her last comment, asking a rhetorical one of his own. "Why do people do lots of things?"

"I suppose you're right about that."

Nikolas stood and walked to the small fridge he kept in the corner of his office, snagging two waters. He handed her one and she took it with a smile as she chewed the rest of her cracker, a considered look on her face.

"You shared with me," she finally said, "so it's only fair I share with you."

"Okay. Shoot."

Although he'd only noticed how attractive she was when she'd walked in, that small, sweet, pixie face sort of blinding him momentarily, he could see the food had restorative properties. Her cheeks had brightened and he could see a gleam in her deep green eyes. All of which only reinforced his determination to get a full meal into her.

"My mother died about ten months ago. She was diagnosed with a fast-growing cancer and didn't have a lot of time there at the end."

"I'm sorry."

"I am, too. She was about to be forty and I'd believed we'd have a long time together, you know?" Nova brushed at a stray tear that leaked from the corner of her eye. "She had me when she was seventeen."

"It's hard to lose a parent." His eyes drifted to the photo of his mother he kept on the corner of his desk. Her vivid smile and warm, compassionate eyes always made him feel like he was looking at love. Or what love was supposed to be.

Generous. Understanding. And the brightest of lights.

"It is. And that was on the heels of my father's passing a few years before." She rubbed a hand over her belly, a gesture he'd seen her now do so often he suspected it was subconscious. "I'd always *thought* he was my father until she told me otherwise."

"That's when you learned about Ace Colton?"

"Yes. Their teenage love affair burned hot and wild one summer. They met while both were on family vacations at a ritzy resort. They'd had an affair before he had to come back to Arizona and the life planned for him here."

"Why didn't your mother ever tell him about you?"

Nova screwed up her face. "It's not going to make any sense."

"I'm a private eye. Trust me, I get told a lot of things that don't make sense. It's why I have a job."

"My mother had her fair share of eccentricities. She was raised in a wealthy family and never really dealt with the real world, if you know what I mean."

"I do."

Nova's description made Nikolas think of his own father and Guy Slater's views on life. Although not Colton wealthy, Nikolas's father had done okay for himself. But the fact that he spent every spare dime he had on his latest obsession had definitely skewed his perception of "what women wanted." While Nikolas didn't share his father's perspective, he had seen his parents' mess of a marriage and wanted no part of that for himself.

"For some reason, she came to the conclusion in her own mind that by not telling Ace she was somehow winning a point against him. At the end of their relationship, he told her that he had a girlfriend waiting back home. He left, she reasoned, so it was his own bad luck he'd never know he was a father."

"She's sort of right."

"Maybe. Or she saved him from a lifetime of responsibility. It's hard to miss something you never knew you had in the first place."

That determined rubbing over her belly changed, her hand settling in place over the front of her stomach. Like she was protecting her unborn child and warding off danger.

Nikolas sensed the change, as well, the air around her growing still. And suddenly, he knew that there was more going on here than a hunt for Ace Colton.

Nova Ellis was running from something.

He'd bet his life on it.

Nova saw the change in him immediately. Although she'd said nothing about Ferdy, somehow, some way, Nikolas Slater knew her secret.

Or sensed it, since she hadn't actually given any specifics.

"I am sorry for your loss. But it's curious you waited so long to come find Ace. Why wait?"

"Like I said, showing up on his doorstep would make him realize what responsibility he'd escaped all those years ago."

"It would also let him know he's a father. Most men would want to know that, even if the discovery upends their life a bit."

A bit?

She wanted to laugh at that even as she considered Nikolas's words. Yes, most men *would* like to know if they were a father. It was why she'd breathed a sigh of relief that she'd managed to escape Ferdy before telling him about the baby. But what if he knew?

Somehow, she didn't think he'd rest quiet if he knew he had a child out in the world somewhere. Nor did she think he'd give up until he had control over her and the baby.

The first few days on the run, when she hadn't thought to turn her phone off, she'd gotten increasingly nasty texts from him. If he was so irate over some texts, how would he be over the baby?

Throat dry, she lifted the bottle of water to her lips.

Would she put the baby in danger if she told this PI about Ferdy?

With that foremost in her thoughts, she opted to keep her own counsel. She'd come here looking for Ace Colton. That had nothing to do with her own failed relationship and poor choice in a boyfriend. And even though she hadn't known about the trouble her biological father was in when she'd started the journey to Arizona, she'd learned pretty quickly that this was the worst time to try and enter his life.

If it was just for herself, she'd put her tail between her legs and leave. But she had a child to consider and had lost the room to be choosy.

Pushing as much brass into her tone as she could muster, she stared Nikolas Slater straight in the eye. "I had my reasons for waiting. But now I have my reasons for looking for my father."

"Fair enough." Nikolas met her gaze, unblinking and direct. It should have made her feel uncomfortable, only it didn't. Instead, she saw something warm unfurl deep in his eyes. "Why don't we go grab lunch?"

"Lunch?" Her voice came out on a small squeak at the same moment the baby let out a swift kick just beneath one of her ribs.

"Yeah, lunch." A small smile ghosted his lips as he stood. "You know. Food consumed at midday."

Was she really willing to give up the precious few

dollars she had on a restaurant lunch? And wasn't it funny that her thoughts had shifted so drastically after only a few months?

There was a time she'd gone out for lunch every day, either with friends at work or with Ferdy down near his office. Dinner had been the same, eating out several nights a week.

And now... Now she was rapidly calculating how she was going to make her last sixty-eight dollars last her until she could pick up some work. Well, sixty-seven after she paid him the dollar.

If she'd used brass before now it was time to use a bald-faced lie. "I know what lunch is but I just had crackers. I'm not hungry."

"I am. And lunch is on me, so if you're not hungry maybe you order something to take with you for dinner."

On him?

"You can't do that. I came to you for help. And you're only getting a dollar." Nova barely held back a wince at the squeaky tone in her voice.

"Consider it an investment."

"In what?"

He shrugged. "I'll come up with something later."

Fifteen minutes later, Nova was still puzzling over what excuse Nikolas Slater would possibly put in his business expenses, as they were being seated at a welcoming pub about two blocks from his office.

He might have kept the confidence of the person who'd hired him to track down Ace Colton, but Nova suspected that his client would be sorely upset to know Nikolas had even spoken to her, let alone spent time with her. Or taken on her case, even if she was a charity.

Nikolas opened the menu their waitress had left for him. "The fish and chips here are awesome. So are the burgers."

Nova's stomach gave an involuntary growl at the idea of a burger but it was the fish and chips that lodged in her mind. She hadn't touched any sort of fish since that morning so many months ago that had preceded her visit to Ferdy's office.

Was it possible she'd rediscovered the taste for it?

Her morning sickness was long gone, but she hadn't risked anything in the fish family for fear of losing it. But now, with the seed of the idea of deep-fried cod and equally deep-fried potatoes having been planted, she found she could think of little else.

When their waitress came back, Nova quickly ordered the dish before she could change her mind, and added a glass of water. The fried food might not be good for her but she could at least keep on top of her hydration. Even if it would mean about eight stops that afternoon for a ladies' room as she hunted for work and a place to stay while she looked for her father.

Nikolas ordered a burger, then waited until their waitress had left, before returning to their earlier conversation. "If you did want to try and reach out, we could connect you with one of Ace's siblings."

An emotion that felt a lot like belonging speared through her chest before she tamped down on her reaction. For the same reasons her father may not be excited to meet her, his family might not, either.

Even if they were somehow okay with having a surprise show up out of the blue.

"That's not really fair to him."

"Fair's got nothing to do with it. He's not here and

you are." He took a sip of the iced tea the waitress had set down along with Nova's water. "I'd say you deserve at least an equal chance to find out about your father as he does about you."

Nova wasn't sure how she'd found one Nikolas Slater, Private Investigator, but somehow, she had. And whatever she might have expected, the man sitting before her didn't match up with a single thing she'd imagined in that short walk from her perch on the town bench to his office.

He didn't mince words, which she appreciated.

He was far too attractive for his own good, with that olive skin and thick, dark curls.

He had an interesting sense of honor, which had come through in the way he'd sneakily got her out to lunch, as well as the way he'd protected his existing client's confidentiality.

Nikolas eyed her over the rim of his glass. "Are you sizing me up or questioning my fashion choices?"

"You're surprisingly charming."

"Surprisingly?" He set the glass down. "Most women just tell me I'm charming."

"Under your spell, no doubt," she added dryly.

"But of course."

She fought the grin at that and kept to her underlying point. "What changed your mind?"

"About what?"

"Before. In your office. You were cautioning me about trying to get into the Coltons' world."

Their waitress returned with their food and, once again, Nikolas showed his discretion by waiting until they were alone before picking up their conversation. "It's my responsibility to show you the options and the angles."

"So you think it's a good idea?" she pressed, curious to realize how badly she wanted him to say yes.

"I don't think it's any sort of idea. But I do know you came a long way and I do know you're Ace Colton's daughter."

"You believe me?"

"I do, but that's beside the point."

Nova reached for a fry. "Why's it beside the point?"

"Because you look like him. A small, petite female version, but the resemblance is clear. The same nose and chin. Same arch to your eyebrows. You're Ace's daughter, all right."

Chapter Three

You're Ace's daughter.

Those words had raced through her mind, over and over, like her new favorite song. Only Nova didn't think she'd ever tire of hearing them.

Lunch passed quickly, the fish and chips as amazing as advertised. And she hadn't had even the slightest hint of a negative reaction to the delicious food, which she took as yet another good omen on the day. The baby had also quieted down, seemingly sated by finally having a solid meal after their limited fare over the past few days.

Nova figured he or she would start back in with the afternoon gymnastics session she'd come to love and look forward to around 4 p.m. each day, but for now, she had a few hours of quiet from the sweet little baby inside.

Which would allow her to focus fully on Nikolas's idea of seeking out Ace's family.

In for a penny...

"Do you have a place to stay tonight?" Nikolas asked, breaking into her post-lunch food coma.

"Hmm?"

"Where are you staying?"

"Oh, I'm good."

Her lunch date stopped being easygoing as Nikolas halted midstride, turning toward her right there in the middle of downtown. "How long are you going to keep up this 'I'm fine' routine you've got down?"

"I *am* fine."

"No, you're not. You didn't have any food for lunch and I know what you were doing by saving half of your lunch for later."

"Just because I'm pregnant doesn't mean I have to overeat."

"Come on, Nova. Be straight with me."

Did she dare? Because there was no way to talk about her situation and lack of ready cash if she didn't talk about Ferdy. She'd deliberately not used a credit card or her ATM card since those texts that had turned threatening, for fear he'd have some sort of tracker on her.

And it had worked, hadn't it? Despite her constant vigilance, she hadn't seen him or any of his colleagues. Even if she couldn't stop looking over her shoulder or avoiding talking too long to random strangers she met.

You can't run forever.

Empirically, she knew that. She did have savings, as well as the money her mother had left her but refused to access anything for fear of discovery. She wasn't destitute and she'd already figured she'd finally have to give in and do something about money when she went to the hospital to deliver the baby.

But for now...

For now she wanted that continued protection of staying off the grid.

You're Ace's daughter.

That additional truth—especially if her father's family accepted her—could mean all the difference. Whatever Ferdy Adler was into back in New York, he'd be hard-pressed to come after her and the baby if she had the protection of one of the most powerful families in Arizona.

Add on a new name and a new life, and he might not even ever find her.

Nikolas still stared at her expectantly and she finally relented slightly. "I do have a way to take care of myself, but I don't have ready access to my finances at the moment." Determined, she continued to brazen it out. "I'm okay overall."

"But not tonight?"

She thought about all the places she'd found jobs along the drive out to Arizona and knew that she'd find something else. She might not get it in the quaint town of Mustang Valley, but she'd find something not too far away. Diners always needed waitstaff. She'd find something to keep her going for the next few weeks while she considered what to do about Ace and his family.

While she went back to regular work and steady meals to keep her and the baby nourished and fed and her mind determinedly off the mess she'd left back in New York.

"Nova, come on. Do you have a place to stay tonight?"

"I will."

"What does that mean?"

"It means I stopped off to talk to you before I continued on with my other plans today. I'm looking for work."

"Which won't pay you in time to shore up a hotel room."

She mentally crossed her fingers and hoped she'd get to work the dinner shift right away to pocket some tips. "I've got a little. I'll get by."

"Why aren't you being straight with me?"

"Why are you pushing this with me? You don't know me. You certainly don't have to worry about my problems."

Even though it was nice that he did.

Whatever else Nikolas Slater might be, she hadn't gotten even the slightest indication that he was a jerk. Or that he'd try to take advantage of her.

It didn't mean she could drop her guard.

After their first date she'd have said the same about Ferdy and look how that turned out.

"Tell you what. I'll make you a deal."

"What's that?"

"I'll go with you while you look for work. I need to do some errands around town anyway, so it's not out of my way. If you find a job, I'll back off. If you don't, you play it my way and take my guest room tonight."

"I can't—"

He held up a hand. "The room has a lock on the door if you'll be more comfortable. I know we don't know each other and I can appreciate you being cautious. But sleeping in your car or at a cheap motel isn't the right alternative. Or safer," he added after a beat.

She wanted to argue with him but Nova knew he was right. She'd done enough of the "cheap and seedy" on her drive west, and while she hadn't run up against any real problems, her pregnant state hadn't even stopped some less savory characters from making passes at her.

"It's a deal. On one condition."

"Tell me."

"You wouldn't give me your opinion before. On if I should or shouldn't reach out to Ace Colton's family."

"Why do you want my opinion?" Nikolas asked.

"Let's say it's sort of like your lunchtime expense."

"My what?"

Confusion stamped itself in his hazel eyes, and once again, Nova felt something flutter deep in her belly that had nothing to do with the baby. He really was attractive. In a roguish, sexy way that was deeply appealing. And nothing like the overly slick, three-piece-suit look she usually went for.

Add on that thick head of dark curls and long-lashed eyes that would make a supermodel envious and she figured she'd better keep her head about her and her hormones off Nikolas Slater.

And hormones or not, there was something about him she trusted. Which was the last thing she needed to be doing after the whole Ferdy mess, but still…there was something there.

The kind way he'd taken on her case and then bought her lunch. Sure, he might be looking to get as much intel as he could for the other case he had on Ace Colton, but he was still helping her.

He'd even acknowledged that she had no reason to trust him.

It was a risk but she needed the help, too.

"Before," she pressed on. "When I asked you why you were paying for lunch, you told me it was an investment and that you'd come up with a way to explain it later."

"So I did."

"Then that's my answer."

"About Ace and his family?"

"Yep. I want your opinion. Sooner or later I'll figure out why."

NIKOLAS HAD TO give her credit, the woman paid attention. She was sharp and smart and she continued to amaze him at every turn.

Even if she was too stubborn for her own good.

And too focused on maintaining her independence to consider the realities of her safety.

No matter how capable she might be, she was seriously pregnant. A reality she seemed to keep ignoring. "When is the baby due?"

"A few more months."

"Wow. That's close."

She rubbed a hand over the large mound that was impossible to ignore. "Not as close as you might think. Especially if you were the one staring down at many more weeks of an alien invasion."

"An alien what?"

She smiled in a way that lit up her whole face, and again, he caught the teasing underneath her words. "There are moments when it feels like I've got an alien growing inside instead of a baby. The way he or she moves or a random foot that suddenly sticks out the side of my belly. A few weeks ago I swear he was doing jumping jacks."

Nikolas smiled back, the idea of a baby inside of her taking on new shape in his mind's eye. Of course he understood the mechanics of pregnancy—both how it happened and what followed on after that exciting first act—but he'd never really considered the experience itself.

Never considered it as a practical reality for himself. His parents' marriage had set a course he had no desire to pursue. And yet…because of his determination not to follow in their footsteps, he'd dismissed the idea of having his own children, too.

Ignoring the sudden shot of remorse that thought ignited, he focused back on Nova. "And your little alien is practicing for entry to earth?"

"When she takes over as alien overlord of the western United States."

"I guess it's as good an explanation as any other." He shrugged. "You've already called the baby a he and a she."

"I don't know what I'm having, so I switch off."

Absurdly pleased by the idea of a small baby, Nikolas smiled to himself. And pulled up short.

Was he actually smiling about babies? And despite his lifetime refusal to enter into commitment, each time he looked at this woman he was oddly smitten.

Nova Ellis had commitment written all over her, from her green eyes to her pregnancy and impending motherhood to the messy braid that fell over her shoulder.

He found her deeply attractive and altogether sexy and...

Whoa.

Where had *that* come from?

He needed to protect her, not have the hots for her. Even if she was wildly attractive in a fresh, enticing way. Despite the seriousness of her situation, there was a lightness about her. She was still able to laugh and find humor in the world around her.

That was a gift. One he saw less often than he'd have liked.

In fact, when was the last time he'd been out with a woman and she'd poked fun at him or at herself? He mentally rolled through the last few years of his dating history and realized the number wasn't just shockingly small, it was zero.

Was that possible?

Even as he thought it, he had to admit that it was. He'd chosen the bright and the shiny over substance.

Most of his dates were incredibly attractive arm candy who accepted his company for a fancy evening out on the town. In exchange, he had a glamorous dinner companion to take to a business event.

Why hadn't he ever noticed it before?

Women only want you for your money, Nikky, my boy. That's all *they want and it gets more and more true with each year that passes. So treat 'em kind and take good care of them but don't get attached and don't expect too much.*

What had passed for his father's words of wisdom echoed in his mind, rattling around with all the finesse of a pinball striking bonus lights, and Nikolas fought to shake off the voice. He'd come to an understanding a long time ago. He might not have liked his father's behavior but his father had genuinely grieved his mother when she'd passed. It had been that moment when he'd finally come to grips with the relationship.

And all his father would never be.

Pushing it all back down in that small space he kept feelings for his father, he gestured Nova forward. "Come on. Let's go back to my office, and we can make a plan to reach out to Ace's family."

"Doesn't he actually have quite a few of them?"

"He does. His family is pretty big. But I'm suggesting a few of his female siblings. His sister, Ainsley, and his half-sister, Marlowe, are who I have in mind."

"Okay." Nova stopped and turned, her opportunity to slow their forward progression. "Even if you still haven't answered my question."

"The one about if I agree or not."

"That's the one."

"You don't miss much, do you?"

She shrugged, those delicate shoulders nearly hitting

her earlobes before dropping back down. "I guess not. The hazard of growing up an only child, spoiled by my mother. I didn't have to share much, and if I wanted to know something, I asked. And, my mother being who she was, pretty much always gave me an answer. Besides, since it was just me, there wasn't a whole lot to distract me when I really got going."

Nikolas considered that and compared it to his own upbringing. He, too, was an only child, and even with his father's intermittent distractions had been fairly doted upon his entire life. Although he doubted that was the sole reason why his mother's passing had affected him so hard, he also knew that was a big piece of it. He hadn't had any siblings to share the grief.

Or to reminisce about all the good times they'd had together.

All those memories lived in his head and that was all he had left. All he'd ever have. That and his father's pithy words of wisdom about what women wanted, of course.

Suddenly sick of his thoughts, he decided to answer Nova. Whether to humor her or because it was important to her, he wasn't sure yet, but he broke his personal rule of investigating and decided to stick his nose into it.

All the way in.

"You want my opinion? Okay. Here goes. Yeah, I think you should reach out to Ace's family. If he was here, I'd suggest you go to him first. But like I said at the restaurant, he's not, and you deserve some closure."

"Thank you. I was hoping you'd say that."

And just like that, she upended him once more. From happy and funny to questioning and serious, to poking at him with a big side of sassy, he'd seen so many facets of Nova Ellis in a few short hours. Yet, here was another one.

Vulnerability.

"I've actually met Ace's siblings. Why don't we go back to my office, and you can give them a call."

FERDINAND ADLER DIDN'T like to be kept waiting.

He didn't like waiting for a meal. He didn't like waiting for a car. And he sure as hell didn't like waiting for news of his traitorous ex-girlfriend.

Standing up from his desk and stalking over to the credenza where he kept several bottles of liquor, he poured himself a generous helping of some of Kentucky's finest bourbon. Tossing back half of it, he slammed the tumbler back onto the countertop, the hit of crystal against thick glass causing a satisfying crack.

Where the hell had she gone?

He'd asked himself that same question for the past few months. The same day the shipment went to hell. He wanted to chalk it up to a coincidence, but something about the timing bothered him.

Had she been a plant all along?

An undercover cop?

Or just another young, naive blonde, which were in abundant supply in New York?

He was depending on that shipment to make his mark and move up into the inner circle of trust with his business associates.

Associates who had not been pleased by the challenges at the port and the delays in getting the prime, grade A heroin they'd been depending on into circulation.

It had come in eventually, and they had grudgingly accepted his apologies when their stock was delivered in full, but it hadn't gotten him that seat in the inner circle he so coveted.

It had also put him several more "tests" behind as a way to prove his loyalty.

He'd done them all, of course. He'd had no choice. The three private flights with cocaine stuffed into false chambers in his carry-on suitcase. The additional money laundering he'd had to add to one of his personal operations down in the East Village. And the hit he'd executed by himself in a dimly lit area of Central Park one night.

Oh yes, he'd done them all and done them flawlessly.

None of it explained why Nova had gone missing the very day the shipment had been held up. A seemingly minor detail that had nagged at him for five freaking months.

He had put his best tech guy on the problem about three days in when it became evident he couldn't find the stupid bitch, his texts going unanswered. Wally had put trackers on all of her accounts, her cell phone, and even attempted to put one on her email.

Yet nothing had hit.

Which had left him in an uneasy conundrum. Had she simply run away? Or had his wannabe boss done something to her? Or worse yet, was she working with the cops, biding her time in some witness protection program?

Regardless of the answer, she had to be punished. And for several months he figured the tracking on her bank account would ultimately give him what he needed to hunt her down and deliver the punishment himself. Only it hadn't, because other than the regular, automatic payments she had scheduled to come out each month from her checking account for her rent and utilities, nothing else showed up.

Her body hadn't shown up, either, killed as an example to him of his mistakes. No one had told him she was dead, or showed him pictures, or produced a body.

So he was now back to door number one, with his questions. He hated loose ends and Nova Ellis was a big, honking loose end.

Why had she run?

What did she know?

And how in the ever-loving hell was he going to find her?

NOVA TRIED TO still her tapping fingers, but no matter where she put them, she couldn't get them to hold still. On her lap, on the arms of Nikolas's really uncomfortable office chair or even on her hips, when she'd stood to pace after getting sick of said uncomfortable office chair.

Was this really happening?

From the time her mother had told her about her father, Nova had imagined what it would be like. She'd spent her entire life up to that conversation believing she was the daughter of Paul Ellis. And it was only after that she was forced to reevaluate everything.

Like did Paul know she wasn't biologically his?

Would he have cared if he did?

Unfortunately, her mother had been in the last stages of her life and getting straight answers out of her had been a challenge. But best as she could tell, Paul had died believing she was biologically his.

Was that why her mother had kept it a secret for so long? To spare his feelings?

Or to hide her deception?

Allegra had told Nova that she'd rushed into a relationship with Paul—an older, handsome family friend who lived in Europe and had been groomed as a suitable love interest from an early age—as soon as the pregnancy from her summer love affair had been discovered.

Even now, Nova wondered how it had all come about. How could she have simply leaped into a marriage with one man to hide from an affair with another? Yet her mother had done it, obviously burying her feelings. By all accounts she had been relatively happy with the decision. She'd grieved terribly five years earlier, when Paul had died in a car accident. And she'd always spoken of Paul Ellis as the love of her life. And Paul had always loved Nova as his own.

Had it all been an act?

Or a way to rewrite history and the pain of a failed teen romance?

As they often did when she thought of her mother's doomed romance, thoughts of her time with Ferdy filled Nova's mind. The past five months had given her a good amount of distance—both physically and emotionally—from the man, and she'd come to understand more about what had made him so appealing.

And why she'd leaped with little understanding of who he really was.

It wasn't something she was proud of, but she wouldn't lie about it to her child. Nor would she hide her baby's paternity from the man she would eventually share her life with. She still had hope she'd find love in her life. Her child would be a part of that family they created, and Nova would tell him or her the truth of their paternity.

She'd accepted that she would never really know whether Paul Ellis was aware she was not his daughter.

She wouldn't go through life doing that to a man who came into her life. The situation with Ferdy might be scary and even embarrassing, thanks to her poor judgment, but if she was lucky enough to find love, she wouldn't hide any of it.

She continued pacing, the movement needed after the heavy lunch and equally heavy thoughts, but her gaze surreptitiously shifted to Nikolas.

Goodness, he really was attractive. Her mother had always thought swarthy men were the most gorgeous of the movie stars, and while Nova hadn't thought she was wrong, per se, she honestly hadn't ever paid much attention. But oh, wow, did she ever now. The dark curls, the olive-colored skin and the five o'clock shadow all did things somewhere low in her belly that had nothing to do with a growing baby or a large lunch of fish and chips.

No, this was a different sort of heaviness. The sort that made her remember, despite all the changes currently happening inside of her, that she was a woman.

Which pulled her up short because—*hello!*—she'd just met Nikolas Slater that morning. And she was having another man's baby. And she was on the run from that same man who was likely a gangster of the first order, even if Nikolas didn't know that part of the story.

But still, she kept sneaking glances at him. And even if she *shouldn't* feel attracted, she *did* feel attracted and there wasn't much she could say to herself to feel differently. Because whatever appealing qualities Nikolas Slater carried in the looks department, he'd proven himself an even better man.

The kindness with which he'd listened to her story about Ace. The confidentiality he'd still maintained with his existing client. Even the sweet gesture of lunch when he figured out how hungry she really was. Even the maneuver he'd just pulled on the sidewalk, negotiating her into a safe place to stay for the night.

All of it had combined to demonstrate that he was a good man.

Nikolas's voice broke into her thoughts. "You ready to make the call, Nova?"

She took a deep breath and resumed a seat in the torture chair. "Can we walk through it once more?"

"Of course."

He turned his computer monitor around so she could see it, then tapped a few notes into a search bar. In a matter of seconds, an image from a society event popped up and Nikolas clicked on it, expanding it so that it fit the screen. The man she recognized as her father smiled back from the middle of the photo, dapper in a tuxedo, with two women, one under each arm. The women's resemblance to each other was easy to see, even without the caption below the picture.

Asa "Ace" Colton poses at the annual Mustang Valley General Hospital Pediatrics Gala with his sisters Ainsley Colton (left) and Marlowe Colton (right). The Colton family are patrons of the hospital and established the gala in memory of Tessa Ainsley Colton, late first wife of Colton Oil CEO, Payne Colton.

"Those are my aunts? Or sort-of aunts?" She swallowed around the lump in her throat, the image making things real in a way it hadn't been up to now.

"I know them both. The blonde is Marlowe and the darker-haired one is Ainsley. They're both good women and devoted to the family. They'll want to meet you, Nova. I know they will."

Nova drank in the image, struggling to believe it could be so easy after all this time. Even if the women in that photo weren't related to her father by blood, they shared history and a lifetime together.

They were still her father's family, which meant they were her family, too. They'd be her *child's* family.

As the reality of that sank in, something she'd been holding onto very tightly crumbled.

The idea that she had to do this all alone.

"Let's make the call."

Chapter Four

Nikolas hunted through his files for the numbers he'd accumulated over the course of building his business. Some contacts he'd known even longer and some he'd acquired through hard work and the daily grind of owning his own firm.

When it came to Marlowe and Ainsley, one fitted the first category and the other into the second.

He'd been a freshman in high school when Marlowe was a senior and he'd known her to say hi at school. After college they'd ended up with some friends in common and he'd see her from time to time at various parties.

As for Ainsley, their relationship had been all business. Her position as one of Arizona's top attorneys and lead counsel for Colton Oil had come with her own sizable work ethic, and there had been any number of cases that he'd helped her on. A surprising number of people looked to a large entity like Colton Oil as a prime fraud target and he'd done work on everything from finding deadbeat dads to helping uncover a well-hidden money launderer working double duty out of one of Colton Oil's refineries.

They had a good working relationship and he trusted

that, just like Marlowe, she'd give Nova a shot to tell her story.

If he had to guess, both would also quickly welcome their unknown niece into the fold.

With both numbers handy, he opted to call Marlowe first. Their vague personal connection, as well as the fact that Marlowe had recently had a baby of her own, just felt like the right place to start.

What he was amazed to see was how Nova seemed to calm now that she'd made her decision.

Although he'd feigned busyness, he'd watched her as she paced his office, one side to the other. Every so often she'd rub her baby bump, whether in reassurance or protection, he hadn't quite figured out.

Maybe both.

But he'd observed it all as she'd mentally gone over the ins and outs of her decision.

He hadn't been putting her on before, either. For all his usual reticence to get involved in his clients' personal lives, there was something about her that made him want to help her out. Assuming her story was true—and based on her resemblance to Ace Colton, Nikolas couldn't see how it wasn't—Marlowe, Ainsley and the rest of the Colton siblings were going to want to know her.

To know the truth of what had come of Ace's failed relationship so many years ago.

Nikolas pointed to the image still looking out from his computer screen. "Marlowe just had a baby. She's still on maternity leave from Colton Oil, which means she'll likely be easier to reach."

"She had a baby?"

"Yep. A little boy named Reed."

"Oh." Nova's puzzlement shifted quickly, her pretty

eyes brightening. "My father was young when he met my mother. I guess it does make sense his family is having babies at the same time I am."

"Marlowe's his half sister and she's also about eight years younger."

"Which means she's just starting her family, too." Nova stared down at her stomach. "Her son will be a bit older than my child. Maybe they can grow up together."

Nikolas knew his adult extracurricular relationships had been just that. Fully adult with little beyond the extra. But something about sitting there with Nova, watching the sheer awe at what was happening to her, got to him in a place he'd believed long buried.

"The Coltons protect their family."

"Assuming Marlowe and Ainsley and the rest of the Coltons are willing to welcome me. Based on the gossip about Ace, he's not a Colton. Which means I'm not, either."

"Let's take it step-by-step first."

Nikolas dialed Marlowe's number, the call going to voice mail after four rings. He left a quick message and considered if he should reach out to Ainsley next when a text came winging back from her younger sister.

Sorry I didn't pick up. Colicky baby and sleepless mama. Talk tomorrow?

Nikolas shot back a quick note of agreement. While he was hesitant to show up at a new mother's front door with the emotional news of Nova's paternity, he was even less willing to drop any whispers of family drama via text message.

Hope the little guy's doing okay. Tomorrow works. I'll call in the morning to confirm a time.

"The baby's a little out of sorts," he said after he hit Send on the message.

Nova sat forward, her attention on the phone Nikolas had already laid back on top of his desk. "Is he okay?"

"Colic sounds like it's having its way with little Reed."

"Poor baby." Nova stood to pace once more. "Maybe we shouldn't bother her with this now."

"I think it'll be fine."

"Yeah, but she's obviously occupied. And the baby needs to get better. I can get settled in and we can try this again in a few weeks."

Nikolas stood and crossed the room, intercepting her on her next path back across the carpet. Settling his hands on her shoulders, he stared directly into her eyes, keeping his voice calm and even. "Nova. It's fine. She and the baby are having a day. She already said we'd talk tomorrow and she'll probably be calling first thing tomorrow before I even have a chance to."

"Okay. I know I'm being flighty about this. I just didn't realize until now how badly I wanted it all to work out." Her voice quieted. "Because the reality of it is suddenly so close and within reach."

Nikolas knew much of his success as a private investigator came from his ability to get people to talk to him. It was a gift he'd had since he was a small child but it wasn't something he'd really given much thought to. Beyond recognizing that he used the skill to garner a nice paycheck, he'd never considered it as a way to get others to open up.

But now, looking at Nova, he wanted to comfort her.

To say the things that would put her at ease.

"Marlowe and Ainsley have had their challenges too, you know."

"How is that possible? They come from such a prominent family. They know they're Coltons."

"That knowledge doesn't always bring security or well-being, nor does it guarantee a smooth life. Things have turned out well for Marlowe now, especially with the baby's arrival, but she went through a very difficult time earlier this year."

"What happened to her?"

Just as she had at the news baby Reed was having a tough day, compassion threaded through Nova's tone and sparked even more deeply within her green gaze.

"In addition to watching her father languish in the hospital in and out of a coma, with no understanding of who shot him, she also went through some personal trauma back in January."

"That's horrible."

Again, Nikolas didn't miss Nova's sincere concern, but he did question what other secrets she carried.

Just like how she hadn't once mentioned a boyfriend or a husband all day. No reference at all to who her baby's father might be. It was a mystery, for sure, and one Nikolas wanted to get to the bottom of.

Setting it aside, in spite of the clanging undercurrents that kept telling him she was facing some sort of personal danger, Nikolas pressed on with the details about Marlowe's close encounter with danger at the start of the year. "It was. She found out she was pregnant, and then suddenly had to deal with a stalker. I haven't talked to her about it directly, but it was common news around town, and Ainsley did share a few things with me. It was a really terrible time for her and her fiancé, Bowie."

"I'm so glad she and the baby are okay."

"We all are." Nikolas waited a moment before pressing on. "The Coltons aren't immune to challenges, Nova. I hope you understand that. I believe they will accept you. Truly, I believe that. Several of them have privately vowed that the gossip about him and the news he's not a Colton by birth hasn't changed how they feel about him. But you need to understand that being part of their world can come with some unexpected attention."

"I guess I do understand that." She glanced down toward the ground before her gaze came back up to land on him. "I am ready for it. I realize prominent families receive more than their fair share of attention. What I don't want is for them to think that their social status is why I've come to find them."

Nikolas gently took her elbow and moved her back over to the desk chairs, settling her into one seat, then taking the empty one beside her. "If I thought that, I can tell you right now I wouldn't be helping you."

"If you're handling a separate case about Ace Colton, you probably shouldn't be helping me at all."

"Don't worry about that. I can handle myself. And I'd rather be the one taking care of an investigation, because I know I'll do it the right way. I'm not on some witch hunt to find some cheap shot of evidence that could get Ace Colton convicted. I'm going to look into things the right way. And I won't allow an innocent man to pay for the crime of another."

It was only as he said those words, conviction coming from a place so deeply inside he wasn't entirely aware it was there, that Nikolas finally understood what had compelled him to take Selina's case. For the past few days, each time he considered her desperate need to find any evidence of Ace's guilt, Nikolas had warred within himself. But now he understood. Now he knew why it had to be *him*.

He would do what was right.

And he would make sure that those in Ace Colton's orbit would be required to do the same.

Nova wasn't sure how Nikolas Slater had landed into her life—or more aptly, how she'd landed in his—but she was beyond grateful she'd found him.

The prospect of depending on him too much still bothered her, but she was doing her best to ignore the small voice that kept telling her she shouldn't take too much. The help he was offering. The home he was willing to open up to her. Even his connections with the Coltons and with him going out of his way to see that she found answers.

Who did that? And what was in it for him?

Even as she asked herself the question, she knew she wasn't entirely being fair. He had a case of his own to work on, and had been more than up-front about what he was tasked to do. Which added yet another thought. Maybe the situation with her was a little like Sun Tzu's famous maxim: "Keep your friends close, and your enemies closer."

Even if that didn't really fit, either.

Only one glance into those hazel eyes and Nova was forced to reconsider. What sort of enemy made sure that she had food? More than that, who but a good person would have seen through her ruse and brazen lie that a package of crackers was more than enough to hold her over?

Goodness, it was all such a jumble in her head. After so many months of depending solely on herself, was it possible she'd lost the ability to recognize simple human kindness when it was offered?

"Those are some awfully serious thoughts I can see flitting through your mind."

Nova glanced around the room, her gaze alighting on a few of the framed articles she saw on the walls. "I didn't see reading minds listed as one of your professional capabilities."

"It's not mind reading when it's as plain as the crinkles on your forehead."

She deliberately opened her lips into a mock O.

"I thought I was too young for wrinkles."

"I believe I said *crinkles*," he said with a smile. "And while you may be young, you seem to have a lifetime of worry piled on your shoulders."

"I'm okay. Really, I am."

"We're going to make sure that you stay that way."

"I do thank you for that. More than I can say. But since part of that is making sure I'm capable of taking care of myself, I'm going to get out of your hair and go look for a job."

"I said I'd go with you."

"I know, but you look busy and, besides—" she let out a small sigh, not sure how to say what she meant without hurting his feelings "—you don't have to."

"Okay. Fair enough." A few crinkles of his own rode Nikolas's forehead as he obviously realized something. "What is it that you do?"

"I used to be a stylist when I lived in New York."

The words were out before she could stop them, the admission opening up any number of avenues for him to press and probe on her former life.

"Why give that up?"

She made a production of pointing toward her stomach. "Let's just say my priorities shifted."

While it was the truth, Nova was curious to see if he continued to press the issue. She hadn't lied. She *did* once work as a stylist. A rather good one, by the number of individuals whom she'd styled and their corresponding press coverage at events. She'd also contributed to several fashion blogs, her articles and suggested recommendations getting a large number of likes and comments.

A strange laugh strangled in her throat.

Likes and comments. Why did it all feel so frivolous now? There had been a time when that attention and confirmation of her professional reputation was all-consuming.

Only now, it all seemed so far away. Like another woman's life.

And in a big way, it was.

A life that she didn't necessarily want to go back to, either.

It was her work as a stylist that had brought her into Ferdy's orbit. She'd hovered in the background at an event for a senior Wall Street executive, keeping watch over the man to make sure he knew how to maintain the air of sophistication and panache demanded by the three-thousand-dollar suit and thousand-dollar Italian loafers she'd dressed him in. Ferdy had attended the same one. She'd been so excited when he'd noticed her, and their ten-year age difference had gone a long way toward adding to the air of worldliness and charm Ferdy seemed to wield.

It had been that same worldliness that she'd excused when he'd appeared to grow bored with a conversation or be a bit too curt with a response. This was the price you paid for dating an older man. One who had business interests and important friends.

How wrong she'd been.

It was only in all the time since that she'd realized how many signs she'd missed. Or flat out ignored. The calls he'd take in another room. The times he'd asked her to make herself scarce when he needed to talk to an associate. Even his vague comments about what he did all day.

For as awful as the past five months had been, there was another part of her that was beyond grateful she'd found out the truth when she did. At least now Ferdy didn't know about the baby. He could chalk her up to being one more young girlfriend in what had to be a long line of them, and she could go on about her business more than two thousand miles away.

Or so she kept telling herself.

Nikolas picked up on her point and if he was curious what had dominated her old life, he didn't say. "I think it's a good thing your priorities shifted. It's brought you here and put you close to your family. There's not much that's more important in life."

"No, there isn't."

She stood then and decided to make her exit when she could. Before she chickened out entirely and took what he offered, sleeping off the tension of the past few months for, oh, about a week in Nikolas's spare room.

And also before he could figure out she'd left more than a few things unsaid and call her on them.

"I'll come back here then? After I've done a bit of exploring around town looking for work."

"You do that."

She picked up her purse and had nearly reached the door when his voice stopped her.

"You're safe here, Nova. I hope you know that."

She only nodded before turning to walk out the door.

MICHELINE ANDERSON RECLINED at her desk at the AAG and considered all she'd built. The Affirmation Alliance Group was the biggest spiritual group west of the Rockies and there had been a time when she had people waiting by the truckload to visit her spiritual center of enlightenment and inner peace.

What bs.

She'd always been rather good at peddling it and had made a damn fine life off it.

Or had, until the past year.

She'd turned the center's motto—"Be Your Best You!"—into a rallying cry for all that was wrong and depraved about the world today and people ate it up. She'd even managed to snag a few B-list celebrities along the way, their ringing endorsements for the AAG skyrocketing her website traffic and the subsequent donations that poured in.

It had all been so easy.

Until it wasn't.

Oh, sure, people were still willing to listen to someone who puffed them up and made them feel good. It was the day she finally realized that little tidbit that she'd been able to unlock the real secret to her success.

She'd spent so many years as a nurse, taking care of other people and cleaning up after them, living a life of drudgery. A noble calling, her mother had told her, when she'd pushed her into the profession at eighteen, determined her daughter would follow in her footsteps.

Noble?

From her youngest days, Micheline had always believed she was destined for so much more, but it had been hard to remember that while cleaning up bedpans and mopping up a floor someone had thrown up on. It was only when she had her son that she'd seen an opportunity that she could seize, in the wee hours of the morning at the hospital.

All because she'd had the courage to switch her own baby with another one born on the same night. That choice had changed her life.

And ensured her child would be a Colton.

She'd bided her time, knowing the choice would pay off some day.

And now that day was here.

Forty years later, that secret was trying to resurface once again. The email to Colton Oil all those months ago had been her brainchild. And it was the start of something so much bigger.

First, cast doubt.

Second, use that doubt to create chaos.

Third…

Well, she was in the process of implementing the third pillar now. Because once you created chaos, there really wasn't anything to do except sit back and watch everything burn.

Chapter Five

Nova picked at the fresh fruit cup Nikolas had snuck into her take-home bag and considered her options. The clever man had both managed to bargain her into staying at his place for the night all while getting antioxidants into her by the shovelful.

And she was too tired and hungry to argue with him.

A fact she resented as she popped another blueberry into her mouth, the kind words of the last diner manager she'd met with still ringing in her ears.

I'm sorry I can't help you. The rush is over and I'm full up on waitresses. I'm happy to give you a shot if I need subs, but right now I can't offer you full-time work.

She'd kept her tone grateful and her attitude respectful, even as the urge to plop onto a stool and bawl her eyes out reared its head.

What else was she going to do? The manager at the diner had been incredibly nice, but Nova figured the woman was a by-the-book stickler. Which meant employment paperwork and a social security number.

Which meant going back on the grid.

Something she knew she had to do eventually. The money and tips she'd picked up on her drive out west had all been managed around places she wouldn't stay long and where minimal questions were asked. But

Mustang Valley didn't offer the under-the-table lifestyle she so desperately wanted to maintain.

Tell Nikolas.

That voice nagged at Nova, over and over, only growing strong after an afternoon spent wandering around Mustang Valley. Although the time hadn't paid professional dividends, she considered it a few hours well spent as she was absolutely captivated by the town, which managed to be both quaint and cutting-edge, all at the same time. The Mustang Valley Mountains that gave the town its name seemed like a protective fortress around the perimeter of the city.

She hadn't known what to expect coming here, the majority of her life having been dominated by skyscrapers and concrete, but Nova was finding it increasingly easy to appreciate the arid land that stretched out everywhere she looked.

When she wasn't looking at that distant horizon where mountains met the desert floor, she was taking in a different sight. One that offered a prominent reminder of why she'd come.

Colton Oil.

Her gaze had been drawn repeatedly to the edge of town, where the large Colton Oil headquarters loomed over the landscape. That was where Ace had worked, along with the rest of the people he'd believed were his family. It was part of his life, which meant it was part of her heritage.

And it was as foreign to her as all that dry land the building sat on.

Had she made the right decision in coming?

Even as she asked herself that, Nova knew the truth. There was nothing left for her in New York. And a nomadic life driving around the country, picking up waitressing jobs, wasn't a life for her child.

Which meant she had to figure out how to survive here.

Her talk earlier with Nikolas about her work continued to fight for space in her thoughts. Was it possible she could find styling work here, in southeastern Arizona? Would someone actually pay her for that? Yet even if they did and she attempted to build a business off a few initial jobs, the baby would be here in a couple of months. She would need to factor in taking some time off, all in the midst of trying to establish herself.

None of it was easy.

And the answers she so desperately sought seemed to hover just out of reach.

Tell Nikolas.

They'd only met that morning. Did she dare risk opening up about Ferdy? Even if she could get past her own personal embarrassment about taking up unknowingly with a criminal, exposing his crimes could put her child in a position of danger.

Do you think you can run away from me?

That had been the text that had finally done it all those months ago. The one that had convinced her she needed to stay on the run all while keeping a watchful eye. Two of them, really.

She'd spent the ensuing months staring at shadows, convinced every one held her ex-boyfriend. And so far it had worked. There was no way she could risk alerting Ferdy now.

Would Nikolas really be able to keep the knowledge of such crimes to himself? Wouldn't he be honor bound to call the cops with her suspicions about Ferdinand Adler?

From a distance, it all seemed well worth doing and she chastised herself for not being brave. For not doing what needed to be done to get a bad man off the streets and unable to hurt others.

But she also had no idea how deep Ferdy's influence ran. Did he have people inside the NYPD? Inside the city government? Would she put her new family at risk, not to mention the fear she already carried for the baby, if she pursued this?

It all roiled around, over and over, and she struggled to make any sense of it.

Midbite on another blueberry, her gaze caught on a small billboard on the opposite side of the parking lot. Although the town appeared focused on maintaining a quaint air and uncluttered landscape, there were local advertisements throughout town, the ads wrapped in tasteful wood frames.

A woman stared back from the image in a professional suit, looking worldly and successful. It seemed like the right match for the headline—"Be Your Best You!"—yet something was off.

Curious, Nova thought, leaning toward the window to get a closer look.

Her gaze drifted over the words and the flowing script at the bottom of the billboard.

Affirmation Alliance Group, Micheline Anderson, founder.

What was that all about?

Nova cursed the burner phone that made searching for anything about as easy as scratching her own back, so she opted for getting her information the old-fashioned way. She climbed out of the car and walked over to the young woman standing under the billboard handing out fliers. She wore a pressed suit like the woman in the ad, leaving a first impression of competence and success.

Until she spoke.

"Hello." The woman nodded, a beatific smile filling her face. The smile didn't stop there but continued on up, shading her eyes with a spacey sort of look that made Nova think of someone coming off a three-day bender.

Minus the bloodshot eyes.

Despite the smile that suggested inner peace and harmony, the woman looked lost.

"I'm so glad you're here today," the woman said, her smile still bright, her eyes still vague and unfocused.

"Well, thank you. I noticed you over here and thought I would come say hello. Stretch my legs for a bit."

She wasn't sure why, but something in her stylist's eye was still bothered by the incongruity of the woman in the ad above her head. She supposed the messaging of being your best self worked well with Micheline's image, but the flowy script and the syrupy message seemed so false and fake.

A point that was only reinforced by a spaced-out, sharply dressed follower.

The woman gestured widely, coming close but not actually laying hands on Nova's belly. "And I see you are beautiful with the bounty of new life."

Although touching her belly had become something of an unconscious habit, there was something about standing before the wide-armed woman that made Nova want to lay both hands over the front of her stomach for protection. Which was silly. Good heavens, it was broad daylight. Yet that urge was there all the same.

Ever since the day she'd run from Ferdy's office, she

hadn't questioned that small itch when it came at the back of her neck.

And it was itching now.

Nova might have teased Nikolas earlier about remarking on her pregnancy, but ever since she had "popped," she'd gotten used to the attention her pregnancy drew. She'd gritted her teeth at some of the people who were too forward, but never had she felt so ill at ease.

All the same, she was the one who'd walked over. So playing along, she said, "I am the luckiest of women."

"Yes, you are. Being your best self." The woman dreamily selected a flier off a stack she had nearby and handed it over. "Living our best lives is our eternal goal."

The sign above the woman talked about that best-self nonsense, too, and Nova wondered what it was all about. Some sort of motto? Or maybe an outward focus to describe what the organization did.

She glanced down at the flier, several New Age words popping out at her as she quickly scanned the page. The words "best self" was on the page at least four times. So were terms like "inner harmony," "personal affirmation" and "life-giving joy."

"Well, thank you for taking the time. I should probably be going now."

"You should come up and visit us," the woman said, gesturing broadly once again, this time vaguely in the direction behind her. "We keep our home at the edge of town, near the beauteous bounty of the mountains."

Oh, goodness, there she was, going on about bounties again. First the baby, now the mountains. Was everything bounteous and beautiful? One last glance into those vague eyes and Nova figured yes, to this woman it probably was.

Life in all its glory.

"I'll definitely think about it."

"Please do. And have a good day!"

Nova was already backing away, keeping a bright smile on her face and offering up a small wave. She hoped she'd looked friendly. It was only when she was seated back in her car that she took her first easy breath.

First the weirdness of that ad, with the woman who didn't seem to quite match. And now the goofy follower, embracing life in all its bounty.

Something was off about those people.

It was only once she drove away, Nikolas's office coming back into sight, that she finally felt the tension ease out of her shoulders.

NIKOLAS SPENT THE afternoon making phone calls, the lifeblood of a PI's day. He'd spoken to several nurses at Mustang Valley General and had questioned the phone company over a few records. He'd even managed to get a hold of Michael Seaver, Ace Colton's new defense attorney since Ainsley's fiancé, Santiago, had recused himself from the case.

He'd pick up tomorrow with a few face-to-face interviews at the hospital, but for now, he was getting ready to call it a day.

An oddly productive one, even if it hadn't gone in a direction he could have possibly imagined.

What were the odds Ace Colton's daughter would walk into his office? Even more intriguing, Ace's long-lost daughter. In what world did that even happen?

Obviously, in his.

He still hadn't figured out his reaction to Nova.

While he wasn't one to leave a person in need in the lurch, he also never considered himself particularly protective. He helped out where he was needed, but he'd never taken such a personal interest in another person.

Why now?

Was it because of the pregnancy? Nova was in a vulnerable state, and while she might try to act tough, no amount of bravado could change the fact the woman was seven months pregnant.

In some way, it was easier to excuse this concern for her by placing it squarely on the pregnancy. It felt detached in some way, like the baby was the only reason he was helping her.

Even if it really wasn't.

Why was he anxious to take care of her?

Pretty women were a dime a dozen. Yes, she was beautiful and he felt some base attraction to her, but that wasn't the reason. And yes, he admired her strength and personal fortitude that had gotten her all the way to Arizona. But that didn't explain why he felt the way he did, either.

No, there was something indefinable that he couldn't quite put his finger on.

Something that had kept him highly aware of her while he was in her presence and continuously curious about what she might be doing now that she'd gone out on her own.

Something that also made him wonder when she'd be back.

He was already anticipating seeing her again.

On a confused sigh he shut down his computer, vowing to keep up the search for clues to Ace's actions and current whereabouts tomorrow. Tucking his computer into the slim leather attaché case he carried each day, he thought about heading out to look for Nova.

It was only in that moment that he realized he didn't have a way to contact her. No cell phone number.

How had he missed that?

Because she hasn't given you one.

That thought struck loud and clear, yet another example of the interesting way she seemed to float around personal details.

Who didn't have a phone?

Only even as he considered it, Nikolas realized he had never seen her pull one out, in all the time they'd spent together that day. Not in his office. Not at lunch. Not even while he'd told her about Marlowe and Ainsley, a search program open on his screen.

Based on the timing of Ace and her mother's affair, he'd calculated Nova must be about twenty-three. No one in their age range lived without a phone in reaching distance. A sort of perpetual appendage to the world around them.

And even if you dismissed needing to be so attached for everyday life, she'd spoken of being a stylist before heading west to Arizona. Wouldn't a mobile phone be core to her success in the field?

Nikolas was nearly out the door when Nova came bustling in. Tension he hadn't been aware of faded away as he took in that petite frame and sweet baby bump. Although he'd watched her run through a variety of emotions today, there was something almost scared in the way she held herself. She wasn't shaking, but it seemed as if she could blow away in a strong wind.

"Nikolas," she exhaled heavily. "You're still here."

"Of course. I said I would wait for you."

She shook her head. "Yes. Yes, you did."

"Are you okay?"

"I was. I mean, I *thought* I was."

"Did something happen while you were looking for work?"

"No, not really. But I guess it sort of did."

Something had obviously shaken her, so he pulled her over to the large couch that sat in his outer office. "Come over here and sit down. Let me get you some water and then you can tell me."

He ran back into his office to get a bottle of water out of his fridge and couldn't easily dismiss the protective feelings that had sprung to life once again in her presence.

Had someone hurt her?

Although she looked well and whole, it had to have been something. And if not physically hurt, had someone threatened her?

The thoughts he had that morning, the ones that made him wonder if she was withholding things from him, came back once again.

Was she on the run from someone? Or maybe there was some nameless, faceless threat after her. Whatever it was, it was tangible and real and he wanted to know what she was up against.

What they were up against together.

Moving back into the outer office, he considered the petite form nearly swallowed by the large leather couch. Although he hadn't quite considered her vulnerable, in that moment he saw it all very clearly.

Yes, Nova Ellis was searching for her father's family. And yes, she was also anticipating the birth of her first child, with all the excitement and anxiety that came at that time of life in equal measure.

But he also saw something else.

He'd already instinctively suspected she was in danger, but now he'd bet his business he was right. It was just a coincidence she'd walked into his office that morning. Nothing other than some odd sort of chance that had put them in one another's paths. Serendipity, his mother would have called it, with a twinkle in her eye.

He might not understand it, but he trusted it.

And as he handed over the water, her eyes wide with all the things she still hadn't told him, Nikolas made a vow to himself.

He would protect her.

No matter what.

SHE WAS OVERREACTING.

In some rational, aware part of herself, Nova knew that.

But she'd felt decidedly irrational since meeting that woman in the parking lot. The one from the AAG. The Affirmation Alliance Group.

Which sounded more and more made up, the longer she thought about it.

Nikolas twisted off the cap and handed over a cold bottle of water. She drank it down, the liquid washing away the dust that had settled in her throat.

"Now. Tell me what has you so upset."

"It's dumb."

"I'm sure it's not."

Although she knew he was only reacting to the way she'd rushed into his office, she now felt ridiculous, having to explain what had her upset.

First she'd showed up out of the blue. Then she'd eaten his food. And now she was about to tell him how a poorly stylized billboard had freaked her out.

Only it hadn't just been the billboard or the strange

dissonance of the woman facing out from it. It was that weird, zoned-out person she'd spoken to. She was... well, she seemed like a *follower*. Like someone blindly trapped in another person's web.

"Yeah, it sort of is."

"Nova. I've been doing this for a while. And I can tell you, when someone walks into my office with wide eyes and an expression that's a cross between haunted Halloween hayride and 'I just got a note from the IRS,' I pay attention."

"I looked that bad?"

"You looked freaked." His large hand wrapped around both of hers where they still held the water. "Tell me what happened."

"What do you know about the Affirmation Alliance Group?"

"Those people out at the edge of town?" He shrugged. "You hear some things from time to time. They have a reputation for being sort of cultish, but more in the 'don't people have anything better to do with their time?' sort of way."

"I guess they're on the edge of town. I don't quite know my way around yet but yes, I think that's it."

"The AAG has a center out there. They're full of spiritual enlightenment and all that crap."

"You think it's bunk?"

"I think it's fine if you want to live your best life. Having it shouted at you from billboards and TV ads feels like overkill. It also feels like it's about a business instead of what it should be. Actually helping people."

"You have a business and you help people."

His wry smile was a little lopsided and it did something funny to her heart. One moment it was beating like normal and then in the next it seemed to flip over on itself.

"Touché."

"Which isn't to say I'm not grateful for your help." She felt a little better having made the joke, some of the equilibrium she couldn't find in the drive back into town returning. "But you were sort of an easy target with that one."

"I guess I was. But what was it about the AAG that had you upset?"

She knew it wasn't fair to tease Nikolas, but no matter how much she tried, she'd always been very good at pointing out things that were incongruous or off-kilter. Perhaps that was what made her a good stylist—she had an eye that didn't miss the things that were out of place. But that also went for comments and statements that didn't match someone's intentions.

Instead of chalking it up to someone else's idiosyncrasies, she'd often comment on the matter before she could check herself.

What surprised her was that Nikolas didn't seem to mind it. Although she was well aware her personality quirk often didn't sit well with others, he seemed to take it in stride, almost amused at the comparison instead of being upset by it.

Unbidden, a memory of one of her last dates with Ferdy came rushing back. They'd increasingly been at odds and it felt like anything she said to him was dismissed or ignored or, worse, jabbed at like some prize fighter in the middle of a ring. She'd gotten better at holding herself back to keep the peace but he'd mentioned something about one of the subway stops closest to her apartment and she'd corrected him.

"I'm off the 18th Street stop, not the 23rd."

He barely looked up from the steak he was sawing, grumbling out an answer. "I've been to your place, Nova. I know what the hell I'm talking about."

"And I live there. I think I know, too."

He did look up then, the knife still in his hand. "Getting mouthy on me?"

"What's the big deal? My apartment's on 19th. I take the 18th Street stop, not the 23rd."

"Right." He set his knife and fork down slowly, his dark eyes like black coals when they finally settled on her. "What's the big freaking deal? You have to mess with me about everything, have to comment on everything?"

"It's where I live. I know the streets near me. That's all I was trying to say."

He stared at her another full minute and all she could think as those dark eyes lasered into hers, like a snake charmer forcing back the cobra, was that their discussion wasn't really about the subway at all. Or where she lived. Or a simple slip of the tongue.

It was about control.

And dominance.

"Nova?" Nikolas's tone was warm and gentle, and at odds with the harsher one that still had the power to fill her thoughts. "We were talking about the AAG."

"Yes, of course." Whatever else those few months with Ferdy had taught her, it was to put on a smile and a happy face, blithely ignoring whatever strange conversation had come before. "I just found them really odd."

"Did you talk to someone?"

"Yeah. After my interview that didn't go at all like I'd planned, I was feeling sorry for myself. I'd driven around for a bit, exploring Mustang Valley, and then ended up parking in the lot of one of the shopping centers past the edge of downtown. You snuck blueberries into my take-home bag."

He did smile at that, the first easing she'd seen in his expression since she walked in. "I did. I believe I also snuck in strawberries and apple slices, too."

"They were delicious, by the way. You may be a sneak, but you're a gifted one."

"So noted." Nikolas nodded, before returning unerringly to their conversation. "So there you were, eating all that good food, and what happened? Did someone approach you?"

"It was that billboard. The one with the older woman. I don't know, maybe she's the founder or something."

"I know the one."

"So here she is in the picture, looking like some sort of giving, altruistic executive. Or supposed to be looking like one. But that's not what I took away from the picture."

"What did you take away?"

"That's the problem. I can't put my finger on it, but here she is supposed to be looking all 'you go be the best you' and compassionate and encouraging. I just didn't see it. Or maybe a better explanation, because it was an ad, was that I wasn't buying it."

"Ads are meant to sell. Most people take a quick, snap impression of what the advertiser wants them to see and move on."

Nova considered that for a minute, finding his description a good one. If she hadn't been sitting there with her car parked in the direct line of sight of the billboard, she likely wouldn't have noticed the incongruity of it all.

It was only as she'd sat there, staring at it, that she'd seen something out of the ordinary.

But it was after the conversation, that strange young woman staring persistently at her stomach as if Nova carried a possible new follower, that she'd felt that strange air of malevolence.

What was really going on at the edge of town at the AAG?

And why did she feel that threat even more keenly than Ferdy's possible reentry into her life?

Chapter Six

Nikolas pulled into the underground garage at his condo complex and kept his finger on the button for the swinging gate door so that Nova could pass in behind him. They'd wrapped up in his office after a long day and he'd told her to follow him before parking in the guest area once inside the gates. After he put his car in his own assigned spot, he'd promised to come back around and help her with her bags.

The conversation they'd had in his office hadn't left his thoughts the entire drive back to his place and he was already planning a call to Spencer Colton, a sergeant for the MVPD, to see how much the man knew about the AAG.

Although he'd never had a reason to look into the organization in the past, Nikolas was mildly aware of them. You couldn't live in Mustang Valley and not be.

To be honest, he had never really given them a lot of thought. But Nova's reaction had him wondering.

Although she'd attempted to brush it off and he'd finally satisfied himself that she hadn't actually been hurt or even overtly threatened, something still didn't sit well. It had been pure instinct that had her running from her meeting with the AAG employee and he didn't like it.

Even if he bought her excuse about an overreaction, there was no way she had made up the panic that had settled deep in her eyes.

Nikolas considered it all as he walked from his car toward visitor parking. Once he had her settled in and ordered dinner, he would spend a little time of his own looking up the AAG. A bit of nosing around and a few discreet searches to see if there was anything to look into a little more deeply.

In the meantime, he wanted to get Nova's mind off her day and thought a hearty meal of Italian takeout might do the trick.

She was already out of her car, the trunk open, when he reached her. "I can help you with that."

"I don't have all that much."

She wasn't kidding. Beyond a suitcase and an over-size travel bag, there was little else in her trunk.

"Is this all?"

"I travel light."

"Awfully light, considering you've been driving for quite a while."

"I don't need much. And I've been trying to save for the baby." She extended her hand and took the rolling suitcase from him. "I haven't seen any real reason to spend frivolously."

And there it was. More of that bravado that suggested she wasn't quite ready to tell him why she'd come all the way to Arizona looking for her father.

Oh, he had no doubt she genuinely wanted to meet Ace and her other family members. That mix of eagerness and trepidation when he'd called Marlowe earlier was real. But as each hour passed he knew that wasn't the whole story.

Only now wasn't the time to push it. So he simply gestured toward the elevators. "After you."

The trip up to his apartment was quick, and in moments he had his key in the lock, opening the door. "I'll get you a key, as well, so you can come and go as you please. The parking garage is a little bit trickier, but there's guest parking outside the gate and I can get you a key fob tomorrow from the building manager."

"I don't want to be trouble."

"Nova. You're not trouble. I'm happy to help you and you can stay here as long as you need."

She rolled her bag to a corner, pushing it out of the way, before she turned back to face him. "Why are you being so nice to me? Please don't get me wrong, I appreciate the help. More than I can say really. But I just don't see why you're going to all the effort."

"You came to me for help this morning. I'm going to give it to you."

"You don't know me."

"I've seen all I need to know."

Although he didn't expect her to magically open up, he was losing his patience when he came to the discussion of why he was helping her. Which was proof it had been a long day and it was time to focus on dinner. "If you follow me down the hall, I can show you where the guest room is."

The wheels of her suitcase bumped lightly over the hardwood floor as she followed him down the hall. "Your place is beautiful. How long have you lived here?"

Nikolas gestured to the open door of his spare bedroom. Flipping on the light, he walked the rest of the way into the room and settled her shoulder bag on the edge of the bed. "About three years. After my business started to take off, I decided I wanted a place in town. My dad and I got along well enough with each other at the house, but it was time to go it on my own."

"I know what you mean. I love my mother and I miss her every day, but I didn't want to live with her. As an adult."

"Exactly."

The talk of her mother seemed to put her at ease and after a few more moments looking around the room she sat down on the edge of the bed. "I didn't mean to sound ungrateful before. I am so thankful to you and I appreciate you having me here in your home."

His earlier frustration faded. She was all alone and trying to navigate a truly unique set of circumstances. It wasn't every day a person you'd just met that day was suddenly opening their home and giving you a place to stay.

"Look, Nova. I get it. I don't understand what you're going through, but I do know it can be hard to depend on someone else."

"It is." Her voice gentled. "But it's nice, too. I hope you know that."

"Know you can depend on me. This room's yours as long as you need it."

He took her in as she sat there. Just like when she'd sat on the overstuffed couch in his outer office, the queen-size bed seemed to swallow her petite frame. Even with the unmistakable signs of her pregnancy, she was still a tiny little thing. There was something about her that made him want to protect her, yet even as he thought it, he knew those feelings weren't actually due to her size.

Because there was also something about Nova Ellis—likely *Colton*—that screamed warrior. The way she was determined to do right by her child. The way she insisted on going after a job. Even in the way she stubbornly resisted taking too much of his offer to help, he saw that strength.

And in it, he understood what it was to feel beholden to somebody else.

"Why don't you rest for a few minutes? I'm going to go ahead and order us some dinner. I was thinking Italian. Does that work for you?"

"Does it work for me?" Sparks of humor lit her eyes and he saw a few more glimpses of the woman he'd welcomed that morning in his office. "Yeah, I think I'll manage."

"Lasagna? Garlic bread? Side of meatballs?"

"I hate to break it to you, Slater, but you're talking to a pregnant woman. That's pretty much the hormonal equivalent of talking dirty."

Her green eyes popped open as she realized what she'd said, and Nikolas could only laugh at the reaction. "I had no idea tomato sauce was an aphrodisiac. But I'll consider myself warned."

She smiled then, before a big rush of laughter spilled from her throat.

Nikolas smiled back, then pulled the door closed behind him. Even if it hadn't been intentional, her comment about the food had reset the playing field between them.

He could only hope that dinner might get him the rest of the answers he sought.

NOVA HADN'T INTENDED to fall asleep. But once she sat down on the edge of the bed, it seemed like she couldn't keep her eyes open. She vowed to herself she would only catch ten minutes, but as she glanced at her watch she realized it was two hours later than when Nikolas had walked out of the room.

"Oh no." She sat straight up in bed, swinging her legs around to the floor. How had she slept so long?

Or maybe a better question. How had she slept so long in a strange place?

Only it wasn't strange. She'd continued to press the point on him that she didn't want to be an intrusion, but the reality was that she felt safe with Nikolas.

You felt safe with Ferdy, too.

Although the thought was unbidden, Nova gave herself a moment to consider the internal warning. She didn't know Nikolas Slater and he didn't know her. She'd leaped into a relationship that had gone horribly bad once.

Was she doing it again?

Or could she thank five months on the run and a progressing pregnancy for adding a level of worldliness she hadn't had when Ferdy came into her life.

Either way, she was here now. All she could do was be vigilant and hope for the best.

And know that she could always go back on the run if she found the worst.

"Might as well go in and help with dinner," she muttered to herself as she straightened the covers. "Or what passes for dinner when you heat it up in the microwave."

Fortunately, she had remembered to slip off her flip-flops before stretching out on the bed, so she slipped back into them and padded out of the room and into the hall. The impressions that she had taken in earlier as Nikolas has shown her to the room now had a chance to take root and flourish. The hallway was decorated like much of the rest of the house—or at least what she'd seen of it—and there were a series of framed black-

and-white prints that ran down the length of the hallway on both sides.

Curious, she stopped to look at them. And saw a variety of pictures from what appeared to be vistas in and around Mustang Valley. In fact, as she peered closer she recognized some of the same things that she had seen today on her drive around town.

The ridge of mountains that rose up at the edge of Mustang Valley, majestically pointing toward the sky.

A close-up shot of the arid land that surrounded those mountains, a small flower peeking up through cracks in the ground.

There was even a close-up of the main street, capturing the life and movement of people as they walked up and down the sidewalks.

It was fascinating to see, all those different types of shots. Most photographers she had met tended to focus on one type of image. Still life, or scenery, or people. But these seemed to infuse all those things—each distinct, yet each part of a whole.

Had Nikolas done these?

Nova continued on the rest of the way into the condo, the hallway spilling back into a great room that was then connected to the kitchen. Nikolas sat in the chair at the table, his focus on his laptop as he typed in a few things. She didn't want to sneak up on him, but she had a chance to look at him quickly before he realized she was there.

Once again, those dark curls captivated her and she imagined running her fingers through them. Would they be soft? She'd bet anything they would be.

A different time, maybe.

Perhaps, if they were different people, things could work out a different way. But for now, she'd have to leave those curls and everything else about Nikolas Slater firmly in the realm of fantasy.

She was an unwed pregnant woman. And while she had no guilt or embarrassment about that fact, she wasn't exactly ripe for a relationship. And he was working on a case that threatened to put her biological father away for life.

They were in very different places, without much of a bridge between them.

So she would take the kindness that he offered. And she would be a model guest. And, if things continued on as they'd started, she'd make her first friend in Mustang Valley.

And that would be all.

He glanced up then, a small smile on his face. "Sleep well?"

"I did. Sorry I slept so long. I intended to grab ten minutes, and well, you can see how that went."

"You and the baby obviously needed it."

"We did."

She moved into the kitchen, where a large take-out bag sat on the counter. "I can warm this up."

"I figured you might want to sleep a little, so I waited to order. Food arrived about fifteen minutes ago. It should be just right, temperature-wise."

"Even better. I'll go ahead and get the plates."

"First cabinet, left of the refrigerator."

Nova found the plates where he promised and took a shot that the silverware would be in the drawer below. Rewarded with the correct answer, she pulled out what they needed and closed the door with a hip bump.

And realized just how long it'd been since she had been in any kitchen at all, preparing to eat dinner.

It was a stray thought. A reminder that even little things proved how much her life had changed.

Shaking it off, unwilling to dwell too long, she took the plates and the silverware over to the table. Nikolas had already cleared off his computer and made a place for them to eat.

Within a matter of minutes, they had a feast set out before them, and Nova was helping herself to a precut slice of lasagna. "This smells like heaven."

"I think you said that about fish and chips earlier today at lunch."

"I might've said that." She tried valiantly, but the smile peeked out anyway. "Okay. Yes. I did say that today."

"Nothing wrong with an appetite."

"I'd like to blame it on the baby, but honestly, I've always loved to eat. Ferdy used to say—" She broke off, shocked that her ex-boyfriend's name had come out of her mouth.

"Ferdy?"

"Yeah. Just a guy I used to know."

"Is that what we're calling him?" Nikolas's words were careful, but she didn't miss his point.

"Call him what you will. He *is* a guy I used to know."

"Right. Fine."

They each finished serving themselves, the easy atmosphere between them gone. Even though the awkwardness couldn't stem her hunger, Nova found the Italian food to be delicious, yet strangely empty of… something.

Unlike at lunch, when they had spoken throughout the meal, dinner conversation was quiet and stilted. She tried to ask him about his afternoon, and to his credit, she got decent enough answers. But something had been quelled when she shut down telling him about her ex.

Empirically, she knew she had a right to her private and personal thoughts. More, she was protecting herself. For all the tentative trust that she'd built toward Nikolas Slater, she still didn't really know the man. And he couldn't know what a problem Ferdy was.

Or potentially open things up if he decided to investigate so that her ex became a more direct threat.

"Would you like anything more?" Nikolas had moved in the kitchen to pour himself a second glass of wine and held up a pitcher of filtered water he left on the counter.

"Sure. That would be great."

He came back to the table and placed his wineglass down before pouring her water. Thinking he had finished, she lifted her hand, accidentally colliding with his. The motion was just enough to push him off kilter and water spilled everywhere as the pitcher faltered in his hand.

Nova leaped up, grabbing whatever she could off the table to mop up the water. "I'm so sorry. I'm so sorry."

When the few napkins they had had with their meal did little to pick up the water, she raced to the kitchen to get paper towels, a supportive hand under her heavy belly. The combination of rushed movements, distended belly altering her center of gravity, and the unfamiliar kitchen, all were enough to throw her off base.

She slammed into the entryway, pain ringing from her shoulder to her elbow and back again as her body connected with the doorjamb.

"Nova!" Nikolas ran to her, pulling her close. "Are you okay?"

His large hands were on her shoulder, stilling her,

and Nova fought against the simple warmth of his touch, convinced it would vanish in an instant. "I'm so sorry. I really am. I'm just so sorry."

Even as the words spilled from her lips, a weird sort of repetitive chant—*"stupid, stupid, stupid"*—kept running through her mind, an unceasing loop.

What had she done? How could she have been so dumb?

She had to apologize again. She had to make it right. She had to calm whatever anger he might have.

"Shh now. It's fine. It's just a bit of water and even if it wasn't, it's not fatal."

The litany of self-recrimination didn't stop but slowly she felt the soothing circles of his palm moving over her back. A bit later she heard the gentle words as he continued to croon to her in comfort.

She didn't withdraw from his touch, but her voice was quiet when she spoke. "I'm sorry."

"I know." He didn't stop the gentle circles but he did move her away from the kitchen toward the large couch in his living room. The overstuffed leather was a match for the one in his office and she abstractly thought the man had good taste.

And that he knew what a couch was supposed to be. Big. Fluffy. Deep. Ready to swallow her whole in warmth and comfort.

Nikolas settled her in before turning to face her, taking her hands in his. "I'm sorry I pressed you at dinner."

"You don't have to be sorry."

"No." His eyes were serious as he brushed back a small lock of hair that had fallen out of her braid and over her eyes. "I think I do."

They sat like that for a few minutes. Normally it made her uncomfortable to be stared at too long, like an object on display. But something in Nikolas's kind, searching gaze didn't bother her.

Rather, for the first time in longer than she could name, she felt as if someone saw her. Actually saw her.

Not as a colleague. Or as a toy to be manipulated. Or, even though her mother had loved her, as the residual effect of a love affair gone unfulfilled.

Nikolas looked at *her*—just her—when they were together.

"I'm sorry if I pushed you in a way you're not ready. We just met this morning and I need to keep reminding myself of that. It's just that—" He broke off, his eyes slightly unfocused before he centered back on her. "Did we really just meet this morning?"

She nodded, the fear that had suddenly swamped her in the kitchen fading to a subtle apprehension. "We did."

"It seems like longer."

"It does."

And it *did* feel like longer. Like she and Nikolas had a genuine connection. As if something inside of her recognized the same inside of him.

Only she'd felt that before. With Ferdy. From that very first date, she'd felt a connection. She'd spent the rest of their time together trying to remember if it had been real and how to get it back.

Because after that first date, they'd never quite replicated it.

"I mean it. I won't keep pressing you. But if there is anything you want to talk about, I will listen. Without judgment or recrimination."

Nova nodded. For all her misgivings, there was a quality in his earnestness that spoke to her. Even the fact that he recognized she was spooked and was willing to back off said something, didn't it?

Tell Nikolas.

Once again, that voice whispered in her head, encouraging her to trust her gut. Only this time, there was an added directive.

Trust him.

Such a simple, tantalizing thought.

One she'd sleep on and reconsider in the morning.

If she was right about him, she'd have someone to lean on. Someone who might even be able to protect her and the baby.

And if she was wrong...

She'd risk him going to the cops and bringing Ferdy down on both of them.

Chapter Seven

Nikolas stared at his computer screen, willing answers to come to life from the depths of its pixels. Although he meant what he said and wanted to give Nova space, he wasn't immune to the signs of abuse. Her response to a bit of spilled water had put him on high alert and he wanted to know what she was up against.

He'd also spent most of the evening picturing her faceless ex, pummeling the man into oblivion.

He didn't want to disrespect her privacy, but a public internet search wasn't exactly a major violation. And hey, he was a PI. Curiosity came with the territory.

Rationalize much, Slater?

He diligently ignored the thought and typed *Nova Ellis* into the search bar. He may be rationalizing but he also needed to understand what she might be running from. And how to protect her if it came to that.

Because now that he had a sense of her vulnerability, there was no way he was leaving her to deal with this jerk all on her own. He might have said it was none of his business, but there had been something in the very depths of those green eyes as he'd wrapped her in his arms in the kitchen that had called to him, way down deep inside.

He wouldn't let any harm come to her or her baby.

The relative uniqueness of her first name brought back several responses on the search and he began clicking on them. Although she hadn't shared her mother's first name, it was easy to see the resemblance between Nova and the woman named in society photos with her as Allegra Ellis.

Nikolas clicked through a lot more of the same. New York charity functions, with both women clad in gowns, their hair done high.

And now she doesn't have a cell phone or enough money to eat.

He considered that fact as he filtered through the photos, each more blue-blooded than the next.

Although he'd thought her beautiful, he hadn't quite pegged her as high society. But there was a subtle substance to her. It had been easy to miss in her eagerness to find her father, but the more he thought about it, the more he saw it. The ease with which she spoke to him was a big clue.

Twenty-three wasn't a child, but most people he knew in that age bracket were still trying to figure out who they were by day while they drank their nights away. Yet Nova had already nursed her mother through the end of an illness and had a child on the way.

Enough to make anyone grow up quickly.

And then there was what looked to be abuse.

He still hadn't figured out if her situation had progressed to physically abusive but there was certainly emotional abuse. He'd bet his PI's license on it.

Ferdy used to say...

Her words over dinner flashed through his mind once more.

Ferdy.

It was a unique name, too. Did he dare look for a

"Ferdy" online? He could quickly string a search query together, her name and the mysterious Ferdy, and see what popped.

His hands hovered over the keyboard, prepared to make one more search when Nikolas stilled.

Nova trusted him.

That trust might have a few guardrails on it, but she was here under his protection and she'd at least settled in enough to allow him to keep an eye on her.

Did he dare betray that?

He wasn't exactly a pro at trust and commitment, but he did know what it meant when someone gave you theirs. His father's cynicism—or heck, even Nikolas's own—wasn't so far gone that he couldn't appreciate what that meant.

Looking up her name online and seeing what came up wasn't the same as going hunting for a name Nova had been plainly mad at herself for using. While he could justify what he'd done so far, something about taking that next step didn't sit well.

He wanted to know more. But he also wanted all her trust, guardrail free.

If he took that next step, he'd be hard-pressed to defend himself.

Curious as to what a fresh day would bring, Nikolas closed the search engine. He jotted down a few notes on a small steno pad he kept on his home office desk. Things he needed to do or didn't want to forget.

His list for tomorrow was already in progress, begun earlier, when he'd wrapped up for the evening.

Call hospital to check status on Payne Colton.
Update call to Selina Barnes Colton.
Consider man named Ferdy.

He wrote down the last in a rush as his computer powered down.

And hoped like hell Nova would tell him what he needed to know first.

FERDY STARED DOWN at the sightless eyes of the man who'd double-crossed his boss, attempting to skim several percent off the top of a very lucrative cocaine shipment, and wondered what his life had become. When had he freaking become a damn hit man?

He was an entrepreneur, damn it. A connoisseur of fine wines and good restaurants and fancy cars.

He was not some run-of-the mill thug who killed when it suited the big boss.

Yet here he was, taking care of business and seeing that the boss's message was delivered with swift justice.

The small park in the Bronx was well lit but not even daylight normally penetrated the deep copse of trees that he'd used to cover up the hit. What he still couldn't figure out was how dumb a guy had to be to follow a near stranger into the trees to begin with.

Ferdy had made some excuse about avoiding late-night joggers and dog walkers and the stupid son of a bitch had shrugged his shoulders and followed him into the darkened area. The additional enticement—that he had some hot kilos he'd needed to unload—had sweetened the deal and in a matter of moments the dumbass was following him into the trees.

The thug had fallen into a pile of leaves and Ferdy was tempted to move a few to cover up the guy but he didn't dare touch anything. Besides, his shoes were soggy enough.

He'd never had a real taste for killing, which might have been why he was good at it. It was a means to an end, nothing more. He was a man who went after what he wanted and if something stood in his way, then he dealt with it. This guy had the bad luck of pissing off the boss and since Ferdy was still trying to worm his way back into good graces, he'd drawn the short straw. But he took no pleasure in the act.

In fact, he'd believed himself above all this, at a stage of his career where he could let others do his dirty work. But that damn shipment had fouled it all up.

Satisfied the thick layer of leaves had masked his footprints, Ferdy walked back to the concrete path that wove its way through the park. His gaze was sharp as he looked for those imaginary joggers but he didn't see anyone. Nor was there a dog walker in sight.

Just him and his thoughts.

Invariably, those thoughts traveled a path back toward Nova.

It galled the hell out of him that he couldn't find her. Her disappearance smacked of disrespect and it wasn't something he would tolerate.

He'd already begun to bore of her before she'd left on her own, those big green eyes often looking crushed after he'd correct her over something. He wanted to keep her in line but he was annoyed he never saw her damn spine. That'd have been fun to beat out of her.

Instead, she looked like a damn sad sack and he was sick of her. Besides, the boss had a pretty hot daughter and he was already thinking of ways he could court some additional favor by marrying in and then continuing to work his way up from there.

All in the family.

Only he still had to find Nova. She was a loose end and he still got an itch between his shoulder blades about why she'd run.

The only reason she'd have done it so suddenly was because she knew something. It hadn't been a coincidence that she'd run the same day the shipment got held up. No freaking way.

Which meant she knew something.

What, he had no idea. Because if she had information, she hadn't bothered to use any of it. His work had continued, unabated. Even that shipment had eventually been sorted out, all to the positive aside from the delayed delivery and the continued need to prove himself as cheap, thug labor.

So what did she know?

He exited the park and heard the distant rumble of the subway. Although he'd rather call a car or jump in a cab, he wasn't going to put himself anywhere near this destination with a credit card payment or someone else's testimony. It was the same reason he'd used cash to head uptown and he'd do the same to ride the subway back down.

Those sightless eyes that had stared up at him from the leaves filled his thoughts once more. He pulled the single ride fare from his pocket and swiped it through the turnstile, heading for the downtown trains.

As he flew down the metal stairs, the gaze in his mind's eye morphed into another one.

Nova, with those sad green eyes, filled his thoughts. Only instead of sadness, he imagined them as they would look.

When they saw nothing—not one single thing—for the rest of her life.

Nova's eyes popped open in a rush, her usual path from dead asleep to wide-awake undeterred by her new surroundings. As this was the second time she'd woken in the bed, she wasn't as surprised as the first. She took in the beige walls and modest furnishings. Tasteful, but bland, was the order of the day in Nikolas's guest room.

And yours for as long as you need it, she quickly reminded herself.

A fair reminder that paint colors and a fancy bedroom suite didn't make a home.

In fact, if she were honest with herself, she had to admit that she felt safer here than she had anywhere for almost the past year. Those nights she'd slept at her mother's apartment, in the last days of Allegra's illness, had been restless and unsettling. Yes, she'd been in her old bedroom but she'd been so scared of what was to come.

And then her time with Ferdy, so wondrous and new at the start, only to turn unpleasant in a matter of months.

She considered it now, secure in a room more than two thousand miles away from him, and wondered what she'd ever seen in Ferdinand Adler. Or how she'd been so incredibly wrong about him.

Why hadn't she left sooner? While she was incredibly excited for the new life growing inside of her, what had possibly possessed her to continue a relationship with the man?

Last night's freak-out in Nikolas's kitchen over the water was a prime example. How had she let things get that bad? So bad that even now, after months away from him, she could get so upset about some spilled water.

While he'd never actually hit her, his terse tone and genuinely dismissive attitude had grown worse in the months they were together. Would it have progressed to physical abuse?

She laid a hand protectively over her belly, concerned

at the idea that her child might have been exposed to something like that eventually.

Worse, she had to admit the truth. Just as she'd spent those quiet, lonely nights during her mother's last days, aware that Allegra wasn't going to get better, in her bones, she knew the same about Ferdy. If she'd stayed— if she hadn't found the reason to run that afternoon in his office—she'd have ended up in a far worse position than she found herself in now.

The thought gave her shivers and she huddled under the covers, her arms wrapped around the baby and her mind whirling with all that still lurked in the shadows.

What was she going to do? She couldn't stay here forever. And what if Ace, or his family, didn't want anything to do with her?

She'd spent yesterday afternoon hopeful that a visit with Marlowe and Ainsley would produce positive results, but what if it didn't? What if…

Frustrated and sick of her own thoughts, she tossed off the covers. Yes, she had a lot to think about and a lot of it was freaking scary. But huddling under the covers?

Ferdy Adler had done more of a number on her than she'd ever imagined if that was how she was going to handle the world around her moving forward. Her child deserved better and so did she.

Within a few minutes she'd brushed her teeth, combed her hair and put on something fresh from her bag. She'd noted a small laundry room off Nikolas's kitchen and she'd ask him if she could do a load of laundry later that day, as well. In the meantime, the least she could do was make him some breakfast. Her culinary skills were somewhat limited but she could manage pancakes and eggs for breakfast.

Nova padded out to the kitchen, finding the door to

Nikolas's room still closed. She took some satisfaction in that and proceeded to the kitchen to bring her plan to life. She easily found the ingredients for pancakes and even lucked out with a package of bacon in the fridge.

Twenty minutes later the distinct scent of heaven began to permeate the condo as the bacon sizzled in the oven. The siren's song had its desired effect and in another minute she heard the distinct click of Nikolas's bedroom door.

"Please tell me you're not a figment of my imagination."

Nova turned from the counter, her head bopping to an internal beat, the act of doing *something* going a long way toward crushing the apprehension she'd woken up with. "I don't know you well enough to bring you breakfast in bed, but I thought it'd be nice to wake up to a meal."

He smiled and Nova couldn't help but notice how his sleep-tousled curls matched the sloe-eyed look he gave her. Goodness, the man was lethal in the morning and that was saying something after how cute he looked last night. But there was something about that sleepy look that still rode his eyes and, oh wow, his five o'clock shadow was positively yummy.

And if this was what a solid night's sleep in a bed not rented did to her, she needed to figure out her future pretty damn quick.

"You thought right."

Nikolas moved into the kitchen. Although she had no idea how he normally walked around his house first thing in the morning, either by usual choice or in deference to her he was fully dressed. An Arizona State University T-shirt and shorts were hardly seductive clothes.

Yet something about the thickly muscled forearms

and the strong calves on display in the shorts made her mouth go dry.

"How do you feel about pancakes?"

"That they're life-giving?"

"I'm not quite sure I'd give flour and a little baking soda quite that much credit, but I do make a mean flapjack."

"You made it, being the operative words." Nikolas walked to the counter and set a cup to brew on his single-cup coffee maker, then turned toward her. "Did you sleep okay? You're up awfully early."

"I slept great. Between the nap yesterday, and a full eight hours last night, I feel better than I have in a long time. Thank you."

"I'm glad."

His eyes, an intriguing shade between hazel and green, narrowed. "It's a big day today. Are you ready?"

"I think so. I felt a little wobbly about it when I woke up, but then I gave myself a pep talk and I feel a lot better."

"A pep talk?"

The moment the words were out, she wished she could snatch them back. What a silly thing to say. Now Nikolas would think she sat around talking to herself.

Or sat around talking herself in and out of things.

Or…or who knew what he thought?

"I do that sometimes. When I'm feeling low. It's silly, I know. But, well, if there's no one else around, sometimes you just need to prop yourself up."

"Do you know how amazing you are, Nova Ellis?"

Heat rushed her face immediately, burning from the middle of her neck on up to cover her cheeks. "For being weird?"

"For tackling the big bad world, and having a child, all by yourself. You know how rare that is, right?"

"I'm not tackling anything."

Before she could say anything else, he came up to her, taking both of her hands in his. "Yes, you are. You aren't afraid of doing the hard thing. Of doing what needs to be done. Don't underestimate that. It's special and exceedingly rare."

The baby chose that moment to kick, a swift jab that hit the edge of her rib. Instinctively, Nova squeezed Nikolas's hands, a reaction against the sharp immediate pain.

"Whoa. You okay?"

Nova gritted her teeth as the second kick quickly followed the first. "Just a bit of morning calisthenics."

"The baby did that?" Those eyes she'd been admiring only a few moments before widened, their shade shifting toward a bright vivid green. "Like, right now? To you?"

"Seeing as how I'm the only one in the room who's pregnant, yeah, it was to me."

She let go of his hands to lay them against her stomach, trying to push her little alien into a more comfortable position. Or at least out of kicking range of her ribs.

"That is so wild."

"It does happen. Especially now that the hotel room keeps getting considerably less roomy."

Nikolas's gaze never left her stomach. "Does it hurt? Every time?"

"No. There are times, if the baby hits me the right way, when there's some pain. Just now, my little soccer-player-in-training caught a rib. But it doesn't hurt normally."

As if on cue, the baby kicked again, but the work she had done to move those little feet paid off.

Nova glanced up, surprised to see the slightest bit of longing where she would've expected dismissal.

"Can I touch?" Nikolas asked.

"Sure." She took one of his hands and settled it on the lower right side of her belly. The baby's latest position made that the most likely spot to feel a kick. "He or she is active this morning, so you shouldn't have to wait long."

"And it really doesn't hurt?"

"No, it doesn't. At first, it felt kind of funny. But because the kicks have grown in strength as the baby has grown, Mother Nature kind of eases you into it."

"It's just so amazin—" Nikolas broke off, his mouth dropping into an O.

The baby kicked again and Nova had the odd sensation of feeling her child kick from the inside and the press of Nikolas's hand from the outside. That large palm, so warm and firm, pressed against her belly. And for the first time since she ran out of Ferdy's office, Nova wondered what it would be like to share this pregnancy with someone.

With a man who wanted the child she carried.

One who wanted her, too.

NIKOLAS SLATHERED HIS pancakes with butter, his mind still reeling over those moments in the kitchen. He'd felt the baby kick.

And man, the kid had some strength in those little legs.

It had been…exhilarating.

And those feelings of protection he'd battled with the night before hit even harder, a reminder that Nova was especially vulnerable right now.

Vulnerable, Slater, as in not someone you make a

move on. You've got too much of your father in you to make another woman live like Mom did.

Nikolas dug into his pancakes, unwilling to think too hard about what it meant that he felt…*stirrings*… for the very attractive pregnant woman in his kitchen.

Or that he felt such a shocking wave of disappointment at his own crappy genes and inability to trust himself to commit.

"Any more pancakes?"

Nova smiled at him as she set a serving plate with more pancakes down on the table. Totally oblivious to the direction of his thoughts.

"Sure. Sounds great." He forked up a few more pancakes, adding butter and syrup to those as well, further dousing the ones still on his plate. "These are great."

"I'm glad. I really do appreciate your help and I thought maybe waking up to breakfast would be a nice way to show you."

He set his fork down at that, his focus fully on Nova. "I meant what I said last night. I really am happy to help you, and I don't see you as a burden." Before she could interject, he added, "But I'm never one to say no to pancakes and bacon. So thank you."

She brightened at that, whatever protest she'd been about to make vanishing. "Good. I'm glad."

The ping of his phone had them both turning to where he'd left it on the counter. Standing, Nikolas saw even from across the room that it was Marlowe.

"Just as she promised."

"What?" Nova asked.

Nikolas nodded toward the phone. "Your aunt. Prompt as ever."

He answered, projecting an air of calm. "Good morning. How's the baby doing?"

"Much better than yesterday. The new formula the doctor suggested was as good as advertised. Reed was able to settle and Bowie and I actually got a whole four hours of sleep."

"That's great. But, um—" Nikolas tried to reconcile her words with how happy she sounded "—only four?"

"Four is great. Four is freaking amazing," Marlowe added. "So what's up?"

Nikolas considered the idea that four hours of sleep was great and figured it might be better to introduce Nova and Marlowe to each other in person.

"I've got someone staying with me. A visitor to Mustang Valley. She's pregnant, and I thought it might be nice to introduce the two of you."

"Is she okay?"

"She's fine, but she's new to town and looking to find a doctor and a few other suggestions as she settles in. I thought you might be able to help."

"I'm happy to. Why don't you head over to the condo around noon and we'll have some lunch?" She gave him the address.

"You don't need to cook."

Marlowe laughed at that. "Nikolas, my dear, sweet man. I've got every restaurant in Mustang Valley on speed dial. It's no trouble at all."

"Nova and I will see you then."

"Nova. What a pretty name. I'm looking forward to meeting her."

Nikolas disconnected the call and turned to see Nova waiting anxiously, her hands fisted at her sides as she stood beside the table. "We're going over there?"

"Yes. For noon."

"You didn't tell her who I am."

"That's not the sort of news you tell over the phone."

Nikolas moved a few steps closer and laid a hand on her shoulder. "Not if you can help it."

"That's a lot to lay on a new mother."

"It's a lot to lay on anyone. But you've lived with it for almost a year. You've held up okay."

Nova laid a hand on top of his, squeezing his fingers. "I have no idea how I looked up and saw your sign. Or why. But I can't tell you how grateful I am that I did."

She squeezed his hand once more before turning and heading back toward the bedroom. As Nikolas watched her go, he considered her words.

It *was* interesting she had found his sign. That she had picked him.

He'd never been one to believe in fate or destiny or anything remotely smacking of the woo-woo stuff. But he did believe in the fundamental intersection of people. The events that shaped lives and the experiences no one could ever anticipate.

Unbidden, the notepad on the desk in his office filled his mind's eye.

Ferdy.

He wondered who the man was.

But at the trust he'd seen reflecting back from Nova's gaze, Nikolas was glad he hadn't done more than wonder.

Chapter Eight

Nova stared up at the luxury condo building before Nikolas made the turn for underground parking. The Mustang Valley Mountains rose up behind them, setting the property off like a gleaming jewel in the bright sun.

"Marlowe lives here?"

"Sometimes. She keeps this place but also lives at Rattlesnake Ridge Ranch with her family." Nikolas smiled ruefully, driving slowly toward the guest parking area. "Or the Triple R, as the locals love to call it, as if we're in the know."

Nova considered that news, memories of her mother's descriptions of the large ranch house weaving through her mind. "That's the big ranch my mother spoke of. They all live there?"

"They do. The town loves to talk about it like it's something out of a movie. Three stories, with individual wings for all of the children, offset by thousands of acres of cattle ranch out their back door."

"It sounds like quite a place."

"I've been there for a few functions but haven't gotten beyond the outdoor pool and entertaining areas."

"It sounds impressive."

"Impressive, and surprisingly warm. All the Colton siblings have made it their home, but Marlowe keeps the condo in town, too," Nikolas said. "I suspect, no matter how large the house, a bit of distance from family is nice sometimes, too."

"I suppose."

Although her mother had never seen the Triple R, Allegra had spoken of it as if she'd imagined it in her dreams. Or, more to the point, imagined it through the eyes of her love. Ace had obviously told her a lot about his home in Mustang Valley and her mother had remembered some of the smallest of details.

The high wood beams and lush leather furniture in the main living area. The industrial-size kitchen that could house all of them for home-cooked meals. Even the ranch itself, thousands of acres and holding so many cattle.

It wasn't until that moment that Nova realized how much she'd made Rattlesnake Ridge Ranch into something of her own personal Oz, waiting for her at the end of her journey, ready to solve all her problems.

Was it that easy?

It hadn't been for Dorothy. In fact, it had been something of a mirage, ultimately sending her away and back to the place she'd begun.

Would that be her own fate? And the fate of her child? A round trip straight back to New York?

Nova rubbed the top of her belly, surprised her own pinging nerves hadn't riled up the baby. Instead, after the morning activity in the kitchen, he or she had quieted, seeming to understand its mother's focus needed to be elsewhere for a while.

As if the baby was ever far from her thoughts.

Nikolas pulled into a guest parking area and turned off the car. He shifted in his seat, turning to face her. "Are you ready for this?"

"As ready as I'm ever going to be."

"We don't have to do this."

"I know. But I've come this far."

"Yes, you have." He reached out and took her hand. "You have come this far. But if we get inside and you change your mind, know there's still time. I'm just going to introduce you as Nova Ellis. You decide if it goes any further."

"Okay."

Nova laid her free hand over his and took heart from the gesture. From the simple connection between them. Whatever came next, she would always be grateful for this man's help. For the way he'd stepped in and given of himself when there was zero reason for him to do so.

"I'm ready. Let's go."

"Let me come around and open the door for you."

She gave him that small moment and it was only as he leaned in and pulled the passenger door open that she saw a few nerves sparking in his eyes, as well.

It only reinforced how much he was doing for her. He did, after all, have a reputation to protect. A business to manage. Yet he'd still stepped in and helped her.

It humbled her, Nova realized, to have found such support. In her mother's wildest dreams, telling Nova to go west to find her father could never have met with this outcome.

Only this *was* what she'd found. Support as high as the mountains that rose up outside the condo.

And quiet strength.

It really was all she needed. With that in mind, she stepped from the car. "Let's go."

Nikolas led the way inside. Nova took it all in, a few people out and about. Each going about their day, totally unaware that something monumental was happening in hers.

Nova marveled at it, and in a funny way, took heart from it, as well. The world would go on turning, no matter what the outcome of her visit with Marlowe Colton would be.

"They cleared us to go up." Nikolas extended a hand toward the elevators. "After you."

"This is quite fancy."

"This is the palace of condos as far as Mustang Valley goes."

"It's beautiful."

"Your father has a place here, too."

"He does?"

"Yes. He hasn't been seen here in a few weeks, though."

Although it was an odd time for Nikolas to drop that news on her, there was a part of her that was grateful for the honesty. Once again, he'd proven that he wasn't pulling any punches with her. Nor was he shading the truth.

But it did make her wonder yet again where her father was. Although everything inside of her rejected the idea that he was guilty of shooting Payne, it was hard to deny how suspicious it was to leave your home the way Ace had done.

She didn't doubt he had a reason, but it was still hard to stop asking why.

It was only as they stepped off the elevator and walked down the hall to Marlowe's apartment that Nova made a singular connection.

Her father was on the run. She was on the run. What were the odds of that?

More, she had her reasons and they were damn good ones.

Was she really going to stand here in judgment of her father, especially since she didn't know what *his* reasons were?

No. No, she wasn't.

Nikolas had barely knocked when the door swung open, a radiant blonde standing on the other side of the door, an infant asleep against her shoulder. "Nikolas. It's so good to see you."

"Marlowe." Nikolas leaned in, pressing his cheek to the non-baby side before touching a light hand to the baby's back.

The man who Nova assumed was Bowie stepped up behind his fiancé. He shook Nikolas's hand. "Good to see you again, Slater."

"Robertson." Nikolas nodded, the last-name thing seemingly terms of respect between the two men, before he turned to the baby. "And this is the little guy, Reed. He does look like he's feeling better."

"Night and day," Marlowe said, her voice low before she glanced toward the door. "Please. Come on in."

Nova stepped forward, mesmerized by the sight before her. She knew she needed to say something but at the moment she was finding it a challenge to put one foot in front of the other.

Did she blurt out the news?

Did she keep it to herself?

Did she...

"Welcome to our home," Marlowe said, before handing the baby off to her fiancé.

She stepped forward, coming closer and closer, and even then, Nova found herself unable to move. The other woman considered her. Her gaze wasn't unkind—far from it—but Nova also understood how the woman had reached the upper echelons of the Colton Oil boardroom.

Marlowe was no one's fool.

But when she extended her hands, taking both of Nova's in hers, there was also an unexpected warmth. Nova's flat-footed anxiety finally receded and she regained the ability to squeeze the fingers that wrapped around hers.

Marlowe stepped back but kept their hands linked, then turned to her fiancé, who had come to stand beside her with their son. "I was curious for the secrecy but now I know."

"Know what?" Nova asked, around a throat dry and tight with nerves.

"That my brother has a secret he's never told any of us."

NIKOLAS LET OUT a breath he hadn't realized he'd been holding. He should have known Marlowe would figure it out. He'd worry what that said about his poker face—or poker voice—later.

But, of course, Marlowe would figure it out.

"Come on in, and have a seat." Marlowe sniffed and wiped at her nose. "It's a big day for all of us."

Emotions were running high but Nikolas didn't get a sense that Marlowe was upset. She'd also had a lot of years of practice as an executive at Colton Oil, and was well able to hide her emotions when needed.

It was that reality that had Nikolas leaning in as they wended their way to the living room.

"You mad at me?" He kept the question casual as they all took seats around a coffee table. Bowie still held the sleeping Reed, but when she took the seat next to him, Marlowe leaned into her fiancé's shoulder, her hand resting on the baby's small back.

"Not at all. But I am curious. About Nova and, to be honest, about how you got involved. You know the rest of the family will be, too."

Nikolas glanced at Nova. The stiffness that had characterized her posture on the way over had relaxed at Marlowe's welcome, only to be replaced with a shyness he'd yet to see from her.

God, how overwhelming would something like this be for a person?

Oddly, while he loved digging into secrets and finding answers for his clients, he realized that he'd spent precious little time thinking about what came after. He found the reasons people behaved as they did, but he'd never considered what happened when those reasons came home to roost.

"How do you know I'm related to Ace?" Nova asked.

"The eyes and the nose. You're definitely his daughter."

Nova smiled, the faint tilt of her lips obvious, even through the nerves. "It's that obvious?"

"Very. The question is, how?" Although he'd remained quiet, Bowie chose that moment to speak up. He wasn't rude, but it was clear from his clipped tone that he carried more wariness and reservations than Marlowe. "You're an adult."

"I'm twenty-three."

"Ace is only forty. That means—" Marlowe broke off, her dropped jaw snapping shut. "Wow."

"He and my mother had a relationship when they were teenagers. Both were on vacation at a resort and, according to my mother's version, fell madly in love."

"Why doesn't he know about you?"

Nova was careful, but to her credit, she gave the same tale to Marlowe and Bowie as she had the day before in his office. The young lovers, meeting while on a carefree summer holiday. Ace's commitments back in Arizona after the vacation was over. And the strange unwillingness Allegra had displayed to tell him about his daughter.

"I didn't know myself until several months ago. My mother—" Nova stopped, the first shot of emotion clearly catching up with her as her eyes filled with tears. "She was diagnosed with aggressive cancer. She shared a lot with me in those last weeks."

Nikolas reached out and took her hand, holding tight as Nova recounted her last days with her mother.

"I am so sorry to hear that." Marlowe cried in unison with her niece as she reached over and took Nova's hand. "And even more sorry you had to go through that alone. That you had such momentous news dropped on you without any warning."

"My mother wasn't subtle on the best of days." Nova sniffed before she laughed softly. "And I know there's a part of her that would have reveled in the drama of all this."

"We have no lack of that around here," Bowie muttered.

Nikolas didn't think the man had fully thawed, but it was also clear he respected Marlowe's judgment, the CEO's acceptance of Nova going a long way.

"Nikolas has shared as much." Nova met his gaze before taking a deep breath. "I understand that Ace has been missing for the past few weeks."

Marlowe and Bowie exchanged a glance of their own before Marlowe took a deep breath. "Nova. What do you know?"

"I know your father is in the hospital, still in a coma. And I can't tell you how sorry I am for that news."

"It was really tough for a while. The doctors weren't sure if he would survive. Stubborn man that he is, he's done that but can't seem to get to that next major milestone of coming out of the coma."

Baby Reed fussed slightly and Bowie stood. He pressed a quick kiss to Marlowe's forehead before heading off to walk the baby to sleep.

"If you need to go with him—" Nova gestured toward Bowie's retreating back "—we can talk later."

"No. He's good. And I like for Bowie and Reed to have their time, too. Reed's bonding with his father just like he is with me." A sweet look came over her face, one Nikolas had never seen before on the very successful, very driven CEO of Colton Oil.

Satisfied Bowie and Reed would be good on their own, Marlowe returned her attention to the conversation. "The doctors are still hopeful my father's going to make a full recovery. What no one can figure out is where my brother plays into all this."

"Do you think he had anything to do with Payne's shooting?" Nova asked.

Nikolas waited for Marlowe's answer to the question, well aware he was currently looking for information that suggested otherwise.

That Ace Colton had, in fact, shot his father.

He'd believed himself well able to handle the case for Selina Barnes Colton *and* help Nova, but was he deluding himself? He believed that he could maintain his objectivity, yet sitting there, staring at the two women who were related to his case, Nikolas was forced to wonder.

Of course, he was worried he'd lost his objectivity on behalf of Selina's case, but what if he was wrong about

Nova? He didn't know her, either, and now here he was, barely twenty-four hours after meeting her, convinced she was Ace's daughter.

Marlowe seemed sure of it, too, even as he began to question himself.

Nova hadn't told him about her background and why she was on the run. There didn't appear to be any evidence of the man who'd fathered her child anywhere in her life.

What if this was a setup?

The part of him that respected his fundamental ability to read people and suss out fakes and phoneys believed himself infallible. But what if he was wrong?

The continued gossip around Ace Colton's parentage had already brought out the phonies. The family had already dealt with a guy named Jace Smith a few months ago. He'd played it cool and fooled the family for a while into thinking he was the switched baby.

Was it possible Nova was more of the same?

The pregnancy was a nice touch, but Ace's history was a poorly kept secret, no matter how hard the family and the execs at Colton Oil were trying to keep it on lockdown.

Suddenly out of answers, Nikolas stood and made a few quick excuses to take a call outside.

Had he made a mistake? He'd taken Selina's case, willing to look for any and all information that pointed to Ace Colton's whereabouts. Then within days, a woman claiming to be Ace's daughter had showed up.

He'd been so convinced Nova was the vulnerable one that he had never considered he might be the one being played.

As he stepped outside the condo, Nikolas took a few deep breaths.

And couldn't help but wonder if he'd been tricked by a pair of vulnerable green eyes and a sweet smile.

"I KNOW NIKOLAS isn't back from his call yet but we don't need to intrude on your day."

"You're not intruding," Marlowe said.

Nova still couldn't believe how well things were going. Or *had* gone, right up until Nikolas got a really weird, serious look on his face and excused himself. He'd looked upset, yet no matter how she thought back through the conversation, she couldn't figure out why.

They'd been talking about her mother, Nova explaining to Marlowe how she'd learned the news of her paternity. And then they'd shifted to discuss Payne's coma and Ace's disappearance. Marlowe hadn't been cool, but that initial wariness had softened a bit as they'd talked.

And then somewhere between Allegra's secretive behavior and the latest on Payne's slow recovery process, Nikolas had checked out. She'd actually seen it happen. One moment he was there, present in the conversation and clearly supporting her. He'd encouraged her to speak and had even patted her arm when she'd talked of Allegra's passing.

And then he'd just…vanished.

Was something wrong that he suddenly had to leave and make a phone call? Especially since she wanted to know more about her father.

"Nikolas seems to have taken to you." Marlowe's voice was gentle. "He's a good guy. I've known him for a long time and the company uses his services, as well. He's honest and fair, which can be hard to come by. Especially in the secrets business."

"Secrets?"

"In my experience, it's rare anyone hires a PI for readily available information."

"I suppose not." Unwilling to come off in any way ungrateful for Nikolas's help, Nova quickly added, "He's been incredibly kind to me. My circumstances are a bit—" she hesitated before pressing on "—strained right now. Nikolas understood that without me needing to say anything." She paused.

"My face may look like your brother's, and my mother may have had an eccentric story, but I think we'd all be better off if we got a DNA test, just to know for sure. Do you have anything with my dad's DNA on it, maybe at his condo?"

"Are you sure you want to do that?" Marlowe asked.

"It's important." Nova nodded. "For you and your siblings. For me, too."

Her insistence on the DNA test seemed to shift Marlowe's last bit of reticence. "My siblings are going to want to meet you, too."

"I'd like that."

Whatever she'd imagined in her mind, this quick push toward another meeting was almost too easy. Nova was hardly in a position to argue, but she had to question how she could stumble upon a man eager to help her, and a day later was sitting in the living room with her sort-of-aunt, who was ready and willing to do the same.

While she took pride in being a New Yorker—and knew that city dwellers often got a bad rap as being too tough—this was a bit different. She'd come bearing the news of a long-ago pregnancy and her long-lost family members were open to hearing her out?

Wasn't it all just too good to be true? And hadn't she learned that lesson with Ferdy?

Conscious of the lull in the conversation, Nova tried to suppress the increasing anxiety and focus on returning the kindness Marlowe had shown.

"How are you finding motherhood?"

"It's wonderful. Tiring and the most difficult job I've ever had, but wonderful." Marlowe gestured toward Nova's belly. "When are you due?"

"Two months."

"If the test comes back positive, Ace is going to be in for two happy surprises. A child *and* a grandchild."

Happy surprises.

Goodness, she'd come bearing quite a lot.

Shifting to a more comfortable position, Nova leaned forward as far as she was able. "Marlowe. I am grateful for how kind you've been. More than I can tell you. But you don't know me. My father doesn't know me. Is he really going to do leaps of joy when he finds out I exist? That I've existed for twenty-three years?"

She stopped, searching for the words that wouldn't make her sound ungrateful for the overt and ready kindness. "I'm just really aware of the fact that I'm dropping a sizable bomb into the middle of Ace Colton's life."

Marlowe cocked her head. Her expression wasn't unkind, but Nova saw the hard resolve that likely made the woman a formidable opponent in the boardroom. "I can't speak for other families, only my own. We take care of each other, Nova. We always have. It's how my siblings and I were raised. Family matters, biological or not."

"Yes, but—"

"But nothing." Even with the quick cutoff, Marlowe's eyes remained kind and warm.

Direct. Simple. Easy.

Marlowe continued on. "What I care about more is

that, if you are Ace's daughter, you know you're not alone any longer."

"I—" Nova stopped and took a deep breath.

This woman was offering everything she'd hoped for, during every single mile of the drive west. Family. Belonging. Security.

Could she really bring all the stuff with Ferdy to their door?

Marlowe had an infant. The family patriarch was in a coma, still struggling from the attempt on his life. Her father was fighting for his own reputation and freedom.

"I thank you for that. And you've given me a lot to think about."

"I hope so. What are you doing for a place to live?"

The sound of the door opening and closing echoed behind them, Nikolas's call evidently at an end.

"I'm good. I'm going to find a little place of my own." She might not be able to afford Mustang Valley but she'd seen enough places on the drive in to town that she knew she'd find something. A job, too.

"You sure about that?" Nikolas's voice lashed her like a whip. "Or do you already have one, as well as an accomplice? Just waiting for you to come home with the goods?"

Chapter Nine

Home with the goods.

What was *that* supposed to mean?

Nova heard the words and tried to piece them together with the dark expression that had settled over Nikolas's face. He'd seemed off when he'd left to take his call, but whatever had ensued in the meantime had seemingly left him upset and out of sorts.

"Excuse me?"

"You heard me."

"I heard you but I don't understand you. What goods are you talking about? And no, I don't have a place yet but as I told you yesterday, I'm going to find one."

"Nikolas? What's this about?" Marlowe asked.

"It just strikes me all of a sudden that Nova's story is rather convenient."

"What are you talking about?" Nova's mind spun with questions. She and Nikolas had spent the past twenty-four hours together and not once had he given any indication that he didn't believe her. And now she was with her family and suddenly he had doubts?

Wasn't he the one who had suggested they come here? In fact, hadn't she specifically asked him for his opinion? She'd wanted that—no, had *needed* that—before making the final decision to have him reach out to Marlowe.

With a solid streak of self-righteous indignation, Nova dug in. "I don't know what your problem is, or why you've suddenly decided you have a problem with me. But I don't appreciate your attitude."

"Well, maybe I don't appreciate not knowing how you got here or where the father of your baby is."

Nova sat back on the couch, his words more shocking than if he had reached out and slapped her. She'd had enough of that with Ferdy's impulsive emotional jabs and she wasn't interested in going back down that road. Ever.

"What does that possibly have to do with finding my brother?" Marlowe inserted herself into the discussion once more. Nova was grateful, because at that moment she couldn't have said anything if she'd tried.

Had she misread Nikolas completely?

Yes, she knew he was curious about the father of her baby. That much had been clear last night, but they had come to a sort of truce over it. He'd seemed willing to leave those questions unanswered, giving her the room she needed to decide what to do about Ferdy.

How jarring to realize there was no truce at all.

A fact made even clearer by Nikolas's plea to Marlowe. "How can you ask that? What if it has everything to do with finding your brother? What if she's working with someone? Jace Smith already made a run for your family. What if she's just a new tactic?"

"I thought she was working with you," Marlowe insisted.

Bowie chose that minute to come back into the room, concern lining his face. "What's going on out here? I just got the baby back to sleep."

"Nikolas has a few questions." Marlowe waved a hand in his direction, before moving to stand closer to her fiancé.

"Well, get them out," Bowie said, his arm coming around Marlowe's shoulders in support.

Solidarity Nova was suddenly envious of as she realized that, once again, she had precious little of that in her life. And certainly not from a life partner.

While she shouldn't have leaped to the conclusion that she had that camaraderie with Nikolas, she had come to believe that he was in her corner. Yet here they were, suddenly on opposite sides.

A small muscle ticked in Nikolas's jaw and for the first time since he'd come back into the condo, Nova saw something other than anger.

Doubt?

Confusion?

Or the sudden realization that he'd been a raging ass?

Nova finally spoke. "I think it's time to leave. I'll go ahead and show myself out."

"Please don't go. I'm glad you're here, and I'd like you to stay," Marlowe said.

Once again, the simple offer stunned her. How was it so easy for Marlowe—someone she'd met an hour ago—to take her at face value? Nova didn't want to be ungrateful, but the roller-coaster emotions of the day had shaken her.

But it was Nikolas's sudden change of heart that had done the rest.

All she could think of at the moment was running. Finding some quiet time by herself, even if she had to do it in her car, and just getting away.

"I drove you over here. I'll drive you back to town," Nikolas said.

"I think I'll be fine," Nova said. "Town isn't that big and it won't take me that long to get to my car. It's parked just across from your office, where we left it this morning. All I need are five minutes to get my stuff out of your place."

"This is ridiculous," Bowie finally spoke up. "Nova, we will take care of getting you back to your car."

NIKOLAS FELT ALL eyes on him and recognized his mistake. Honestly, he'd realized his error the moment he'd stomped out of the house under the guise of making a phone call. Yet something had kept him going. Some small flickering flame, growing bigger by the moment as his thoughts gave it air and room to breathe.

"I can take Nova back to her car. She and I can discuss a few things while we're at it."

"I don't think that's a very good idea," Bowie said.

Nikolas hadn't come here to pick a fight, nor had he come with the expectation he would bungle things so badly. "Nova's things are still at my house. I do think that she and I should talk alone, and then I'm happy to bring her back here."

Bowie and Marlowe both looked at Nova, as if waiting for her assent. It took a moment and Nikolas bore up under Nova's scrutiny as she considered his offer. Although he had seen a myriad of emotions from her over the past twenty-four hours, he hadn't yet seen betrayal.

That was exactly what he saw now.

And he had no one but himself to blame.

"I'd like to go get my things. And I'm fine if Nikolas drives me back to his house."

"Why don't you plan to come back here later?" Marlowe said. "We'd love to have you stay with us until we get everything sorted out."

"Thank you, but it really is important to me to find a job. I did some looking yesterday and I'd like to do a bit more this afternoon."

"Look for the job and then come back. Please," Marlowe added.

"Okay." Nova's eyes widened. "We also need to set up a DNA test like we discussed."

DNA test?

Nikolas kept his focus on her. "What test is this?"

"The DNA test I told Marlowe I wanted to take. The one that will prove if I'm Ace Colton's daughter or not. The one that will make sure we're all making the right decisions here."

Everyone except him.

Shame filled him.

Nikolas made it a point to be thoughtful and measured and even-tempered in his work. So how was it that in a wild blaze of confusion, he could so easily throw all that away when it came to Nova Ellis?

"We still have Ace's DNA. From the test that was done between him and my father," Marlowe said. "It would be easy enough to take Nova over to the lab and test against the same sample."

"You have a DNA sample?" Nova asked, her attention shifting back to Marlowe. "Why? I know there's been gossip about Ace but did you really believe it?"

"She doesn't know?"

Nikolas knew Marlowe's question was directed at him. And suddenly, he had to admit that Nova Ellis hadn't been the only one keeping secrets.

"I'm handling a case for Selina. I didn't think it was appropriate to say anything about the paternity test."

Marlowe's gaze was direct and pointed, her attention fully on him, even as she kept her seat like a sentinel beside Nova. "What does Selina have to do with any of this?"

"She hired me to find your brother."

"Under whose auspices? And for what reasons?"

Marlowe's edges may have softened with her engagement and the birth of her son, but the woman was still a highly competent business professional. And it was that boardroom badass who faced him down now.

"She claimed it was for the good of Colton Oil." Nikolas knew he had to navigate this carefully. "She said that as PR director of the company, she needed to understand what you were dealing with."

"And you believe her?"

"I'm not saying Ace is guilty and I told her as much. I'm not looking for guilt. I'm looking for the truth."

"And it didn't strike you as odd that my father's ex-wife is the one looking for the dirt?"

"I took the case and I'm willing to see it through. Ace's guilt or lack of it is irrelevant."

Nikolas might have a lot to apologize for, but he wasn't going to apologize for doing his work. He'd had one of Mustang Valley's best-respected professionals in his office, asking him to work a case. Whether he thought the subject was innocent or guilty had no bearing.

He would do his job.

"Nikolas? What is this about?"

Nova had been quiet up until now, leaving the inquiring to Marlowe. But she obviously had more than a few questions of her own.

"I know you said you had taken the case. You were very up-front about that. But what does that have to do with my father's DNA? And why were Payne and Ace given a DNA test? I thought all this business was nothing but malicious gossip."

At Marlowe's nod, Nikolas laid it out. "It's not gossip. Or maybe a better way to say it is that it is fact that has been gleefully repeated."

"But how could it be true? I don't know much beyond what I've read online, but as I understand it, Ace was Payne's first child with his late wife. A loving marriage, by all accounts."

"It was. My father loved Tessa. But there was—" Marlowe broke off, her dark brown stare direct and challenging.

Nikolas knew the subject was concerning, but he didn't know what had Marlowe's eyes narrowing like that.

It was only as those brown orbs widened once more that something seemed to dawn on her. "You don't know about the email?"

"What email?" Nikolas and Nova asked the question in unison.

Marlowe glanced between both of them before her earlier anger seemed to fade. "Why don't I start from the beginning?"

MORE THAN ONCE over the past few months, Nova had felt a bit like Alice down the rabbit hole. Traveling through strange lands on the run from Ferdy and knowing that her body was changing daily with her pregnancy had added a degree of the surreal to her life that had never been there before.

But now? In this exact moment? She had to be some weird combination of Alice down a rabbit hole, through a looking glass and then traveling into orbit. She'd found an outcome so unexpected that there could be no other explanation.

She listened quietly as Marlowe outlined the email that had come in to all of the Colton Oil executives back in January. A tell-all email from a masked sender that spoke of Ace Colton's birth. An email that had come to them all before Payne's shooting.

And the fact that, at only a few hours old, Ace had supposedly been switched with another baby in Mustang Valley General's maternity ward.

"Did you believe it?" Nova asked the question first, but she could see Nikolas was curious to do the same.

Marlowe shook her head. "No one wanted to believe it. It just seemed so odd and far-fetched and out of the blue. If my brother had been switched, why did it take so long for it to come out?"

Her question hung there, absolutely valid, yet still unanswered. It was Nikolas who finally spoke up. "But *was* he switched?"

Marlowe looked to Bowie for support, before nodding in the affirmative. "Yes. That was what the DNA test was for. It's a requirement that the CEO position at Colton Oil is held by a Colton by blood and Ace was CEO. We needed to know Ace's paternity or risk violation of the company's governance documents."

Marlowe finally stood and moved to Bowie's side. "Ace isn't a biological Colton. He's not Payne's son. Based on what they can do with DNA, they've ruled him out as a biological sibling of Ainsley or Grayson, too."

"Which means he's not Tessa's son, either."

"No." Marlowe shook her head. "That horrid email was correct."

Whatever Nova had expected to hear coming here, the idea that her father wasn't who he thought he was, or who *she* thought he was, was the last straw. She glanced around, suddenly desperate to get *out*.

Out of the condo.

Out of the company of these amazingly kind people.

And possibly out of Mustang Valley altogether.

She'd come here trying to find her family, only it turned out they weren't *really* her family. The fragile hope that had been building since the moment they walked in vanished.

And in its place was an emptiness that was somehow colder and even more bereft than what she had carried before.

She wasn't Nova Ellis. Paul Ellis had never been her biological father.

But apparently she wasn't Nova Colton, either.

Who was she? What name would she give her child? Where would they go?

Nova struggled out of the deep cushions of the couch. Nikolas leaped forward immediately, his hand outstretched to help her to her feet. Nova took the help—there was nothing she could do but take it—and then dropped his hand as soon as she was steady.

"Marlowe. Bowie. You both have been too kind. I'm going to go now. I think that would be best."

"You will come back, won't you? There's more to the story and I think you should know what's going on." Marlowe stepped away from Bowie's side and moved in closer, pulling Nova into a hug. Although Nova knew she was putting up an emotional wall, she couldn't deny the woman's hug and gentle words meant something.

And the idea that there was *more*? Nova was having trouble processing this news, let alone anything else that would shake the tenuous ground beneath her feet even harder. "I will. But I need a little bit of time to think."

"I can understand that. What we just told you is a lot to take in, on top of all that you've already had to come to grips with. But there is something I want you to know."

"What's that?"

"Ace is my brother. I feel that way, and so do all my brothers and sisters. That email, or a DNA test, can't change that. More, it *won't* change that."

Nova didn't know what to say. The fierceness and the absolute loyalty to the man they had always called brother was humbling to witness.

"What it also will not change," Marlowe continued, "is that you are a part of our family, too. Ace is my brother. You are, too, if you are his daughter. The child you carry would then be Ace's grandchild. We would all be a family."

A large lump settled in the middle of her throat. Nova wanted so desperately to take what was being offered. To bask in the glow of family and know innately that she belonged.

Oh, how she wanted that.

Only something held her back.

The DNA test that would prove Ace was her father, but would also prove she wasn't a biological Colton.

Ace—a man she'd believed was a good, upstanding person—was on the run, suspected of trying to murder the man he'd spent his life calling Dad.

And all of it was happening under the horrible cloud of fear she'd carried all the way from New York.

Why had she ever come here?

"I do hope you know how much I mean that," Marlowe said before giving her one last hug. "Family is something you make, not just something you're born to."

Nova nodded, still numb. "We should go now."

Nikolas led the way to the door. In moments they were back in his car, navigating through Mustang Valley. The town looked the same as it did before. Empirically, Nova knew that. Only this time, when she looked at the mountains that rose up in the distance, and the sun that warmed the earth, she saw a desolation she hadn't noticed before. A heavy shadow from the mountain. And a sort of scorched earth from the sun, which had turned the land brown and cracked.

She'd come here and she was too close to giving birth to leave.

But it had become impossible to think that this place would ever become home.

Nikolas didn't say anything as they drove; he just kept his eyes on the road and seemed to accept the now-awkward silence between them. She caught him glancing over at her from time to time in her peripheral vision, but she didn't have the energy to turn and meet his gaze. Nor did she really want to.

The man owed her nothing. If anything, she owed him. For his hospitality with his home, the generosity of sharing his food, and his willingness for a short time to help her. She wouldn't think of the fact that it had felt like the two of them were forming a connection. Nor would she give any breathing room to the hurt and anger that still lingered from the way he had turned on her.

Nikolas pulled up beside her car, which she had parked in one of Mustang Valley's public lots. She still needed to pick up the few things that she had left in his guest room that morning, but she wanted to use the remaining afternoon hours to look for a job. Determined to tell him as much, Nova turned in her seat.

And came face-to-face with a look of misery so pro-found it shook her to her core.

"Nikolas? Are you okay?"

"No, I'm not. I'm sorry is what I am. Deeply, deeply sorry."

It was what she had wanted. An apology. One she knew she deserved. Yet somehow, sitting there staring at him, she felt her anger evaporate. "Thank you for that."

"It's only what you deserve. I shouldn't have doubted you."

"I wouldn't put it that way." She tilted her head, con-sidering the overwhelming barrage of thoughts that re-fused to let up. One after another, they rolled through with all the force and power of a high-speed train. "You didn't have to give me the benefit of the doubt. I would've appreciated it if you'd saved your doubts spe-cifically until you asked all your questions."

"That's just splitting hairs."

"No, it isn't. You don't know me. I don't know you. I came to town with nothing but a story. On some level, if you didn't have a few doubts it would make me won-der about you."

"Do you have doubts about me? About who your father is?"

"Yes."

Her response hit its mark, but it also generated the first smile she had seen on his face since the moment he had stood and left Marlowe's condo for his supposed call. "Direct as always."

"There really isn't any other way to be."

"What doubts do you have about me?" he finally asked.

Nova considered his question, and with it how much

she should tell him. Clearly, Ferdy was a question mark between them.

"I'm worried that, no matter how hard you try to keep things separate, my situation will spill over onto your case as you try to find Ace."

"But I told you I can keep them separate."

"Which would be fine, if they *were* separate."

When he didn't say anything, Nova continued. "I'm worried that you jumped in to help me, even though you don't know anything about me. And that I'll get hurt because of it. And what if Ace isn't even my dad?"

He didn't respond, but neither did he avert his gaze. He maintained the direct stare, those hazel-green eyes steady and focused.

Meeting his eyes and taking it all in—from his behavior yesterday, his warm, generous and selfless actions, to his doubts today—Nova knew she had to make a choice.

She could either trust him and trust that things would work out or she could continue to leave him in the dark and allow all the reasons that she was on the run to fester in his mind.

"What I'm worried about is that if I tell you the truth about the baby's father, it's going to put us all in danger. You. Me. And most of all, my child. Can you understand that? Do you understand now why I am afraid?"

"Nova. You have to know I wouldn't do anything to put you or the baby in danger."

"You say that now. You believe it. Just like last night, you believed that you wanted to help me. Only today, your mind suddenly told you otherwise."

He shook his head. "No, it's not the same. I know it's not the same. You have to believe me."

She wanted to. She wanted so badly to believe him. Just like she wanted to believe Marlowe and the idea that she could have a family here in Mustang Valley. Just like she wanted to believe Ace Colton would welcome her with open arms when they finally met.

Only, the Coltons weren't her family.

And Ace might be a stone cold attempted murderer.

She *wanted* to believe that Nikolas could make things right.

But how did you make things right against the threat you never even saw coming?

That was really at the heart of it all.

It was those things you never saw coming that did the most damage. Her mother's illness. The truth about her father. Ferdy's betrayal.

She'd gotten quite good over the past year at dealing with the things that she hadn't seen coming. Maybe it was time to trust herself and make the leap.

"Nikolas. I do believe you."

"Then tell me. Tell me what has you so scared."

Just like the day before, when she'd sat outside Nikolas's office on the sidewalk bench, the baby kicked. Hard enough to make a point and timed well enough to push her into gear.

She'd leap.

And if it was the wrong choice, then she'd figure it out and run once more. She'd gotten pretty damn good at it, after all. She could take care of herself and the baby.

"For the past five months I've been running from the father of my baby. He doesn't know I'm pregnant. As far as I know, he doesn't know where I've gone. It has to stay that way, on both counts."

"Why are you running?"

"Because the man I trusted, the man I created a new life with, he's not a good guy. In fact, I think he may be a very bad man."

Chapter Ten

Nikolas had dreamed up more than a few scenarios in his head about Nova's situation. Between his job and his generally curious nature, he'd done quite a bit of thinking on who this Ferdy guy might be that Nova had mentioned at dinner.

Never, in any of his imaginings, had he suspected the guy was a criminal. And a big one, by the sounds of it.

But as Nova spoke, telling him of her relationship with this Ferdy, the way they'd met and fallen for each other, Nikolas evaluated each piece. The way the man's behavior had changed after that great first date to becoming verbally abusive. The subtle and not-so-subtle signs she could recall now, after the fact. And then the big reveal, the day she'd gone to tell him she was pregnant and he'd been upset and angry about a drug shipment he was trying to shepherd into the Port of New York.

"Have you told anyone else about this? About your suspicions?"

"No. No one. I can't."

"Why not?"

"Because Ferdy can't know about the baby. He may not care about the baby specifically, but there's no way he'd want me and his kid out there on our own, out from under his thumb. Especially now that I ran. He'll figure out that I know about him."

"You can go to the police."

"No!" Nova's hand gripped his forearm across the cupholders between their seats. "No. That's exactly what I didn't want to have happen. He's hidden his deeds this long. Hell, I didn't even know about them. I can't go to the police. What if he has some cops in his pocket and that's how he's getting away with things?"

"Okay, okay. No police."

Nikolas knew she was afraid, and he knew he needed to manage this carefully. But that depth of fear was something even he hadn't anticipated. She'd obviously had a lot of alone time these past five months. To fear that going to the cops would make things worse didn't speak well of her ex—and he already thought pretty poorly of Ferdy.

"You promise?" Her eyes were still wild, the hurried tones of her voice a match to the terror he could see in their depths.

"Yes. I promise."

"I thought—" She broke off, a look of misery paring deep lines into her forehead. Even as youthful as she was, Nikolas could see the way the emotional pain mapped itself on her. The hunch of her shoulders, the stiffness in her back as if she might be ready to break. "I thought if I came here and changed my name and became a Colton, I could make it all go away. It seems silly now to think that. But they're a powerful family and I guess... I guess I thought I could hide inside of all that."

"You're not entirely wrong. But you've been determined to go off the grid, and in order to change your name and start a new life, you're going to have to go back on it."

"I know. I've known that, regardless of meeting the Coltons. I'm going to have my baby in a hospital. I won't risk him or her to any other environment." She blew out a breath, the few wisps of hair around her cheeks blowing in that soft breeze. "I have money. That's the weird part. I have money that my mother left me, and I also have some that I've saved from my own job. I'm not destitute. But—"

"But to touch any of it would mean an electronic record."

"Yes, it does."

Grit. Determination. Uncommon strength.

Nova had all of those things and so much more. Once again, Nikolas thought of his own behavior earlier when they were at Marlowe's. "I am truly sorry. About before. You didn't deserve my judgment."

"I think we can put that behind us."

"Can we?"

"Yes, we can. I can."

"If you can be so open-minded as to put that behind you, can I ask you to be open-minded about something else?"

She shifted again in her seat, seemingly to find a more comfortable position, and Nikolas realized how unfair it was to keep a seven-months-pregnant woman stuck in the front seat of a car any longer than necessary.

"But before I ask you anything, can we please go to your office and finish this conversation there?"

The worry lines that had so recently tugged at her mouth had vanished as her lips quirked upward. "Do you think we can maybe order some lunch while we're at it?"

"I'll give you a better option. Let's go get lunch first."

He wasn't sure how she did it, but just as he'd observed yesterday, Nova had an amazing ability to move seamlessly between things that were very difficult and things that were surprisingly easy. It was enticing, he acknowledged to himself.

And wildly attractive.

Most women of his acquaintance were all too happy to hold a grudge, or even in best-case scenarios, simply pout. She did neither of those things. And he got the feeling that when she said she wanted to put the unpleasantness of the afternoon behind them, she meant it.

He got out of the car and came around to the passenger side to help her out. He reached for her hand, clasping his fingers around her much smaller one, as a zing of electricity shot up his arm and on into his chest.

Yep, there was no doubt about it. For all his protective feelings and all of his ready desire to help her, Nikolas also couldn't deny the fact that he saw her as a woman.

And as he helped her out of the car, he remembered something else.

She was alone and vulnerable. Which meant he was just going to have to keep those feelings to himself.

NOVA FOUGHT THE urge to rub her palm as they walked back toward Nikolas's office. She found him attractive and had from the very first moment. But something had shifted between them in the car.

Something that had nothing to do with her case or her problems and everything to do with being a woman.

As she imagined herself leaning forward, pressing her lips to the lush fullness of his, her fingers flexed over that hard, beard-shadowed jaw, Nova slammed smack into reality.

Was she that desperate for any sense of connection after her experience with Ferdy?

Even as she thought it, Nova recognized just how unfair she was being to herself. Yes, she had made a horrible decision when it came to Ferdinand Adler but it didn't mean she'd lost her ability to make good decisions.

What about the last five months? She'd done okay and she'd be damned if she was going to let herself forget that.

But Nikolas…

Would it be so bad to imagine something developing between the two of them? Oh, sure, now wasn't the ideal time. And what man really wanted to take on a woman and another man's baby? Not one she'd ever met, no matter how sweet and caring.

But maybe, somewhere down the road. After she was settled and had gotten into the rhythm of motherhood.

Maybe…

"You want that burger we talked about yesterday?"

She might be fighting an attraction to Nikolas, but she had no such compunction about beef. "Um, yeah."

"Then let's go. We'll grab some lunch and we can talk about what we're going to do."

What we're going to do.

Nova had already been hurt once and it would do her good to keep her heart in check and not allow those words to sing in her mind, propping her up and making her feel as if someway, somehow things would work out.

She was still jobless, homeless and, based on the news that morning, Colton-less. No matter how well-intentioned Marlowe was, nothing could change the fact that Nova wasn't a blood relation to these people she'd come so far to find.

But neither was she alone. And it was helpful to remember that, too.

An hour later, Nova had to admit what a good plan lunch was. Still full from her double cheeseburger and feeling slightly self-righteous that she'd ordered salad instead of French fries, she laid her napkin on the table. "You haven't said much, but I can see the wheels turning in your head."

"I'm thinking about a few things."

"Such as?"

"It started out that I was thinking about what an ass I was earlier, but then I realized that jackass move might pay a dividend or two."

Intrigued, Nova leaned forward. "Tell me more."

"I told you that I was looking for Ace."

"A fact you've been honest with me about from the beginning."

"Right. But what I realize now is that Selina hasn't been. She didn't give me all the facts."

Curious about this woman who sounded so opposite from Payne's first wife, Tessa, Nova gave Nikolas the space to continue processing, saying nothing.

"Selina never mentioned that email Marlowe told us about."

"Does it matter? It's obviously the catalyst that made them all realize that Ace isn't Payne's son."

"But who sent it? And why now, after all this time?"

"Maybe somebody who came into the information?"

"Maybe. Or maybe it's somebody who's been waiting and is finally ready to make a move."

Nova was happy to be a sounding board for his ideas, but none of it answered the bigger question to her mind. "If somebody wanted to say that Ace wasn't really a Colton, then they have to know who really is."

"Who really is what?"

"The switched baby."

Nova saw the moment the light went off. "Of course. That's it. I've been sitting here thinking it was Selina trying to make a play for the senior office. But maybe it's the heir, wanting to come back and take his rightful place."

"You thought Selina might be guilty somewhere in this?"

"I had to consider it just now. You saw Marlowe's reaction when I told her Selina wanted me to look into the situation. But the heir makes way more sense."

The double cheeseburger she'd gleefully eaten sat like lead in her stomach. "Wait. Wait one second. You took this case. You took it on."

"So?"

"So how do you suddenly decide the person asking you to do the work might be guilty?"

Nova felt like her thoughts had become a tennis match. Innocence or guilt. Comparisons of every situation to Ferdy, then quick reassurance that things were nothing like her time with her ex. Even a simple conversation had seemingly gone sideways.

"Look, Nova. It's an unfortunate reality of my work but just because somebody hires a PI doesn't mean they're innocent."

She tried to look at it from his perspective but had to admit it seemed like a rather callous way to make a living. Did everyone have an angle?

And was that why it had been so easy for him to assume she did, too?

Questions without answers. Or maybe put in a better way, answers she didn't necessarily want.

"If I turn it another way, I can also understand exactly why Selina hired me. Putting aside her family connections, the woman has a huge job at Colton Oil. She's responsible for all public relations for the company. That's a massive responsibility to sit on one person's shoulders. And it's not like the oil industry hasn't had its fair share of bad press."

"I guess."

"Guess all you'd like, and I'm cool with whatever opinion you have either way, but she has a right to protect her professional interests."

Maybe that was what was really bothering her.

She'd driven over two thousand miles, zigzagging across the country, with some sort of black-or-white outcome in her head. She'd find her father, and he would either want her in his life or he wouldn't.

There hadn't been any gray in that equation.

No question marks.

No scales to weigh one side versus another.

How odd, then, to realize that Nikolas Slater lived with those scales every single day.

NIKOLAS DROVE TOWARD his condo and, for the second day in a row, Nova followed behind him in her car. He was still surprised she was willing to even talk to him, let alone come with him to his home after the time they'd spent at Marlowe's and his subsequent behavior. Only she claimed to be over it, forgiving his behavior even as she'd made it quite clear how his lack of trust had made her feel.

Then they'd gone to lunch and he'd felt they'd settled on more even ground. Only to have another round of conversation at lunch forcing him to reconsider that, too.

He hadn't missed her discomfort as they discussed his suspicions about Selina. And it didn't take an investigator's license to know that she wasn't fully on board with his methods.

Why did that bother him so much?

He had tried to shrug it off, claiming that he was more than comfortable with her opinions, but if he were honest with himself, it did chafe a bit to see that disappointment in her eyes.

Especially when it settled so squarely on him.

He had never felt the need to apologize for his job, and he had no interest in starting now. But did she have a point? Even if he put the idea of conflict of interest aside, there was something suspicious about Selina Barnes Colton. The woman was a barracuda, and while she appeared to fancy herself some sort of wheeler and dealer, she wasn't exactly hard to read on the surface.

It had been clear from their initial meeting that she wouldn't be sad at all to see Ace go to jail for the attempt on Payne's life.

Did she feel that way, regardless if Ace was innocent?

Nikolas drove through the gate to his underground parking garage and saw Nova pass through the gate, as well. He'd given her a key fob that morning so that she could come and go as she needed to.

So here they were. Facing a second night in his condo with nearly everything changed between them since they'd left that morning.

Nova met him at the garage elevator and had already pressed the up button while she waited for him to join her. "What was that other thing that Marlowe said earlier?"

"One other thing?"

"That there was more information. I wasn't ready to

hear it at the time, my only focus on leaving, but I remember. She said there was more to tell us."

Now that Nova mentioned it, their conversation with Marlowe resurfaced in his mind. "It sounded like it was more news about Ace."

"I got the same feeling. Like they've learned a few things since getting that email."

"We can call her. Go back over there."

"I'm one step ahead of you." Nova waved a small phone in his face. It was the most basic of the basic, and it had no bells and whistles, but the small device looked like it could make phone calls.

"Where did you get the phone?"

"It's a burner I bought somewhere in Iowa. I was starting to feel really pregnant and I realized I probably needed to have something. You know, in case of an emergency."

They stepped into the elevator, and once again Nikolas was struck by her ingenuity and the amazing bravery that she had shown over those long, long months.

Without thinking through the impulse, or barely even registering he had one, Nikolas leaned in and pressed his lips to hers.

What had started as impulse quickly flared as her hand came up to rest on his shoulder. Heat and need—the sort that might stay banked for a surprisingly long time—suddenly sprang to life with all the ferocity of a blaze.

And Nikolas was more than willing to be consumed.

The elevator rose steadily to his floor but Nikolas was unaware of their movement. He was unaware of anything except for Nova.

He'd been so careful with this up to now. It wasn't right to have feelings for a client. Even less right to act on them. And she was…vulnerable, in a way he'd never understand.

Or had never understood before.

Yet try as he might to pull away, the meeting of lips and the even more tantalizing mingling of tongues had him rooted to the spot. The hand she'd initially placed on his shoulder drifted up toward his head and he heard the softest moan as her fingers ran through his hair.

Somewhere in the steady blaze, they'd reached his floor and the elevator doors gave a light ding as they swung open. Nikolas lifted his head, that ding seeming to punctuate the moment.

What was he doing?

He shouldn't be kissing her. And she shouldn't be kissing him back. And they shouldn't…

Nikolas took her hand and stepped off the elevator, effectively shutting down the quick rush to judgment that had sprung up in his mind.

He'd worry about this course of events later.

Right now, they needed to call Marlowe and get a plan together.

Nikolas opened his door and gestured Nova through. She still hadn't said anything on the walk to his door from the elevator and neither had he. What was there to say?

I'm sorry.

That was great.

It won't happen again.

No, no and *hell* no.

It was better to stay quiet and let the reality of kissing Nova Ellis live on in his mind. Besides, why would he jinx the opportunity to possibly do it again?

"I need to go get a few things from my desk. I'll be right back."

He didn't wait for an answer but headed down the hall to his home office to grab a notepad and pen. They had discussed so much that he wanted to write it all down and see if anything jumped out at him.

It was only as he reached for a legal pad on his desk that he saw the notes he had left himself the night before.

Call hospital to check status on Payne Colton.
Update call to Selina Barnes Colton.
Consider man named Ferdy.

In the light of a new day, he was glad he hadn't done a search for Nova's ex. He wasn't entirely sure why he'd held back last night, but he was very glad he'd left well enough alone. Nova needed someone she could trust with her secrets. He might not have demonstrated his trustworthiness earlier, but he was determined that would be a one-time slip.

She could trust him. And they would figure out what to do about this Ferdy fellow.

Together.

It was the one thing he could give her. That he could truly promise her. He'd keep his word.

Legal pad in hand, he headed back out to the kitchen. She offered up a wry little smile as she waved at him with an apple in her hand. "Sorry. I was hungry." He thought he heard her add in a muttered voice, "I knew I should have had the fries."

Holding back any suggestion he'd heard that last bit, he said, "Nothing to be sorry about. Anything in the house is yours. Please know that."

"I do know that. Thank you."

Nikolas looked at her for another minute and realized she had effectively removed any lingering awkwardness between them over the kiss. Their ongoing discussion about food, and her consistent hunger, had given them a chance to refocus. And once again, she awed him with her ability to read people and to understand a situation.

To understand how to shift things just enough so they could move forward.

Normally he'd take something like that as the gift it was and back off. They'd shared an impulsive moment—one not meant to be repeated. And yet...

Unwilling to fully let the subject of the kiss drop, he moved up in front of her, closing the space between them to barely nothing. "Do you?"

"Do I what?"

"Know that you can have whatever you want?" He bent down and, holding her hand still, took a bite of her apple, smiling as he did. "But you might need to share a little bit."

Chapter Eleven

Sierra Madden sized up her opponent and considered what she knew. It was a favorite game—one that she'd honed after a lifetime of boxing—and she enjoyed playing it against prospective clients.

The aim of her little game was to see just how much she could find out with the fewest questions.

Take the woman opposite her, here in the booth at the heavily used diner about twenty miles outside of Mustang Valley.

Selina Barnes Colton.

The woman had reached out to have a meeting, intimating on her call that she wanted to hire Sierra to find someone. The who, of course, was the interesting part.

Selina's former stepson, Asa "Ace" Colton, who was wanted by the cops.

The man had been the subject of endless news stories and quite a bit of gossipy speculation over the past few months. Ever since his father, Payne Colton, was found shot in his office and Ace had gone to the top of the suspect list for the crime.

A crime whose victim hadn't woken up to name his killer. An attempted killer who may or may not be a man who had recently discovered he wasn't his biological son.

For her money, Sierra didn't get a guilty vibe from Ace, but it ultimately wasn't up to her to decide. That was the funny thing about being a bounty hunter. The only thing she had to decide was whether or not to take the job. Once she made her choice, the rest was up to someone else.

Sierra had read all the news stories, of course. There weren't many in Arizona who hadn't. But for some reason, she'd found herself lingering overly long on the incredibly attractive heir to the Colton Oil fortune—even one who was accused of murder. There likely hadn't been a filed photo of him at this point that hadn't made its way into news stories and she was convinced she'd seen damn near every one of them.

Sierra didn't believe in fate, nor was she superstitious, but it still struck her as odd that Selina Barnes Colton had somehow come looking for her. It was a question she planned on asking when the time was right.

For now, she held off while she considered the other pieces she did know.

Selina was the ex-wife of Ace's father. For reasons no one seemed to understand, despite their divorce and his moving on to a third marriage, Payne had kept the woman on and given her a rather high-ranking position at Colton Oil. Selina was in charge of all public relations for the behemoth company.

She also seemed to have a rather sizable ax to grind with her former stepson.

Oh, she'd said all the right things on their initial call when Selina had reached out to set up the meeting. She'd talked of her "deep desire to bring Ace back to his loving family, keeping him safe at home while they hire the best criminal defense attorneys." Words that, while kind and caring on the surface, had carried a twisted, sort of manipulation when she'd actually spoken.

That inconsistency alone had Sierra on high alert. But it was something more—some strange, undefined air of malice about Selina—that had kept her in her seat and unwilling to look away from the woman claiming she'd pay big for Sierra's services.

Sierra had discovered boxing in her teens and had used the sport to hone both body and mind. You learned a lot about yourself when you took a punch and you learned even more when you figured out how to throw the right ones in return. She knew when an opponent was going to feint a move, when they were getting tired and breathing through their mouth and when they were looking somewhere over your shoulder, eyeing their next move.

Selina had been doing that last one since they'd sat down. A move that made Sierra's survival instinct kick in.

Every. Damn. Time.

"And you want me to find your stepson?"

Selina's lips tightened as if she'd just tasted the lemon that sat beside her cup of tea. "Ace and I don't refer to one another in those familial terms."

"Oh? What do you use, then?"

"Our first names suffice."

Fine, Sierra thought. She'd take the bait and play along. "What if Ace doesn't want to be found?"

"That's a silly thing to say. He should want the love and support of his family."

You keep selling that word, "family," but I'm not buying it.

Only Sierra didn't say that. And with the rigid smile

she kept in place, she knew her body language hadn't suggested it either.

"He's a grown man." Sierra considered the photos she'd seen of Ace Colton through the years. *Grown* was an understatement for the attractive, vibrant man he'd become. "A successful one by all accounts, too. Surely he can keep his own counsel."

"Ace needs to come home to his family." Selina took a sip of her tea, the delicate move at odds with the calculation in her eyes. "I was told you're the best and that you always get your man."

"I do."

"Then why all these unnecessary questions?"

Sierra had to give the woman credit for landing a strong, sure jab on that one. She needed this job, no matter how skeptical she wanted to be about the Colton woman's motives. She hadn't believed her personal life could get more challenging after her father passed away, but she'd been wrong.

So wrong.

And she did need the money Selina was prepared to pay. Twenty-five thousand paid off a lot of debts.

"I like to know what I'm up against."

As an answer, it seemed to placate the woman in front of her. But as their conversation spun out, Sierra hammering out the expectations of her work, she wondered what she was getting into.

Would this fix her problems?

Or create a whole set of new ones?

NOVA HUNG UP with Marlowe, once again surprised by how easy the other woman was to talk to. Not that she'd call her "Aunt Marlowe," but it was still so novel to think of her that way. A part of her still questioned if there was a falseness to it until she took a DNA test, but she pushed it down.

She still thought of Paul Ellis as her father, after all. The man had raised her and loved her, and that meant more than biology when she thought of the man she'd called Dad for nearly two decades. They'd had a wonderful relationship and she'd spent a lot of time since hearing her mother's news about Ace considering how she could—or should—think of Paul. He might not be her biological father, but she'd never dismiss her wonderful memories of him.

Or the subtle guilt that she was somehow erasing him by looking for her biological father.

Marlowe's attitude and continued insistence on the definition of family had given her some clue, though, on how to move forward. Family was what you made. And Paul would always be the wonderful man who raised her.

Always.

Taking heart from that truth, Nova focused on moving forward.

Marlowe had stressed once again on their call her personal conviction that Nova's DNA test would come back as a match with Ace and that, despite the recent discovery of Ace's own parentage, the Coltons were Nova's family.

And they were all there for her.

As an additional sign of that solidarity, Marlowe had invited her and Nikolas over to the Triple R that night for dinner with her and Bowie as well as Ainsley and her fiancé, Santiago Morales. The rest of the Colton siblings were off at other functions and Nova was strangely glad of that. It was all still so new and she wasn't sure she could handle an evening with all of Ace's siblings and associated significant others.

Nikolas looked up from the laptop he sat with at the kitchen table. "How'd the call go?"

"Good. We're going to the Triple R for dinner."

"That's a great idea. You can see the family home and get a feel for where everyone spends so much of their time."

Nova thought about her mother and the way Allegra had spoken of the Triple R. She'd be so excited for Nova to go there and to meet more of the family. Nova could practically hear her mother's voice, chattering away as they discussed outfits and hairstyles.

It looks like you got your wish, Mom.

Nova fought back the lump of tears that clogged her throat and focused on Nikolas instead. "I think she's still a little mad at you."

"I wouldn't expect anything less."

He might have expected it but Nova hadn't. "Really?"

"Of course. And since I'm still a little mad at me, too, I can hardly blame Marlowe for feeling that way."

"I told you earlier that it's fine," Nova said. "That I'm fine."

"Maybe you are."

"Why aren't you okay with that?"

Nikolas let out a hard sigh and ran a hand through his hair, ruffling those curls she now knew were baby soft. "Because I'm not used to second-guessing my instincts. It bothers me that I did. More than that, it bothers me that I questioned them with you."

Nova wasn't particularly used to apologies. As an only child, she hadn't had siblings to fight with and then apologize to when things got out of hand. And she and her parents had always gotten along quite well, the occasional fight notwithstanding. But this… This was something different.

"Thank you for telling me that."

Nikolas had been jotting notes intermittently on the legal pad beside his computer, but he laid his pen down and gave her his full focus. "You're welcome. And you should know I'll try very hard not to do it again."

"I believe you."

She took the seat beside him and looked at the notes he had scribbled down. "Your handwriting is atrocious."

"Why, thank you."

"I'm serious. This is like serial killer scrawl if I've ever seen it."

"And the compliments keep on coming." His hazel eyes crinkled as he smiled and Nova fought the urge to reach out and touch the line of his jaw. That perpetual five o'clock shadow was so tempting.

She might be able to control herself around his temptingly strong jawline, but she couldn't hide her laughter. And just like that, the tension at the prospect of meeting another of her father's sisters faded.

"What exactly did you write down?" She turned the pad toward her but could make little sense of what was there. "Because yeah, I see what looks like words but I'm not taking anything away."

"I've searched all articles about Ace, Payne or the Colton family since Payne's shooting."

"And what did you find?"

"Not much that's all that substantive, despite the amount of coverage. The speculation about Ace's parentage has been covered, but not in any real depth. Colton Oil had evidently done a good job of keeping the information on lockdown. Where it is mentioned, it's referenced by anonymous sources, which makes me say that the mercurial Selina Barnes Colton has been doing her job."

"And doing it well." Nova scanned the list once more now that she knew what she was looking for. "How often is that angle of the non-heir referenced?"

"A few times. It's kind of set up to leave a question in the mind of the reader, before every reporter goes on to say that no one has been accused of any crime against Payne. Or had until the recent arrest attempt after the gun was found in Ace's home."

"Do the articles say there are any other suspects?"

"No, and that's the strange part. I know the MVPD has been working this case. They haven't simply assumed that Ace is responsible for the shooting."

"But the news doesn't seem to think so."

"Apparently not." Nikolas tapped his pen on the notepad. "You have to admit, the family aspect is what makes the story juicy."

Was that how people would look at her? As a juicy story, fueling local gossip and speculation. The long-lost daughter, arriving back in town and pregnant, as well.

"You look sad all of a sudden."

Nova traced a circle on the edge of the notepad with her fingertip. "I was just wondering if that was how people would look at me. As a story to gossip about."

"Some will. That's human nature. And when you have a family as prominent as the Coltons, people do look. And watch. It comes with the territory."

"Now who's being honest?"

Although he'd kept his physical distance since their kiss, Nikolas reached out to her now. "I told you I can't be anything but honest with you. And you should be prepared for the ways that your life is going to change."

"I thought being a mother was going to be the big change in my life."

"That will be, too. The biggest of the big. And it's going to happen along with your new family dynamic. It's a lot all at once."

Nova shifted the hand resting on her lap to her belly. She increasingly didn't have a lap to speak of, the baby's growth and development continuing to change her body in the most obvious of ways. Up to now, Nova had considered all of it a mental preparation for motherhood. The day-by-day changes in her body that would prepare her for the major changes in her life.

But the reality was that in a few short months, she would have a child and she'd never go back to her old life. She'd never be just Nova Ellis. Or Colton. Or whoever she ended up being.

"Nova?" Nikolas's voice was gentle. "Was that a bit too honest?"

"No." Nova pulled herself from the lingering thoughts. "You're only saying what I already know. My life is changing. It has been, really, since my mother's diagnosis. And each step that's come since keeps making that more and more clear."

"You don't just mean the baby, now, do you?"

"No. Like you said, the baby's the biggest of the big, but everything for the past year has been sort of big."

Nikolas had grown quiet, his expression taking on a faraway look before he reached out and closed the lid of his laptop. She sensed that he was working up to something and gave him the space he needed.

"I lost my mother five years ago."

Nova mentally did the math and realized Nikolas had lost his mom at the same age she'd been when she'd lost hers. Much too young, as far as she was concerned, even as she knew you were never old enough for that terrible event to take place.

"She was an amazing woman. She believed in me and supported me. And she did it all with a smile, even when she probably didn't feel like it."

"What do you mean by that?"

"My father loved her. Loved us both. But he wasn't exactly a faithful husband."

Nova thought about her own mother and Allegra's teenage affair with Ace. How she'd quickly rushed into a relationship with Paul Ellis after Ace had broken her heart. Had Paul ever known that he wasn't biologically her father? Had her mother shared that with him?

Questions that would never be answered, even as Nova wondered how people built relationships with each other. How they committed, day after day, when there was the potential for such large secrets between them.

Hadn't Ferdy proved that? He carried secrets that weren't just painful, but illegal, too.

It was a wonder people found each other at all. That they created and built and *stayed* in relationships for a lifetime.

"Your mother knew, obviously?"

"She did. I often think that's why she didn't want more children. She never came out and said it, but I think it was easier on her to focus on me and not think about sharing one more bond with him."

"But she loved him?"

"Totally. And died heartbroken because while he loved her, he never loved her all the way. He never gave her all of himself. He never found a way to put her first."

"Do you think that's what it's about? Putting someone else first?"

"I think it should be. But I don't know that it often is."

Nova thought about that, wondering what it all meant. Humans were innately flawed, but that didn't mean there wasn't good in people. But how did you know? Certainly not everyone was Ferdy, hiding criminal activity. A lot of them were men like Nikolas's father, just finding their way through life. Stumbling—terribly sometimes—but not all the way bad.

It was hard to understand and it made her think of her own father. Allegra had believed Ace had feelings for her, yet he'd left her at the end of their summer fling. Was that the inconstancy of youth? A character flaw? Or just the strange vagaries of how life went sometimes.

Why was it all so hard to understand?

Holding back the mental sigh, she gave Nikolas her full attention. "I'm sorry. But thank you for trusting me with this."

"I just—" Nikolas stopped, those curls flopping against his fingers once more as he ran a hand through his hair. "I thought you should know that. Slater men are a bad bet. Hell, a lot of men are a bad bet. But that doesn't mean you're not entitled to happiness and a future."

Nova wasn't sure how, but their conversation had seemingly leapfrogged from life-changing events to family pain to an underlying warning to steer clear of a relationship with him.

That warning lodged somewhere underneath her breastbone, but Nova ignored the feeling, vowing to think about it later. They barely knew each other, so she had no reason to be upset.

No reason at all.

Of course, her conscience whispered, there wasn't any reason for him to say it, either.

Was it because of their kiss in the elevator? The one

he'd initiated? Maybe he was really warning himself and Nova was simply caught in the crossfire.

Whatever the reason, Nova heard the warning loud and clear. She stood at that, her focus just above the top of his head. "I'm going to go lie down for a bit and then get ready to go over to the Triple R."

NIKOLAS SPENT THE better part of an hour continuing his online searches as well as digging through a few databases he had access to via his investigator's license. Nothing had provided much beyond what he already knew, but he was grateful for the distraction.

What was wrong with him?

If he'd been looking for a calm, cool, collected way to tell Nova that they couldn't kiss again, he sure as hell hadn't landed on one. Instead, he'd ham-fisted his way through his family sob story and then warned her off like she was some sort of girl, fawning over him.

He wasn't a repeat of a youthful Ace Colton, caught up in a summer romance. And for all her seeming innocence, Nova wasn't her mother, locked in the wonder of a first romance at seventeen.

He'd been the one to kiss her, after all. It was hardly fair to suddenly assume she felt some wild, crazy attraction.

Only something had begun to shift in him as they'd sat there. He'd listened to her talk of her life changes and the baby's impending arrival, and in that moment, he'd seen himself doing that all *with* her.

Being there.

When she finally met her father. When she went into labor. And most of all, when she sat there in the hospital, propped up against the pillows, holding her child serenely in her arms.

He'd seen it all, and seen himself clearly in the scene with her.

And that scared him beyond all rational thought.

He didn't know this woman. As early as today, he'd wondered if she was playing him like a fiddle. And now?

Now he was fantasizing about her baby and spending time with them once the little one arrived?

He was Guy Slater's son, after all. He didn't do long-term relationships or permanence or, heaven forbid, real, true love. He did short-term and easy. He'd seen how his father's behavior had ravaged his mother and he wasn't interested in repeating that mess. Because of it, Nikolas had always been careful. He didn't get into relationships he couldn't easily get out of, and he'd become a champ at selecting women who expected a fun, casual date, not someone permanent.

So why now?

And why Nova Ellis?

She was the exact opposite of the sort of women he usually dated. The pregnancy aside, everything about that petite frame and long braid that fell down over one shoulder and those vivid green eyes spoke of permanence. Forever.

And when he talked to her, he could see it, too. This wasn't a woman content with the casual. She might be young, but his mother would have called her an old soul. A person who saw the world around her for what it really was, even as she continued to find the good in it.

His mother would have liked Nova. He could envision his mother sitting at the table with them, talking of deeper things beyond the weather or the latest gossip around town. And in the same vision, he saw

Nova holding her own, talking of the things in life that truly mattered.

He *saw* it, damn it.

And while his mother might be gone, Nova was very real and very much here. She deserved someone who could both appreciate those traits in her and encourage them. Not do to her what his father had done to his mother and betray the beauty in those gifts.

Which only reinforced his words earlier. He might have been ham-fisted in his approach, but he'd been honest. Nova Ellis Colton was a bright, shining light.

And he well knew he couldn't have any part of it.

Chapter Twelve

Although something had whispered to Nova that she should drive herself to Rattlesnake Ridge Ranch, she'd ultimately acquiesced to having Nikolas take them in one car. Bowie had offered earlier to take her home and she assumed the offer would still stand if needed.

Which wasn't like her, but, well, a woman had a right to change her mind when her feelings were hurt.

And hers were.

She had told Nikolas she forgave him for his freak-out at Marlowe's earlier that day and she'd meant it. A few minutes thinking through his perspective and she'd innately understood why he had panicked. He didn't know her and he had no reason to believe *her* reasons for being in Mustang Valley.

But to warn her off like he did? Over a kiss?

Well, that had her pissed.

Nova stared out the car windows at the vista that surrounded her. The three-story ranch house was visible in the distance, but it was the land that really captivated her. As someone who had been born and raised in New York City, she found the idea that there could be more than a street width between buildings mind-boggling. And here, for as far as she could see, was land.

Although Payne Colton and his family ran Colton

Oil, she also understood that Rattlesnake Ridge Ranch was a working cattle farm. A rather successful one, by all accounts. It was an interesting juxtaposition, the cowboy-like nature of owning a farm along with the corporate responsibilities that came with running an oil company.

One more thing that fascinated her about the Coltons.

Nikolas pulled up in front of the house into a small parking area. With as many family members who lived here, they needed more room than just a standard two-car garage. As reinforcement of that, Nova saw several cars already parked in spaces.

"Well. I guess this is it." Nova turned to Nikolas and she unbuckled her seat belt. "Time to meet more of the family."

"They're going to love you."

"That would be nice. But for now, I'll settle for getting through the evening."

Nova didn't want to be ungrateful, but she was still smarting from Nikolas's reaction earlier. It wouldn't do to get her hopes up that suddenly she was walking into a family reunion. A strong, self-effacing thought that carried her as far as the front door.

The thick, magnificent entryway was flung open before she even had a chance to knock.

"You must be Nova!" A pretty woman with long, chestnut-colored hair beamed at her through the doorway. "I'm Ainsley. I've been so excited to meet you."

With barely a hello in return Nova was pulled into a tight hug and once again that sensation of being Alice down the rabbit hole struck with full force.

Was it possible that people could love so unconditionally? Could accept her so simply?

Based on the strong, welcoming circle that enfolded her, Nova had to believe the answer was yes.

"Come on in. Don't let me leave you standing out here." Ainsley waved them both in, shooting an eye toward Nikolas as she did. "Good to see you again, Nikolas."

"You, too, Ainsley. How are things?"

"They're better now."

Nova followed Ainsley deeper into the house, marveling as she went. While the image her mother had painted in her stories of the house had been from nearly a quarter century ago, Nova could see how things had been contemporized. The living room was still an impressive centerpiece to the house, the paneled ceiling rising two stories above them. She suspected the furniture, the rugs and the wall hangings had likely been updated from the way they were initially described. Things were rustic yet carried enough modern sensibility to seem fresh instead of outdated.

In spite of its size, the room was warm. Homey. And even if her entire New York City apartment could fit into this room, it didn't feel cold or spare.

Perhaps it was the people who lived here? The ones who, even now, surrounded her and talked to her, not at her.

"Marlowe and I still can't quite believe you're here. But I can see it. I can *so* see it."

"See what?" Nova asked.

"The resemblance. It's like I'm looking at my brother. A far more beautiful and feminine version of my brother," Ainsley said with a wry smile, "but I can see Ace."

She didn't miss the fact that Ainsley still referred to Ace as her brother, and she gave Nova the courage she needed to press on. "I'm sure it's been hard on all of you, to have him missing and your father in a coma."

"You have no idea," Marlowe said, setting drinks down on the coffee table. "Our brother has always played oldest when it suited him, taking the quiet and stoic route when he needed to, but this is new, even for Ace."

"He's been through a lot, Marlowe." Ainsley reached for one of the iced teas on the coffee table. "Finding out about his birth the way that he did. The way we all did."

Although he had been quiet up until then, allowing the sisters to direct the conversation, Nikolas finally spoke. "How did he take the news?"

"It was difficult, of course. To spend your whole life thinking one thing, and then find out that you were someone else. And all from an email, no less. But we told him." Marlowe looked at her sister before shifting her attention back to Nikolas. "We told him that it changes nothing in our eyes."

"Sweetheart, we talked about this," Bowie interjected. "Your feelings may not change, but it's still a lot for Ace to go through."

"I know. I just wish—" Marlowe broke off. "There's so much happening. So much good. Reed's arrival. Our engagement. Ainsley and Santiago getting together. All the siblings, really, finding their place. Finding love. I'm just sorry he's missing out."

Although it was obvious the discovery of his birth had shaken Ace, Nova had to wonder if there was a little more to it. To Marlowe's point, things were changing in the Colton family. Relationships, new babies. It was a lot of change—albeit wonderful change—but to add that on top of your own personal confusion must be difficult.

Nikolas handed her one of the sparkling waters that Marlowe had set down on the coffee table. It was a simple gesture but it was enough to break some of the cool tension that had existed between them since his comments at his kitchen table.

"Thank you."

Nikolas didn't say anything, just nodded, but she had the feeling he understood some of what she was thinking. "Marlowe, you said earlier that there was more to Ace's story. I'm ready to hear it. All of it."

"You didn't tell her?" Ainsley asked Marlowe.

"We covered a lot of ground earlier." Marlowe smiled at her sister before shooting a supportive glance toward Nova. "I didn't want to bombard the poor woman with too much."

Nova appreciated that subtle support and decided right there on the spot that Marlowe would have been the perfect older aunt. Able to keep a confidence and more than willing to cover for her if she'd missed curfew. The added wink Bowie shot her from where he sat beside Marlowe only sealed her fast-growing affection for the pair. "I think I'm ready to hear the rest now."

"I think we left off after the email and the paternity test."

"Yes, that's right." Nova braced herself for whatever might be coming next, well aware nothing had been normal up 'til now.

"Our cousin, Spencer, is a sergeant with the MVPD," Ainsley began. "He's been working the case professionally but that hasn't stopped the rest of us from looking into things. Both Marlowe and I have been focused at work trying to uncover where the email might've come from."

"Did you find anything?" Nova asked, realizing

they'd left the subject of the email open-ended earlier at Marlowe's condo.

"Eventually. It took a bit of digging but Colton Oil keeps some great people on staff in our IT department."

"Darling, we can discuss the merits of IT work later. I think Nova wants to know what's going on," Santiago Morales said, his rich voice soft with both love and pointed affection to keep Ainsley on track.

Ainsley leaned over and gave him a quick kiss before pressing on. "Of course. So we ultimately did trace the email."

"Who did it?" Nova asked, aware that hacked emails and anonymous tips took this whole situation up a notch.

Ainsley nodded. "IT traced it to a dark web account. The sender is some guy by the name of Harley Watts. Spencer has him in custody but he won't talk."

Dark web. Jail. Secrets, lies and subterfuge. Nova's head spun at the idea of it all. What was really going on here?

Marlowe picked up the thread from Ainsley. "Since my father's shooting, there's been a tremendous amount of pressure on Ace. The question of whether or not he'll be able to ascend to the CEO role. The questions around his kidnapping at birth. And then of course my father's shooting and subsequent coma."

"A lot for anyone to take in," Nova said. And it would be, but from what the sisters said, there was way more that had happened since those horrible days back in January.

"He's tried so hard to keep his focus solely on Dad, as we all have, but the hits just keep on coming." Ainsley reached for Santiago's hand, twining their fingers together. "That's how we met actually. Last month, someone tried to frame Ace, planting the gun used to shoot my father under the floorboards of his home."

"Framed, you say?" Nikolas asked. Although he'd been steadily focused on the conversation, this new news had him moving to the edge of his seat on the couch. "You know who did it?"

"We don't know yet. We've been working on it and so has Spencer. The call is suspicious in and of itself. But the ballistics did prove that was the gun used to shoot Payne." Santiago shook his head. "Nothing about it has been an open-and-shut, though. We still have no idea why Destiny Jones, whom Ace said he never met, gave the tip to the police. Or how anyone even got into Ace's apartment to plant the gun."

Whatever she'd expected coming here, the depths of depravity and cruelty the real killer was determined to mete out surprised her. And with that surprise came another reality: Ace's siblings were all convinced of his innocence.

Nova rubbed at her arms, the warmth of the room fading in the reality of what her father faced.

What they all faced, really.

"Is that why Ace went on the run?"

Santiago nodded. "We think that's the reason. The ballistics look pretty bad."

"Even if we all believe, without any doubt, that he's innocent," Ainsley added, her hand tightly linked with her fiancé's.

Nikolas took off his sport coat and settled it over her shoulders before resuming his seat beside her on the couch. Nova didn't miss the pointed look Marlowe shot toward Nikolas, or the softening in her dark brown eyes.

Point to Slater, Nova thought with no small measure of satisfaction.

As Nova snuggled deeper into Nikolas's jacket, she recognized one more thing. That look confirmed something else. Marlowe Colton really would be an awesome aunt.

And an even more awesome person to have in her corner.

NIKOLAS TOOK THE jacket Nova handed back to him and set it on the couch as they stood to walk in to dinner. He'd wanted to know more of Ainsley and Santiago's story about the planted gun, but one of the cooks had announced that dinner was ready, putting a temporary end to the conversation.

Once again, his mind played through the details Ainsley and Santiago had shared. A planted gun? That suggested an additional layer of malice and trouble he never would've expected out of this situation. And while it was a simple leap to say that Ace was a prime suspect because of the ballistics match, the man wasn't dumb. And the anonymous tip from this Destiny Jones didn't sit well with Nikolas, either.

He'd done a lot of digging into Ace Colton's life and he couldn't figure out who besides his siblings was close to him. He wasn't married and hadn't been in a serious relationship for some time. Even if he was squiring dates around town, was he really bringing them back home and showing off a gun used to shoot his father?

It just didn't play for him. Not when you thought through the actual logistics of how someone would come to know of a gun hidden in the man's home.

Which led him straight back to the idea that Ace was framed, the gun planted for easy discovery.

Did Selina know about it and elected not to tell him? She certainly hadn't mentioned a gun—planted or otherwise—when she had come to speak to him about Ace. And his police contacts were playing it close to the vest. They'd confirmed a gun was discovered in Ace Colton's home, but no one had even whispered the idea that it might have been planted.

He had been wary about this case from the beginning, and as each point was added on a running checklist of "guilty" or "not guilty" for Ace Colton, Nikolas had to admit to himself that he was growing increasingly uncomfortable.

Especially if it put Nova in the crosshairs.

What would a killer, hiding in the wings, do if he or she suddenly knew that Ace had a child? And not just a child, but a child who was about to deliver Ace's first grandchild.

That would be some awfully powerful motivation to pull Ace out of hiding.

Bowie saw him lingering at the doorway and came over to talk. "You okay, man?"

"Yeah, sure, I guess."

"You don't sound very sure."

"What do you make of this whole planted gun thing?"

Bowie appeared to understand his underlying question without being asked and motioned Nikolas to a small butler's pantry to talk. "I haven't liked it from the start. Ace and I have never been particularly close, especially being rivals from different companies. But I've always respected the man, and I've always felt he respected me in return."

Nikolas understood that. Bowie's role as the head of Robertson Renewable Energy had always put him at odds with the Colton family. Even the fact that he and

Marlowe had gotten together had added to the gossip gristmill around town.

Bowie continued on. "But it's never sat well with me. The idea that the guy shot his father. Even if you take out the email about Ace's birth and the whole paternity test, it's a stretch. You spend your whole life thinking of this man as your father and suddenly in a matter of days you pick up a gun and shoot him? I just can't see it. Especially because he is such a decent guy. Tough in business, but fair."

Nikolas had felt the same and had said as much to Selina in their initial meeting. Regardless of the confusion and shock Ace Colton might've been operating under, it was a huge leap to assume that he would pick up a gun and shoot Payne.

"And the plot thickens if somebody's trying to frame him."

"Bingo. That's what Marlowe and Ainsley have been so determined to figure out. Who would have a motive for framing their brother? If they find that, then they figure out who had the motive to shoot Payne."

Although he hesitated to ask, Nikolas knew the question would only continue to nag at him. "Do you think it could be Selina?"

"Much as the woman gives me the creeps and makes me question Payne's judgment to keep her around, I don't think it's her, either. She certainly benefits if Ace is out of the picture. She probably thinks that she can better direct whoever might be selected CEO in his place. But it's an awfully big leap to go from calculating bitch to cold-blooded murderess. I don't think she has it in her."

Nikolas wasn't quite so sure about that, but he re-

·spected Bowie's opinion and would add it to his weighing of the situation.

She might be capable, but that didn't mean she was capable of murdering her ex-husband. Besides, there was something in Selina Barnes Colton that had Nikolas thinking if the woman did decide to shoot Payne, she'd see the deed through rather than leave before knowing if the man was well and truly dead.

She didn't strike him as a woman who left loose ends.

"What are you two doing out here?" Marlowe found them in the pantry and gestured them back toward the dining room. "Everything's on the table."

Nikolas followed Bowie and Marlowe into the room, his mind reverting to where he'd started. A hidden killer couldn't know about Nova's connection to the family. She'd already run from danger in New York.

What had she possibly run in *to* by coming to Mustang Valley?

NOVA CLUTCHED HER stomach at the laughter that infused the conversation at the table. For all their talk of being a couple of old, boring lawyers, Santiago and Ainsley had kept them all in stitches throughout the meal. Although they claimed to have only met recently, there was a sweet kinship between them that spoke of both bone-deep attraction as well as soul-deep friendship and affection.

It was heady to observe something so private, yet so obviously *right*.

And she couldn't help but wonder if she'd ever find that herself.

The baby kicked and Nova rubbed a discreet hand over the little foot jabbing against her ribs. No matter how sad she felt from time to time about the end of her misguided relationship with Ferdy, she would never regret her child.

Never.

Just as she and Nikolas had discussed, her life was about to change in so many new and amazing ways. Her child was a blessing and she needed to focus on that and not worry about where her next relationship would come from. Or if she was going to have another relationship at all. She wanted to be a good mother and create a good life for her child. That was what mattered.

All that mattered.

Especially with Nikolas warning her off their kissing and everything.

A fact she'd done her damned level best to forget about for the past two hours. Even if she was failing miserably at that by thinking of their kiss oh, about every other minute. Neither did it get any easier each time she looked at him, his strong jaw and juicy lips a constant reminder of just how good he was at kissing.

And how long it had been since she'd actually been kissed.

Shifting her attention back to Ainsley and Santiago and off Nikolas's lips, Nova was eager to hear more from the cute couple. "How did the two of you meet?"

"Santiago was Ace's lawyer. Is his lawyer," Ainsley added. "Since I'm the in-house counsel for Colton Oil, Ace called both of us about the planted gun."

"And we ran with it from there," Santiago said.

"And by run with it," Marlowe added, "they mean they pretended to be a married couple up at the Marriage Institute. It's connected to the AAG."

At the mention of that horrible place Nova's gaze sharpened. "You went there? To the AAG?"

"That's the last update in the convoluted story of our family," Marlowe said. "We have little doubt Micheline was the one to switch the babies."

That strange sense of foreboding that Nova hadn't been able to shake yesterday when she met the woman from the AAG rose back up in her chest, a sort of clawing panic she couldn't define. Was it really possible that was where her father had actually come from? Worse, was it possible that the AAG "lifestyle" and those people were a part of her heritage? Part of who she was?

Was that why she had reacted so badly?

Yes, that young woman had given her the creeps. But Nova's reaction had been wholly disproportionate to the actual conversation. Even as she had known that, she had just felt so odd, staring up at that billboard and then speaking to the woman who acted as if she was in a cult.

"What did you find out?"

"Santiago and I posed as a couple going up there for counseling. Our intention was to see what we could find out."

"Why do you think Micheline is connected to Ace?" Nikolas asked.

"The police have traced it back. She used to go by the name Luella Smith. Up until forty years ago," Ainsley added. "She was a nurse in the hospital the night Ace was born. A nurse who was also pregnant at the same time and disappeared days after both Ace and her own baby were born."

The shock at the news that her father was possibly related to the AAG founder was hard enough. But if she had been pregnant, too, what was the possible motive for making a switch? "But why would she do that? If she had her own baby, why would she give it away for another?"

Although it would be hard to process the story under any circumstance, being pregnant added a dimension that made it even harder to fathom the shocking news. "I mean, what you're talking about is crazy. This woman had a baby of her own and then switched them? Why?"

As a recent mother, Marlowe obviously understood her distress and came around the table to sit beside her. "Nothing about it makes any sense. But we can only assume Luella or Micheline or whatever we want to call her had some sick, twisted reason to switch her baby with a Colton."

"It really doesn't end, does it?" Nova asked the question in a daze, the calloused cruelty of the idea cutting through her like a sharp knife. Was it really possible? If Ace was her biological father and Micheline was *his* biological mother, then that made that woman her grandmother. A woman who'd switched her own child at birth.

The realizations speared her, one after the other, one wound worse than the next.

What was she really a part of? And what sort of awful DNA was her child inheriting? A criminal father and a psycho grandmother.

"Nova?" Marlowe asked, her voice gentle. "Are you all right?"

Was she all right? "I can't believe it. Any of it. The layers of betrayal. The ripple effects of such a long-ago act."

Just as he had before dinner, when he had shared his sport coat, Nikolas reached for her again. "If you'd like to leave, I can take you home."

"What home? I came to Mustang Valley thinking I would find one, but all I'm finding is lies."

Nova fought at the tears that welled up and dashed

them away. She would *not* cry. Not in the face of so much kindness. So much caring that these people had shown her.

But she also questioned how she could stay.

"I know this is hard to process. We've had some time and we're still struggling with it," Ainsley said from across the table, the concern written on her face as clear as the compassion that practically rolled off Marlowe in waves. "But you do have a home here. With us."

"I appreciate that more than I can say. Truly I do. But none of you know what I'm running from."

"Why don't you tell us then? We'll listen. We're here for you."

Nova let Ainsley's words wash over her before turning to Nikolas. She didn't need to say a word because he already knew the question. In the quiet nod of his head, she understood what she needed to do.

She would never be free of her life in New York—would never find a way to set her child free of it, either—if she didn't trust these people.

Shifting her gaze from Nikolas, Nova looked around the table. At Marlowe beside her and her fiancé, Bowie, where he sat in solidarity across the table. Then on to Santiago and the kind understanding in his green eyes. And then on to Ainsley, the eager welcome she'd greeted her with at the door still there, only now it was layered with compassion and understanding.

How could she stand up to so much understanding and acceptance?

And suddenly, Nova realized it was pointless to try.

With a final nod back to Nikolas, she took a deep breath.

"I guess it's time to tell you all, then. I have a story of my own."

Chapter Thirteen

In the end, it had been surprisingly easy to tell them all about Ferdy. About her run from New York and her zigzagging trip across the United States. Even about the fear that he'd find her somehow and come after her.

What hadn't been easy, Nova realized, was to say goodbye.

She and her "aunts" had hugged in the large foyer of the Triple R, each promising to spend more time together. They'd also invited her to come stay at the ranch in the meanwhile, but she'd opted to take a rain check on that. She couldn't take advantage of Nikolas's kindness forever, but she didn't feel it was right to just accept without talking to him.

Besides, leaving meant she wouldn't see him as much, and despite the talking-to about the kiss, she wasn't ready to give up on him.

Which was probably her most misguided decision of the evening but hey, a girl could dream.

"You're quiet." Nikolas made the turn into town, off the road that had taken them out to the Triple R.

"Just thinking." Nova murmured the words.

"Tonight was a lot to take in."

"It was. I thought the news earlier at Marlowe's, that

Ace wasn't really a Colton, was the hard part to digest. Guess I was wrong."

Nikolas hit the button for the gate to his underground parking lot. "I guess we were all wrong. Seems there's a lot more going on under the surface than anyone really understood."

He pulled around to his parking spot and cut the engine. She nearly had her door open when he laid a hand on her forearm, stilling her. "Are you really doing okay with this?"

"I have to be."

"Nova. That's not an answer."

"What other answer can I have? It doesn't really matter what I thought on the drive out here from New York. It doesn't matter what idyllic image I had in my mind about finding my birth father. All of this is real. His blood connection to a crazy psycho. The fact that he's not a Colton. I either accept it or I run away with my tail between my legs. And in case you haven't guessed, I'm not particularly fond of doing the latter."

He smiled at that, his expression the response she had hoped for in her attempts to lighten the mood. "You really are amazing."

Without questioning herself, Nova leaned forward and pressed her lips to his. It was part need, part experiment, and she wasn't going to apologize for it. For all his attempts to try and warn her off earlier, she wasn't oblivious to the sparks that flared between them.

It was time to test them out. And oh boy, were they worth a spin.

The same fever that had gripped them earlier that day in the elevator took hold again, only this time, they had the space to leisurely explore each other. There was no rising elevator, and no elevator doors waiting to ding open and effectively end their kiss.

There was just the two of them, ensconced in the quiet of his car.

Her gamble paid off. Nikolas was as into the moment as she was, and it was a matter of heartbeats until his hand came up to rest at the base of her neck, his fingers drifting tantalizingly over her nape. The lips that she had fantasized about during dinner were strong and firm, pressed against hers and reminding her of needs she had believed long dormant.

He ran his tongue along the seam of her lips and she opened for him, gasping at the firm pressure. Feelings pulsed through her, beating in time with her heart, caught in the rhythm that they made with each other. Her breasts, already heavy from her pregnancy, added the additional weight of desire as her nipples pressed against the cups of her bra.

Goodness, did this man know what he did to her? How he made her feel?

The baby chose that moment to kick hard enough to bring a gasp to Nova's lips.

"Are you okay?"

"I'm fine." Although she didn't exactly want to dismiss her child, it felt like a bit of a mood killer to tell the man you were kissing that your little alien had decided to get in on the fun.

The desire in his eyes was rapidly fading, replaced with concern. "Are you sure?"

"Yes, of course."

Her little traitor kicked again and it was enough to have her drawing a breath, sucking air in between her teeth.

"Nova, come on. What's going on?"

She finally gave in, the awkward position they were both in and the way they had to lean toward each other over the center console forcing the issue. "It's the angle I'm sitting in. I'm twisted just enough that the baby has easy access to my ribs."

"Why didn't you say anything?"

"It wasn't a problem until the cute little alien woke up."

"Calisthenics time?"

"Apparently."

The baby kicked again and she finally gave in, twisting so that she faced forward. At the same time she shifted the little one just enough so that the kicks met something other than bone.

"Can I?" She looked to her left and saw the eagerness that painted his face. "Can I feel?"

"Sure." She took his hand and placed it against her stomach, the baby actively performing for its audience.

"That is amazing."

"An amazing mood killer." She didn't want to be resentful. She was well aware parenthood came with a lifetime of moment killers. It was the price you paid for the amazing little human entrusted to your care.

But did it have to start already?

Something flickered in Nikolas's eyes, now a deep green as they reflected back at her inside the darkened car. She couldn't quite name the emotion, but she saw something. It was only when he leaned in closer, contorting himself so that he had to move his body completely over the center console, that she sensed his intention. Once again his mouth met hers, his tongue a hot brand against her own.

And once again she responded in kind, her body shockingly sensitive to his touch.

They stayed like that for several long moments, mouths fused as the kiss played out in glorious, vivid color, his palm still pressed against her fetal soccer player.

Long minutes later, when they were both breathless, he finally lifted his head. "I don't think the mood was killed at all. Do you?"

A FEW HOURS LATER, Nikolas couldn't sleep and had opened his laptop for company. It had been late when they'd arrived home, and despite wanting to spend more time kissing Nova, he'd figured retreat was the better option.

Especially because it was killing him to think about her, asleep just down the hall. Not that he'd act on it, but that didn't mean he wasn't thinking about it.

Damn, but what a roller coaster. She had been thrown several significant curve balls over the past forty-eight hours and had managed to dodge, bob, weave and all around field them like a pro. He was awed by her and not just because he was attracted to her.

A fact he was increasingly coming to grips with because there seemed to be no other alternative.

The light knock on his home office door pulled his attention and, as if he'd conjured her up, Nova stood in the doorway. "I couldn't sleep."

"Me, either." He gestured to the small love seat up against the wall beside the desk. "Have a seat."

She was still wearing the same outfit she'd worn to the Triple R, suggesting she'd spent the past hour in her room, as wide awake as he was. "What are you working on?"

"I wanted to look a bit more into Micheline Anderson and the AAG."

"That creepy place."

"Yes."

"Is it wrong to realize that while I wanted to know my birth family, if that place is part of it I think I might have been better off not knowing?"

"Unfortunately, all I have for you is my good ol' special brand of honesty. Homegrown and easily dispensed."

He got the requisite smile out of her at that before she added, "Lay it on me."

"There's no way we can put that genie back in the bottle."

"Succinct as always."

"I'm your man."

The easy humor between them fled as his words sunk in. It had been a joke, but after their make-out session in the front seat of his car, it hit a little too close to the truth.

He was increasingly thinking about being her man.

Which was ridiculous and stupid and likely a sign he should pack her up and send her over to the Triple R to stay with her aunts, just like they'd offered.

"Did you find anything?"

"Not much. I've reread the background on the place and I looked up some of the tax filing information, as well."

"What did you find?"

"They seem legit. They'd gained some real favor a few years back but that's faded. Even though they're not really in vogue any longer, the worst I could find was a few snarky comments about them on social media."

"And that's hardly a sign of anything."

"No, it's not. If a post isn't snarky, is it really a post at all?"

Nova eyed him. "Is that sort of the same as a 'tree falling in the woods' philosophy?"

"You bet."

Nova leaned her head back against the sofa. "I remember those days. Playing on social media and reading whatever the latest drama was that someone got into. It's been a while and I guess I have to say I really haven't missed it."

Her comments brought back home to him what she'd lived with for the past five months since leaving New York.

"You've given up a lot."

Her eyes popped open and, in that moment, he saw some of Ace's features in the set of her mouth and the shape of her eyes. "Not as much as some."

"I'm not talking about some. I'm talking about you."

"I guess I did." She stared down at the belly that both defined her and seemed to add a goddess-like, ethereal quality all at the same time. "But he or she is worth it."

"Or course they are. It still doesn't change the fact that you gave up a lot."

She laughed and he didn't miss the sharp edges. "Do you know what I was thinking in the car? Before, when we were kissing?"

"That I was a god among men?"

He got another laugh at that, noticeably softer this time. "About the baby, I mean." When he just waited for her, she continued on. "When the baby started kicking, interrupting us, I thought, geez, kid, could you just give me a few minutes to myself?"

"And I bet the baby kicked even harder."

"Pretty much. I mean, this is my baby. All I have in the world, and I thought something like that."

"You're going through a lot of changes. That doesn't make you a bad parent-to-be. It makes you human."

He knew it was coming—he'd sensed it from the moment she'd stood in the doorway—but it was still something of a surprise when her smile drooped and Nova fell into copious, weeping tears.

He moved to sit next to her, wrapping his arms around her and pressing her head against his chest. "Go on. Let it out."

Her emotions whipped high and strong and her small fingers clutched at the front of his shirt as she cried. Although he didn't know every reason for her tears, he knew quite a few and so he just settled in to wait out the storm.

And remained oddly grateful that he was the one she trusted enough to break down in front of.

"I'm sorry for that." Her voice was quiet and muffled against his chest, but her tears had subsided to a series of soft hiccups.

"Why are you sorry?"

"Because the front of your shirt looks like you just came in out of a downpour."

"I'll dry."

"Ferdy never liked—" She stopped at that and he waited, curious if she'd keep going. It was only when she let out a small sigh that he knew she was ready to share. "Ferdy didn't like tears. And it was okay because I've never been a big crier anyway. But there, in the first few weeks of my pregnancy, before I even knew I was pregnant, I was crying a lot. Hormone central, really."

He let her talk, and tell him of an afternoon on the couch watching an action movie her jerk ex wanted to watch, when she'd started crying.

"And he was all like, what the hell are you crying about? And that only made me cry harder."

Nikolas had never considered himself a particularly violent person. He knew how to take care of himself, but his glib tongue and easy smile usually got the job done far easier and without any bloodshed. His or anyone else's.

However, in that moment, picturing her curled up on a couch watching some bloody, gory action flick and then being reprimanded for showing any sort of emotion, Nikolas would have gladly gone several rounds with the bastard.

He continued stroking Nova's back, glad he could give her some comfort in the midst of an emotionally stressful situation. But it was only when her hands went slack against his chest, a sign that she'd drifted off to sleep, that he finally spoke.

"He doesn't deserve you. He never did."

NOVA WASN'T SURE how long she'd slept but when she woke she was curled up on the big couch in Nikolas's living room and there was a blanket over her. Which was a far cry from the small love seat she'd fallen asleep on.

Or the strong chest she'd fallen asleep on, for that matter.

Sitting up, she glanced around. A light burned over the stove, giving enough glow to extend to the living room that she could see by. Other than her shoes, which were set neatly against the base of the couch, she was fully dressed.

A light still spilled out of his home office and it drew her. She padded to the door, still in a sort of hazy waking state, and still curious about the time.

So it was a surprise to walk in and see Ferdy's face smack in the center of the large monitor Nikolas kept above his desk.

"What are you doing?"

Nikolas glanced up. His shadow of a beard had grown darker over the past few hours, giving him a dangerous, roguish look, but it was the sharp glint in his eye that really stopped her. She shifted gears, no longer curious to what he was doing and very concerned that something had happened. "What's wrong?"

"I've been looking up your ex. That guy is serious trouble and I haven't even found the really incriminating stuff. All I've been able to hunt up is innuendo and suggestion."

"Where'd you find him?" She moved closer into the room, her gaze fixed on the monitor. It was strange to see Ferdy's face again after so many months of only seeing him in nightmares.

"You'd be amazed at some of the dark holes those in less savory businesses deal in."

"The dark web? What Harley Watts used to send the message to the Colton Oil board?"

"You know what the dark web is?"

"I've read at least a thriller a week for the past months. Yeah, I know about the dark web." She perched on the edge of the love seat. "How much time do you spend on the fringes of the internet?"

"As little time as possible, but I do use the tools at my disposal and this is one of them."

"I had no idea you were such a rebel."

Although she'd meant it as a joke, the comment came out a bit more pointed than she'd intended.

"I wish I could tell you my life was squeaky clean, but I deal in a shadowy area. I'm not law enforcement, which gives me some latitude that the law doesn't have. At the same time, I live with the knowledge that the law doesn't have to go easy on me if I break it."

"A shadowy middle ground."

"It is."

Since going on the run from Ferdy, there were moments when Nova felt she'd lived an entire lifetime from the day she overheard him in his office. But sitting here with Nikolas, she acknowledged something else.

She could divide her life with Mustang Valley as the reference—before and after coming here. She'd initially believed it was before and after Ferdy. Or before and after pregnancy. Or even before and after her mother's death. And all of those things were momentous.

But there was something here. Something in finding her way to Arizona that had truly changed her in irrevocable ways even more profound than her circumstances.

Did that mean she was finally where she belonged? And if she was, didn't she owe it to herself to make a full break? To find a way to solve her past and put it behind her.

"Can you find out more? In any of the databases you use?"

"Find out what?"

"Things about Ferdy. His work. His criminal associates."

"If he hasn't been arrested for a crime it's going to be harder. We may be able to make up a sort of panel of known associates if we dig hard enough. Try to find dirt across all of them and make a connection." Nikolas quieted, his gaze never wavering off her. "What you overheard in his office will be a necessary piece."

"To put him away?"

"Yes. And to get someone to listen to you. They have

to have some sort of reasonable proof that the man did something. A group of unsavory friends doesn't quite do it."

"I know."

And she did know. Way down deep, it was that knowledge that had haunted her since the day she walked out of his office, so careful to keep her steps breezy and light. So determined that anyone who'd seen her would think she was simply out for the day and had popped in to visit her boyfriend.

But she knew that there would come a day when it would all catch up to her. When the need to do what was right was going to have to outweigh her personal safety. Because she didn't just suspect him or think the worst.

She *knew* the worst.

"Can we start small? A few places where I can refamiliarize myself with his life and see if anything comes back to me."

"What did you have in mind?"

"I was thinking about our conversation earlier. About social media. For all his potential bad dealings, Ferdy loved being out and being seen around town. Maybe there's something there. Someone he took a photo of."

Nova had already considered the events she had attended with Ferdy. He was always glad-handing someone and he loved any opportunity to have his picture taken for a photo op.

Would one of those give them the answers they needed?

"No discretion, eh?" Nikolas asked. "Being that public with his less savory friendships."

"I think it's a real possibility. Besides, if he thought he had things set up so he wouldn't get caught, he wouldn't think to worry about a photo op here or there.

But between that and what you're digging up, we may be able to put him with some other bad actors."

"It's worth a try."

"Of course, I'm assuming he and I are still connected on social media. If we are I can nose around to my heart's content."

"You want to give it a try?"

Now or never.

"Yeah, I do. I'd use my phone but I've deliberately kept it off for fear of being tracked."

"Log in via desktop. I know it's old school, but it still works."

Nikolas stood up and gestured to his seat, giving her room to maneuver at his laptop. She sat down and placed her hands on the keyboard, surprised to realize how easily it all came back. Her password was one of her easier ones and she logged in. Several hundred notifications waited for her in the upper corner of the screen.

"Wow. You can tell I've been away for a while." Nova glanced at the notifications but ignored them. She'd look through them another day.

"You've had reason to be."

"Okay. Here goes." She tapped Ferdy's name into the search bar, pleased when a small check confirmed they were still "friends."

She immediately went to his photos section, scanning for anything she might recognize as a function or a group of people.

Nikolas gave her room to work, setting a pen and notepad beside her, and she quickly became lost in the exercise. He'd done a lot over the past few months. Images of him in a tux filled several thumbnail photos and she clicked into several, curious to see if anyone else was tagged in the image.

Most of the pictures were of him or him and a date. Shocked that the photos didn't upset her more, she kept on clicking, searching for something she could use.

And then hit the motherlode.

"Here. Look here." Nikolas was already off the love seat and leaning over her shoulder. "These people. I don't know them but I recognize them from being around. The first time Ferdy and I met, he was talking to these people before he introduced himself to me. And this one." She tapped a man with white-blond hair and vivid blue eyes. "He's been at functions. He's distinctive and hard to forget. He also has an accent. It's charming—" She broke off, memories of a long-forgotten evening springing to mind. "Only it's not. It's sort of harsh underneath, as if he's sizing up everyone and everything around him."

"Is it tagged?" Nikolas leaned over her shoulder and hovered the mouse over the photo. No name popped up but he took a screen grab of the image. "We'll see what we can do with that."

The warmth of his body enveloped her as he tapped a few commands to save the photo. Even though Nova knew she was tempting fate, looking up Ferdy and somehow putting her intentions into the ether, she couldn't deny that it felt good to act.

To find some way to put the nightmare behind her.

It didn't seem so bad with Nikolas at her back, his large body shielding her from harm.

THE CALL CAME at 3:10 a.m. Ferdy rolled off the slut he'd picked up at a club the previous night and read the name on the screen.

Wally.

The bitch was so blitzed out on pills and booze she'd never hear him, so he didn't bother closing the door as he walked naked into the living room. "This is Adler. It better be good."

"Oh, it's good." Wally launched right in. "I found her. She logged into a new device to check her social media. Who'd have thought the one password you knew would actually pay off. It pinged me as soon as she logged in, confirming the IP address and making sure she was legit on a new device."

Yeah, Ferdy thought. Who knew? He might not know much about the tech mumbo jumbo, but he understood what an IP address was. And he very much understood how you could use it to find a real one.

"Where is she?"

"Arizona."

"Where?" he asked, already envisioning their reunion.

"Mustang Valley, Arizona."

Chapter Fourteen

Nova and Nikolas got into a rhythm over the next week. She'd found a part time job with a small boutique on the main drag of Mustang Valley and spent her days there while Nikolas went to his office. The time in the shop was so affirming, connecting her with her old skills and helping her feel productive again.

All within a few storefronts from Nikolas's office.

She'd also begun a tentative relationship with Marlowe. The new mother had invited her over for a late lunch at the end of Nova's first week in the shop. Marlowe had talked about Reed and her pregnancy. Nova had been able to ask questions and chat with Marlowe as if they were friends, which meant more to her than she could have ever imagined. It also made her realize just how alone she'd been these past months, experiencing her pregnancy almost in a vacuum.

"You sure you don't want to move into the Triple R?" Marlowe asked. Her kindness was evident in her smile, even as her head was bent as she stared down at her nursing son.

"It feels wrong, somehow. Especially since the test results aren't back yet."

Although the Coltons wielded considerable influence in Mustang Valley, they hadn't been able to force the issue of the DNA test due to a large, rush job project that had come down to the lab from the state. The lab promised to work as fast as they could, but by the last estimate, an answer was still at least a week away.

"We can help you, Nova." Marlowe's voice was gentle, but shot through with the implacable steel Nova had come to associate with the woman.

Nova smiled at that but kept up her steady refusal. "Besides. With the way your family has been coupling up lately, you'd think you all would be way more focused on minimizing outside distractions."

Marlowe did laugh at that, color high on her cheeks. "Bowie and I can find any number of ways to distract ourselves. I don't need to give that gorgeous man one more excuse."

The conversation was funny and easy and Nova was already considering how she was going to work up to her next question—about getting her stylist business going locally—when Marlowe dropped one more *distraction*.

"So you and Nikolas. Is anything happening there?"

"Oh. Well, we… I mean, um, we—"

Marlowe interrupted her, leaning as far forward as the infant on her lap would allow. "So something *is* happening. I knew it! Ainsley told me to stay out of it, but I knew I was right."

"No, really Marlowe, nothing is happening."

Those dark eyes that knew how to command a boardroom bored full force into her. "Nothing at all?"

"I thought Ainsley was the attorney?"

"It's in the genes." Marlowe waved a breezy hand. "Spill. You like him—that much is obvious. And he likes you, too."

"You think so?" Nova heard the unmistakable notes

of hope in her voice and quickly tried to put the ki-bosh on it. "Because he's just helping me. Really, we're friends."

"Friends." Marlowe actually sighed. "I think I used that excuse for a while with Bowie." She smiled down at her son, a beatific smile on her face. "And you can see how that turned out."

"Yes, I can. And there's one small difference. On top of how you both feel about each other, that baby *is* Bowie's son."

Nova hadn't realized just how much that fact weighed on her until the truth spilled out.

"Oh, honey." The teasing vanished entirely from Marlowe's voice, replaced with a feminine understand-ing that went to the heart of the matter. "Do you hon-estly think that matters?"

"I didn't think so. And most of the time I *don't* think so," Nova said. Her child was not either less than or some sort of burden to be borne. "It's just that every time I question if there could be something between us, I can't help but feel that it's a lot for Nikolas to take on. Here he was, a little over a week ago, a carefree bachelor. And then I came along and sort of dropped into his life."

"Life does sort of work that way. The things we can't plan for, and all."

"I know. But is it fair to add on having designs on the man? I've got a large set of responsibilities on my own. And it's just—" Nova exhaled heavily, frustrated by the wishy-washy answer that simply was *not* her. "It's a lot for a guy to take in, is all."

"Don't you think Nikolas is capable of making that decision for himself?"

"Of course he is. I just don't see why he'd want to."

"Nova Colton!" Marlowe's voice shot across the room. It was the first time she'd actually heard anyone formally address her as a Colton and Nova's head snapped up at Marlowe's bark. "How dare you say that."

"I—" Nova tried to hold off the tears but no matter how hard she tried to stare upward and swallow hard around the lump in her throat, the tears were faster. She'd have blamed it on hormones but there were no amount of hormones that could make up for the shot of warmth that bloomed in her chest. "No one's ever called me that."

"My mother was a champ at calling me by my full name when she was upset and challenging me on my bs." Marlowe's voice was gentle. "I thought I'd give it a try."

"Reed's in for quite a ride in another ten years."

"You bet he is."

Nova laughed through her tears. "You're a bit of a nut, you know that?"

"Yeah. But don't tell anyone. I sort of like my reputation as the scary head of Colton Oil."

"I won't."

And she wouldn't. Because some way, somehow, in the midst of the chaos that was currently her life, Nova had found a friend. Despite all her confusion over Nikolas and her future, Nova took heart from that simple fact.

She wasn't alone.

NIKOLAS MADE THE last turn out of town to head up to the AAG. He nearly missed it, he was so wrapped up in the voice coming through the speaker in his car.

"Come on, Spencer. You can't be serious."

"When am I not serious?"

Nikolas knew that for the truth, the MPVD sergeant one of the most serious and dedicated cops he knew. "So you definitely think the AAG is a cult?"

"Yes. All this ridiculous good day stuff is like a sign. My team and I have had them on our radar for years but that marriage institute seminar Ainsley and Santiago attended added more proof. The members of the AAG are brainwashed. And when we do get our hands on one of them they stay locked up tight as a drum."

"Like Harley Watts," Nikolas pressed.

Spencer sighed, but didn't question where Nikolas had gotten his information. "Exactly. The man's not talking."

Although much of what he'd uncovered so far suggested the same, Nikolas still wondered how the AAG had stayed off of everyone's radar for so long. Heck, they'd even come into town a few months and played key roles in helping the recovery efforts after the earthquake that had hit this part of the state.

Loony and a little brain-washed, sure. But an actual cult?

"Look, man," Spencer said. "Just be careful. I'm not crazy about you being there either, for the record. But I also know I can't stop you."

"I'm not working against you."

"Yeah, I know. It still doesn't mean I have to like it."

"How about if I promise to fill you in after my visit?" Nikolas asked.

"Deal."

Nikolas disconnected the call as he drove up the long, sweeping road to the AAG center. For all the initial welcome, including the friendly face at the front gate and the pretty rose bushes that flanked the entrance, things changed quickly as you drove further inside.

Despite the flowers and seeming look of warmth and welcome, the campus had a compound-like feel. It made Nikolas think of Nova's comments about the incongruity in the ad. That inconsistency played the same way on the actual property.

He'd spent the past week, in between looking into Ace's whereabouts and giving Selina ongoing updates, figuring out his approach to Micheline Anderson. Spencer had reluctantly given his help and Nikolas knew much of that was because he actively worked to be a good partner to the MPVD. Spencer Colton didn't pull any punches and if the man was looking for a way to catch Micheline Anderson and her enterprise, Nikolas knew he needed to be careful.

Because something rang false about the AAG's owner and founder and it was time to find out why. Was it because she was the former Luella Smith? Or was she simply a bad seed who'd become conveniently tied to the mystery of Ace Colton's birth? Since wondering about it was all he'd managed to do, Nikolas figured it was time for action.

If he could get a DNA sample from Micheline while he was at it, he wasn't above trying.

He'd called earlier that day to schedule his appointment and had stuck as close to the truth as he could. Yes, he was a private investigator with a practice in Mustang Valley. He was investigating the disappearance of a local resident and he believed there may be a connection with said resident and Micheline.

What he hadn't expected was to get an invitation for that afternoon.

Again, was it brazen and brassy? Or stupid and misguided? Or did the woman really have nothing to do with what was going on down in town?

All questions he hoped to find answers to.

One thing he hadn't questioned was the desire to keep Nova out of her orbit. They'd discussed it, and despite the fact she'd initially wanted to come along, she'd reluctantly agreed to stay away. He wasn't above using the baby's safety as a bargaining point to force the issue but it hadn't come to that.

If Micheline was playing a dangerous game with Ace's history, the last thing she needed was to know the man had a daughter and a soon-to-be-born grandchild in the mix. He'd gotten the added reassurance from Nova that she would stick close to the Coltons while he managed the rest of his investigation and it gave him a tiny measure of comfort that she was being looked out for and watched over.

Even if you should be the one watching over her.

That small, insistent flicker of desire hadn't left him, even though he'd done his level best to avoid being too close to her as they'd settled into a routine together. But he hadn't been able to do anything with the steadily growing need to protect her and the baby.

Nikolas filed it all away as he walked into the AAG. It was time to put his game face on, and mooning over Nova and her "little alien" as she liked to refer to the baby wouldn't do. Even if he'd increasingly taken to calling the baby "little alien" in his mind, as well, and thinking about what the kid would look like when he or she arrived.

He'd even caught himself searching online for a crib and baby furniture the other night after she'd gone to bed.

Focus, Slater. Scary self-help guru now, baby shopping and imaginary diaper duty later.

A woman at the front desk greeted him as he walked

in. He took in the wide-open, well-lit lobby and the sayings of affirmation, like "Life your best life" and "Your drive for spiritual enlightenment starts here," that lined the walls. He even saw a sign that read Keys to Your Happiest Life, with ten daily affirmations written beneath it.

While he wanted to give the place some credit—anything that tried to help people find the strength within should be applauded—there was just something so palpably false about the surroundings. The pseudo psychology seemed overdone and the environment was so calm and sterile as to suggest a brightly lit funeral parlor.

"Welcome to the Affirmation Alliance Group. How may I help you?"

The voice belonged to a pretty blonde who manned the front desk of the center. She had bright blue eyes that made Nikolas think of an angel and her smile was equally warm and bright.

Nikolas moved closer to the desk and put on his most professional smile. "I'm Nikolas Slater. I have an appointment with Ms. Anderson."

"Micheline is in a session right now. Can I get you anything to make you comfortable?"

Nikolas could have sworn something dark flashed in those baby blues as the woman took his measure, but it was gone as quickly as it came and all he was left with was the vague sense of having been flirted with. Which was silly because she'd not moved from her place behind the desk, nor had she touched him. And she'd hardly said anything suggestive. And yet...

He shook it off. Whatever was going on in this place, he'd come with a set of expectations of bad dealings and fake facades, and it wouldn't do to add a layer of paranoia on top.

"I'll wait then, thank you."

Nikolas moved away from the desk and kept his gaze on the welcome center. He made a show of reading the various affirmations but was also using the time to get a gauge on the building's security. He could see several cameras positioned in various corners, ensuring anyone who entered would be recorded.

Once again, not something to overtly get concerned about. Businesses couldn't be too careful and closed-circuit cameras were a way to ensure they had a solid record should anything happen on their property.

The blonde moved up beside him, her big eyes wide as she spoke. "I'm Leigh. Leigh Dennings."

"It's nice to meet you, Leigh. Nikolas." He extended his hand to shake hers, allowing his hand to linger briefly on hers. The move was subtle and not overtly creepy, but when she gave him a broad smile, it reinforced that sense that she was lightly flirting.

"Why don't you come with me, Nikolas? While you wait." She gestured toward the large affirmation poster he'd seen when he walked in.

"This is what we're all about here at the AAG. Here. Let me show you." She extended a hand and pointed, game show style, at the list of ten affirmations that ran from top to bottom. "Everything is about being your best self. Living your very best life."

"That's wonderful to hear. And a noble cause, too."

"Oh, yes. Micheline is such a guide for all of us. She teaches us all in her ways, encouraging love of self as a pathway to love of others."

Although his initial impression had been that the pretty Leigh was relatively sharp, he was starting to wonder. She did not quite match the description of the spacey AAG woman Nova had met in the parking lot, but there was definitely a bit of brainwashing going on here.

"How long have you been a part of the AAG, Leigh?"

"Two years."

"And before then? Are you from Arizona?"

"I don't talk about the time before then." For once he heard something other than blind devotion in her tone. Disgust? Fear? He heard both when she spoke once again. "I'm a different woman now."

Nikolas sensed that focusing on Leigh's time before coming to the AAG would shut her down, and he needed the opposite. "It sounds like you found your home here."

"Oh, I have. I most certainly have."

An image of his strong-willed mother filled his mind's eye, and in the back of his mind he heard her teasing voice. *My silver-tongued boy. You always know just what to say.*

He'd never hoped for his gift to work more than at that moment. "You look very familiar to me. Do you spend much time in Mustang Valley?"

"I was named Miss Mustang Valley."

"That's where I recognize you from. What an honor to have been chosen." Nikolas leaned in, his voice conspiratorial. "They certainly picked the prettiest girl."

A small blush colored her cheeks, but instead of reacting naturally to the compliment, she kept up those robotic answers, saying, "The honor was mine."

The hand she'd settled on his forearm as she walked him to the affirmation poster was still there, and once again Nikolas had the subtle sense she was flirting with him, even though there was something stilted and off about her attempts. He might've thought her out of practice, but that wasn't quite right, either.

It was as if she did know how to flirt, yet was holding herself back.

"Well, now that you've received such an honor, I'm sure the modeling gigs will quickly follow. I suppose you'll be leaving here soon."

The hand dropped from his arm. "I would never do that. I would never leave Micheline."

"But I thought winning Miss Mustang Valley was one of the ways you were being your best self?" He feigned confusion. "It's an honor."

"It is an honor. But being my best self happens here."

Leigh stared at him once more, and Nikolas wasn't sure if he was being sized up or if he'd frightened her with the idea that she could leave if she wanted to. Perhaps both?

"Well, then I guess that is the AAG's gain, and Mustang Valley's loss."

The stiffness in her body faded, and she relaxed back into the conversation, her hand once again going to his arm. "What brings you here today to the AAG?"

"I'm afraid I can't share the purpose of my visit with Micheline."

She leaned in, her lips near his ear. "Oh, come now. Won't you tell me?"

It was the first full-on flirtation he'd gotten, and Ms. Dennings didn't disappoint. She was close enough that her hair whispered against his cheek and her breasts brushed lightly against his biceps.

"I'm afraid I can't. Client confidentiality and all that."

She put on a pretty little pout. "Well, I guess I can accept that reason."

"But maybe you would let me take you out sometime?"

Throughout his career he had never really gone much

for false behavior such as this—limiting it only to times when it was absolutely necessary to get information on a case—but there was something different about this time.

In this instance, Nikolas just felt bad.

Was it because he pictured Nova, waiting for him at the end of the day?

While she had a lot to do with it, he admitted to himself that it was something else.

There was something about *this* woman that bothered him. It continued to nag at him that there seemed to be some aspect preventing her from leaving. It set off his antennae, and he wondered if, when this was all over, there would be a way to get Leigh some help.

The woman's seeming blind devotion was concerning. While Nikolas had no interest in actually taking her out, he would see to it that she got support if they truly uncovered bad practices up here. And based on Spencer's intel, it looked like there was no way Micheline was innocent of what happened behind the scenes in her center.

"Leigh."

Another voice suddenly speaking her name had Leigh standing up straight and putting a bit of distance between the two of them. "Yes, Micheline."

Nikolas turned to see a tall, sleek woman come toward them. She looked to be in her mid-sixties, with a sweep of blonde hair that capped off her trim figure in another one of those power suits. "I understand my guest is here."

"This is Mr. Slater, right here with me. Let me introduce you."

Nikolas was walked back toward the front desk,

Leigh's hand still in a proprietary place on his fore-arm, as if she were afraid he'd float away.

He took the gesture in kind, keeping his smile broad and even, as if he was enjoying the feminine attention. As covers went, playing the roguish playboy rarely went wrong.

And it had the added benefit of an easy dismissal when confronting a calculating woman.

Go ahead, Micheline. Assume all you want that I'm no threat.

Nikolas was careful to keep his gaze bland, adding one last leering grin for Leigh before she turned him over to the AAG founder.

"I understand you made an appointment to see me, Mr. Slater. Something about a case."

"Thank you for seeing me on such short notice."

"What would you like to discuss?"

"I'd prefer to discuss my business in your office."

If she still thought him a clueless playboy, the press for privacy noticeably had her reconsidering. She wasn't shy about giving him the once-over, her gaze hard, be-fore a warm smile was back in place as she nodded her head. Without any further comment for him, she turned to Leigh. "Mr. Slater and I will be in my office. Please see that we're not disturbed."

Hurdle one cleared.

Nikolas followed Micheline to her office, glancing at more of the silly posters on the walls. Micheline seated herself behind a large desk, her crossed legs visible be-neath. She was an attractive older woman, with a strong bearing about her. As he stared at her, taking in both her facial features as well as her overall body language and position, Nikolas couldn't help but wonder if this was Nova's grandmother.

Nova was much smaller, her petite frame more of a match to the photos he'd seen online of her mother instead of what he knew of Ace Colton. But that didn't mean there weren't other resemblances.

Their eyes appeared to be the same shape. And there was something in the shape of Micheline's face that suggested a similarity to Nova's. It wasn't a complete stretch to see a resemblance. In fact, once she began talking and he observed the movements of her hands and the set of her shoulders, it wasn't a big stretch at all.

She reached below her desk and he heard the distinct open and close of a small fridge. "May I offer you a water, Mr. Slater?"

"Thank you." He nodded, inordinately pleased when she pulled a bottle out for herself, as well.

After handing it over, she started in. "I must be honest, this is something of a surprise. I'm rarely visited by private investigators." Her smile remained serene but there was nothing but flinty resolve in the set of her shoulders and the hard granite of her gaze.

"I realize my visit might be a bit of a surprise. But I was hoping to talk with you about Ace Colton."

The granite never wavered, nor did the semi-smile that hovered about her lips. The only clue he had that she'd even responded to the name of Colton was the subtle tightening of her fingers against each other, where she had them clasped in front of her on her desk.

Point Slater.

"Another curiosity seeker, are you, Mr. Slater?"

"Excuse me?"

"I think you're well aware of my meaning. The Coltons have been harassing me for the better part of six months, convinced I've got something to do with what's happened to their oldest son."

"Don't you?"

"How or why would a humble businesswoman like me have anything to do with a powerful family like the Coltons?"

"A lot of people feel differently on the matter."

"That doesn't mean they're right."

Point Anderson.

"There are rumors that you worked at Mustang Valley General during the time Ace Colton was born."

Once again, she remained completely calm, her demeanor showing no sign of faltering. Nor did she make any move to open the bottle of water. "It's hardly a rumor. I was a caregiver before opening my center. I make no secret of that."

"Under a different name."

She waved a hand. "Names are a tie to the earthly plane, nothing more. Our spirits are bigger than names. Bigger than labels."

Nova's continued press about the incongruity of Micheline's image in the ad struck him anew. He'd only been in her presence for a matter of minutes, yet here was a woman who knew what she was about and who understood the role she was playing.

Flawlessly.

"I appreciate your distinction, but I'm referring to the earthly plane at the moment."

"What a waste."

Nikolas ignored the interjection and pressed on. "Didn't you have a son when you worked at Mustang Valley General?"

"It's no secret I have a son. It's an unfortunate reality that he and I are estranged."

"Why?"

"Jake left home at seventeen. He and I have had very limited interaction since then."

"So you basically haven't spoken to your son in twenty-three years?"

Micheline's mouth dropped into a frown and it was the first crack in the serene, powerful image she seemed determine to portray. "I find it curious you know so much. I'm afraid that once again, I'm feeling rather harassed by your visit and your line of questioning."

"I'm sorry. It's important I get answers for my client."

"I'm quite sure whatever answers you're seeking won't be found here."

"Maybe yes, maybe no. Harley Watts also worked for you."

"Harley who?" Micheline's smile was broad, her stare devoid of any recognition, but Nikolas would have bet his next year's salary she knew exactly who he spoke of.

"This isn't that large of a place. Surely you know all about the IT guy. You know the one? Recently arrested and even now sitting in a Mustang Valley jail cell?"

"I'm afraid I can't comment on the personal lives of my employees. Even the ones no longer working here."

Before he could question her further, Micheline was up from her desk and moving around the office. One by one, she pointed toward various affirmations, rattling off a personal story about what she'd learned from that particular phrase and how living by that had changed her life and those of the AAG members.

She was both entertaining and riveting, and in the act he could see how she'd done well for herself with the AAG. Nothing quite seemed to touch her. No suspicion of guilt. No accusation that would stick. Nothing seemed to penetrate the veneer of wellness being paramount.

It was fascinating, really. And in her impassioned

speech he could see why she'd done so well with her business. Whatever else the AAG was—and he was already envisioning his report back to Spencer, free of charge—there was an enticing sales pitch here that had clearly captivated a lot of people for a very long time.

It was strange, certainly, yet at the same time, he recognized the act for what it was. A woman in the midst of self-protection, ensuring the dangers of the world remained at bay.

Wasn't that what his mother had always done with his father? Taken him back so that she wouldn't have to face the real ugliness of going out on her own.

Was that living?

Because suddenly, Nikolas had to acknowledge that he made similar choices. His weren't about safety as much as about self-preservation. He'd watched his parents' marriage combust on a powder keg of emotion and betrayal.

And he feared to ever risk himself in the same way.

Which said volumes about him and his own view of the world.

And which also kept him from giving fully into his feelings for Nova.

It was that knowledge that had him abruptly standing. The sudden movement and obvious end of the meeting added another crack in Micheline's façade. Anger skirted the edge of her gaze as she stared at him from across the room.

"Mr. Slater? Is something wrong?"

"Not at all, Ms. Anderson. I won't waste any more of your time. I've gotten all I came for."

The whirling dervish that had moved around her office in a rush of restless energy stilled. "And what was it you came for?"

"The truth."

Chapter Fifteen

"And what did she say then?" Nova had enjoyed the story, laughing throughout a late lunch in his office as Nikolas regaled her on his time with Micheline. She had hung on every last word of his story on the visit to the AAG, a mix of shock and humor lacing her questions.

"She said that she hoped I found inner peace."

"What a strange woman."

"Pretty much, but what else could she say?" Nikolas dug a piece of garlic bread out of their take-out bag as Nova finished grabbing plastic forks and knives from the second bag. "It was clear she wasn't going to answer my questions about Ace."

"Or working at Mustang Valley General."

"Exactly. But it does reinforce the discussions I've had with Spencer. Even if Micheline Anderson isn't part of this situation with Ace, she should be watched. Carefully."

They settled into their seats in his office, using his desk as a table between them.

"Did you get any DNA?"

He finished chewing a bite of garlic bread. "Nope. She pulled out two bottles of water as if she'd have one with me, but never opened hers."

"Damn it. That would have been the smoking gun right there. Then we'd know."

"Which she has to know, too. If she is the one behind the switch in the hospital, *and* she was in the medical field, she'd have to know how easy it would be to do a DNA test."

Nova let out a huge sigh as she spooned some baked ziti on her plate. "I just hoped you'd get something out of her."

"I did meet one of her followers."

"Oh?"

"The woman who mans the front desk. She gave me the same sort of brainwashed vibe you got from that woman in the parking lot."

"I sense a but in there."

"Well, yeah. She seemed brainwashed, but not nearly as spacey as you described your girl. It was like there was this other person trying to get out."

Nova's gaze narrowed. "What other sort of person?"

"A normal, red-blooded woman."

That gaze widened once more before Nova slammed a hand down on the desk. "Oh my God! You flirted with her!"

"I didn't—" Nikolas felt the wash of flame sneak up his neck and onto his cheeks. "I mean, I didn't—"

"You so did, but that's beside the point. Did it work?"

"I'm not sure."

"Why not?"

"Micheline came out and that was the last I saw of Leigh Dennings."

Nova dug into her meal, her gaze thoughtful. "That's one more thing about that place that just does not make sense."

"*One* more?" Nikolas asked, emphasizing the number. "Try about a million, with the most damning of all coming from the Harley Watts email to Colton Oil."

Nikolas had worked the email angle on his own, digging deep ever since Marlowe and Ainsley had shared his name at dinner. While Watts came up squeaky clean on any background checks, his reputation was pretty solid in some of the darker corners of the internet. The guy knew how to work a keyboard and Nikolas had found a few references to his hacking skills before he must have joined the AAG.

And then his former employer had clammed up, too, claiming she had no idea who he was.

"You know what I mean. It's like everything about that place is an image distorted by a warped mirror. Everything looks right until you look too close."

It was a great description and once again reinforced the way Nova's design mind thought in images and pictures. He realized that he'd shortchanged the work by not tapping into that.

"I want you to look at something later for me," Nikolas said.

"What is it?"

"I pulled up a bunch of details off the AAG website. A brochure in pdf form as well as a few images they have posted. You might see something I can't."

"Okay."

They settled into companionable silence, just as they had for the past week, and Nikolas thought again about that baby furniture he'd looked at online. She was less than two months away from delivering the baby and they were both going to need a permanent place to stay. Marlowe had taken Nova to her doctor a few days before, and despite the length of time between her last checkup and this one, the obstetrician was pleased with her pregnancy and the baby's development.

Things were moving along. And somewhere along the way, he'd begun to take an incredibly proprietary view toward Nova and the baby.

A view toward something more permanent.

Funny way of showing it, Slater. You haven't even kissed the woman since last week.

But he'd wanted to.

Before he could carry that thought to its logical conclusion, the door in his outer office slammed open. Belatedly, Nikolas realized he hadn't locked it after the food delivery arrived. He got up to deal with whomever was there.

And came face-to-face with a seething Selina Barnes Colton, who strode toward him on sky-high heels that set off a pair of killer legs.

"Just what do you think you're doing?"

Nikolas stared down the formidable woman. She was still incredibly attractive, her marriage to a much older Payne ensuring she'd become rather rich at a young age. To all who knew him, Payne was much happier with his third wife, Genevieve, a woman who was both closer in age and temperament.

But it was Selina who'd made her mark.

"What can I do for you, Selina?"

"You can get off your ass and get my case wrapped up."

"I've called you every day to keep you apprised of the progress."

"You've called me every day as a CYA and I don't appreciate it."

Nikolas knew a ranting client when he saw one so he gave her the space to complain, waiting until she'd gotten her litany of perceived sins out. She'd nearly finished when her gaze sharpened on the entrance to Nikolas's office. "Entertaining?"

"I have—"

He never got out "company" because Selina was already marching into the office, her voice rising several octaves as she caught sight of Nova. "Why is *she* here?"

"Excuse me?"

Although Nikolas knew how to placate a client, he wasn't going to stand for anyone mistreating Nova. He was about to say as much when Selina whirled on him once more.

"What are you playing at, Slater? Who is this woman? I've already seen her twice this week hanging out with my stepdaughters."

"Ex-stepdaughters, you mean?" Nikolas clarified.

Selina ignored the distinction. "I've seen this woman with Marlowe and Ainsley. Who is she and what are you doing with her?"

There was no way in hell he was giving up the news that Nova was likely Ace's biological daughter, so he sidestepped the question completely. "This is my friend, Nova Ellis. She's new in town and I introduced her to Marlowe and Ainsley."

The screech subsided to a mild roar. "That's awfully convenient. You have a *friend*," Selina spat the word, her feelings on Nova's status more than clear, "and you decide to introduce her to Ace's sisters. That's an awfully large conflict of interest, don't you think?"

"I thought you hired me to investigate Ace. Not your stepdaughters." If Selina wanted to play the family card, he'd toss it right back at her.

"*Ex*-stepdaughters. And my point is valid. Where are your loyalties?"

"To the truth."

Whatever Selina was about to say vanished, her jaw snapping shut at his point.

"We are both looking for the same thing, aren't we?" Nikolas pressed.

"Of course we're looking for the same thing," Selina finally agreed.

"Then perhaps you'd like to know more about my visit today to the AAG."

For her part, Nova remained quiet throughout the exchange and didn't seem to have any need to interject into the conversation. And with the dangling opportunity to hear more about the AAG, Nova might as well have been invisible to Selina. "Of course I'd like to know more."

"Why don't we continue our discussion in the outer office?"

Nikolas filled Selina in on his visit and the continued concerns that the AAG wasn't what they seemed.

"You know I have little regard for that 'be your best self' stuff. Why does someone need to pay some organization to find that?" Selina huffed.

"Everyone finds their own way in their own time." Nikolas wasn't about to dismiss those who didn't have the shark-like instincts of Selina. "What I'm more concerned about is that you knew there was an email sent from an AAG member, yet never told me."

Selina's smile was reminiscent of that shark as she stared back at him, innocence personified. "That's why you're the best, Nikolas. You're so good at finding all the clues and I didn't need to betray my knowledge of a highly confidential matter involving the Colton Oil company."

As strategies went it was a smart one and, once

again, a reminder not to estimate Payne Colton's second wife.

Which led him to his final area of concern. While he'd been open to whatever this case threw at him, there was one piece that had increasingly bothered him.

"Maybe you can answer one more question for me."

"I'll answer what I can."

Cool, calm and vague. Yep, she was a business executive all right.

"There's still the matter of the gun found in Ace's apartment. Ainsley and Santiago have been working on that matter, as well as the MVPD. It's moved Ace up on the suspect list."

"Which is exactly the reason I wanted you to investigate him in the first place. The goal here is to determine who shot Payne."

"I'm well aware of that. But there is something about that gun I can't quite wrap my head around."

"What's that?"

"A gun is magically discovered under Ace's floorboards and suddenly you show up at my door asking me to investigate the man. You didn't have anything to do with putting it there, did you?"

That calm, cool visage crumpled as Selina began to laugh. "Oh, Nikolas, you do have an imagination."

Nikolas didn't see what was so funny about any of it and held his ground, not even cracking a smile. "In my line of work, I like to think about it as considering all the angles."

Selina's laugh continued on, but she finally sensed that he wasn't laughing with her. "You're serious."

"As serious as the coma that still has Payne Colton in its grip. And equally as serious as ensuring the wrong man doesn't go to prison."

"That is why I hired you." Selina moved up closer and laid a hand on his cheek. "You are a sweet young man. And I can promise you this. I might not have any deep, abiding affection for my former stepson, but I didn't frame him or set him up. If he tried to do in poor Payne, that was all his own doing, not mine."

Selina laughed again, shaking her head. Her hair was still perfectly styled around her face but she'd laughed hard enough to make her mascara run. She ran the tips of her fingers under both eyes, wiping away the last vestiges of tears. "You are thorough. It looks like I made the right choice after all."

Damn straight you did.

Only he didn't say that. He waited until she collected her purse and shot one last glance toward his office door. Then she turned on her heel and was out the door as fast as she'd sailed in.

Nikolas was still processing the visit when he heard a soft voice behind him.

"Whatever possessed you to take a job for that woman?"

Nikolas turned to face Nova. "It's *my* job. People hire me to find answers."

"Yet you didn't tell her who I am."

"That's not her business to know."

Nikolas knew he played a dangerous game. He'd known that since Nova walked into his office and told him who she was. He'd believed himself well able to manage the conflict between Nova's identity and Selina's case, but he was forced to again question that belief.

He'd dodged a bullet today, but he suspected Fate had several more loaded in her gun.

It was about time he started to accept the distinct possibility that he was going to have to face down one of them.

FERDY WATCHED THE high-heeled woman hightail it out of the PI's office twenty minutes after she'd stomped in. He wondered who she was, but after the quick visit, chalked her up to a client, nothing more.

He'd been watching the place for a few days, surprised by how easy it had been to run down Nova in this little Podunk town. The IP address Wally had tracked down had paid off, and he'd found the condo complex his IT whiz had triangulated. A day watching the comings and goings at the complex had easily produced Nova, her head peeking above the dash on some old car.

She looked good. He hadn't seen her full-on yet but that face staring out over the dash was prettier than he remembered and she looked happy.

Too bad she wouldn't be for long.

He'd had a long time to think about what he'd say to her and, for starters, he wanted some damn answers. Why'd she leave and what did she know?

The town was a piece of work. He'd driven it from one end to the other, trying to find the right place to drag her for their little conversation. He needed some room to work and privacy and, most of all, a place to dump the body once he was done. There was a small park near the end of town that he thought would work but he wanted one more look at it.

He also needed to figure out who this PI was.

It was clear Nova was shacking up with him. Had she told him what she knew about Ferdy or had she tried keeping it all to herself? He wasn't opposed to killing

the bastard but he needed to minimize his presence
and two bodies got even more notice than one. People started connecting the dots with two bodies and he
wasn't interested in having any of those dots lead back
to New York.

The boss had finally given him a decent opportunity to prove himself again and he needed to get home.
Much as he'd have liked to stick around and play with
Nova for a few days before he got out of town, he had
work to do.

And in the end, dead was dead and that was all that
really mattered.

He settled back into his seat. The piece of crap sandwich he'd picked up at a convenience store was a far
cry from one of his beloved subs but he ate it anyway
to keep up his strength. Once he got back to New York
and managed the next job shipment coming in, he could
dine on an eight-course meal of caviar and steak if he
wanted.

Right now was a means to an end.

He unwrapped the sandwich, the scent of oil and vinegar wafting back at him. He bent his head to take a bite
and when he looked back up, he saw the door opening
again to the PI's office.

The guy walked out first. Tall, dark hair, solid
build. He wasn't heavily muscled but Ferdy figured he
wouldn't go down easy. Nor did he think this one would
be easily lured into the woods like that recent job in
New York. One more reason to find out what she'd told
him and how much he knew.

He reached for his phone to take a picture when Nova
stepped through the door.

The sandwich in his hands fell, splattering oil and
vinegar all over his slacks, but Ferdy didn't notice.

All he saw—all he *could* see—was the large mound of her stomach that preceded her out the door. The PI held the door for her and he didn't miss the way the bastard looked at his woman.

And for the first time in five months, Ferdy had an idea of just why Nova had run.

ONCE AGAIN, NOVA was forced to consider another facet of Nikolas's life she hadn't expected. This whole job with Selina Barnes Colton had her wondering about the realities of his work.

He'd proven himself to be a good guy. She didn't question that.

Not one single bit.

But his job did involve a strange, shadowy place she still couldn't fully understand. Nor could she fully comprehend how he seemed more than comfortable with living and working in those shadows. Which, she acknowledged to herself, was a bit hypocritical, based on her history with Ferdy.

But this wasn't about her. It was about Nikolas and whether or not she was comfortable with his choices.

"You're quiet. Everything okay?" Nikolas had helped her into the car and then come around to his own side. It was only now, as he started the car, that Nova realized just how loud her thoughts felt, closed up in such a small space.

"I'm thinking."

He smiled, but even from just looking at his profile as he pulled out of his parking space and navigated the traffic, she could see that it didn't reach his eyes. "You've been thinking ever since Selina showed up."

"You said the reason you didn't tell her who I was is because it's not any of her business."

"Because it isn't."

She'd been thinking about it since the woman came screeching into Nikolas's office, seeking answers.

"Did you mean what you told her? That you wanted the truth?"

"That's my only goal. I don't take on cases to hurt people or to ruin their lives."

"But what if that's a by-product?"

The drive through Mustang Valley didn't take long and they were nearly to Nikolas's condo. "Is that what you really think of me?"

"No, I don't. And that's the problem. I'm trying to reconcile the man I've come to know with the private investigator who takes on cases for horrible people."

"I'm sorry if you think Selina's horrible but you're going to need to get used to her. She's part of the Colton family, no matter how hard it is to understand why Payne's kept her around."

"But she believes my father is guilty."

"Which is why I'm working to find the truth. I don't believe a planted gun is sufficient evidence that he did Payne harm."

"And you don't think the fact he ran is proof, either?"

"Not really. Like I told you before, I can work in the shadowy areas law enforcement can't. I'm going to keep digging because the more time I spend on this the more I lean toward the 'Ace Colton is innocent' column."

"Are you just saying that to placate me?"

"I'm saying it because I want the truth."

Nikolas pulled into his parking spot and cut the engine. He shifted his attention fully toward her. "Nova, look, I realize that it's something of a leap to take me at my word, but hear me out."

"Okay."

"I realize that my job has something of a duality

in it. Right and wrong aren't nearly as clear-cut in my world as it is in law enforcement and, as I told you before, that gives me some leeway in working my cases. What it also means is that to be the man I want to be, I can't ever forget that."

"I understand. It's just that…" She let her words fade off, not sure if she should say what she really felt or keep dancing around the truth of the matter.

She wanted him. But she couldn't quite get past the fact that she'd leaped quickly with Ferdy and was now paying the price.

Was her judgment off when it came to men?

Or could you question some of the things a person did because you wanted to better understand them, yet still care for them?

Because she wanted him. And she wanted to know that he wanted her in return. Not because he felt sorry for her. Or because she was a stepping-stone in his case investigating her father. Or even because she was handy.

That he wanted her. That he saw *her.*

As if sensing she stood on a precipice, Nikolas suggested they move inside, and she agreed, following him toward the elevator. Their ride up to his apartment was quiet and she kept wondering if there was an easier way to say what she wanted.

No, Nova amended to herself. What she *needed.*

Nikolas unlocked his door and gestured her through and Nova went straight to the kitchen, getting herself a glass of water.

"Nova, are you okay?" Nikolas followed her in.

"I'm fine. Good. Just thirsty. Would you like something to drink?"

"I'm good." He stood at the counter, staring at her as she drank down the glass of water.

He waited until she was finished before he pressed.

"Are you sure? Because I get the feeling there's something you want to say to me but you're holding back. I'm good with what I do for a living. I can handle your opinion and not break."

"That's not what I'm afraid to tell you."

"What are you afraid of then?"

She set the glass on the counter and walked over to where he stood. Moving in close, she placed her hands on his chest and stared up at him. She knew she took a risk and she also knew that in a few short months her life would change yet again with the baby's arrival. But now. Here. She just wanted to take something for herself.

Just for herself.

"I'm afraid that this will all be over soon and I won't get a chance to tell you how I feel."

"Nova, I—"

She stepped up on her toes and pressed her lips to his, effectively silencing his words. She didn't want rejection right now, even though she knew he was well within his rights to give her one.

Only…

She'd caught glimpses. Since that very first day together, she'd had moments where she would swear he felt he same. Where the heat in his eyes was all for her. Just for her.

It was the hope from those small flashes that beat in her chest now.

His fingers were gentle but firm on her upper arms as he held her still, pulling back from the kiss. "Nova, I don't want to take advantage of you."

The hazy fog that had wrapped around her at their kiss lightened. "Advantage? But that's not how you should feel."

"How should I feel? You're here. Under my protection and pregnant. What else would you call it?"

And that was when Nova heard it. The very thin thread of control that he was hanging on to. It wove through his voice, quavering low in his throat, and Nova knew exactly what to do.

"I want you. Me. Nova. The woman. Not pregnant Nova. Or on-the-run Nova. Or illegitimate-Colton-daughter Nova. Just me. The woman who wants to be with you."

"I'd like that." He swept the tip of his finger over her forehead, pushing away a lock of hair before tucking it behind her ear.

"Make love to me, Nikolas. Please."

That tender look faded, his hazel eyes going wide. "Can we? I mean, I don't think that we. Um. Well, it's just that—"

He stopped and Nova couldn't hold back the light giggle that rumbled up in her chest. "Yes, I can do that. We can do it together. In fact, it's good for me."

"Excuse me?"

"Most pregnant women are lucky enough to get regular sex. It's healthy and normal."

"Oh. Wow."

"It doesn't gross you out?"

The confusion that had lit his gaze only moments before faded, replaced with something she couldn't quite define but would happily look at every single day for the rest of her life.

"Not at all. And don't you even think it. Not for one single minute."

And she wouldn't.

She had far more pleasurable ways to spend her minutes.

Chapter Sixteen

Nova followed Nikolas down the hall to his room, her body humming with anticipation. She wanted this. Wanted him. But now that she was faced with the chance to have exactly what she wanted, she was suddenly attacked with a case of shyness.

Although she'd peeked into his room in passing through the condo, she'd never actually walked in. The masculine furnishings were impressive, the large wooden furniture dominating the room.

She wasn't a total innocent, but as she looked around, collecting herself, she had to admit another truth to herself. She hadn't actually had sex since she'd found out she was pregnant. Ferdy hadn't been her first, but the sex had begun to taper off after those initial halcyon days when they were first together and getting to know one another.

She'd obviously gotten pregnant, the outcome of a broken condom from an old pack in her bedside drawer, but they'd only had sex a few more times after that. After that she'd been so sick during the early days of her pregnancy that she'd begged off several events.

And then she'd gone on the run.

So here she was. With a new man and a body she

wasn't entirely sure what to do with. All the bravado she'd had in the kitchen faded at that reality.

"What is it?" Nikolas moved in close, the top few buttons of his shirt open at his throat where she'd managed to undo them on their walk to the bedroom. Dark hair was visible through the open shirt and she wasn't sure she'd ever seen anything sexier.

"Nova, if you want to stop, we'll stop. Now or any time."

"I don't want to stop."

At the clear concern, Nova remembered her exchange with Marlowe that morning.

Is it fair to add on having designs on the man? I've got a large set of responsibilities on my own. It's a lot for a guy to take in, is all.

Don't you think Nikolas is capable of making that decision for himself?

It struck her in that moment just what Marlowe had meant. For all the responsibility she'd faced over the past year, very little of it had been the result of factors within her control. Because of that, she'd learned to control the things she could around the chaos. Her life. Her attitude. Even the slow and steady drive west had been another act of taking charge of her life.

It was fine to take responsibility for her own life, but in learning the lesson, she needed to do the same for others.

And assuming Nikolas didn't know what he wanted was a bad place to start from.

"I don't want to stop at all."

He smiled down at her before bending his head and murmuring against her lips. "I don't want to stop, either."

True to his promise, he didn't. From the slow drift to the bed, their clothes coming off one fascinating piece at a time, until the point he laid her down on top of the covers, Nova felt as if she were in a dream.

An erotic, amazing dream, but a dream all the same.

Had she ever been with anyone who so innately knew what she needed?

As each piece of clothing fell, his hands found more of her. She thought she'd be embarrassed when her bra finally came off and all of her swollen, heavily pregnant body was exposed, but he only stared down at her in wonder. For a moment, his hands settled on her stomach and she saw that wonder take on new shape and dimension before he looked back up at her.

The baby had quieted after dinner and wasn't moving, but she felt the connection. The protection he offered them both and his amazement at the new life that grew inside of her.

And then the moment shifted once again, the focus back to the two of them. Nova reveled in how he made her feel. Tentative strokes grew stronger as he asked what she liked and she responded with the truth in a mix of breathless moans and the laying of her hand over his to show him the exact spots that felt like heaven beneath his hands.

He spent long moments on her breasts. Always a sensitive part of her body, she felt herself nearly falling over the edge from just the play of his tongue and hands against her flesh. And then he shifted, touching that most intimate part of her and Nova shattered, flying into a million pieces as he coaxed her response.

On a hard cry, she let herself go, safe in the knowledge there was nowhere else she wanted to be.

Nikolas held Nova close as the last of her orgasm whipped through her. He supposed he hadn't quite believed her when she'd said that sex was good for pregnant women, but now that he looked at her, her color high and a healthy glow suffusing her cheeks, he had to admit she knew what she spoke of.

It was humbling to realize all the body could experience. And where he'd been worried he'd have a difficult time making a distinction between the woman and the baby she carried, it has been incredibly easy—natural, even—to focus solely on her.

Even as he took caveman-level satisfaction at her climax, he knew he needed to hold himself in check. She was learning what her limits were and he was figuring out how much he could press and push and coax to bring her pleasure.

Which made the sure, steady hand reaching out to take him in her palm that much more of a surprise. "Nova. We don't have to…"

His words faded as pleasure shot through him, lighting him up even as his body tightened in anticipation. He laid his hand over her, stilling her movements before she finished a show he wasn't even sure they should kick off.

And then she was kissing him, the same goddess he'd watched take her pleasure shifting focus to give him the same. Whatever potential anxiety he'd had about them being together faded at the explosive desire that ripped through his body.

Had he ever felt like this before?

In that moment he could no more conjure up the image of any woman who'd come before her as he could remember a time he didn't feel this way.

Such was Nova's power over him.

And how startling to realize that he wouldn't have it any other way.

"Please, Nikolas." She whispered against his ear, her voice breathy. "Let me."

In the same way he'd trusted that she'd tell him if there was something she didn't like or want, he trusted that she'd continue to know her own mind and could manage what she felt comfortable with.

A cool breeze blew through the windows he'd left open that morning before leaving and Nikolas relished the way that air coated his skin, slick with sweat and hot from what built between the two of them.

But it was her whisper against his mouth as they kissed that notched that heat several degrees higher. "I want you. All of you. Now."

He nodded and extended a hand toward his end table and the condoms he had in the top drawer.

"We. Um. We don't have to if you're, you know, okay." Nova's eyes widened. "It's not like I can get more pregnant. And I've been to the doctor. Once I found out about Fer—" She stopped as if unwilling to say her ex's name in bed. "Well, let's just say I made sure I got tested for everything. So I'm good."

He'd always made it a personal practice to do the same, both in safe sex and in ensuring his ongoing wellness, and smiled down at her. "I'm good, too."

"So, you know, if you want, we can skip the condom."

"I'd like that."

While he had no issue with her pregnancy—if anything, she was even more desirable than he could have imagined—her size did ensure they would need to maneuver a bit differently. Shifting so they lay facing each other, Nikolas pulled her close, placing her leg over his hip.

"I believe this is the position the sex manuals call 'beached whale.'"

Despite the sensitivity of the moment and the cliff his body hovered over, Nikolas couldn't stop the rolling laughter. "Oh, they do, do they?"

She smiled back at him, impish sparks filtering through her green gaze that was hazy with passion. "I believe so."

"I have to say it's a first-time position for me."

"Me, too."

He settled himself at her entrance, his body straining to be inside of her. He bent his head to kiss her, lingering over her lips. "A first I've no doubt I'm going to love."

Nova's arms came around him, her soft sigh echoing between them. It was only as Nikolas entered her body, the culmination of the intimacy and connection they'd had from the first, that he realized something else.

He'd been right about loving being with her.

But it was only in that moment, as the movements of their bodies pushed them both over the edge of pleasurable oblivion, that he knew he actually loved *her*, too.

NIKOLAS WAS STILL getting used to his new reality— and the idea that he was in love with Nova—the next morning.

He'd rolled over to pull Nova close, marveling in his mind how he'd fallen so hard and so fast—only to run his hand over a cold fitted sheet. She'd been up for a while if the bed didn't have any remaining body heat and he was about to go look for her when his phone rang.

"Slater."

"It's Marlowe. The lab called this morning. They've got the results."

"I thought it was going to be another week."

"They had a break in what they were working on and rushed the job."

"Did they tell you?" Although he'd gotten used to the idea that Nova was Ace's daughter, the test would be the final piece of proof they could all rely on.

"No. They insist on giving the news to Nova in person. And as the father's family member authorized to get the results, I have to go with you."

"What time can you be ready?"

"I'm already ready." Her smile telegraphed through the phone lines a buoyancy he'd rarely heard from Marlowe Colton. "But how about if I meet you there at ten?"

"See you then."

Nikolas dragged on a pair of jeans and padded out to the kitchen. Nova wasn't there and he almost called out her name when he found her in his office, seated at the laptop.

"Hey."

"Hi." Her big green eyes seemed to suffuse her face and she offered him a shy smile. "Good morning."

Even with making love twice more the night before, Nikolas recognized the signs of some morning-after apprehension. Unwilling to leave her with another moment's concern, he walked over to her and bent to press a kiss to her lips. "Good morning yourself."

He lingered over her, amazed at how easy it all was. He'd never gone in for the whole commitment thing and owned that he was more than gun-shy based on his father's ill-advised example, but he never expected it would be so easy to get past it all. Apparently a lifetime of behavior didn't have to dictate your future.

Especially when someone came along who was more than enough.

That was what he'd never understood about his father's behavior, Nikolas realized now. His mother was a wonderful, loving woman. A truth Guy Slater acknowledged whenever he spoke about his late wife. Yet something had still kept him looking, always keeping one eye out for the bright and the shiny.

And never realizing that what he had was bright and beautifully shiny all on its own.

Nova was that. All of that. Warm and beautiful.

And absolutely wonderful.

While he might feel that way, he wasn't sure if she was ready to hear it all. So he focused on her instead. "What are you looking at?"

"I've been thinking about your conversation with Micheline. I know it seems like a long shot, but I wanted to look through any interviews she may have given or any other photos there may be about her. See if anything sparks." She chewed on her lower lip, her gaze dipping to the computer screen. "And honestly, I was curious to see if I could find any resemblance."

"That's a good idea." He moved in closer and couldn't resist leaning in to kiss her once more. "On both fronts. Although I think I've got a better idea, and it doesn't involve an internet browser."

She smiled at that and lifted her lips to kiss him back. "I like how you think. But I do have a question for you."

When he only nodded, she smiled and said, "Is there a reason I keep getting retargeted with baby furniture ads?"

"Hmm. That's interesting."

"I thought so, too. It's happened ever since I pulled up an internet browser."

There was a part of him that knew he should feel a little embarrassed, yet he couldn't seem to find it. He cared about her. Based on his revelation the night before, he even loved her. And he loved the baby. He'd already begun to think of them as a threesome, just the way he'd observed Marlowe, Bowie and Reed together.

"Let's just say I wanted to be prepared. And maybe, in the course of that preparation, I've done a little browsing online."

Her teasing smile faded, her brows knitting together. "You do know what you're asking, right? A brand-new baby is a lot to take on."

"I know."

"It's a lot to take on when you plan for it. It's a whole different matter when it's with someone you barely know."

"I know that, too." He bent down and pressed a kiss to her forehead. "But I also know something else."

"What's that?"

"I'd like you to consider moving in here. More, I'd like you to consider staying with me. Bringing the baby back here once it arrives. I'd like you both to live with me."

She stood, pulling him close into a tight hug. "Oh, Nikolas. That is so much to offer. It's amazing, but it's so much."

He hugged her back, pulling her tight against his chest. He wanted it all so badly—more than he could've ever imagined. "Is that a yes?"

"Yes!"

He hugged her tighter, and in the process bumped a few files off his desk. He bent to pick them up so she wouldn't inadvertently trip on them, and set them down to restack later, his steno pad down on top.

Her gaze drifted, and he saw the moment she took in what was on the page.

Consider man named Ferdy.

"Nikolas? What is this?"

"My to-do list."

She leaned a bit closer. "It's dated the day we met."

"Yeah." He sensed they were on dangerous ground, but he had no idea why. "What's the matter?"

"Why would you have written this down? About Ferdy? Why'd you put him on your to-do list? I told you that we needed to be careful and discreet. Heck, at that point I hadn't even told you about Ferdy other than a slip of his name at dinner."

"I know. And I didn't do anything about it. I had written it down because I wanted to make sure I remembered it."

"And you didn't look up any information? Then? Before I told you everything."

Wherever he thought this conversation would go, the immediate flare-up wasn't it. Particularly since they had just been wrapped up in each other, envisioning their mutual future. "Nova. What is this about?"

"It's about the information I trusted you with."

"Yes, and I handled it properly. I made notes to myself, and that's all I did."

He saw her gaze waver, shooting back to the notepad, before shooting back up to him. "So that's your answer, right there? Like it makes everything okay."

"Excuse me?"

"Just like yesterday. With Selina. You're perfectly comfortable operating in those shades of gray."

Selina? What did any of this have to do with Selina? Nikolas felt himself being backed into a corner and all he could do—all he could think to do—was go on the offensive. "A point I have been honest with you about from day one. Further, I gave you full disclosure of my work and my caseload when you still had every right and opportunity to walk away."

"That's right. There you go, practically with your hands up and your voice all smooth and easy, like there's no problem at all."

"From my point of view, there isn't."

"I guess we'll just have to differ on that."

Nikolas had no idea how the conversation had gone so far sideways. Especially from nothing more than a few scribbles on a notepad.

"The reason I came to find you is because Marlowe called. The lab has your results back and we need to meet her there at ten."

"I guess I'd better go get ready, then."

"Yeah, I guess that's a good idea."

She slipped away from him, exiting the room without turning back. Not only didn't he understand what had her so upset, he was equally unable to understand where he was the bad guy in all this.

He hadn't betrayed her trust. And the fact that she couldn't see that stabbed a pretty big hole in his own.

THEY'D BEEN TALKING about baby furniture. About moving in together. About the future.

How did it all go so wrong?

Nova felt like she carried some blame for it, only she couldn't take back what she said. Nor could she change how she felt. Nikolas did operate in a shade of gray. He also knew how to use that silver tongue of his to make it all work out okay.

But was that so wrong?

As they drove toward the lab, Nova couldn't stop asking herself that question.

Nikolas made no pretension about who he was. He'd been up-front from the moment they'd met and he'd acted properly toward his current client in what he shared.

Even the day before, as he'd talked about the visit to the AAG, he was careful to relay Micheline's behavior, but not its bearing on his investigation.

So what was it? What had her spooked?

Was it just seeing Ferdy's name, so starkly written in Nikolas's scrawled handwriting? Or was it something else?

Something that had everything to do with an incredible night spent in his arms and an overwhelming case of emotion she wasn't entirely sure what to do with.

He'd asked her to move in. He'd looked at baby furniture. He wanted the baby.

Weren't things moving too fast?

Just like with Ferdy.

Maybe that was what seeing his name in black-and-white had really meant.

She'd made a mistake once. What happened if she did it again?

The lab was a nondescript building in a Mustang Valley business park. As she looked at the low and squatty structure, she couldn't believe that the entire course of her life would be decided from within its walls.

Which was both silly and oddly profound, she thought as she worked her way out of the car.

Nikolas had pulled them up to the building's portico to drop her off, the parking lot nearly full at that hour. Over the past week he'd taken to coming around and opening the door for her, and while she really wanted to stand her independent ground, her stomach was getting too big to argue the point.

She held his hand as she got out and was oddly buoyed when he clung an extra few seconds before dropping hers.

Maybe the morning hadn't been totally unsalvageable.

Maybe.

"I'll just go park and be right back."

She didn't say anything, just watched him walk back around the car and climb in.

Those black curls that captivated her so much picked up the slightest breeze and Nova thought about the night before. She'd spent the night in his arms. She'd touched every inch of him, as he had her. He hadn't seemed put off by her pregnancy. In fact, he'd told her how beautiful she was and how lucky the baby was to have her as its mother.

It had been tender and sweet and had brought a light sheen of tears to her eyes that he saw her wholly as a woman, yet appreciated and understood and even celebrated the life that grew within her.

"Damn hormones," she muttered as she dug out a tissue from her purse. Between the coursing hormones and the wild swings of emotion over the past week, she'd taken to shoving tissues in her purse each day, and now tugged at one of her stack. She'd inadvertently tossed her wallet on top of them and had to juggle her heavy purse to pull out the small scrap.

Her focus caught on the tissue, she wasn't paying much attention to the broader parking lot.

It was only as she pulled the tissue free that she glanced up, the sudden sound of a car engine and squealing tires registering somewhere in her mind. A large black SUV swerved madly through the parking lot. And as she watched in disbelief, seemingly safe on the sidewalk, she realized one other fact.

Despite the narrow confines of the portico, the SUV was headed straight for her.

Chapter Seventeen

Nikolas found one of the last spots in the parking lot and had jumped at it, lost in thought and the rote mechanics of parking the car. He'd gone over and over his discussion with Nova in his mind, replaying the words.

And the angry frustration that had characterized them.

He didn't want to apologize. Moreover, he didn't have anything to apologize for. He couldn't change who he was, nor was he going to offer excuses for his job. He was good at what he did, damn it.

Why should he justify his work choices?

All good questions but ones that had very little validity in the face of a frustrated partner who was scared and scarred by recent events.

Something he'd do well to remember.

Like a deflating balloon, his selfish anger faded. Yes, they'd still need to work through this. He was still a PI and there were still going to be cases she didn't like.

But…those cases weren't going to be the investigation of her father. Perhaps he could give a bit more credence to that aspect of the situation.

Focused on making it right, he continued walking toward the lab, oblivious to what was around him until he heard the simultaneous squeal of tires and Nova's scream.

Registering them both at the same time, he took off at a run. As he moved, the building seemed to get farther away instead of closer, and he took in the image of a large SUV bearing down on her small frame, the whole scene like a tableau.

One that was about to become grisly as she stood all alone on the portico sidewalk.

Nova's scream echoed in her head but as she stared at the SUV, nothing else but the noise seemed to register in her mind. A mixed sort of confusion gripped her, a mental cry between "what was happening?" and "move!"

Self-preservation finally won out as it became evident the SUV wasn't just out of control, but purposely bearing down on her.

And Nova ran.

As quickly as she could, she bent her legs to manage her center of gravity and raced for the front door. Unless the manic driver was determined to actually drive into the walls of the building, all she had to do was get to the door and get inside.

She'd worry about what came after once she got there.

With a tight hold on her stomach, she moved. The engine kept getting louder and louder, but she refused to turn around.

She just kept going.

Like the day she'd run from Ferdy's office, one foot in front of the other. Like that long drive to Arizona, one mile after another.

She didn't think or give herself time to second guess. She just moved.

Somewhere she registered shouting. She thought she

might have been the one screaming. But she ignored it all, her sole focus on those doors.

The squeal of tires echoed once more and the backdraft off the SUV as it drove by floated over her skin, blowing her hair around her face.

But it never hit her.

As her hand grasped the door handle, she turned to see the SUV swerving as it took the last curve of the portico at top speed. Lurching once again when it came to a sharp left out of the parking lot toward the street.

And then Nikolas was there, his arms around her and his lips pressed to her ear as he held her. "Are you okay?"

"I'm fine."

Physically she was fine. Whole and untouched, which meant the baby was whole and untouched.

Safe.

She wanted to take heart in that. And she wanted to believe that they'd *be* fine.

Only she couldn't get past the understanding that safety was an illusion and any safety she had felt was a thing of the past.

"That was Ferdy. I know it."

"How do you know? Did you see him?"

"I know, Nikolas." She turned toward him, fisting her hands into his shirt before resting them against his chest. "I know it."

"Shh now. We'll figure it out."

"He's here. He found us. Me and the baby."

THE MOMENT MARLOWE ARRIVED, Nikolas met her and got her settled with Nova in the lab director's office and then went off to find the security team. So close to the building, they had to have video of the area under the portico and he was determined to get a visual on Ferdy Adler and make sure the whole damn town knew to look for the bastard.

There was still a chance it was just a confused driver, but Nova's depth of conviction and his own view of how deliberate the move appeared had him falling on the same side she did.

Adler had found her.

How had it happened? He cycled through the past week. He'd managed every protocol he knew to work his searches. There was little chance an actual search would or could flag anyone's radar, so how had the man found them?

He'd been absent and out of her life for five months. Then, suddenly, Nova shows up here and he finds her?

No way.

So he'd keep looking. Keep trying to figure out how they'd tipped the guy off.

And he'd do everything in his power to keep Nova safe.

MARLOWE HAD TAKEN charge the moment she walked in, sitting with Nova in the director's office and calling for support from Colton Oil security.

"I'm just mad I didn't think of doing this before."

She'd berated herself since coming in, every comment some variation on that same theme.

"Marlowe. You couldn't know. How could any of us know?"

The truth was that they couldn't know. Couldn't know Ferdy would find her and come for her.

But how?

She thought about her credit cards, untouched in her wallet. The cell phone that was still dark and unused in her purse. She'd been so careful. She hadn't done anything that would have tipped him off or given him a way to find her. And find her so easily.

Yet he had.

Had Nikolas done something? One of his searches or requests for information.

Something dark settled in her chest as she ran that one through her mind. How easy it had been to leap to that conclusion. To assume it was him and the tools he used in his work.

And with that, their fight that morning came rushing back to her.

"What's the matter, Nova?" Marlowe asked.

"Me. Nikolas." She struggled to put it into words. She'd had a lot of time to herself these past months and had learned to keep her own counsel on absolutely everything. Did she dare let someone else in?

Ask for an opinion that wasn't her own?

"Nikolas and I had a fight this morning." Nova corrected herself. "An argument, really."

"I can see things have progressed for you two."

"They did. And I wanted them to. And then this morning, I messed it all up."

"I find that hard to believe but why don't you tell me."

She described the brief note about Ferdy. The concern that Nikolas had betrayed her and, more to the point, the concern that his job had those frustrating dark places.

"Look, I don't claim to be an expert on love. I am so grateful I found Bowie, but who knows what would have happened to me if he hadn't come along?"

"You'd have found some other person who was right for you."

A funny look came into Marlowe's dark brown eyes. "I'm not so sure about that. Bowie Robertson was hardly 'right' for me in just about every way possible."

"That's hard to see when you're together."

Marlowe shrugged. "Maybe so, but it doesn't change it. We were enemies from competing companies. We had different backgrounds and different paths in our careers. Moreover, we both saw the world through vastly singular lenses."

"Yet you found a way to come together." Although Nova more than appreciated the listening ear and the reality that no one's relationships were as easy as they appeared on the surface, she couldn't help but press Marlowe. "And you both make it work."

"All I'm saying is that sometimes there are other forces greater than us that bring us together. If I hadn't gotten pregnant with Reed... If that hadn't put Bowie and me together...maybe we wouldn't have found our way."

Although it didn't change her conviction that Marlowe and Bowie belonged together, her aunt's comments did give her some food for thought.

The forces of the world acted on you in a variety of ways. That didn't mean that they didn't or couldn't lead you to a wonderful outcome. In fact, sometimes it was the challenges in those forces that brought you where you needed to go.

Which was all well and good for the people who'd already found their way, but that didn't mean things would work out for her. She cared for Nikolas. If she'd allow herself to think the word, she might even admit that she loved him.

But she'd leaped too easily with Ferdy and was now paying the price.

She certainly didn't think Nikolas was a bad man, so on some level the comparison wasn't a fair one. And yet at the same time, her bigger fear was that the feelings she had now were something of a mirage. A shiny package of emotion that was nothing more than a box of glitter.

Quickly opened, and even more quickly dissipated.

Nikolas barreled into the director's office. "Come on down to security. There's something I want you to see."

NIKOLAS TOOK IN the authoritative stance of Spencer Colton, sergeant for the MVPD, his faithful K-9 companion by his side, and hoped like hell the man could work off the slim information they had in order to put out an APB.

Spencer and Marlowe hugged and then Marlowe made quick introductions between Spencer and Nova, giving the two of them a chance to finally meet. Spencer's work on Ace's case had kept him busy the past few weeks and he was one of the few members of the Colton family whom Marlowe hadn't yet wrangled for a visit to meet their newest family member.

His dog, Boris, also took an immediate shine to Nova. The canine seemed to sense her anxiety and had taken up a spot beside her, refusing to move.

"I'm sorry we're meeting like this, Nova." Spencer was calm and caring, but Nikolas sensed the impatience quivering beneath the surface. "Slater filled me in on what you think is going on but I'd like to hear it in your own words. Both what happened this morning and then everything you know on Ferdinand Adler."

Nova recounted each piece to Spencer. Nikolas had been impressed with the MVPD lead's help on the AAG situation, but his reassuring manner with Nova reinforced every good thing he'd ever heard about Spencer Colton. He asked questions confidently and without agitation, leaving them all with a sense that he had things firmly in hand.

"And you've had no contact with him since that day you left New York?" Spencer asked.

"No." Nova shook her head. "None at all. I've deliberately lived in a way that I'd be hard to find, too. No credit cards. No bank accounts. I've broken contacts with my former job and all friends. I ran and disappeared."

Until a few weeks ago.

Nikolas considered that, shocked to realize that the first moment Nova had attempted to put down roots, Adler had found her.

Spencer shifted everyone's attention to the large bank of security screens filling one of the walls of the room. After a few taps on the control center keyboard, images filled several screens. He'd preset several camera captures and various angles were up on screen. Although it was hard to see anything from the side of the SUV, the tinted windows obscuring the driver to nothing more than a profile, the last camera in the portico got a clean shot of the driver through the front window.

"That's him."

Spencer moved into action, directing one of his officers positioned at the door to put out the APB. "Confirm that we have every reason to believe the suspect is armed and dangerous."

FERDY HAD ALWAYS known that waiting to hear the sound of sirens meant you were too late. It was why he'd barely gone a mile from the squatty medical building when he dumped the SUV. He'd get farther on foot and he already had another car waiting for him in one of the parking lots in Mustang Valley. It was time to put the second part of his plan in motion.

He'd watched enough this week to know Nova would come back to town with that PI. He'd already set a little surprise for the guy at the office and once he sprang that, it wouldn't be hard to snatch Nova away.

And then he'd be done with her.

The baby had given him some pause, he wasn't gonna lie. The idea he might have a son was an awfully powerful motivator to keep her alive. At least until she had the brat. But in the end, he knew it was too risky. She'd formed some attachments here. Which meant people would be out looking for her and he didn't have time to wait around. He needed to get back to New York.

And what was he going to do with a baby anyway?

Nope. Better to make a clean break and be done with it all. She'd been a blip in time. A relationship that had taken a turn for the worse. End it all and start fresh. His future was way too bright to get bogged down in a past that had been nothing but trouble.

The sirens got louder before passing him in a blur, racing back toward the lab.

The police didn't seem to pay him any notice and that was by design. He had dressed in the same vacation gear he'd seen people around town wearing. Shorts and hiking boots as well as a T-shirt and hooded sweatshirt for climbing up into the cooler mountain air. A standard-issue backpack was slung over one shoulder, full of regular old hiking equipment. He'd bought it all a few towns away, satisfied that he'd look the part, even if he felt like a total loser. Who cared about this crap? He got all the fresh air he needed on a walk through Central Park and he had zero interest in climbing a mountain. But the hiking gear might come in handy. The rope seemed pretty sturdy and he was going to need something to keep Nova still. And the small pickax he'd picked up could make a wicked sticker if he needed extra backup for his gun.

While he'd like nothing more than to make her suffer, he simply didn't have time. He'd get the information he needed out of her, enjoy scaring her as he did, and then get rid of her.

Revenge was sweet, but the money and prestige waiting for him back in New York were sweeter.

It was time to get this done.

NOVA HAD TO give him credit, Spencer Colton didn't waste time. In less than fifteen minutes a bulletin was out for Ferdy's capture and his picture had been circulated within a fifty-mile radius. No one going in or out of Mustang Valley was going to get by without some serious scrutiny from the MVPD and Spencer had shifted his attention to manage the matter personally until Ferdy was caught.

What came after… Nova knew they'd deal with that, too.

Ferdy was now a wanted man and she'd shared enough detail to contribute to a warrant. She'd have to keep sharing that information, ultimately testifying to what she knew.

It was inevitable.

"You doing okay?" Marlowe had sat faithfully beside her while Nikolas and Spencer worked, taking it all in but saying little to interfere.

"I think I am. It's finally going to be over and that's saying something."

"You'll get this behind you and have a chance to

move on. To look forward to the baby's arrival and all that's still to come."

Although Marlowe didn't say it, Nova heard the rest of that sentence.

With Nikolas.

Was that possible?

She wanted to believe they'd find their way forward, but there were still so many unknowns. They had a lot to figure out and she wasn't above questioning if they could see their way to the other side. Marlowe had meant well with her comments earlier about how she and Bowie had found each other, and there was a small, hopeful part of Nova that believed she and Nikolas could find the same.

With that hope beating in her breast, she smiled at Marlowe. "We're here. Do you think we should look at the test results?"

"I think that's a great idea."

Marlowe had settled a large manila envelope on the security console beneath her purse and crossed to pick both up. "Here you go."

Nova stared at the envelope, well aware her future was inside those thin sheets of paper. The truth of her past was there as well.

On a soft sigh, she settled it all in her lap and called Nikolas over.

"What is it?" He was in that serious mode she'd observed when he worked, yet his eyes were soft as he stared down at her.

"It's time to find out."

He nodded. "It's time."

Nova opened the package, surprised to see how very few pages it must take to change a life.

And then read the truth.

TEST CONCLUSIVE. SUBJECT A AND B ARE
BLOOD RELATION, 99.9% CHANCE OF PAR-
ENT AND CHILD.

Parent and child.

Nova laid a hand over her belly, the truth of it all
settling in.

She was Ace Colton's daughter.

Her future had been decided.

NIKOLAS WASN'T SURE how to comfort Nova. He'd suggested they stop for some lunch but she'd shook her
head, uninterested in going anywhere public. Understanding, he then suggested they order in and go back
to his office to wait for news from Spencer.

Marlowe had offered to come along but Nova had
sent her on her way, directing her to spend time with
baby Reed. Nikolas hadn't missed their exchange and
something had cratered deep inside him when he'd overheard Nova's whispered goodbye to her aunt.

Hug him. Hold that sweet baby tight.

Those words had haunted Nikolas, proof that the
morning had fundamentally altered Nova's view of the
world. Up until now, every discussion of Ferdy had been
just that—discussion. But now, there was a reality that
had sobered them all.

And had made it clear how dangerous he really was.

Because of that, Nikolas didn't expect to see and
hear Nova's usual chatty countenance—and he well
knew they still had to work through the implications
of their argument that morning as well as the news of
Ace's paternity. Even knowing that, there was something in the wide-eyed ghost who sat beside him in the
car that cut him deep.

Since the first moment she'd come into his office, Nova had radiated vibrancy and happiness She was bright and warm and in a flash of a moment, her ex had taken that away from her. He'd even taken away the joy of her learning about her father.

Ferdy's intentions had been clear. Even if Nikolas hadn't watched it with his own eyes, the various views on the lab's cameras had shown it in multi-angle detail. That SUV was driven with the intention to kill Nova and her child.

Their child.

No matter how willing Nikolas was to embrace the child Nova carried as his own, the baby was biologically Ferdy's. A fact the man was obviously unmoved by, considering his actions.

Something cold settled in Nikolas's bones. He and Nova might have a lot to work out, and he might need more time to prove to her that his business wasn't an obstacle between them, but he would not let anything happen to her. More than that, he had no idea what he'd do if something happened to her.

Get her settled in your office, lock the doors and you can discuss it all.

Nikolas came around to the passenger side and helped her out, observing the same zombie-like visage in place as she stepped from the car. They moved quickly but she didn't let go of his hand and he held tight, pushing as much support as he could through touch.

In moments he had them both inside his practice, pushing through the door, then closing it and adding a firm snap of the lock. His office wasn't big and he could see through to his inner office. Something hovered in the doorway, and his attention was drawn to it immediately.

"What is it?"

"Sit here." He settled Nova on the sofa. "I want to look in my office. I'll be right back and then we'll call for some lunch."

She took a seat, her eyes downcast and tired, and Nikolas headed for his office. The flashes he'd seen were a line of sticky notes, several attached to his door-frame. He knew they hadn't been there before and as he moved closer to read the scratch on them he saw that there were several more, making an arrow to his desk.

Following along from the doorway to his guest chair to the top of his desk, Nikolas read the various messages. Words like *Information*, *New York*, *Investigation* and *Details* were all written, like a path leading him to his computer. And the last one had an arrow and was stuck to his laptop.

He'd followed them all, curious as to who had done this and why. Someone with answers? Someone working with Adler?

His natural determination to get answers had him moving to the chair, dropping into the seat to wake up his computer. It was only as he sat that he heard the click.

Adler stepped out from behind the door, gun in hand. "Boom."

Nikolas was nearly up when something registered in the words.

"I wouldn't move if I were you. Otherwise that fancy leather chair you're sitting on is going to leave a very large hole."

Heart pounding, Nikolas dropped his gaze to the

seat and saw the edges of something large wrapped beneath his chair.

Adler never even attempted a smile. All Nikolas could see was the steady, cold calculation deep in the man's eyes. "It's exactly what you think it is. And so long as you stay in that seat, it's not going to go off."

NOVA BELATEDLY HEARD the conversation, that familiar voice whipping through her with shocking force. The heaviness that had ridden her limbs since they left the lab shifted, uncoiling inside of her and moving her into action. Her immediate thought was Nikolas, followed quickly by running to get help.

But it was Nikolas's scream that had her moving.

"Run, Nova!"

Despite the heavy, distended weight of her body, she moved. Fumbling with the lock, she felt the dead bolt give way and tugged the door open, slipping through as fast as she could. All she had to do was get someone's attention. That thought kept her going as she pushed through the door, holding her belly as she ran, screaming for help.

Go.

Run.

Move.

The words were a litany in her mind. *Don't think about what's behind, just keep moving forward.*

Even if her heart was breaking because Nikolas was behind.

And then it didn't matter any longer as a heavy arm came around her shoulders, pulling her back abruptly.

Nova stumbled but before she could even get out a scream, big hands were over her mouth and the harsh scent of aftershave rose up in her nose.

She would have tried anyway—would have clawed and scratched and kicked to get her and the baby away from him—but it did no good.

The small prick flashed a shot of pain into her upper arm. His next warning was unnecessary as the hallway leading into Nikolas's office from the outer entrance increasingly swam before her eyes.

"Scream and you're dead. That means the baby, too."

Chapter Eighteen

It wasn't real. It couldn't be.

Only it was.

Just like that day, so long ago now, when she'd lain on the floor of Ferdy's office bathroom and listened to the words he spat at his business partner.

Words that had told her how guilty he was. And just what a bad man he really was.

Nova knew this was coming. Hadn't she expected it each and every mile since leaving New York? The growing child inside of her or the increasing distance hadn't made a bit of difference. Ferdinand Adler was always out there. Always lurking. Like a monster from her nightmares.

Only there was no waking up from this.

No magic set of words that would change the fact that she carried the child of a madman.

A madman who wanted both of them dead.

Pain swam in her head, the aftereffects of whatever he'd drugged her with. Her mouth was full of cotton, even as her bladder threatened to give way. She already visited the bathroom on what felt like auto-repeat this late in her pregnancy—however long she'd been out had only added to the urgency.

Maybe she could use it to her advantage.

She was tied up in the back of a car, her hands behind her back as she lay on her side.

"Beached whale" filled her mind once more, only instead of the sweet and funny connotation the words had taken on in her lovemaking with Nikolas, this time they did nothing but bring tears to her eyes.

She was helpless. And her child's life depended on all she could do in whatever time she had left.

She had to reason with him. Had to give him some way of understanding that she'd do anything to keep the baby safe. The rest could come later. Her Colton family would come for her.

Nikolas would come for her.

Assuming he ever got out of the office Ferdy had rigged with a bomb.

Good Lord, what had she wrought? Had she really been that desperate all those months ago that a few dates with this man had somehow had her seeing stars?

And how wrong had she been, to feel as if her relationship with Nikolas was at all the same. To even question that what she felt for him—the power of those feelings and the reality of all they'd shared—was at all the same.

She *loved* Nikolas.

And whatever she had felt for Ferdy—even before she knew about his behavior—was nowhere close to those feelings.

Some relationships worked out and others didn't. But going in with the best intention—and the assumption your significant other *wasn't* a violent criminal—were the sort of stakes it was worth gambling on.

Nikolas Slater was a good man. He'd shown her nothing but care and concern and bone-deep compassion since the day she'd walked into his office.

Why had she questioned a single second of it?

"Good. You're up. Took you long enough." Ferdy spoke through the open front driver's side window. He looked different than the last time she'd seen him. He'd traded a dark silk suit and black dress shirt for outdoor gear. It was an odd look on him and gave her the same sort of creeps as looking at that billboard of Micheline Anderson.

It didn't fit.

Just like he didn't fit here. Nor did he fit into her life.

She had no idea how long she was out but if she went by her bladder it had to be nearly an hour if not longer. "I'm up and I need to pee. Terribly."

He laughed at that, his eyes dark with menace. "You're not going to live long enough to care."

Nova had no idea how to play this. There simply was no charted territory called "negotiation with psycho ex." So she did her best to breeze through it and keep as much of an upper hand as she was able to, stuck on her side with her hands tied.

"I assume you want answers?"

"You bet your damn ass I do."

"Then you're going to need to let me up to go to the bathroom. Otherwise I'm going to make a mess of your car."

He seemed unfazed by the ask but shrugged and came around to get her out. He was rough as he dragged her inert form from the back seat but did relent and take the duct tape off her wrists. She breathed through her nose at the immediate sting but said nothing. She was going to do her level best to get out of this, but if for some reason it all went sideways, she'd be damned if she'd come this far in her life to end as a simpering fool.

"There's a bush over there." He gestured with his gun. "Stay where I can see you."

She said nothing, just marched over to the small wooded area he'd pointed to. It wasn't easy, but she found a way to position herself and hold onto the bush for support and found a way to take care of business. It also gave her time to think. Outrunning him wasn't an option. On a good day in her top fighting weight she'd have been hard-pressed to outrun him. He had at least eight inches in height and wasn't wearing the slick shoes he normally wore.

And she wasn't in top fighting weight. She was a seven-and-a-half-months-pregnant woman with a lower center of gravity and fat ankles.

"So bargaining it is," she muttered, pulled up her panties beneath her flowy maternity dress, tap-dancing as to what she might use to stall him and get him out of the woods.

She hadn't covered every inch of Mustang Valley, but based on the position of the mountains she sensed that she was on the east end of town. An area well used by hikers, if some of her local reading was accurate. She was torn between alerting someone for help and hoping no one came anywhere near their path.

She had no doubt Ferdy would shoot to kill anyone who got in his way.

She'd done as he'd asked and remained in his line of sight. As she tromped back toward him, she took in the sight of his large form, broad shoulders and bull-like physique.

Her only chance was to use brains against his brawn.

And hope like hell he fell for it.

NIKOLAS SCREAMED ON the inside as he did everything he could to move the process along. Nova's real screams still echoed in his mind and even though it had been less than an hour, all he could think of was the face of the madman who had her in his grip.

How had he been so stupid?

He knew Ferdy was after her. How had he let the man get so close? Close enough to strike at Nova and set a bomb?

"It's simple but effective." Marlowe's twin brother, Callum, lay beside the desk chair on his back, suited up in the same protective gear they'd had Nikolas put on, a flashlight in one hand as he went over the bomb. "Pressure set, so the moment you sat down it activated."

"And I let him lead me right to it."

He'd uttered something along similar lines about every thirty seconds for the past twenty minutes as several MVPD team members worked around him. It was Callum, though, whom Spencer had called in to help. The former Navy SEAL turned bodyguard knew basically everything about everything and he'd diagnosed the bomb situation—and what was needed to defuse it—faster than anyone else on the MVPD team. Not that they weren't good, but Callum was better.

And Nikolas was beyond grateful for the help.

"Can you defuse it? And in the meantime, can you get Spencer out and after Nova."

"Already on it, Slater!" Spencer hollered as he came back into the office, also clad in the heavy protective gear. "Every officer I have is canvassing the block for any footage. Your cameras lose them as he drags her to the parking lot across the street."

"Figured." Nikolas gritted his teeth at the helplessness of it all. Each minute they sat there was wasted time.

Nikolas leaned as far forward as he could, his gaze steady on Spencer Colton. "He's not going to let her go."

The no-nonsense cop he'd seen all day faded away. In its place was a compassionate man who understood the stakes. "I know. It also helps that we already had the perimeter set for the APB."

There wasn't any more that could be done and Nikolas knew it. Damn *it*, he knew it.

And still he struggled to sit still and let Callum do his work.

"I've got the area cleared and we've got everyone here in gear," Ace and Ainsley's brother, first responder Grayson Colton, called out as he came into the office to stand beside Spencer. He spent most of his time working with local law enforcement in and around Mustang Valley.

"Everyone out of range?" Spencer asked.

"Yep." Grayson nodded. "And I've got first responders on scene."

"Good." Spencer nodded before turning his attention to Callum. "How much more time do you need?"

"You tell me when you're ready. This bitch is mine."

Spencer refocused on Nikolas. "You know what to do."

"Yeah. Callum walked me through it."

"Step-by-step. You take it one step at a time and let him deal with the bomb."

Nikolas nodded. "I understand."

"We found them!" The words echoed through Spencer's body transmitter and Nikolas nearly moved before Callum slammed a hard hand around his ankle to hold him still.

"Not so fast, Slater."

Spencer took the call and Nikolas's heart broke at the words spilling through the body speaker. The woods on the edge of town. A hiker spotted them from a distance and called it in remotely but did not approach.

Spencer barked out the order that the hiker not engage and moved his team into action.

"Let us do our job, Slater," Spencer shot back at him before aiming a glance toward Callum's prone form on the ground. "You do as he says. We're going to go bring her back."

Nikolas prayed Spencer was right.

He had no idea what he'd do—or who he'd be—if Nova and the baby didn't come back all right.

NOVA CAUGHT THE flash of something high in the mountain but kept her gaze firmly on Ferdy as she moved toward him. She put some extra pregnancy moves into the motion, bowing her legs so she waddled more heavily and keeping a hand on her lower back.

What he didn't know wouldn't hurt him.

And if it gave her the slightest opportunity to run down an ounce of compassion in the man, she'd take it.

"What is all this?" Ferdy waved at her with the gun, the business end tracing her body from head to toe and back again. Nova felt herself flinch and fought to keep her movements steady and even.

"I'm pregnant, Ferd."

"Yeah. I got that. Is it mine? Not that guy you're shacking up with?"

"The baby is yours."

"Who is he?"

Interesting. No asking about the baby or any details. Just a leap to who Nikolas was.

"Someone I met a few weeks ago. Someone who's been helping me get on my feet here."

Ferdy sneered. "Looks like he's been doing more than that."

She had no interest in riling him up any further, and the more she downplayed Nikolas the more she hoped Ferdy would believe her that no one knew why she'd run.

"In two weeks' time?"

A leering grin split his face. "As I recall you and I moved pretty fast."

She ignored the stab of revulsion at that reminder and continued on. "My mother talked about this place before she died. I thought I'd come check it out as a place to raise the baby."

"What have you been doing in the meantime?"

"Working and driving my way across the country to get here."

She could see him chew on that for a minute.

"I didn't want to be a burden or place the responsibility for the baby on you."

"It's my kid."

"An *unplanned* kid." If babies could hear what their parents said while they were in the womb, Nova prayed that hers would also innately understand her only goal was getting them both to safety. "I thought for a while what to do about it and then realized that I'd just leave. New York's too expensive and that way we wouldn't be in your way."

"And that's the only reason?"

She mustered up the most wide-eyed look she could manage. "Yeah, why? I didn't want to burden you with it and I figured just leaving would be the cleanest break."

"Clean?"

"Yeah, Ferd. No attachments and no responsibilities. Why?"

"Nothing. No reason."

Nova saw the calculation race across his face, the mix of "what does she know, what doesn't she know?" hardening his jaw. Digging down deep and praying there was something left inside of him that wasn't completely evil and twisted, she moved quickly, leaning forward to hold her stomach.

"What's wrong?"

"The baby. He's been kicking like a madman and I'm not sure what's wrong."

Ferdy came closer, confusion filling his face. However he expected to manage this conversation, the talk of the baby and her reasons for leaving had obviously softened him.

Now she had to play it out.

Although she didn't want to break eye contact, she bent again, willing him closer so she could get a better look at that glint of light she'd seen up on the mountain.

Twisted over, she added a few more moans for good measure and it was enough to get him closer. As he stepped physically close enough, she latched onto his free hand, squeezing hard. "Oh no!" Moaning harder, she added a little shriek. "I think my water broke."

"Your wat—"

He stumbled closer, the gun still firmly lodged in his hand, but Nova hung on and wailed, "It's too early. The baby can't come this early."

"Get up!" He screamed the words, but she pulled on him again, this time harder on his free arm. It was enough to pull him off balance and gave her a chance to look up on the mountain.

The glint she'd seen was now a line of MVPD officers. She made out Spencer in the distance and did her level best to send the proper signal.

On a hard scream, she let go of Ferdy's arm and stabbed him hard in the eye with her fingers.

Then she put up her hands and ran, screaming all the way, "Help!"

NIKOLAS HEARD THE screams and saw the swirling push-pull of two bodies playing out in the clearing. He'd driven hell for leather out to the eastern edge of town, a wash of images racing through his mind.

Images of holding Nova safe in his arms fought with his worst fears and he was nearly mindless as he drove, gripping the steering wheel until he vaguely registered the ache in his fingers.

And still he drove on. Ninety. One hundred. As fast as he dared, whipping toward the edge of town.

He raced for the duo, no idea what he'd do against a gun. His only consideration was getting to her. Putting himself between Nova and the man who'd come to kill her.

They'd come so far. She was still alive and the police were here and he was here.

Finally.

Nikolas screeched to a halt, slamming the car in Park and leaping out of the driver's side. He dashed toward them, stopping short when the large body in front of him stiffened just as a loud crack rent the air.

The man who chased Nova stilled and fell, a sniper's shot fatal.

And Nova continued to run.

Nikolas gave no thought to the body, just sprinted around Ferdy's motionless form until he could get to Nova.

She screamed as his arms came around her, fighting and struggling against his tight hold. "Nova! Nova!

It's me, Nikolas." When she still didn't stop, he held on tighter and planted his feet. "Nova! Baby. I'm here!"

She finally quieted at that, her eyes going wide as she twisted to look up at him.

He'd managed to stop their forward movement and could hear Spencer and his team swarm down from the mountain behind them. Paying them no mind, he held her, pulling her close and pressing her head against his chest. "Shh, now. You're okay."

The small form that had so recently been in wildcat mode pressed against him, her arms wrapping around his neck as she clung to him. "Oh, Nikolas. I thought… I mean… I didn't know if you were—" A heavy sob fell from her lips. "You told me to run but all I could think was that I was leaving you."

"It's all right now. We're both okay. And you did exactly what you needed to do. Getting you and the baby to safety was all that mattered. All I wanted."

"I'm sorry I left."

"And I'd have been mad at you if you'd tried to stay."

"But there was a bomb. And Ferdy was there. And you're okay!" She said that last part in a rush, as if finally realizing that he'd gotten free of the danger.

"Callum Colton knows a thing or two about bombs and knew how to take this one apart."

"Oh, okay." She still clung to him but her arms softened a bit as she stared up at him. "I guess I'd rather belong to the family who knows how to take them apart than the ones who put them together."

"Then I'd say you've come to the right place."

Although she'd made the joke, it finally sank in that Nikolas was standing with her and Ferdy was not. "Where is—"

She tried to twist around but Nikolas held her still. "There's no need to look."

"Is he dead?"

"One of Spencer's snipers shot him down."

"Oh." She pressed her face back against his chest before lifting it again. "I need to see. For my own peace of mind. And for closure. For my child."

He understood. She'd been on the run for nearly six months. Living in a state of emotional turmoil even longer.

Closure meant more than visual comfort.

He held her close as they walked back toward Spencer. The MVPD team was moving around Ferdy's body but hadn't yet covered him and Nova stopped a few feet away.

"All that muscle and bravado, gone."

"I'm sorry."

"I am, too. He could have chosen another life. Another way of living." She took a deep breath and turned away. "Do you know, he didn't even ask me about the baby? Nothing beyond whether it was his."

"Again, all I can say is that I'm sorry."

"Maybe I will be. Someday. Today I'm just grateful to Spencer and his team."

Spencer's K-9, Boris, raced over to her, planting himself beside her. "Hey, baby." She bent down to pat his head.

Nikolas moved them away from the clearing and the police. Once they were far enough away, Boris still keeping close, Nikolas pulled her to his chest once more. "I didn't tell you before. I'm sorry for our fight this morning and I'll do whatever I can to make it right. But I love you, Nova. I want you and the baby and I want you to move in with me. I want to make a life with you."

"Oh, Nikolas, I want that, too. Even as I said it, I knew I'd pushed unfairly. We'll find our way. We'll figure it all out. Because I love you, too."

"We'll figure it out together."

"Yes, together." She lifted her head for a kiss, their lips meeting in warmth and something that felt a lot like permanence. The old Nikolas Slater would have turned tail and run.

The man he was today knew he'd not only found his future, but there was nowhere he wanted to go if Nova wasn't by his side.

Epilogue

Three weeks later, Nova stared down at the emerald cut engagement ring on her left hand and marveled at all that had happened in the past few weeks. She was continuing to grow by the day, the baby kicking and positively thriving as they marched ever closer to her due date.

Each night, she and Nikolas spent their time wrapped up in each other. And then each day the man had been a shopping fiend, ordering so much baby furniture online she finally had to lay down an ultimatum.

He either needed to stop or she was moving into the Triple R. It was part threat, part practical argument. If he bought anything else, she feared they'd no longer fit into his condo.

Even as she knew they could make anything work, the barb had hit its mark and they'd—thankfully—only had three packages delivered that week.

Ferdy's death had hit her more emotionally than she'd expected. Not that she was upset he was gone—especially as the extensive nature of his crimes continued to come to light—but she did care about his death as far as it affected her child.

She knew they'd both be better off in the long run, but it didn't change the fact that new life was coming into the world that he had been a part of creating. It was going to take some processing, and her obstetrician had recommended a wonderful therapist who was helping Nova work through the strange mix of freedom and guilt, neither of which had fully faded away.

It had been her therapist who'd recommended she take another step. One she'd finalized just the day before.

She was no longer Nova Ellis. She was Nova Colton, in the eyes of her new family *and* in the eyes of the government.

Nikolas came up behind her, his strong, solid arms wrapping around her. She and her belly still fit within them, but if she kept growing like she was, she doubted he'd be able to do it for too much longer.

"Hi," she whispered as she leaned back and pressed a kiss to his jawline.

"Hi, yourself."

She tilted her head slightly toward the floor. "I know I've said no more furniture, but maybe we can get one of these rugs?"

"Sure." Nikolas bent down and kissed her temple. "Why?"

"I can't see my very swollen feet when I stand on it."

He continued to take her pregnancy jokes in stride and told her repeatedly that "beached whale" had taken on a new meaning in the way she kept using the term. A joke that had them making googly eyes at each other regularly, and that Ainsley had finally poked her about earlier.

"Let's sit down and you can put them up on me."

She wasn't going to argue and did just that as Spencer and his fiancée, Katrina, who were visiting their Colton cousins, came into the room. Spencer's K-9 chocolate Lab, Boris, trotted in behind them and immediately came to stand guard beside Nova. She appreciated the silent support more than she could have ever imagined.

She also loved his soft head and the way he'd lay it against her when he was nearby.

Although he usually wore a look of all business, Spencer smiled brightly as he wrapped an arm around Katrina and then sat down opposite them.

"Hey, Slater. Heard you had a run-in last week with Sierra Madden?"

Nova vaguely remembered Nikolas saying something but she'd been so forgetful lately. With all the new names she was learning she was still struggling to keep up.

"I did." Nikolas nodded. "She was coming in for a meeting with Selina as I was going out."

Spencer frowned. "She gets around."

"Selina or Sierra?" Nova asked.

"Both, but I was referring to Selina."

Nikolas shrugged. "I was just in her office to deliver a check, and I have to say, I'm thrilled she's not my direct problem anymore. I told her I'd found nothing to implicate Ace and that I was giving her the money that she'd paid me back, minus expenses."

"She pissed about that?"

"Not mad enough not to take the money." Nikolas grinned before shooting Nova a wink. "And I'm fine with that."

"So about Sierra?" Nova pressed, curious why the woman's name was familiar.

"Apparently Selina is still peddling her crap about wanting to find your father and make sure he's well cared for. Sierra's a bounty hunter and, as she likes to say, 'she always gets her man.'"

"Do you think she'll get my father?"

"I think she's going to find Selina had motivation for hiring her and it's not necessarily about finding justice. Ace doesn't match the body type that was seen on the video footage the night Payne was shot. And the bank teller who called in the lead about the gun is now missing."

"Slater's right," Spencer said. "Destiny Jones has been missing for a few weeks now. I finally had the good sense to actually share the information I had with Nikolas and showed him the footage, too. Your man here's got a good eye and I think I'll keep working with him, instead of keeping him at arm's length."

Nikolas kept a firm hand on her ankle, his reassurance absolute. "I think your father knows exactly what he's doing. Sierra Madden can't change that."

Nova couldn't help but smile at that. "So he'll be okay."

"I've no doubt about it."

Although she still anticipated the day she and Ace Colton would finally meet, Nova couldn't deny how good it felt to get to know the rest of the family. Secure in the knowledge she belonged with them, she smiled as she watched the rest of the Coltons slowly file into the party.

It was that image that carried her through the evening. Past thoughts of her father, out there somewhere nearby. Near, but still not quite a part of her life yet. And the baby, so soon to make an appearance, anticipated and already loved.

And then there was Nikolas and the lifetime that stretched out before them.

"You okay?" He pressed a kiss against her forehead as Clan Colton seemed to get up as one to traipse into the kitchen for dinner.

"I'm good."

"You're quiet. You not overwhelmed by all of this?"

She still hesitated for a minute. She'd gotten what she'd wanted as she drove west. A new life and a future for her child.

How was it possible she'd gotten love, too?

"Sometimes it's a little overwhelming."

"Families have a way of doing that."

She hesitated, wanting to say this exactly right.

Perfectly, really.

"But it's all wonderful, even when it's a little big to take in all at once."

"I think impending parenthood is supposed to be big and a little overwhelming."

"But it's perfect because it's us, Nikolas. You and me and the baby here soon."

He pressed a kiss to her forehead. "You never told me what you thought about the names I mentioned this morning. Ashley and Avery are great girl names. Especially now that the OB told you what you're having."

"I already know what I want to name her."

"You do?"

"Yep." She nodded, awestruck at the love and happiness that welled inside of her as she thought about their future.

Together.

"Clara. After your mother."

Although she'd rarely seen him speechless, Nova was pleased to see she'd managed the feat.

"You've given me love and a life I couldn't have ever dreamed of, even a few months ago. I want to name our daughter after the woman who made you the man that you are."

Tears sheened his eyes, turning them a vivid green. "I'd love that."

He took a deep breath, gathering himself.

"You've done the same for me, Nova Colton. You've given me a life I didn't even know I wanted. And now it's here and I couldn't be happier."

He pressed a kiss to her lips, willing the action to say as much as was in his heart. "I love you. Forever, Nova."

"And I love you. Forever, Nikolas."

* * * * *

COMING SOON!

We really hope you enjoyed reading this book.
If you're looking for more romance, be sure to
head to the shops when new books are
available on

Thursday 14th May

To see which titles are coming soon, please visit

millsandboon.co.uk/nextmonth

LET'S TALK
Romance

For exclusive extracts, competitions
and special offers, find us online:

📘 facebook.com/millsandboon

🐦 @MillsandBoon

📷 @MillsandBoonUK

Get in touch on 01413 063232

MILLS & BOON

THE HEART OF ROMANCE

A ROMANCE FOR EVERY KIND OF READER

MODERN

Prepare to be swept off your feet by sophisticated, sexy and seductive heroes, in some of the world's most glamourous and romantic locations, where power and passion collide. **8 stories per month.**

HISTORICAL

Escape with historical heroes from time gone by. Whether your passion is for wicked Regency Rakes, muscled Vikings or rugged Highlanders, awaken the romance of the past. **6 stories per month.**

MEDICAL

Set your pulse racing with dedicated, delectable doctors in the high-pressure world of medicine, where emotions run high and passion, comfort and love are the best medicine. **6 stories per month.**

True Love

Celebrate true love with tender stories of heartfelt romance, from the rush of falling in love to the joy a new baby can bring, and a focus on the emotional heart of a relationship. **8 stories per month.**

Desire

Indulge in secrets and scandal, intense drama and plenty of sizzling hot action with powerful and passionate heroes who have it all: wealth, status, good looks…everything but the right woman. **6 stories per month.**

HEROES

Experience all the excitement of a gripping thriller, with an intense romance at its heart. Resourceful, true-to-life women and strong, fearless men face danger and desire - a killer combination! **8 stories per month.**

DARE

Sensual love stories featuring smart, sassy heroines you'd want as a best friend, and compelling intense heroes who are worthy of them. **4 stories per month.**

To see which titles are coming soon, please visit

millsandboon.co.uk/nextmonth

MILLS & BOON
MEDICAL
Pulse-Racing Passion

Set your pulse racing with dedicated, delectable doctors in the high-pressure world of medicine, where emotions run high and passion, comfort and love are the best medicine.